To Kristen

DARK FUTURE

Welcome to the
future + hope
many more books for
us both

KC Klein

DARK FUTURE

KC Klein

AVONIMPULSE

This book is a work of fiction. The characters, incidents, and dialogue
are drawn from the author's imagination and are not to be construed
as real. Any resemblance to actual events or persons, living or dead,
is entirely coincidental.

DARK FUTURE. Copyright © 2011 by KC Klein. All rights reserved
under International and Pan-American Copyright Conventions. By
payment of the required fees, you have been granted the nonexclusive,
nontransferable right to access and read the text of this e-book on-
screen. No part of this text may be reproduced, transmitted, down-
loaded, decompiled, reverse engineered, or stored in or introduced
into any information storage and retrieval system, in any form or by
any means, whether electronic or mechanical, now known or herein-
after invented, without the express written permission of Harper-
Collins e-books.

EPub Edition October 2011 ISBN: 9780062113795

Print Edition ISBN: 9780062117045

10 9 8 7 6 5 4 3 2 1

This book is dedicated to my wonderful husband, Jim.
Thank you for believing in me even when I didn't believe
in myself. And to my girls, mamma loves you.

ACKNOWLEDGMENTS

This book would have never seen the light of day unless I had a few people to thank along the way. Much appreciation goes to my agent, Jill Marsal, and my editor, Esi Sogah, for believing in me and this book. Thank you to the ladies at WriteSpot: Julie Ellis, Jo Gregory, Kathleen Grieve, jj Keller, Lynnette Labelle, Theresa Sallach, Jenn Thor, and Dee Ann Williamson for teaching me so much about the craft of writing. Thanks to Kris Tualla, Tes Hilaire, and Nora Needham for your unwavering support and great advice. To Pam for being the best friend and cheerleader a gal could ever have, and last but not least, a huge shout-out to Erin Kellison whose wise critiques and loving advice have never been wrong.

DARK FUTURE

CHAPTER ONE

My eyes popped open and my heart thudded against my chest. I scanned the familiar shadowed shapes of my bedroom. Dresser, mirror, closet, the blinds on my patio door. Nothing, all familiar, all quiet. But why my rush of panic?

I had heard a sound. Was it the swish of a door being closed or the beeping of buttons being punched on a keypad? Had someone punched in my code for my home alarm?

My pulse tripled in time, while my cowardly body froze in fear. Dredging up courage I shifted my gaze a half-inch to the right, straining to see past the heavy cream curtains that obscured the door leading to my backyard. A soft yellow light glowed around the perimeter. My motion-detector lights had clicked on.

No need to panic. Probably just a cat . . . but the beeps?

Dammit, maybe I dreamt the noise. Did downing a half package of cookies increase the chances of carb-induced nightmares?

Ignoring the cold bead of sweat that coursed down my side,

I turned my head and read the neon blue of my digital clock—4:30 A.M.

Swallowing, I strained to hear over the swish of my blood being pumped past my ears. But I *had* heard something. No way would I have awakened from a deep sleep in the middle of the night for no reason. I needed to investigate. A mature woman would.

Maturity was overblown.

I wiggled farther under my Egyptian cotton sheets and pulled them under my non-blinking eyes. Nothing to be afraid of. Just some car alarm being reset from the outside.

A soft click of a light switch echoed through the stillness, and a sliver of light peaked out from under my bedroom door. Terror clawed at my throat. I shot a glance back to my bedside table—empty. Damn, I'd left my mobile phone in the kitchen.

Someone was in my house.

I sat straight up in bed and . . . froze.

Get up. Get up.

Shoes sounded on the tile down the hall. I had a choice. I could lie here and be murdered on my sheets, or die standing. Decisions. Decisions. Terror clawed its way up my throat, and all I wanted to do was throw the covers over my head. Instead, I flung off the blankets and leapt out of bed. Bloodstains on cotton are a pain to get out.

Weapon . . . weapon, I need a weapon.

I dropped to my knees and searched for the bat I kept under my bed. My fingers brushed cool metal. I grabbed the bat, straightened, and ran toward the door. Clad only in a pink tank top and Hello Kitty panties, I prayed I didn't end up in the coroners' lab with a cheerful cartoon stretched across my rippled behind.

My bat rattled against the wall as I watched the doorknob turn. I braced myself, ready to swing, but I couldn't feel my arms. The door opened quick and hard, slamming me against the wall. Before an *umph* even left my mouth, a hand reached around and disarmed me.

I was flipped, driven face first into the wall, my right arm bent high at an odd angle. White pain sliced through my shoulder. A thigh jammed between my legs. Fingers grabbed tight to my hair, and cranked my head back.

A taut body pressed flush up against mine, and the scents of fresh-turned earth and sweat washed over me. Hot breath warmed my ear as images of rape and death exploded in my mind.

"Kris, I need you to listen to me." A female voice whispered calmly.

Shock zipped through my nervous system. A woman? How did she know my name? I tried to turn my head, but a painful yank to my scalp had me back to my intimate kiss with the plaster.

"We don't have a lot of time. Everything I say is of extreme importance." Her voice was soft, but edged with steel. She spoke with authority, like a commander leading troops into battle. *Poor troops.* She paused, then a heavy sigh. "Unbelievably, the future of the world rests on your . . . pathetic shoulders."

Her voice was familiar, yet not. I scoured my adrenaline-filled brain for a match, but all I could think about was one slight move and my arm would snap.

"I am going to let you go now. And Kris, it's imperative you remain calm. Do you understand?"

I nodded, since my mouth was too dry to form words. The piercing hold to my shoulder was released, my hair freed. I turned and marshaled enough confidence to swallow my own spit, but no courage could be mustered standing braless in juvenile panties.

The light from the hall didn't fill the room, leaving the shadows bold and far reaching. Her darkened form stepped back to the opposite wall near the light switch. She reached out and flipped it on.

A face identical to my own stared back at me.

A scream ripped from my throat. I jumped back. My head slammed hard against the solid wall, and then I slid down to the floor.

My vision blurred around the edges. I refocused, then gasped, couldn't help it. I stared at . . . me.

The woman glaring at me in her take-no-prisoner stance was my identical twin. Except, I didn't have an identical twin.

If the fashion police ever got a hold of her, they would've revoked her visa. Her failure to use an ounce of originality was criminal. Her black tank top looked like it had been ripped and the ends tied, showing off her washboard stomach. Form-fitting, night-camouflaged pants and black combat boots completed her uniform.

Her hair was longer, but with inexcusable inches of regrowth showing dark against her blonde hair. She stood with her feet wide, hands fisted, one on each hip. Her arms were ripped with muscles, shoulders broader than I'd ever seen my own. She was tougher, stronger . . . edgier.

We both stared at each other. She and I were the same, yet not. She was tan; I had a phobia about sun bathing. Her hardened blue eyes were punctuated with thin lines; I carried wrinkle cream in my purse.

Her gaze traveled to my tangled mop of hair, down to the tips of my French manicured toenails. Disgust marred her already strained features.

I raised my eyebrows, and then in a streak of obstinacy I'd never outgrown, I wiggled my freshly painted toes.

Her gaze, as inviting as a newly dug grave, leveled with mine. "God, I'd forgotten how young you are. And the panties . . ." she shook her head, "embarrassing."

I couldn't agree more. I scrambled off the floor and slipped on a pair of sweats. With both of us standing face to face, there was no denying the similarities; I had a double, except the body was better.

Or had I gone crazy? Neither option left me giddy with relief.

"Who are you?" I asked. I had to be dreaming; this was a better third option.

She didn't answer, instead ran over to the bathroom, flipped on the light, and opened my sliding closet doors. She yanked out a duffel bag from the top shelf and began riffling through my clothes.

Dreaming or mental breakdown, I was sure both roads started out pretty much the same.

She dashed over to my dresser and pulled out my sports bra and black running shorts. She threw them at my head. "Put these on. We don't have much time. We need to leave."

"Where . . . why?" Crazy I may be, but one thing I knew—I wasn't going anywhere with this woman.

"You'd never believe me, so you're going to have to trust me." Her behavior bordered on manic as she dived into my closet and threw every one of my shoes across the room. I hovered near the corner, not sure if I should call the police or a hospital with padded rooms.

"Where are your freaking running shoes?" she yelled, glancing over her shoulder at me.

The crazed leer in her eyes scared me. And I realized that though I may've become a new member of club insane, she could've run for a place on the board.

"In the bathroom," I said meekly. That's where I left them when I stripped before showering.

"Of course," she said, smacking her palm to her forehead. "You never put anything away."

She disappeared into the bathroom and it took every ounce of gumption I had to slide my feet in the direction of the door. If I made a run for it, would she catch me? She had that chiseled look of a sprinter.

She was back before I took two steps.

"Why aren't you dressed?" she asked and leveled me with the steel blue of her eyes.

I took a deep breath. Maybe there was a small part of her brain that could still respond to logic. "Look, I don't know who you are or why you're in my home, but you need to leave before I call the police."

She pulled out a gun. And damn if it didn't look like she knew how to use it. The barrel was aimed somewhere in the vicinity of my head. She jerked it up and fired a shot that blew out a nice-sized hole in the plaster.

"What the—" I ducked and threw myself behind the bed for cover.

"Next time it'll be for real. Now. Get. Dressed."

I peered over the mattress, first at her, then toward my new skylight. "Hell lady, this is Scottsdale, not South Phoenix. The neighbors here call the cops for gunshots."

"You'll be gone by then." She shrugged. "But damn, I'll be here. Hell. Don't make me use it again. A body is a lot harder to explain than a bullet hole."

She tucked her gun into the waistband of her pants and began dismantling my medicine cabinet, throwing things at random into the duffel bag.

Okay, note to self: You can't reason with Crazy. I stripped and put on my running clothes. Things might go better if I played along. At least I'd avoid getting shot at. "Who are you?"

This time the question stopped her. She leaned over, bowed her head, and braced her hands on the bathroom counter. She shuddered, as if suppressing a sob. Then she found me with her gaze in the bathroom mirror. "I'm you, Kris. But from the future. I've come back to send you forward."

In the harshness of the bathroom lighting I could see the dark circles under her eyes, and the permanent downward turn of her mouth.

For a moment her eyes glistened, but she blinked, and her cold dead stare was back. "I failed. I don't know why, but I failed The Prophecy. You need to go back and do the cycle again. We've done this before, but this time you have to do better. Better than me. You have to save him."

"Save who?" I could barely get the question out. My stomach twisted with a sick sense of déjà vu.

Her shoulders were bunched around her neck, and she shivered as if plucked from an ice storm, though her skin glistened with sweat. She had the look of a woman on the edge, and only sheer grit kept her from jumping.

"ConRad. I've killed him. And now you have to go back to the very beginning, back to when he first met you and get it right."

CHAPTER TWO

My better-body-double or BBD, as I was calling her, drove my car at a reckless speed along the semi-deserted highway. I sat in the passenger seat, bracing myself against the dashboard and clutching a duffel bag heavy enough to include the kitchen sink. Daybreak was imminent as the dark sky lightened to a blue-black.

My BBD seemed overly concerned with the approaching dawn and kept glancing to the eastern horizon, muttering things like, "running out of time," and "she's got to go back."

"So, the future huh?" I'd been trying to reason with her for the last five minutes, but it wasn't working. I didn't believe any of her deranged talk, but playing along seemed the best avenue of getting information. "Your weapon, it doesn't seem very advanced. The gun you're toting is pretty standard of what's on TV. What, there's no 'set the laser to stun, Scottie,' in the future?"

I thought my joke was pretty darn funny considering the circumstances, but my BBD shot me a glance that quelled all humor. I could almost believe that she was my future-self, except for the eyes. They were stone cold and so very callous. Every time she shot me a look, my skin crawled.

"The future, it's not like that. It's not . . . better," she said, focusing back on the road.

"What do you mean?" Her tone of impending doom was starting to wear on me.

"Do you remember our grandfather and how we would go and visit him during the summer?"

I nodded. I'd given up on rationalizing how she knew intimate details about my life. Crazy was a river you just floated along on.

The summers with my grandfather were some of my favorite memories. The days filled with sweet tea, fly fishing, and no one worrying when you stayed out past dark.

"Do you remember how he would talk to us about the end of the world? How we were living in the last days?"

I nodded again, not really understanding where this was leading. Grandpa had been a pastor at the local church. He hadn't taught brimstone and hellfire, but he was concerned about "Judgment Day," as he called it.

"Well, it happened, Kris. Armageddon is for real. And the future is *not* better."

A shudder crawled along my skin. Whatever this was—a delusion, a psychotic episode, a carb-induced nightmare—she believed it. In her mind the end of the world was the absolute truth.

We turned into a deserted parking lot that led to the hiking paths up into the mountain preserve. The trail head was marked with a sign asking dog owners to pick up after their pets, along with a supply of "doggie bags" for the forgetful owner. A copper water fountain and empty horse trough filled in the rest. She parked the car and turned off the ignition, then focused her attention on me.

"I don't want to tell you too much. I don't want to bias your decisions. You just need to have more . . . integrity, more trust." She ran both hands through her hair and slicked back the disheveled mess. "Ah, I wish I knew, but I don't. This time it has to work."

"Tell me too much? You haven't told me jack. What has to work this time?" Wisps of apprehension swirled in my belly. This woman looked too familiar and knew too much for me to keep dismissing her. "Is that what I'm supposed to do? Stop Armageddon from happening?"

"No." She shook her head. "That's already happened. You'll be too late for that."

She spoke with a conviction that only an eyewitness would have.

"Jesus," I said.

A bitter laugh flowed from her lips. "Oh, how I wish, but *he's* already come and gone, so the world will have to make do with you."

Great. Only a savior fits the job, and instead the world gets a surgical intern.

I unzipped the duffel bag, curious at what she deemed vital for my "do it better this time" quest. A glass jar of pasta sauce, no noodles, a half dozen cans of baked beans, one tuna—no can opener. I dug some more, dental floss, a wad of tissues, a box of Band-Aids, and a lone tampon.

"What am I suppose to do with this?" I lifted the bag to show her the contents.

She seemed as shocked as I about what made it into the duffel.

"Okay, so you never perfect the skill of packing under pressure." She grabbed the bag and threw it into the back seat. "All you really need is what you've put in your fanny pack."

She looked at me as if expecting me to do something.

"Now what?" I asked.

"You go."

"Go where?" This was insane. Was I really contemplating doing what this woman was telling me?

"Go out there." She pointed toward the trail head. "Go climb the mountain. Go for a run."

"And then what?"

"Don't worry. The 'what' will happen. Just go. Dawn is almost here. We don't have much time."

I arched my eyebrows in disbelief. "So you're really going to make me do this?"

"Yes, dammit. Just go already. Are you always this annoying with the questions? Go. For. A. Run. Is that specific enough for you?"

I had enough of her attitude. I opened the car door and slid out.

"Wait!" she shouted, before I closed the car door. "One more thing."

I hunched over so I could peer at her through the opening.

"Don't tell ConRad that you saw me. Or anyone else for that matter. He doesn't believe in The Prophesy. When you first meet him, he's very suspicious and very . . . um . . . angry. So if he believes you're a spy—he'll kill you."

And this was the man I am supposed to save? The whole story was nuts. I mean, she kills him and then he possibly kills me. This made no sense. Of course, that's the definition of insanity.

I couldn't help feeling sorry for her. I always had a tender spot for crazy people, my mother for one. It might not be pretty, but hey, insanity happens.

"Let's talk?" I said. "We can make our way over to the hospital. Get you a nice warm shower and a hot meal." And then whatever colored pill that would make you uncrazy.

In one quick move she pulled out her weapon, and I was staring down the barrel of a gun for the *second* time in my life.

"Don't make me put a hole in your arm."

But this time I wasn't scared. Twisted logic traveled both ways on this mentally unstable freeway. "You wouldn't shoot me. It would be like shooting yourself. And how stupid is that?"

Yeah, right back atcha, babe.

"I've lived through worse. The question is—have you?" Her voice back to command mode.

In that second I believed her. She oozed of hard core. But me? Nope, I didn't do pain well. I slammed the door. "You're crazy, Lady! Absolutely nuts. You belong in a padded room where they give you drugs. Lots and lots of drugs."

She opened her car door and barreled toward me, gun waving. I froze, second-guessing my impeccable logic that she wasn't going to kill me.

The gun cocked with a sickening click. She aimed, then shot the ground by my feet. I screamed, threw my arms over my head, and did the one-legged dance.

"I'll give you a five-minute head start, and then I'm coming after you. And so help me God, if you're not half way up the mountain, I'll make you dig our grave, and I'll put us both in there myself."

CHAPTER THREE

Both feet hit the ground in a clumsy sprint up the rocky path. After about five minutes, the death threat of oxygen deprivation and a gunshot to the arm were neck and neck.

I braced my hands on my knees and sucked wind. Blood started flowing to my brain again and rational thought returned. I'd been up this trail numerous times. I used to run this every other day after work, and I knew two things for sure: There was a parking lot on the other side of the mountain, and the mobile phone in my fanny pack was useless until I left the preserve. I just had to keep ahead of her . . . and pray she wouldn't commit her suicide and my murder.

My breathing slowed to a more normal rate, and I continued up the trail at a less death-defying pace. The moon had set, but the stars were bright enough that I could make out the dirt trail and was able to avoid tripping over the majority of the rocks.

It was a few miles up the mountain and down to the other parking lot, so I settled in for long run. The landscape was in deep shadow, but I knew this place. This was home.

The desert was an acquired taste like that of strong coffee or an aged whiskey. Ancient cactus and enduring mesquite trees made their home in a hostile and thirsty ground. I had a sort of hard-earned respect for a land that held fast to the heat of the sun like a mother would her newborn baby. Because despite the cover of night, the temperature still kissed the nineties.

A tingling of goose bumps trailed along my arms, spreading to the thin skin over my skull. Endorphins flowed to my brain and aligned my thoughts like a completed puzzle. Either time travel was possible and everything my BBD said was true, or something way more plausible—I was off my rocker.

Yeah, there was no escaping; crazy ran strong along hereditary lines. Some families are bent. They're just made that way. There are things a Freudian couch and a handful of antidepressants couldn't fix—though a bottle of vodka usually made a damn good attempt. After all, it had been my mother's favorite form of therapy.

The toe of my shoe caught, and for one second I was suspended in air, the next sprawled across the dirt trail. My knee stung as I turned and sat on my butt to pick out the pebbles digging into my skin. My ankle throbbed. I flexed my foot and winced. No broken bones, but possibly a pulled tendon. It would be smarter to wait and finish the trail in daylight, but a crazy woman with a gun was as good of motivation as any.

The sun was trying to peek over the distant mountain range, throwing pinks and purples across the sky. Twenty feet away, in a shallow ravine, a mesquite stretched wide, offering protection from the coming heat. A joke of shelter really— more of a tease, but I pushed to my feet and limped closer.

Black spots obscured my vision. I rubbed my eyes with the

heel of my dirty palm. Instead of dissipating, the spots grew and multiplied. The edges around the holes crinkled like fire, burning gaps in the atmosphere, like cigarette holes to paper.

I shook my head and tried to clear my vision, but the black holes metastasized, eating away the sky like a cancer.

Then vision faded altogether. Nothing. Darkness.

I bent over and lowered my hands to my knees. Dizziness rolled through my stomach in a wave. I reached out to steady myself against the trunk, but instead of rough bark, my hand flailed wildly around, meeting nothing but air.

I lost my balance, tipped forward, and fell into darkness.

CHAPTER FOUR

Pain. God, there was pain. Every joint ached. Every muscle seemed stretched beyond its limit. And cold. When had it gotten this cold? I opened my eyes. Where was I?

And then like an animal sensing fear, I knew something was wrong. Black. There was nothing but oily blackness. Was I still outside? Had I been passed out that long? I turned my head toward the sky expecting the soft glow of stars and the moon, nothing.

I struggled to a sitting position, stiff from the cold ground. I fanned my hands out groping in the dark like a twisted game of blindman's bluff. The tips of my fingers brushed against a dirt wall. I scooched and placed my back against the rough coolness. At least my butt was safe.

Something wasn't right. Every cell in my body seemed to beat out one message—run. But I couldn't see my hand in front of my face, much less run away.

It was as if the blackness sucked out all light and sound. There were no low hum of passing cars, no blare of sirens. Even a quiet desert was never this silent. No chirping crickets or rustling leaves. No scurry of life. Just my harsh panting—loud even to my own ears.

And the smell. I drew a deep breath of air trying to identify the scent. No sage or rosemary, or even the metallic smells of the city, but something off, foul, like . . . decay?

Panic wrapped around my heart and squeezed. As a doctor I'd smelled this before. It was an odor that came with the job as much as the scrubs and pagers. Death.

Only decomposing flesh could emit such a foul stench.

The rancid smell grew and burned my nostrils. I slapped my hand over my nose and struggled to swallow the taste of rot, as it slicked down my throat.

God, let it be a dead animal and not some corpse lying here next to me.

The thought shot me to my feet—scraping my back along the rocky wall. I stood legs apart, hands fisted and ready to do battle. The body might have fallen here and died of natural causes . . . or something else might've killed it.

Darkness chipped away at what little courage I had. I shook so bad, my legs could barely support my weight. But there was something I was missing, something that my muddled brain had forgotten.

"My phone," I cried with relief. I'd thrown my phone in my fanny pack before I'd left the house. And maybe, just maybe, I could get service. Cold and numb, my fingers grappled with the zipper and finally won. I recognized the smooth plastic, but fumbled and dropped my lifeline with a sickening thud.

"Crap," I sobbed.

I fell to my knees and did the universal hand-pat-sweep in complete darkness. Moving in wider and wider circles, I crawled forward. But the phone evaded me, as if the darkness had devoured the small black rectangle for breakfast.

Good God, where is it?

My imagination ran rampant with the image of a decayed body, complete with missing limbs and only half a face. I was certain I was within a hair-span of sticking my hand into a pile of squishy flesh.

A breeze blew past my ear—a mere shift in the wind? Then, a touch to my shoulder, not hard, more like a brush or a . . . lick?

I stopped my frantic search, and slammed myself back. My hands braced against the rock behind me, nails trying to find purchase in the hard dirt. Frenzied, I wiped my shoulder and my fingers came away wet and sticky.

I turned my head from side to side, desperate for any source of light, when a heated, moist gust of air blew into my face. My hair fluttered around my face as my chilled body warmed. I sucked in and drank the smell of the fetid air as it washed over me. Gagging, I tasted remnants of last night's cookies, and swallowed them . . . a second time.

Adrenaline levels spiked. I froze and did the only thing I could think of—I prayed.

God please let this tacky moist stuff be from the only mature pine tree in all of Scottsdale, growing in the only deep crater on this mountain preserve because God, if I'm not here alone, I'm truly going to piss my pants and pass straight away from sheer terror.

I didn't get an answer. Prayers didn't work that way, just the sound of me hyperventilating in the dark.

In the distance, a circle of neon-blue light appeared and crept steadily toward me. The light skimmed across the red-packed ground, gliding over jagged rocks and shallow furrows. The harsh florescent glow surrounded me, turning my skin an unnatural blue. Then slowly, the circle widened, revealing the ugliest, most terrifying creature I'd ever seen.

I screamed.

Chapter Five

Its body was made up of gray scales the size of salad plates that overlapped, forming like a well-fitted armor. A viscous blue substance coated the scales, creating a sucking sound with each inhale. My gaze traveled up and locked on a pair of predatory eyes that constricted in the neon glare. A football-shaped head bent low, toward me.

Its mouth unhinged, mere inches in front of my face, baring long knife-like appendages. Blood-stained teeth were slick with stringy saliva, billowing as its heated breath blew in my face. White mucus, glowing blue in the light, dripped from its claw-like hands. The beast was huge, at least ten-feet tall, round and fat like a well-fed tick. But it was the black intelligent eyes that captured my attention. Its piercing stare crossed all communication barriers, relaying to me one message . . . prey.

The gurgling in my throat signaled the death of my scream.

Its head lowered and bumped my cheek with its flattened face. Two slits in the front opened and closed, as it inhaled my scent. Its head rose, eyes fluttered back as if in ecstasy. Then it lowered and came back for a longer sniff.

Terror had nothing on me. I'd done terror; terror was two floors *up* for me. I knew in mere seconds I would pass out . . . just hoped it was soon enough.

The sound of rocks crashing came at me from the side. Out of the blackness a man hit me hard and solid in the stomach.

There was no contest. I was weak and slow; he was strong and fast. I was slammed to the ground, the wind knocked out of me.

Blackness enveloped us as the neon circle of light went out. Panic surged through me as I struggled against the heavy weight across my abdomen. *Run. Get out of here.*

Rough whiskers abraded my cheek and his harsh breathing rasped in my ear.

"Stop fighting," he hissed, then shifted and pulled my face tight against his neck. The scent of sweat, metal, and male heat reached me as I fought to breathe.

"Now!" he shouted, at some unknown signal. He seized my arm and pulled us both to our feet, almost dislocating my shoulder in the process. Gunshots splintered all around us, streaking through the night like bolts of lightning.

I decided, if this was my last moment on earth, I didn't want to see death coming. I squeezed my eyes shut. A coward to the end.

"Move!" His shout was barely audible above the chaos crashing around my head. Machine guns fired. Men screamed. Then a primal animal roared so loud and high-pitched that I tried to break free to protect my ears.

The man was having none of my self-preservations. He pushed me up over a crumbling rock wall, his hands squarely on my butt and thighs. I clawed at the dirt and rocks to gain leverage. Finally, over the wall I moved forward on hands and knees, desperate for distance. Within one panicked breath the man was there, pulling, forcing me up into a dead run.

Within four strides he jerked me to a stop and let go.

Free of his support, my feet skidded out from under me. I landed hard on my butt, fire splintered through my tailbone. My teeth smashed together biting my lip. I rolled onto my side, gagging on the taste of metal, warm and thick, as the blood mixed with my saliva.

Stricken with no sense of direction, I froze alone in the dark.

With the *rat-a-tat-tat* of machine guns punctuating the night with their sharp bursts of light, I could see other men, their faces streaked with black, hovering and firing behind what little coverage there was. Then *he* was back again, wrenching me as if I was a mere inconvenience.

I could barely stand—the throbbing in my lower back made my legs quiver. I hobbled a few steps and collapsed to my knees.

"Get the hell up. Now!"

I shook my head. My lungs were on fire. "Who are you?"

"If you can talk, you can run," he shouted.

I tugged back on my arm, but his grip was relentless. It was either run or be dragged. With sheer strength of will, I forced myself to my feet.

A brain-jarring explosion erupted from behind. Heat singed my back as the blast propelled me, throwing me through the air. My body skidded to a stop along the ground.

I trembled. I didn't want to rise again, but the man refastened his hold and gave no mercy.

He hauled me across the hard-packed dirt. I stumbled to my feet, forced to run blind in the darkness.

My chest ached, lungs burned. I'd no idea how long we ran. My body slowed. My oxygen-starved brain no longer obeyed orders. Willing to beg for mercy, I wondered if God had answered my prayer or the Devil himself.

The man pressed harder and I knew I had my answer— *Antichrist.*

I picked up the pace.

Finally, we slowed to a stop. My hand brushed along a large smooth boulder. Then he freed his savage hold to my arm.

I collapsed. Every bone liquefied from sheer exhaustion. Grateful for the reprieve, I dug my fingers into my cramping side.

"Wait here," he ordered.

Fine with me. I flipped on my back and gasped for air. I doubted I'd live through the next few seconds, much less the rest of this day. Stealth was so not my priority.

"Quiet," he whispered, harshly.

Unable to utter a word, I shot a middle finger in the direction of his voice. Granted, he did just save my life, but he'd been none too gentle about it.

He laughed, but it sounded hoarse. Like that part of his vocal cords had about as much use as my treadmill. Of course, he'd been able to see all along. When we were running, he had me swerving all over, possibly to avoid objects.

I dropped my hand with a thud, too exhausted to care if I'd forgotten to be grateful.

"It's the damn thin air," he said. "I forget how thin the atmosphere is till I have to run a mile in it. Stay here. Let me make sure she's gone."

Female? Something that vicious had a gender? The thought of it breeding caused a cold shiver to pierce my heart.

As soon as he was gone, I wanted him back. True, wishing the Antichrist back smacked of pure crazy, but lying waiting in the dark for monsters wasn't exactly a sane plan either.

"Let's go." He took my hand and led me up a rocky hillside. After a few shaky steps, he pulled me into a crouch alongside him. A flare of light broke the darkness blinding me for a second. When my vision cleared, I saw the florescent stick he used to illuminate a small dark tunnel. The harsh blue light played havoc with his features throwing them into shadowy contrast, all but one, the piercing blueness of his eyes.

"Did anyone else survive? Are all of your bodyguards dead?" He had pushed a pair of night vision goggles on top of his head and rubbed his face, smearing dirt and sweat across his brow.

Bodyguards? "No," I shook my head, "no one else."

"What do you mean no one else? As in you are out here by yourself?"

I nodded, hoping it was the correct response. I desperately wished I knew which response was.

"What the hell kind of irresponsible goddess are you to come out here all alone?" he growled as his hand gripped my wrist.

If his voice was harsh before, then it had just dropped to a whole other level. Even with the sweat on my skin, I felt chilled. What was it about his question that made me nervous? His tone? His actions? Didn't matter; I followed my gut and did a favorite diversion tactic and asked one of my own. "Who are you? Where are you taking me?"

I tried to keep my tone light and ignored the way his hand ground my ulna and radius together.

His fingers snapped open as if my skin burned to the touch. He moved back a fraction of an inch; his eyes narrowed into slits.

"Why do you ask questions you should know the answer to?" His voice hinted at hesitation, as if he was afraid of my reply.

Something about my response had changed him. His suspicion rose between us like a physical barrier, brick by thick brick trapping me in. Well, he wasn't the only one. His questions scared the crap out of me. Why would I know who he is and where we were going? Yeah, I trusted him alright—about as much as I did a Rottweiler, in a locked room with a steak tied around my neck. I put my hand up in a gesture of peace. "Listen, I appreciate you saving me back there, but I'm not going anywhere without a little information."

There, I did it. I took matters firmly in hand.

With the merest of shrugs, he side-stepped and pushed me aside. Then placed the glow stick in his mouth and crawled into the dark cave on the side of the hill.

I stood gaping in disbelief as he vanished into a mountain. Oops, my bad, I hadn't realized the conversation was over.

My desire to follow through the coffin-like hole was neck and neck with working a double shift in the emergency room on New Year's Eve. But as I watched the light get fainter and fainter, the pendulum swung in the opposite direction. I sure didn't want to be left in the dark and with whatever the hell had been chasing us.

"Hey!" I shouted. Desperation threw my voice into a higher pitch. "Wait for me."

No answer. It was either the arrogant jerk or the monster. I made my choice and crawled after the florescent glow.

Soon the tunnel widened enough for me to stand. I'd lost track of the moving glow stick, but decided there was only one direction—forward. I rounded a corner and saw a bright light, an opening, glowing comfortingly in the dark. I rushed forward.

The tunnel led to a large cavernous room. The walls were made of dirt and rock as if a large mountain had been hollowed out. Other tunnels led off into the distance, larger than the one I'd come from, more like hallways. Computer equipment on dented metal tables and large screens dominated the front of the room. Machine guns lined the walls, and something I'd seen used as a grenade launcher in an action movie took up space in the back.

To the side of me, I caught a glimpse of the only splash of color among the multitude of grays and browns. A set of red metal doors were off to the side, guarded by five men with guns, barring the entrance or exit to whatever was behind those doors.

The sound of guns being locked and loaded whipped my head in the opposite direction. Another set of five heavily armed soldiers crouched down, each with machine guns pointed directly at me.

I froze mid-motion. There must have been a misunderstanding. I was not the enemy. The thing outside was.

No sudden moves. No sudden moves. Look . . . friendly.

I plastered a smile on my face so big I could feel my lips crack. I hoped to appear nonthreatening, but knew I failed. My sports bra and shorts were ripped and dirty, and I knew my eyes held a crazed, deranged glare. I'd be better off channeling Nicholson. *Heeeerrre's Johnny.*

I scanned the room, desperate for the sight of the man I followed through the tunnel. Or was it down Alice's rabbit hole? I searched scowling faces trying to locate the severe blue eyes I'd caught a glimpse of earlier.

I found them on the face of a thirty-something looking man with short dark blonde hair and a six-feet-tall muscular frame. He stood behind the five men, hands planted on hips, feet spread wide in a military stance.

His icy glare directed at me.

Cold blue eyes blazed from his harsh face. I had no problem interpreting his thoughts. He'd like nothing better than to have me skinned, stuffed, and my head mounted on a wall. The fact that he could do the deed, and no one would stop him, was obvious. He exuded predator power—as natural to him as a lion stalking a poor, defenseless lamb.

"Waiting on your order to fire, Commander." One of the soldiers took out a hand gun and leveled the barrel at my forehead.

Geez-us. Really? What is it with me and guns today?

My heart slammed into my chest wall. This was it, death by a shot to the head.

"No! No fire!" I shrieked holding my hands up in a universal sign of surrender. I wished I'd had a white flag. I would've waved it like a cheerleader's pom-pom at homecoming. I sent a pleading look to the man who apparently no longer wanted to save my life. He had to realize I was no monster. I widened my smile and was sure my crowned molar showed.

His lips didn't even twitch.

If his glare could alter temperature, I would need Arctic gear. I waited—afraid to hear the command that would end my life.

"No." He shook his head slightly from side to side, sparing me no more than minimal effort. "Take the prisoner to the Holding Cell."

CHAPTER SIX

Holding cell? Prisoner? When did this happen?

In shocked silence I watched as if outside myself as two soldiers took hold of each arm and led me through a series of tunnels. We walked further and further down into the bowels of the mountain. Some of the tunnels were lit with copper mesh wiring glowing with a pale yellow light, while others were dark or lit only by torches stuck into crevices along the wall. The air was thick and damp, enough to frizz my hair. The odor of moist earth and rotten eggs, hinting at sulfuric gas, made me want to gag.

I was deposited in a cell, formed by a natural depression in the rock wall, and enclosed by rusty iron bars cemented across the front. The men locked the gate and took their leave, but not before lighting a nearby torch.

So grateful I was not to be left in the dark, I nearly shouted a thank you. I pushed my back against the wall and inched down to the floor. I placed my head in my hands and took slow deep breaths. Panic brewed, threatening a full-out attack.

This sort of thing was not supposed to happen to me. I

wanted to be back home with my comfy pillow and down comforter. To wake up to the smell of gourmet coffee that was set to brew at seven every morning. I wanted to wake up and realize this was all a dream. I wanted . . . I wanted my mom. God, I missed my mom. I'd *always* missed her, but going back home wouldn't fix that. Nothing would.

Think Kris, think.

This all had to be connected. My future-self sending me up a mountain trail at gunpoint was all for what? What had happened? All I remembered was dark holes burning in my vision and then falling. . . . Was that it? Did I go forward in time? She said the "how" would take care of itself. How did she know that would happen? But, of course, she said we've done this before. She knew because she'd done the same thing herself.

A cold prickling crawled over my skin. She told me I had to "save ConRad," whoever the hell he was. And what else? Oh yeah, that he was angry, and if he thought I was a spy, he'd kill me.

The thought had my ulcer calling loudly for attention. I wrapped my arms around my middle. My story had to be above suspicion. I'd just hoped he'd buy it.

I woke with a start. A large burly face covered in curly, red hair hovered inches from mine. Fat, pink lips were slapped between a coarse mustache and thick beard, reminding me of two slabs of salmon sushi.

"Get up. Time to see the Commander," his breath stale and voice chipper, as if going to see the Commander was the same as a long awaited trip to Disneyland. He didn't wait for my response, just grabbed my arm and hauled me to my feet. Another soldier, a walking brick wall with a buzz cut, met me outside the cell and attached to my other arm.

I snorted—like I was a threat. They outweighed me by about two hundred pounds . . . each.

"What's your name?" I asked, not really caring, but wanting to draw out my journey to the Commander as long as possible.

"00215," said the curly, red hair man.

"What?" That wasn't a name; it was a number.

He looked down at me with surprise, then a knowing smile. "Oh, you're a sly one all right, but I won't be fooled. No worries though, the Commander will get it out of you."

My foot stumbled, and I would've fallen if not for the two hammerheads clasped on either side. They dragged me down a long dirt tunnel, supported with metal beams, and stopped at a nondescript door. Two other soldiers stood outside, presumably guards. Who exactly did they think I was—Jet Li? Inside sat a wooden table, two chairs, and a wad of copper wiring focused directly on one seat. I swallowed hard; I knew exactly which seat was mine.

The room was an interrogation chamber fresh out of a scene from a spy movie. Gray plastered walls, dirt floor, utilitarian-ugly. I was told to sit and wait for the Commander.

All alone, the minutes crawled. My eyes fell upon a cockroach the size of my palm as the bug walked, too fat to scurry, across the ceiling.

Did they keep them as pets?

I wondered if this was a new species. And what did they feed on—human flesh? The image didn't help my panic-induced imagination in the least. My mind caught on the possibilities of torture, played out every scenario, from witch dunking to bamboo under the fingernails. I'd buckle under them all.

Come on, Kris. You're tougher than this, my inner cheerleader rallied, but then I remembered who I was and shook my head. *Nope. No, don't think so.*

The air chilled my skin. Gooseflesh spread over my arms and across my stomach. I glanced down and groaned. If I *had* to be interrogated, I wished I'd worn something confidence inspiring. Something with protection—I had too much delicate, pale skin exposed. Instead, I was half clothed and, crazy as it seemed, I couldn't stop sucking in my belly.

The door opened. The Commander entered.

He was the same man who'd saved my life or sentenced me to prisoner status, depending on which way you looked at the situation. As strung out as I was now, I choose the latter. I'd had a small iota of hope that there were two commanders, but I'd always been genetically predisposed to misfortune.

Screw the genes that gave me good cholesterol; I needed lucky blood coursing through my veins.

My gaze followed him as he walked over to the opposite chair and took a seat. His presence filled the room. Even the walls seemed to be under his command as they drew in closer. This didn't help the pools of sweat that were collecting under my arms.

The Commander, on the other hand, seemed to have braved the death-defying experience quite well. His short blonde hair was wet, possibly from a recent shower. A clean brown cotton T-shirt was pulled tight across a broad chest, short sleeves drew taut over well-defined arms. His muscular legs were clad in basic army camouflage and tucked into black military boots.

A serrated knife, the size of my forearm was strapped to his thigh.

Okay, so he'd taken the class entitled "How to intimidate your foe with your attire."

He'd probably even used a toothbrush. Seeing as I would've committed a minor misdemeanor for a toothbrush, my resentment started to outweigh my fear. I glanced at his face, not surprised that his expression seemed to be carved from granite. Strong nose and chin placed squarely between the sharp rising and falling planes of his cheekbones. Small lines crinkled around his eyes and a furrowed brow completed the picture.

In some circles he would be considered handsome, if one liked the arrogant, brooding type. I, personally, was partial to the laid-back surfer dudes, mostly because a surfer would never glare at me with such hostility. The Commander, on the other hand, looked like he wanted to singe the very skin from my body.

His eyes disturbed me the most—icy blue, cold like they'd seen countless inhumane things. Callous things that could erode a person's soul.

I stiffened my spine. I sat here, convicted without even the benefits of a trial. None of this was my fault. I'd done nothing to initiate my time travel, and the only thing I'd experienced from this man was rudeness and borderline aggression. I was the victim here, pulled from a dark hole with bullets flying, chased by a monster, and treated like a prisoner. I'd done nothing wrong, and I was sick of being treated like I had.

"What is your name, rank, and serial number?" His voice was rough, as his eyes narrowed.

Silence was my response. We glared at each other—me on guard, him with animosity. I held my own for a few *very* tense moments—then blinked. Out of the two of us, he would always win the staring contest. I swallowed hard, my tongue suddenly thick, and put on my false bravo.

Show no fear. *Yeah, right.* "I'm cold, dirty, and have had nothing to eat or drink in hours. I haven't even used a decent bathroom. I am sorry . . . Commander, is it?" My voice had the same edge to it that I used with unruly patients. "I'm just not feeling in the most cooperative mood."

He didn't say anything, his face a mask of chiseled stone. Then he stood and walked out. A few minutes later two soldiers appeared—the same two that escorted me here. I'd already nicknamed them, Red and Tank. They carried in a bucket of water, soap, a change of clothes, and something resembling food.

The water sloshed as they sat the pail down, soaking into the dusty ground. "You have ten minutes," Red grunted, as they walked toward the door.

Stunned, I never actually believed my requests would be granted. After they were gone, I pushed the wooden chair against the door handle, barring their entrance, and stripped out of my clothes. I grabbed the bar to wash and took a quick sniff. Ugh, no flowery scents here.

I scrubbed my body down with the tepid water and coarse soap, ignoring the sting from my cuts and abrasions. Time being short, I threw on the apparent standard uniform, khaki tank top with camouflage army pants, over my wet skin. The pants were too big, but there was a belt in the pile, so with some creative alterations they stayed in place. Finished, I removed the chair, not wanting to push the Commander's sudden benevolence.

I pulled up a seat and examined the pile of brown goo on the plate, aka food. My gut churned, not up to the task. I pushed the plate aside and downed the glass of water. The water was lukewarm and went down with a mineral taste, stale and gritty, unsticking the back of my throat. I wished I had a gallon of the stuff.

A short while later the Commander entered, along with my two new favorite soldiers, who removed all the stuff including my dirty clothes. Once again I was left alone with my antagonist.

"Are there any other accommodations that we can get for you?" he asked in a pleasant voice. I was in no way fooled. "Let's try again, shall we?"

I nodded.

"Good, now what is your name, rank, and serial number?"

"I don't have a rank or serial number. I don't belong in this . . . this . . . military," I said, gesturing with my hand to indicate the entire compound.

His eyes narrowed, apparently not liking my tone. "How could you not be in the military? Everyone is required to be in the military . . . that is, if you're human."

The word *human* seemed to resonate off the walls, impregnating the air with suspicion. If I was human? What the hell did that mean?

"I don't have a rank or number, but I do have a name. It's Kris Davenport." My voice sounded strong. I was impressed.

"Where are you from?" He stepped closer to the table, minimizing the space between us.

"Scottsdale, Arizona."

"What's your occupation?" He lowered himself on the opposite chair and perched forward.

"I am a doctor, surgical intern actually. I work at the County Hospital." My gaze was plastered to his every move waiting for signs of attack.

The room fell silent. He leaned back, crossed his arms, and stared. "What were you doing out there last night?"

"Jogging." I lied, knowing the lion wanted to lead me like a docile lamb, only to turn around and spring.

"Why are you lying?" he said the words slow, cold, and calm, as if he did this every day. I, new to the whole interrogation thing, tried to wipe the sweat from my palms on my pants without him noticing. "I'm not lying. I'm telling you the truth."

He stood and paced the floor.

He was agitated—I didn't care. Okay . . . yeah I did—knowing I was the focus of his anger scared the crap out of me.

"I see," he began. He stopped pacing, turned, his gaze level with mine. "Let me tell you why I don't feel up to playing this game. Why I don't feel up to spending all day going over your bull of a story. Last night, we detected a female outside the compound on our surveillance system. We thought that this was strange since the only exit to the outside planet is heavily guarded, as you saw when you were brought in.

"Stranger still is the fact that you are a female, and since no female has ever been out on this planet without an armed escort, we thought we would investigate. And what did we see?" His voice went a notch lower—a degree colder. "You, screaming your head off, standing mere inches from the biggest alien life-form we've ever seen."

He came over, slapped his hands on the table, and lowered himself a mere inch from my face. "We lost two soldiers out there. Both were my good friends. One was killed when he was thrown; his head split open on a rock. And the other was sliced in two by the alien's claw."

I drew back into my chair, trying to create distance. As his voice grew louder, I felt myself become a little smaller.

"So . . . this is why I don't feel like playing the usual game of waiting you out, toying with you, threatening you until you break. Because you will break . . . my prisoners always do." He said the last sentence slowly as if he relished the breaking.

"So I suggest you get motivated, cut the lies, and get right to the truth. Because if not, I am willing to speed up the whole damn process." He withdrew his knife and flung the blade deep into the wood of the table. The ivory-carved handle stood on its end, vibrating slightly waiting for his next move.

I suddenly became motivated.

"Listen . . ." There was a desperate ring to my voice I didn't bother to hide. "I'm telling you the truth. I don't know what happened either. One moment I was running and the next I woke in pitch black with something breathing hot putrid air in my face. I—"

He cut me off with the raise of his hand. "Enough!" His voice boomed. "I am a patient man, but you are pushing me beyond my tolerance."

Ha! Patient? I think not. He'd only been in the room with me for five minutes and already he wanted to kill me. Better revisit that virtue buddy. But for once, I wisely kept my mouth shut.

As if reading my thoughts he straightened and took a deep breath. "Let's try this again, your rank . . . serial number . . . and your real name." Each of his words ground out through clenched teeth.

"I've told you my real name, Commander. It is just Commander, right?" I asked, trying to keep the conversation light.

"I am the Commander in Chief of this compound. Just Commander to you. A very select few, like the ones you are responsible for killing last night, call me ConRad. I'm the head of this compound, and nothing is done here without my order. Nothing goes on here without my knowledge."

ConRad? OMG ConRad! Waves of hot and cold slammed through me. This was the man I was supposed to save? I must've gotten something wrong. Maybe missed something with all the gun waving. I'd gotten the impression that my BBD felt sorry for killing him, possibly even guilt-ridden over it. I was a doctor. I saved lives for a living; but if he went into cardiac arrest right here, I'd have no problem stepping over his body and running for the door.

I assessed him for about the hundredth time, and he looked about as fit as any man could. My scenario didn't have a chance in hell. So now, who was going to save me from him?

I fluttered my hand up to my throat suddenly nervous. *Lie or die, sweetheart.* I needed information. "Where is this place? What is this compound?"

His eyebrows arched.

Apparently I was wrong; his face wasn't made from chiseled rock since it didn't crumble from such an expressive gesture.

"How do you *not* know what the compound is?" Suspicion flowed off him. His gaze bore into mine seeming to measure every nuance of my expression.

I closed my eyes, then opened them. Exhaustion made my head heavy. "Please?" I didn't sound quite like I was begging. Okay, yes I did.

Nothing. Silence. He stood, stared, and took in every detail as if he hadn't seen a human in twenty years. Then, as if information was as valuable as water in a parched desert, he doled it out sparingly. "This compound is the last defense that stands between us and the annihilation of the entire human race."

All right . . . a little melodramatic to me, but he didn't seem to be the joking around type. "What are you talking about 'the annihilation of the entire human race'? Sounds a lot like a bad sci-fi movie." I laughed nervously.

His eyes widened, nostrils flared.

A nervous tingle spread in my belly. Apparently sarcasm wasn't the crowd pleaser it once was.

"Who are you? Better yet WHAT are you?" He took hold of the huge hunter's knife, crossed the table, and in a blink slammed me into the wall. The wooden chair clattered uselessly to one side. No defense, no barrier, just me against a violently strong man.

I couldn't breathe. His muscled forearm pressed against my windpipe. I went for the knee to the crotch move, but he was too quick. He pushed both legs between mine. Pinned my arms with one hand above my head.

"Where did you come from? Who sent you?"

I saw spots. Strangled animal sounds came from my throat.

He let up ever so slightly. "Answer me or I swear I will slice your throat here and now just to make sure."

He had whispered the words. A gentle caress to my ear, but I believed every one of them. "I don't know . . . I just . . . I was running, and I think I must have passed out. And when I woke up, it was . . . it was . . . dark, I swear. No one sent me."

PleaseGodpleaseGod, let him believe me.

My toes danced trying to gain purchase on the dirt floor. "My name is Kristina Davenport, and I am a surgical intern at the hospital and . . . that's it, I swear."

"See, I will make this easy for you." His voice so husky I had to strain to hear him. "There are only two possibilities. One . . ." he took his forearm away from my throat, sheathed his knife, and held up a finger, "you are telling me the truth, and you really don't know how you got to this planet. Or two," second finger went up, "you are an alien life-form who has learned how to shape-shift into human form in order to penetrate our defenses."

Alien life-forms. Shape-shifting. What was he talking about? But, out of those two choices, it didn't take a genius to figure out which one to pick. "The first one," I agreed, sucking in sweet air like an addict gone too long between fixes. I plastered myself against the wall, trying to make myself small, to take up less room, since he took up more than his fair share.

"Well, if that's the case, then we will just have to subject you to a mind-invasion interrogation to see if you are telling us the truth." His lips brushed my cheek, his breath tickled my neck as he spoke.

Ahh . . . I didn't know what a mind-invasion was, but I didn't want to find out.

"Nope," I said, shaking my head as vigorously as I could. "No need. Since I've been telling you the truth, there's nothing to find out. No mind-invasion, no alien life-forms, just plain old me." I had to stick with my story. My BBD told me he'd kill me if he thought I was a spy. What she failed to mention— which was adding up to quite a lot—was he was freaking crazy.

"But, I think it's the latter," he continued like I hadn't spoke, the lines around his ice blue eyes settling deeper into his chiseled face. If faces told stories, then his was one I didn't want to know. An orphaned kitten wouldn't find mercy at his hands. "I think the aliens have finally learned to shape-shift and you're the result. What better decoy than a . . . woman?"

He said the word *woman* with a low growl deep in his throat. Never had I heard the word spoken quite like that before, almost possessive, like he had a claim on me. I shivered on the inside. My skin felt turned inside out, raw nerve endings exposed, pulsing in the breeze.

I'd never been more aware of being a woman than in this moment.

His woman.

I gasped, shocked at the thought. What was wrong with me? I couldn't seem to think with my soft breasts pushing against his hard chest; my body flushed against the unmovable planes of his stomach and thighs.

His hand came back to my throat, stroking the underside of my jaw. Though the pressure was light, there was a strong undercurrent of menace. A calloused thumb scraped the sensitive skin, letting me know he could snap my neck.

Oh, I knew he could kill me, but I also knew something else. Something my brain couldn't access. It wasn't a memory exactly, but more of a gut reaction, an impression of familiarity. I clenched my jaw, pushing the uncomfortable feeling aside.

"Now," he said, his voice barely a whisper, "there are a few ways to tell if you're human or if you're . . . not. One is the smell." Deliberate, as if a connoisseur wine taster, he buried his face deep into the curve of my shoulder. His lips and nose skimmed my skin, leaving a small prickling of heat in his wake. He inhaled and captured the essence of me, in my hair, my ear, even my breath.

I trembled.

He relinquished his hold on my neck, grabbed a fistful of hair, pulled and exposed my throat. My body arched more fully against his. My breasts had no protection except two thin layers of cotton that chaffed my sensitive nipples. Rock-solid legs rested between mine. His hardened desire pressed against my own heating center. His face shifted back to my line of vision. Eyes scrutinized me as if memorizing every curve, every angle. "Too sweet to be alien."

His voice called to my blood as it pumped the word— *yes*—through my veins, luring me to give up . . . to surrender. I panted—struggled against his iron-clad grip on hair. On tiptoes I strained to . . . what? Push away or to get closer? I was confused. All the signals screamed that he was a dangerous, knife-wielding, crazy man, and yet my body wept with relief as if I'd come home after a long, strenuous journey.

"The second is the taste." He opened his mouth. A pink tongue peeked out and deliberately touched a tiny scar that boarded his upper lip. Then, slowly, he lowered his mouth and licked me, from the top of my shoulder to my neck, jaw, and swirled around my ear.

A warning trigged internally, too much, too . . . intimate. My heart flopped into my stomach and shook me from my trance.

"Mmm, you taste human. Like salt or more like . . . warm sunshine?" He pinned me with his gaze. His eyes spoke a primal language. Desire warred with anger; need against punishment.

I looked away. Embarrassed. Violated. His body crushed mine, suffocating in its nearness. I couldn't move. I couldn't even breathe without crushing my breasts against him. I always considered myself strong and physically fit, but he subdued me with barely any effort. Heart racing, I panicked.

When I was little, my two older brothers used to torment me. Pinned me down, sometimes for minutes, sometimes hours. The feeling of no control would break me—complete powerlessness always did. I used whatever weapon was available; whatever maneuvers would give me a fighting chance. This was no different. I turned my head, opened my mouth against his neck, and . . . sunk my teeth in.

He cursed. Grabbed hold of my shirt, picked me up, and slammed me back against the wall.

A painful whoosh came from my lungs. My vision rocked—brain swished inside my skull.

"You bit me." He sounded shocked.

My head hurt so bad I had to blink hard to keep my eyes in their sockets. "You licked me," I shouted back.

He assessed me, aqua blue eyes hooded with thick, long eyelashes, for what seemed like an eternity. "I will ask you one more time. Who are you?"

"I've told you everything." My voice sounded desperate, tired, even to me. "I went running and fell into the dark . . . I'm a doctor at a hospital. If you don't believe me, just call them. I've worked there for years."

He stood still, his body hard against mine, creating an insurmountable barrier. His face so close I could see his pupils enlarge, almost hiding the hard blue of his irises. The rage in him lived and breathed. One hand ran along my scalp in a mock caress, grabbed hold of my hair and pulled.

"Liar," his voice barely a whisper, the knife was back . . . shaking at my very exposed, very vulnerable artery. "There hasn't been a hospital anywhere on Earth since the year 2075." And in one efficient movement, he drew the knife across my throat.

CHAPTER SEVEN

Oh God, this is it!

A burn sliced across my neck. I wrapped my hands around my throat to stem the flow of blood.

A warm wetness trickled down my skin, my palm, in between my clamped fingers. I was afraid to swallow, afraid to feel my blood slip away as I died. I gasped at him, my breath rapid and shallow. This man had killed me, cut my throat like some animal left to choke on its own fluids.

Tears of self-pity blurred my vision. For some stupid reason I'd never thought he'd hurt me. Terrify me—yes. Manipulate me—yes, but never murder. I blinked to clear my sight, tears squeezed from the corners of my eyes. I was beyond caring that he would see me cry. What was pride when you only had seconds to live?

I clenched down on my hitching sob. I never thought I'd die like this, in some dank, gray room, wearing coarse, military clothing, my only companion a psychotic maniac.

ConRad eased back and released my hair. His hand curled

around to the underside of my jaw. The course pad of his thumb dried the wet trail on my cheek. His glanced down at his thumb and forefinger as they rubbed together seemingly puzzled by the moisture. "My job is tough, and I offer no apologies or excuses, but I had to be sure. Aliens don't bleed like us. I needed to know you were human."

A murderer with a profound sense of responsibility. Wonderful.

"So you killed me!" I shouted. I placed two fingers against my carotid artery and took my pulse. Was the rhythm racing or . . . thready? Were those white lights in the distance? Had it become harder to breathe? *The end, the final finale.*

"What?" He stepped back and wiped the blade on his pant leg before sheathing the knife in its holster. A *tsk* sound came from between his closed lips. "Barely a scratch. You won't even see the mark in a few days."

I pulled my hand away from my throat and glanced down, amazed at the thin smear of blood on my fingers. With hurried movements I palpated my trachea, then the cartilage around my larynx. I swallowed a few times. All seemed to be in normal working order. The cool breeze of relief swept through me, followed by a blister of hot rage that sprang forth and flamed my face.

"You complete jack—" The words I used to describe him wouldn't have been fit for even a hard-core rapper to use. If my mother had heard me, she would have reached for a bar of soap. And I was just getting started.

The Commander must have thought so too. He raised his hands in mock surrender. "Hey, was that all in English? There were names I don't even think I know the meaning of."

A small smile played across his face, crinkling the corners of his brilliant blue eyes. It had a way of making him appear younger, almost charming. But then again, the Devil is said to appear as an angel of light.

"Well, next time you think someone just killed you, let's see how you react," I snapped in my defense.

He nodded. He had justified himself once—he wouldn't do it again.

My heart still thundered as I pulled in my first full breath. I rubbed my hand across my chest. Was I up to these life-or-death situations? Forget monsters or murders—I would die from a common old heart attack.

I needed space. Proximity to this man put me on edge. He seemed to drive me to my boundaries and then test my resistance. My hand raised and pushed on his chest. I needed room. I needed space to breathe without his scent—soap, metal, heat—flooding my nostrils.

ConRad didn't budge. His chest was as unforgiving as any rock mass. Then he stepped closer. My arm, worthless against such power, bent and became trapped between our bodies. His gaze locked with mine, nostrils flared, eyes focused and heated. His larger frame hovered and crowded.

Something happened; something had changed. He was on the attack. My belly twisted and my throat dried. His face so close, lips within licking distance. His breath fanned my cheeks. His scent made my mouth water. *Just a taste . . . just one taste.*

"What if I'm wrong? What if the aliens are more advanced than even I thought? Or maybe . . ." his voice turned rich and deep, like a red wine, "I'm just looking for a reason."

He spoke the last under his breath, almost as if he was being pulled along against his will. I could sympathize.

He was so tall I put a creak in my neck to watch his expression. I placed my palm flat against his broad chest, and I could feel his muscles shift as his arms came to either side of my head, pressing his hands against the wall.

Trapped again.

"A reason?" I swallowed. I couldn't seem to follow a simple train of thought. Primal words diffused through my brain . . . open . . . more . . . yes.

His mouth parted, a tongue swept along his full upper lip leaving a shimmer of wet behind. "It's been a long . . . long . . . long time since I've had a woman."

His words rolled through me, seeping into my raw nerves like a rum punch. My mouth eased forward. The promise of his flavor . . . consuming.

His eyes burned, transfixed on my neck. He bent his knees, lowered, and rubbed his hips against mine. His hands slid to my scalp, massaging. Then he grasped my hair and tilted my head exposing my neck—stretching my wound.

My breath escaped in a pant. My mind warred with my body as my muscles unfurled, preparing for surrender. He looked at me as if I was dinner . . . no dessert. He was a man kept alive on bread and water for so long, pushed to the edge—on the brink of rushing the line.

He lowered his head.

Time lingered. Heartbeats ceased. Then a tongue, warm . . . wet . . . slow, licked my wound. A sting erupted as his tongue drew across leisurely from one end to the other. More suggestive than a caress, more intimate than a kiss. The gesture reeked of possessiveness, of ownership, of a . . . branding.

He lifted his head and rolled his tongue around his mouth. "You taste like human." He said, and then ground his hips into mine. "You feel like human."

My God, he's crazy. But I couldn't stop my legs from going weak. My arms clutched around his shoulders, afraid my knees would buckle if I let go.

"Silly little girl, found all alone in the dark." His mouth was beside my ear.

Addicting chills spread at his seductive tone.

"You cost my men their lives all because you were at the wrong place at the wrong time. Or were you? Maybe it's all a trick, maybe they've found a way to make you look, feel, and taste like a human. But I wonder . . ." He whispered as he gently kissed the corners of my mouth. His tongue bathed my parted lips.

I licked the moisture; savoring the flavor of salt, metal . . . blood. My body went from hot to cold to . . . burning. A smoldering fire began in the pit of my stomach, scorching its way south.

"I wonder," he began again. "I wonder if they made it possible for you to come like a human."

An emotion of the purest form swept through me, an uncontrollable urge to weep. A low moan escaped from the back of my throat. *Please ConRad, it's been so long. I thought I lost you.* Something cool and smooth dragged underneath my shirt, lightly past my ribs. His knife. The blade skimmed my skin down to my waist. With a small flick of his wrist, he cut the belt holding up my fatigues.

A shock of cold air hit my bare thighs, and my brain snapped awake. I didn't know this man, and another realization following hard on the first—I wasn't wearing underwear.

Warning bells triggered. Not just ordinary "hey, wait a minute" alarms, but all out *Halt! Stop!* Warning bells. "Wait!" I squeaked, but to no avail.

His hand clamped down on my bare behind. His breath came in gasps—body trembled.

"God, you're so soft . . . so very . . . female." His words . . . reverent. His mouth . . . everywhere. My temple, neck, and hair were bathed in prayerful administrations. His hands slid down my bare legs and hiked them around his waist—removing my pants with a decisive snap. One calloused palm rounded my hip and settled deep between my thighs. He groaned, bit my lip, and tugged. "You're so wet. So ready for me."

I wanted to deny the accusation, but couldn't. Not when his fingers slid deep inside me—easy, willing, no resistance. My hips bucked against his hand. How could I be doing this? How could I have let this go this far?

Then his fingers moved . . . and I ceased thinking at all.

Hips rocked, forcing his hand deeper—drawing him closer. *Don'tcomedon'tcomedon'tcome.*

My mind reared back from the loss of control. A roaring tidal wave of pleasure swept through my body, jolting me to the core. A moan slipped past my lips.

He covered my mouth with his hand and buried his face in my neck. He growled, animal-like, visceral.

And damn me to hell because I responded.

I shook, the spasms of my orgasm rippled through me.

Reds and blues shot through the darkness behind my eyelids. My muscles, strained to the breaking point, finally shattered. Sweet relief rushed through my body. Tears threatened again, but this time from the feeling of safekeeping, of being in a place I never wanted to leave.

Only our ragged breathing broke the silence. Neither of us moved. My legs wrapped around his hips, his hand across my mouth—my face flamed, ears burned. He gazed into my eyes and for the first time saw me . . . really saw me.

There was a sense of déjà vu, of familiarity, then something else that went way beyond. I could see myself through his eyes, but as if looking in the past. Like each life was a reflection, and I stood peering down a hall of mirrors.

He unclasped my mouth and tenderly stroked my cheek. His forehead lowered and rested on mine. "I didn't mean . . . I didn't think it would go this far. Kris?" He hesitated.

I had no strength. No energy—he had consumed it as if he had every right. But did he? Had I at one time given him my heart and my body?

I didn't think he hesitated often, but it didn't matter. I couldn't look at him. I couldn't pretend everything was okay and have a conversation while his fingers were still deep inside me.

"Please," I said as I limply pushed on his arm. ConRad's fingers slipped out of me and rounded my thighs. Wetness trailed along my hips as his hands lingered there. He reluctantly let go and lowered me to the ground. I stole a glance at him. His breath came in hard; an expression of strained control lined his face. I understood completely.

I broke eye contact, slicing my gaze to my feet. I reached for my pants and pulled them around my waist. The cut belt lay useless on the floor.

I left. I picked up my clothes and shredded dignity and walked toward the door. What else could I say? What could I do? I had seriously thought ConRad was going to kill me, and yet he'd just brought me to the best climax of my entire life, pinned against a cave wall.

Shameless.

Chapter Eight

I flung the metal door open, ready to force my way past the two guards previously posted there. Instead, I stumbled out into the harsh orange glare of the corridor undeterred. They were gone. What had ConRad said—something about there was only one way in and one way out, which was heavily guarded.

Didn't matter. I'd find a way.

I staggered down the concrete tunnel and tried to run, but my head spun like I'd had one too many rounds at the local bar. Smooth gray walls surrounded me, and I braced my shoulder against one, concentrating on staying upright. I had to get out of here. I needed to get back to my sugar-coated life, one that didn't have monsters and mean men who cut me just to see if I would bleed.

The thought caused my neck to itch with awareness. My hand brushed the skin and my palm came away with a thick smear of red. The wound had begun to seep.

I was bleeding again. Which, I'm sure had nothing to do with the freaking gyrations against a damn cave wall. I closed my eyes, the vivid picture of how I must have looked with legs wrapped around ConRad seemed to have been branded into the back of my eyelids.

With my forearm I wiped the sweat that coated my skin and slicked my hairline. I wasn't sure if the moisture was from my recent aerobic activity or the thick, heavy air that smelled like cooked eggs and wet earth. I trembled as I continued down the hall.

This wasn't happening. My day hadn't consisted of being sniffed by an alien, treated like a prisoner, interrogated by a mad man, sliced to assure I bled, and then brought to a withering climax. I had disastrous days before, but this one marked the official D-day of my life.

"Do you need help?" The voice was soft and melodic like ice melting in a glass of sweet tea. A young girl about sixteen or seventeen had skipped to a stop. Her straight blonde hair swung like a gold curtain past her delicate shoulders. Blue eyes widened with interest as they peered out beneath fringed bangs. She hadn't escaped the imposed military uniform, green camouflage tank top, and army pants, except the one flare of originality—white tennis shoes instead of combat boots. She was petite, a little taller than my shoulders, but her stature was one of confidence that only the truly young, not yet beaten down by the world, could maintain.

I saw my lifeline and grabbed it.

My hand snaked out and caught hold of her wrist, pulling her in close. I placed my face a mere inch in front of hers so there'd be no confusion. "Where's the exit? The way back home? I need to get the hell out of here!"

Her body reared back, arm twisting under my hold. Terror ringed her eyes as they scanned me from head to toe—then toe to head. I could only imagine what she saw. A half-crazed woman, drenched in sweat, and bleeding. With a death grip on a pair of overly large combat pants that, with a mere slip of my fingers, would tumble to my ankles, leaving me half naked.

Right, that's all I need—more exposure.

I relinquished my grasp, shocked at how grotesque my bloodied palm print showed against her pale skin.

"Sorry," I mumbled, my voice hitching on the simple syllable.

"We should get you to the infirmary," she said leaning forward and inspecting the wound on my throat. "It doesn't look like much, but you don't want to take a chance with infection, especially down here." She grimaced and held out her hand by the way of introduction. "By the way, my name's Quinn. What's yours?"

I swiped my dirty palm along my pant leg and shook her hand. I blinked my eyes, surprised by the sting of emotion. A few kind words and I was ready to collapse, crying on her shoulder.

"Kris."

"Hmm . . . odd name," she said with a slight narrowing of her eyes. Quinn turned and began to walk down the corridor, then glanced behind her to make sure I followed. "We take a right here, and then it's just a little further."

I shot a look around, trying to get my bearings. Everything appeared the same. Dark, dingy halls with copper wiring strung across the ceiling, poorly illuminating hard-packed dirt floors and industrial walls. Thick steel arches reinforced the dirt ceiling every few yards, presumably to prevent the ceiling from falling in and burying us alive. My finger tugged at the collar of my shirt. "How do you know where you are going? This has the feel of a human-sized rat maze."

"Well, now it's like a second home, but in the beginning . . ." She shrugged, turned, and tapped her hand on the steel arches where large black numbers glistened with condensation that ran lazily down the column. It was so humid even the metal sweated.

"There are markings on each passage where they split— basically four main hallways that connect with each other. Of course, there are other side tunnels, but until you get to know the basic four, don't bother with them. Just remember, if you get lost, always try to find your way back to tunnel one, which will bring you to the center of the compound. Here we are . . . just through these doors."

If the two silver doors had ever been tended to, they'd long ago lost their shine. Dingy metal and dirt-smeared, they were haphazardly wedged into the side of a mountain. Surprisingly, the hinges were well oiled as the doors swung easily open. Quinn held one door back for me to follow.

My feet slowed to a stop as I stared in disbelief at the so-called infirmary.

The same lighting that hung throughout the compound was here also, thin copper wires giving off a gloomy orange glow. Each wire alone didn't provide much light, but when numerous lines wound back and forth, the effect was more substantial. But even in the dim glare, the infirmary left much to be desired.

Below the lighting was a mesh net strung across the ceiling. The net was secured on all sides and drooped toward the middle, presumably to prevent boulders from falling and crushing recovering patients. Thoughtful.

Metal cots were overturned; some with a few, thin, dirty mattresses draped over them. Wooden tables, stained brown with dried blood, lined one wall. A few pathetic chairs stood, or didn't, depending on the number of legs. And against one wall, a rusted-out metal cabinet, whose doors hung in a saddened lopsided way, completed the room dedicated to healing.

I had entered a furniture graveyard. I wondered if burning the furnishings would release their tormented souls. Sure couldn't make the place much worse.

Didn't matter, not my problem. The sooner I got patched up, the sooner I'd be on my way. My BBD might have commissioned me with a responsibility, but it didn't mean I had to accept. Besides, the only one here who needed saving was me.

I walked over to the cabinet and pried open doors caked with dirt and rust. Browsing the contents, my gaze settled on a few nonsterile gauze pads, some bottles of alcohol, and a locked metal box—nothing impressive. I picked up the box and shook. It was light, seemingly empty with small pieces clacking against the sides. I searched the dented shelving for a key and saw none.

I turned to Quinn and held up the box. "What are these?"

"Microbiotics. Careful, we only have a limited supply. We need to make sure we have enough for the goddesses."

I rolled my eyes. Goddesses—give me a freakin' break. *Don't ask, Kris. Not your concern. Don't*—but, of course. . . .

"What's a goddess?" My voice a low monotone. I may've been interested if my capacity for surprise hadn't already been flatlined.

"How do you *not* know what a goddess is?" she asked, studying me as her eyes arched in surprise.

I shot her my deadpan glare.

She quickly held up her hand. "I know . . . I know. You are sick of everyone answering a question with a question. Well, goddesses are not really goddesses in a strict sense of things. I mean we don't worship them or anything, but they are treated like precious glass dolls, a little too carefully if you ask me."

Quinn's fingers entwined with the hem of her green army shirt, fraying the seam. She shrugged. "Anyways, that's a whole other topic. Basically, the short version is the goddesses are regular women who have developed, or were born with, special gifts. Each gift is different, but they are all used to strengthen our defense against *them*." Quinn pointed to the earthen ceiling, her tone hushed. "In fact, lately the goddesses seem to be our only defense."

I assumed she was talking about the monster, or as ConRad said, alien. I was all for whatever was in my defense against the hideous beasts. What were they anyway? Where did they come from? I inhaled and prepared to drill Quinn with my questions, curious despite myself.

"The ironic thing is we were the ones who searched the aliens out." Quinn plopped herself on top of a wooden table and began swinging her legs back and forth, squeaking the wood with each kick. Her bare hand ran the length of the scarred wood. I barely contained shouting warnings of splinters and staph infections.

"I mean how many years did humans try to contact intelligent life-forms in outer space? Well, we contacted and *they* came, but we almost annihilated the entire human race in the process."

Annihilation of the entire human race? This was beginning to sound like a bad rerun of a *Stargate*. I hated sci-fi.

"Here, let me help you with that." Quinn jumped from the table and took the metal box out of my hand. She fished a key from around her neck. "ConRad gave me the key for safe keeping before he went on the mission to rescue you. I'm glad," Quinn smiled mischievously and unlocked the box, "I conveniently forgot to give it back to him."

Tipping the box on end, she reverently cupped a small pinkish rectangle in her palm. The pellets looked like pieces of candy, the type I had jammed in my PEZ dispenser as a kid and eaten out of Superwoman's head.

"This stuff is great. This medicine kills all the bugs and takes away the sting." Quinn crushed a pellet and smeared some on my neck and then wrapped a thin layer of gauze around my throat. She stepped back, hands on hips and examined her handiwork. "There, that should do the trick. You have to be really careful of infection here. The underground heat and damp encourage cuts to fester."

"Is that what you do?" I asked, impressed with her knowledge. "Work in the infirmary?"

"This place?" She swept her hand in a circle to encompass the whole mess of a room. "No—no one works here. It's more like a self-serve. But we lose a lot of good men down here to infection, so the know-how is just common sense." She glanced at her feet as they traced small circles in the dust on the floor.

"And a lot of good women too," I added. I was a feminist to the bone and it was a habit—albeit an irritating one—to always add the female version to the scenario.

"What?" Quinn raised her head, her art project on the floor no longer as fascinating.

"Women too. You know, you must've lost a lot of good females to infection, not just men." I studied the empty shelves and began to take inventory. A mental supply list formed of what I would need to get this place up and running.

Dammit Kris. Focus. You are not here to get this place going.

I glanced back at Quinn taking in her wide eyes and gaping mouth. "What?"

"Who are you?" Bewilderment colored her words.

What was I supposed to say? Whenever I told the truth, nobody believed me. I finally learned the hard lesson—I kept my mouth shut.

"You haven't listened to a word I've said, have you?" Quinn leaned forward, her body tense, face pale. "I told you the microbiotics are for the goddesses. No woman has ever died of infection here at the compound. The women get the medicine. Oh man . . ." She shook her head and shuddered. "If a goddess ever died of infection, the Commander would have a . . . a . . . I don't know a word strong enough to describe his reaction, but it wouldn't be pretty."

"I don't understand. Are all the women goddesses? I have only seen men—soldiers and you, of course. So where are all the females?" My teeth slid edge to edge. What had ConRad said? Something about a woman being the best decoy?

"Where are you from?" she whispered as if coaxing me into confession.

"Oh, I don't know . . . Planet Earth." I laid on the sarcasm, but my voice rose despite my best efforts. "Where are you from?"

I was sick of everyone thinking I was some sort of alien spy.

Hadn't ConRad proved I was human? My ears heated at the memory of my pleading, his name quivering on my lips.

Quinn stared, mouth slightly open.

"Look," I said and rolled my eyes, "if I knew where I was, I could better answer where I'm from, right?"

More staring. A bikini wax was less painful. No, correction. A full Brazilian was an easier undertaking.

Quinn stepped closer and adjusted her long hair over and around her ear. In that one moment, she looked years older than I had originally thought. She touched my neck again and shook her head. "Men, they can be so stupid sometimes. I could've told him you weren't an alien. Your energy's too bright."

My breath hitched in disbelief. How had she known about ConRad's accusations? Did she know what had happened afterward? My ears started to pulse.

Quinn stared off in the distance as if she'd heard something. "Come on, he's looking for you."

"Who is?" I asked.

"The Commander, of course," she said rolling her eyes, seeming to test the gesture for the first time.

I narrowed my own. Was she mocking me or . . . mimicking? Hard to tell.

Quinn grabbed my hand and rushed me through the swinging metal doors. "We need to hurry. He's upset."

Great, *he's* upset. Not hard to imagine, considering his standard M.O. was pissed and royally pissed. I slowed my pace. Quinn tightened her grip and yanked on my arm as she dragged me along the twisting tunnels. Before we even rounded the corner I could overhear ConRad's gruff commands.

"Where the hell is she? And keep this covert. I don't want the Elders here breathing down my neck. But find her. NOW!"

My body jerked in response to ConRad's order. I shot a pleading glance at Quinn, desperate for intervention.

Apprehension trumped over the pity in her eyes. She leaned closer. "Show no fear," she whispered.

Easier said than done. Regardless, she was right. I wasn't going to back down. His anger appeared to intimidate everyone, but it wouldn't make a coward out of me. Taking a deep breath, I squared my shoulders and stepped forward.

There stood the Commander in Chief. He had my previous guards backed against the wall, sheer intimidation keeping them pinned. He seemed oblivious to the sweat tracking down his face, as if he was above the discomforts of mere mortals. ConRad's profile was rigid, seemingly birthed from the surrounding mountain itself. He was a walking study in simmering rage being kept tightly reined in with stone-cold control.

Wasn't that how one describes a sociopath? God help me if he had body parts stuck in a freezer somewhere because I'd be next, squished between the frozen peas and empty ice cube trays.

I knew immediately when ConRad became aware I was near. I didn't so much see his reaction, though he ceased barking orders, as sensed it. It was a heightened cerebral awareness, a rising of hair along my arms, the feel of blood rushing through my veins. And I knew it was the same for him. As any woman would—any woman who had let a man smell her scent and relish her moans.

In a hushed second we were alone. Quinn and the soldiers had fled, leaving me desolate like Daniel in the lions' den with only faith as his shield. Of course, this time the lion wasn't restrained and my shield of faith . . . a bit tarnished.

ConRad pivoted toward me and stilled. Our eyes held, communicating a wave of heat.

I broke first. I was on no such terms where sharing impregnated stares across a room with this man was appropriate. He was dangerous. It was best I kept that in mind.

"Are you alright?" he asked softly.

Could it be . . . was it possible he'd been worried about me? I'd prepared myself for a scorching set-down, not consideration. My cheeks warmed with insecurity. After our last encounter, I felt overly exposed. A sensation I wasn't taking kindly to. "I'm fine."

He stepped back with a nod, allowing me to see the entrance to the interrogation room. "It will be fine, I promise," he said reassuringly, raising his hand in invitation.

My throat constricted as my earlier anxiety returned. I could almost hear an inaudible pop as my chances of escape burst. I hesitated, searching his face. The sincerity etched in the crinkle-lines along his eyes, and the kindness belying his fierce gaze had my feet crossing the threshold. I sat at the pitted wood table, absent the knife, as he took the opposite chair for himself.

"You must realize by now why your presence here is such a concern."

"I realize nothing," I said, "except that I've been treated like a prisoner, interrogated as a spy, and in general bullied into submission." I arched a brow. "Have I missed something?"

ConRad leaned back in the chair and folded his arms across his chest. "Things will go better for you if you cooperate."

"Yeah, because things have gone great so far," I said, rubbing my neck. I may have a penchant for drama, but I really had been scared that he was going to kill me. It's not something a gal was willing gloss over.

"This way of speaking that you do—this tone in your voice, is it your attempt at humor?"

Great, he's beginning to sound like my mother. "Are you telling me sarcasm hasn't hit this world of 'Cavemen Gone Military'?"

I copied his mannerism by folding my arms to match his.

"Hmm . . . there it is again. It's . . ." he paused for a moment, "annoying."

Yep, about sixty minutes ago he was telling me I tasted like the sun and now he found me annoying—lovely.

"Regardless," he continued, now all business. "We need to know where the portal is. It's a matter of life or death, not just for us at the compound, but the entire human race."

This question again? We had come full circle, but the "annihilation of the entire human race" thing had started to sink in. My run-in with the monster, an . . . alien was still too real. I had deep scrapes along my hands and knees to prove it. "I've told you everything I know. All I remember was passing out and then waking up with a foul stench and a monster breathing in my face. If that was a portal, then I have no idea how I came across it or how it works." Then a thought came to me. "What if we went back to where you found me and tried to activate the portal? All I did was walk through; maybe that's all it would take."

He dismissed the idea with a quick shake of his head. "It's too dangerous right now to attempt a discovery mission. Besides, my men and I have walked every inch of this planet and we never came across any portal."

I nodded my head, but somehow I already knew that I was the key to activating the portal.

His glance flickered away, and then sliced back. "That's why I enlisted a help of a goddess. There may be things you can't remember, but we still need in order to assure mankind's safety."

Wisps of unease began to curl through my belly. I still didn't trust this man. I was becoming less and less judgmental of my BBD's decision to knock him off. Of course, that was not something I wanted him to know. "And how do you propose to get that information?"

He uncrossed his arms. Concern flashed in his eyes, but immediately it was replaced by cold indifference. This was a man who would get the job done and not waste energy on regret. "It will all be over soon."

Chapter Nine

What the hell was that supposed to mean? If this was another death threat, then I was about willing to slice my own throat in order to stop the suspense of it all.

My head snapped to the side as the door opened, and five very capable looking soldiers, armed with machine guns, marched in. Buzz cuts and camouflage galore, the men displayed a uniformed front resembling cutout paper dolls. Their stance military ready, their guns in front for easy access. The soldiers' gaze darted around the room as if ready to address any threat. Apparently finding none, they opened their ranks in a half circle, enabling me to see what they were so jacked up over.

There in the center, protected like a lamb among lions, stood a tall, willowy figure in dingy white robes. Her shoulders were stooped, gray hair long and unkempt. Her head was cast down as if in deference so I couldn't see her eyes, but my wisps of unease grew and encircled my heart with a constricting grip.

ConRad had shot to his feet at their entrance. Giving his full attention to the woman, he gave a small bow. "My utmost gratitude for coming."

Gesturing to the woman, ConRad looked to me. "This is Aura. Aura, this is Kris. Aura is a goddess, one of the most powerful in the compound, perhaps in all of civilization. Since you're new here, I'll explain a few things. All goddesses, when first their powers are perceived, are isolated from any human contact so they can more aptly focus their senses within. Very few humans are allowed to even speak with a goddess, but since this is such an extreme case, we made an exception."

He turned his attention back to the robed figure. "Aura, do you know why you are here?"

"Of course I do," she snapped. "I wouldn't be a very good goddess if I didn't."

My eyes darted back and forth between ConRad and the goddess, trying to piece together their relationship. Hadn't ConRad said he was the Commander at the compound? So who was this woman and why did he treat her with such respect? Respect that was sorely lacking in his treatment with me.

"Then thank you again for coming," ConRad said, with a reverence and moved to the side.

A path cleared between her and me. The very air seemed to part. There was a strange pulling sensation from this woman, as if invisible tethers were being thrown out from her soul and hooking into mine.

Aura stepped out from her protectors and the soldiers scurried out of her path, almost as if they were afraid to touch her. Gliding over she sat on the chair ConRad had vacated, all the while her head still bent with stringy hair obscuring her features.

Something wasn't right. What had ConRad threatened

earlier—mind-invasion? Chills rose on the back of my neck and ran along my arms. My desire to flee was so strong that my limbs became paralyzed in contradiction.

She slowly slid her palms, fingers knurled with age, closer to me along the table. She unbowed her head, and for the first time I caught sight of her face.

I got a vague impression of papery-thin skin that crinkled and sagged over delicate bones. But it was her eyes. Her eyes transfixed me, fusing my flesh to the metal chair and birthing a fear in my heart like I'd never known.

There was no color . . . just huge black pools swimming amidst the hollowed orbital cavity. No iris, only black from lid to lid. Only a person whose soul had been taken and replaced with something darker could have eyes like that.

My breath caught. A rush of adrenaline unfroze my muscles as I sprang from my chair, and then just as quickly hit a solid wall of flesh—ConRad. He'd come up behind me and very firmly pushed on my shoulders, lowering me back into my chair. His hands splayed gently along my throat as a silent reminder that I was not going anywhere.

I turned my head, my gaze clashed with his. There was no way I was going to stay and participate in this interrogation. I may be under suspicion, but I had cooperated with his demands. I told him everything I knew. I wasn't a hostile witness and shouldn't be treated like one.

"We need answers, Kris. This is the easiest way." His voice was quiet, as if we were the only two people in the room.

"For you or for me?" I'd little doubt the easiest way for him was not necessarily the same for me, but I couldn't help focusing on his eyes. Was that kindness in his normal blue eyes, with the normal pupils and irises?

I cut my gaze away, disgusted at myself for reading into the slight softening of his face. I was here because of this man. No one was holding a gun to his head, and like he'd said earlier, nothing goes on within this compound without his consent. It was crazy to trust a man who only a few hours ago I thought was going to kill me; but then again, lately my instincts were off.

I braced myself and glanced back at Aura. Her lips stretched into what I assumed was her attempt at a smile, but browned teeth paired with the black eyes turned the expression grotesque. How deep did this mind-invasion go? Would she be able to "see" my omission about my BBD?

"Don't be scared child. I'll protect you. Lay your hands in mine," she said, beckoning with a slight upturn of her fingers.

As unreasonable as it sounded, I believed her. Hadn't my BBD said that I needed to be more trusting? Besides the odds of me not obliging were zero at best—with five, make that six, armed men ready and willing to make me obey.

I slid my hands into Aura's dry, cracked palms, her skin warm against my chilled flesh. She began to breathe slow deep breaths. Soon my lids became weighted. I lost the battle to keep them open. All the tension flowed out of my body. My jaw, head, and shoulders felt heavy; my whole frame drooped. My muscles became liquid, yet tingly and light at the same time. With each breath I went deeper and deeper into a black abyss. Hues of blues, purples, and greens swirled before my closed eyes. A cool breeze stirred from outside my body and forced itself deep down into my lungs. I felt a pulling, slight at first, then with more persistence, toward my hands, then out of my body all together. At first I struggled, but the urge to let go was too tempting, like slipping into a hot bath after a twelve-hour shift. Relinquishing control, I floated on the gentle breeze as it hovered around me.

I won the fight against my eyelids and pried them open.

God, I'm tired.

My head was lying on the table on my crossed arms. Had I fallen asleep on my desk at work? It wouldn't be the first time I'd catnapped among the mountain of charts. I raised my head, scrubbing my hands over my face. For all of two seconds there was sweet oblivion—then the swell of horror came crashing in like the final wave over a drowning man. *I'm in enemy territory. There's no one here I can trust.*

I rocketed out of my chair. It crashed to the floor behind me. I slammed my back to the opposite wall, palms flat, heart racing.

I scanned the room, it was empty, except for him—ConRad.

"You're all right. You're fine," he whispered, sitting rock still, hands in surrender mode as if calming a wild animal.

I didn't believe him. Something happened. I was changed. My skin felt unfamiliar, and my very bones seemed to have laid within someone else's body.

"What happened?" I shook my head, tears blurred my vision. Why was I crying?

"Do you need to lie down?" Concern flashed in ConRad's eyes. "Aura said you'd be tired."

Aura? Who was Aura?

Then the synapses in my brain began to fire and I started to remember—the gray old woman, the soul-sucking black eyes.

"What did she do to me?" My voice cracked as I wiped the tears off my cheeks.

"Kris, please . . ." His voice trailed off as he stood and took a step toward me.

"No, don't touch me!" I yelled, raising my palm to fend him off. "Don't come any closer."

Why was I acting like this? What was wrong with me? I didn't trust ConRad, but if he really wanted to hurt me, he would have done so already. But I couldn't help feeling threatened . . . exposed. I needed a few minutes to reconstruct my defenses.

He froze, eyes widening by my response. "Kris, you are safe here. I wouldn't hurt you. You're under my protection now."

"Whatever," I said, my voice caustic. "All you've done is harm me. I don't believe you."

He paled as he took in my words, heightening the contrast of the blue of his eyes against the white of his face. "Of course, that's how you would see it."

He bent and righted the chair and gestured for me to take a seat. "Sit. You look about ten seconds from crashing to the floor."

I felt like it too. Now that my heartbeat dropped from dangerous levels, black clouds crowded the sides of my vision. I found my chair and sat, taking deep breaths to prevent myself from passing out.

ConRad took his own chair and mirrored my breathing.

"Aura did a special treatment on you, something we call *retrieval*. She has special powers that allow her to access information from people."

"Was this the mind-invasion you threatened me with earlier?" I tried to keep the edge out of my voice. I didn't want him to know how betrayed I felt by his actions.

"Yes, but she did this in a much kinder way. More of a coaxing than an invasion, the other way can be much . . . harder." There was a slight clenching of his right jaw muscle, but otherwise he was motionless. I'd begun to read him better—the more agitated he became, the stiller he was.

"She read my mind?" The thought made my throat thick.

"That's an oversimplification, but . . . yes." His eyes settled on mine with the last word, letting me know he wouldn't hide behind excuses.

I wouldn't have believed him, except I sensed I'd been invaded on some level. Like I'd been stripped naked and left to weather the elements alone.

Everyone has their weakness—the thing that they're most afraid of. Some people don't even know what theirs is—but I knew mine. It was the belief that became the foundation of what I built my life on—don't let 'em in. Even though I was a medical intern, I'd kept myself free from emotional attachments. Feelings for patients were kept in their place. Outside of work there was no time to foster emotional attachments. Keep things simple; that was my motto. No one gets inside my head without my permission.

My hand fluttered up to touch the sudden throbbing at my temple. I was sick of being vulnerable, sick of being left out in the cold. I didn't know how to protect myself, and worst of all I didn't know who I could trust.

"How could someone do that, especially without my consent? I need answers. Where the hell am I, and why am I here?" My voice had lost its calm demeanor, instead bordered on hysterical.

She'd been in my head. What had she seen?

The room spun and closed in on me. "Who are you? Who are all these people? What are you doing hiding inside a mountain? And what is that creature that attacked us?"

"Alright, alright . . . calm down. I know you have a lot of questions. This all seems very strange to you." He pulled his seat closer and took hold of my folded hands. "We don't have all the answers, but let me start with what we believe might have happened."

ConRad's thumb ran along the inside of my wrist, then he stopped his administrations and lifted his head, pinning me with his stare. "We believe that you might have traveled through space and time."

Well, duh, but I kept my mouth shut.

"I know it sounds crazy, but we've heard tales of people doing this in the past. I didn't believe it, but now . . ." He was close. I could feel his breath as it fanned my cheek. The man had no concept of personal space—I needed room. I broke his hold, twisting to release his grasp on my wrist. He got the not so subtle hint and sat back in his chair.

I, on the other hand, needed more than a hint. I needed the truth.

I raised an eyebrow. "Really? That's what you've come up with? Okay fine. So *if* I traveled in time, where am I now?"

His eyes narrowed at my tone. He could've probably counted on one hand how many people stood up to him and lived to tell about it.

"You want answers?" The man who had gently caressed me was gone, in his place was the Commander bent on getting what he wanted. "How's this for answers? This is your future.

"Look around," he said, crossing one ankle over the opposite knee and circled his finger in the air. "Pretty isn't? Sometime after 2020, scientists learned how to harness atomic power. With that knowledge all the new satellites were equipped with UFCs. With more power and longer range we were able to make contact with IL—intelligent life. They came, they conquered, and the human race nearly died in the process.

"The war, the Global War, surpassed anything ever seen in the whole history of mankind." ConRad stood and began to pace the small width of the room. "Our planet was destroyed, billions of people were killed. Most of our technology was lost, not just decades of it, but centuries. It was as if the world was thrown back to the late eighteen hundreds. The aliens' consumption of raw materials caused the Earth's core to heat up. We know that most of the land is underwater, but we're not sure how much. What remains is one mass of land that barely supports the few thousand people left—or at least that's how many we think are left. Earth's settlement may be located north of the equator, but with so much of the planet uninhabitable, we just can't be sure. According to legends, at one time there were huge blocks of ice floating around the northern part of the planet, but I don't see how. All I do know is that we inhabit the only dry land, and there's only water as far as the eye can see."

"Oh God," I said as a new thought struck me, "tell me this

isn't Earth. Tell me this barren, cold, dark place isn't home."
Tears welled up in my eyes. How could humans let it get this
far? Why didn't someone step in and urge caution?

"No, thank the goddesses. The planet you saw outside this
compound is a whole other story. We don't have to get into all
that today. I know you're tired." He seemed drained also, the
lines on his face had etched in a little deeper, the corners of his
mouth pulled a little tighter.

I had passed over the boundary of tired long ago and now
seemed to be smack in the middle of delirious, but the need to
have answers was too great. Knowledge was power. I couldn't
stand the thought of being vulnerable any longer. "No, I want
to know, need to."

He stopped pacing and zeroed me with his gaze. "It's why I
live in this God-forsaken mountain like a rat in a hole. It's because this hell is a portal planet, a way to travel through space.
Dark Planet is the last defense against the aliens. The main
function of our society—or what's left of it—is to protect the
portal. If the aliens are able to break through, then the whole
human nation will perish. I know I keep saying that, but it is
true. It's a numbers thing—we don't have enough bodies left to
sacrifice again."

I cringed at his use of the word *sacrifice*, as if the aliens were
some type of gods needing atonement.

"So that's it, the sordid truth of why we are living like animals and getting our butts kicked by giant cockroaches with
teeth." He'd turned and faced the wall, hands on hips as if the
retelling of history made the facts more gruesome.

I couldn't believe what he was saying. Intelligent life? Global
War? Billions of people dead? I put my head in my hands,

squelching the childish desire to cover my ears. If everything he said was true, then the Armageddon that my grandfather warned about had happened; the world as I knew it was gone. I felt a churning in my stomach that had nothing to do with the persistent cloak of fatigue that had been draped over me since my late-night visitor.

"So then why am I here?" I blinked rapidly to dispel the burning in my eyes.

"Hell if I know." He faced me again and ran both hands through his hair. "Aura told me that you passed through time and space. She also said 'someone' sent you. When I pushed for more information, she said that all I needed to know was that you are not a spy. Damn goddesses, they get so cocky sometimes. Do you know who could've sent you?"

I shook my head, but got that sick guilty feeling in my stomach.

He sighed. "Of course not, why would anyone tell me the truth. I'm just the Commander of this hell hole."

And for one second I felt sorry for him, and then it was gone.

He shook his head. "There are myths about time travel, but I want to be crystal clear on my thoughts here—they're just that, stories. But hell, if someone talks against the myths and prophecies that are spewed out by the Elders and goddesses alike. That kind of talk can be construed as heresy and before you know it, you find yourself buried up to your neck with a bunch of people throwing rocks at your head."

My God, what if he was telling the truth? What if all of this wasn't a dream and this really was the future of the human race. And with all our advancements, this is what our race had come to. Capital punishment and heresy? Shock thickened my brain, making his words hard to digest.

ConRad took two steps and braced his hands on either side of the table, crowding me with his presence again. "But there is one thing I do know, and that's that you came to this planet through some type of portal, and it wasn't the one under my guard. So where is it? Because if you're hiding information about another portal and the aliens find their way through, I'll cut you up and feed you to them myself."

Okay, so he scared me—a lot, but hell if I was going to let him know it. "Oh, another threat from you, how original. And here I thought we had moved past that to, I don't know, dirty looks?"

ConRad leaned in close, a sly smile slithered across his face. "Oh, we can move past that if you like. Right on to the part with you moaning my name, legs clasped around my hips."

Ahhh . . . jerk anyone? Because only an arrogant prick would bring *that* up. And there was the crux of the problem. He believed I was hiding something and I saw him as a bully who used his authority to get what he wanted. But if I was sent here to enlighten his views, it wasn't happening today. An overwhelming fatigue permeated through my muscles. The fight seemed to have been leached out of my body. "I don't know. I just don't have any answers for you."

ConRad backed off and nodded, sensing I was physically and mentally done. He stood and opened the door. "Soldiers, escort Ms. Davenport to her quarters, we're done for the day."

Relieved I wouldn't be spending another night in "cave jail," I stood and stifled a yawn.

As I started towards the door, I turned and stopped. I

hadn't missed the point of how vulnerable I had been, lying unconscious outside, among the killer aliens. ConRad had put his life at risk and two of his men had died protecting me. "Commander, thank you. Thank you for answering all my questions, and . . . thanks for saving my life."

The corner of his mouth lifted, which I assumed was his version of a smile, and nodded.

"Call me ConRad."

"Okay, ConRad. By the way, there were large floating blocks of ice. They were called icebergs."

His eyebrows popped slightly as if contemplating a whole new concept. "Good to know."

Was it? I always thought knowledge was power, but now . . . now all I wanted was to go back home, open a bottle of wine and lose myself in a trashy novel. *Yeah, it was good to know.* I hoped he was right and walked out the door.

Chapter Ten

Bits of white floated in a puddle of red. I didn't want to get my princess slippers wet. They were my favorite, but there was blood everywhere. Mommy had told me to stay in bed, but I had to help. The red on my hands made grasping the small bits so hard. They kept slipping. There were so many pieces. How would I ever get her back together? I wasn't scared though. She'd be alright. I just had to get all the small, white pieces back together and she'd be fine, and then I could wash off all the blood—so much blood.

I sat straight up in bed, panting. Tears wetted my cheeks like always, the images lingering on the inside of my eyelids long after I'd awakened. I checked my hands. No blood. Instead, a fine white dust coated my palms, clothes, and hair. What the—?

I jumped out of bed and frantically brushed at my clothes and hair. Where did this come from? A tremble from above answered as a new fine mist of dust rained down on me. I threw my arms up to cover my head. Earthquake!

I slammed myself against the concrete floor and belly-crawled under the bed. Not being a Californian, I hadn't cut my teeth on fault lines and mud slides. I couldn't remember the safety protocols. Was it take cover in a bathtub or was that for tornados? The mild sifting settled and I poked my head out from behind folded arms. I scooted forward and shot my eyes to the ceiling, a ceiling made of dirt and rock. I sighed—really, since when is plaster such a modern advancement? I crawled out on my hands and knees, glad no one was around to observe my display of courage. I couldn't help it if some people didn't understand my utmost respect for safety—my own, of course.

Last night when the soldiers showed me to my room, I was delirious with fatigue. My gaze fell upon a small cot. I made a beeline and passed out face down. I hadn't bothered with a tour at the time, not that one was needed. I sat back on my legs and with a small turn of my head, took in the whole room. Covered in dust was a small bed of army-green wool blankets and a hard pillow. Along one wall was a brown metal desk and chair, and crammed in one corner was a set of tall army-green foot lockers. One had a lock on it, and the other was open with a folded set of what looked like camouflaged pants and a shirt the color of pureed spinach. Oh goodie, the exact duplicate of what I was wearing. Apparently, when ConRad said billions of people had died that included every person with a fashion sense.

On the other side of the cot, tucked behind a partial wall, was a toilet—minus the seat—and a white sink with a small mirror hanging on a nail above. I went over and pulled the cord above the toilet. It flushed.

I closed my eyes, and said a small prayer of thanksgiving that this hollowed out mountain had indoor plumbing. My eyes traveled around the small bathroom. And then added a postscript to the big Guy above—toilet paper, please.

With a steadying breath, I took a peek in the hazy mirror, and then stifled a small scream. The soft blonde curls I religiously tamed at the hairdressers had rebelled and puffed into something akin to a blonde afro. Dark circles, and lord help me, puffy bags beneath my eyes like they'd never known wrinkle cream. And my complexion, once my labor of love kept up with daily masks and chemical peels, had dulled and paled.

Screw this. It's time to go home. However I came through, they can just send me right on back. Set the dial to good ol' year 2010 and beam me home, Scottie.

The question was how. And of the two people who might know the answer, I was willing to talk to only one—Quinn.

I turned on the silver faucet to wash my face and knocked over a plastic cup with a toothbrush and silver tube of toothpaste into the sink. This room had been occupied, and whoever they'd booted out must have left in a hurry. I shrugged my shoulders, beggars can't be choosers, and laid claim to the toothbrush. Sorry sucker, life bites.

I ripped off the layer of gauze around my throat and smoothed my hand over the healthy skin. No marks, no scab, just baby-new skin where once the knife's edge had marred. One thing was for certain; in the future, they knew their antibiotics.

I left my "hovel sweet hovel" with relief, and I rounded the corner, intent on my mission to bleed Quinn for answers. Men bustled about the tunnels with machine guns strapped to their backs and their black combat boots leaving tracks in the dust. They seemed oblivious to the quaking above their heads. I, on the other hand, screamed and ducked beneath every metal arch, hovering until the dust settled. Consequently, I was given a wide berth.

I followed Quinn's directions, sticking to the path marked with the number one and came upon a set of metal doors. A soldier ducked through one, and a din of rumbled conversations slipped out past the swinging door.

I sighed—this was as good a place as any. Pushing through the doors, I scanned the room for Quinn. But instead—there were men, lots and lots of men. They clustered around tables and benches, shoveling gray goop into bowls and drank from white mugs. The noise of clicking spoons against plates, gruff laughter and murmurs of conversation hushed as heads swiveled to take in the new arrival. About fifty pairs of eyes widened at me. My feet stilled and grew roots that burrowed deep into the base of the mountain.

The echo of a dropped spoon as it vibrated against the concrete floor cut across the room. I knew I could make an entrance, but still . . . I did a quick check of myself. Yep, still clothed—hadn't miraculously become naked since leaving my room. With a super quick check around the room, I realized, ah, no Quinn here. I shuffled, at least one of my feet, in the direction of the door when I caught a glimpse of a steaming carafe, glistening among white mugs, on a back table. Could it be? The elixir of life—the nectar of the gods—coffee?

I needed to find Quinn, yes, but first things first. By my calculations, it had been about forty-eight hours since my last caffeine fix. My addiction was a tightly controlled thing; it needed to be fed black coffee often and in copious amounts.

My nose signaled my brain, immediately sending happy endorphins bouncing through my caffeine-atrophied veins. My boots tripped on themselves in their quest to carry me toward the Promised Land, parting soldiers as if the men were merely the Red Sea. Snatching a cup and carafe, I poured the black liquid to the rim and took an appreciative sniff, savoring the aroma. The first sip was strong, almost bitter. I pushed the liquid down my throat, my eyes watered as a burn traveled and pooled in my belly. Damn. That. Was. Bad. I looked at the side of the pot for a warning label that should've read "Caution: will grow ridiculous amount of hair on chest if consumed in large amounts."

I closed my eyes and contemplated one more sip. Had I mentioned I was an addict? Besides, braiding chest hairs sounded like fun.

An audible gasp shook the room. My eyes snapped open. Soldiers posed as if frozen within a photograph. One man had stilled his hand mid-shovel to his mouth, creamy goop sliding off the spoon and plopping into the bowl. The so-called coffee turned solid in my stomach. Not a very welcoming crowd. My brain refocused into three simple tasks. Get out of here. Find Quinn. Go home. In that order, no more distractions. With my mug warming between my hands, I held my head high and made a hasty exit.

Outside in the hall I breathed a sigh of relief. With a reception like that, I might have to consider ordering room service. I smiled at the thought of ConRad bustling a linen draped cart into my dirt-den and presenting me with croissants and gourmet coffee. I wondered if he was on the menu, but then again, I'd never acquired the taste for shark.

After a solid twenty minutes I found myself back at the command center. I could've made it in half the time, except I cowered with every mountain shudder. I needed to get home. I wasn't made for this life. My idea of roughin' it was staying in an RV without a five-star restaurant nearby. I had convinced myself if I went back to the original place I'd come through, then I could get back to my time. I just had to persuade Quinn to help me get out of the compound. Of course, there was the small, pesky detail of the carnivorous alien, but one step at a time.

The command center was a huge hollowed out space free from any metal support beams. Soldiers milled about checking weapons, monitors displaying black screens with blinking green cursers were on the metal tables. A loud digitized beeping rose above the low hum made from a crowd of people. It could have almost been a normal workplace—well, a workplace back before Bill Gates invented Windows and DOS was a viable computer program. And everyone had a machine gun strapped to his back and there was something that looked like a missile launcher pushed against the wall. So maybe normal was stretching it.

To the right of the rows of computers was the heavily guarded tunnel—the one I had crawled through seemingly a lifetime ago. Five men stood armed and ready in case anything bigger than a small rat came their way—even then the rat would go the way of target practice. On the opposite side of the room were the large red double doors I had noticed earlier, with another group of soldiers standing battle ready and on guard. With all the fire power in one room, I was hoping that happy trigger fingers weren't contagious?

And of course, in the center of it all was the Commander. If the command center was the pumping heart of this compound, then he was the brains. Standing in front of a huge wall-length computer monitor, he seemed to be the eye in the middle of a storm. As men ran from station to station, he was stillness, projecting an aura of power. I stopped and stared; my jaw slacked. He was a wonderfully made specimen. All tall muscular form, biceps bared and glistening, and a six-pack subtly defined in a tight, damp tank top.

My respirations quickened, and a bead of sweat traced the skin between my breasts. I cut my gaze away from his body and concentrated on his face. He wasn't as old as I'd first thought. The slight lines around his eyes and forehead weren't from age, but from stress and fatigue. As he turned and glanced at the images flashing upon the screen, his eyes narrowed and his jaw muscles clench. And why not? He literally had the weight of the world on his shoulders.

My drooling presence must've become obvious, since ConRad turned and caught me with a diamond hard stare. My breath hitched. Could he glare at me with any more coldness? He dismissed me with a curt nod and turned back to the wall-sized computer screen.

I turned away, embarrassed. To be caught staring at him like some starstruck groupie was not the image I wanted to portray. I walked away and headed to the one room where I might feel more in control, in my element, the infirmary.

Before I could push through the swinging doors, there was Quinn running to meet me with a crazed leer in her eyes. "Thank the goddesses I found you. Where've you been?"

She grabbed my hand and hauled me into the infirmary. "I've been looking all over for you. Hurry, we don't have much time."

"What's going on? What happened?" I set my coffee cup on the nearest table to distract me from the all too familiar clenching in my gut.

Something was wrong. Quinn's appearance had altered in some way even from a few hours ago. The change was subtle. I couldn't quite put my finger on it, but she looked older, as if she had aged ten years over night. My hand wanted to brush the blonde hair that stuck to her cheek, but I kept it firmly at my side. *Don't get involved. Not here to make friends. You're here to get home.*

"Quinn, what's going on?" I yelled to be heard as the ceiling groaned and quaked, showering us with dust and small pebbles.

"It's them," she mouthed or shouted; I couldn't tell. Of course, my lack of hearing could've been because I kept throwing my arms over my head expecting a cave in.

"It's them. The quaking. They want in," she said, pointing to the ceiling, her eyes wide as small pools.

"Them, as in the aliens, *them*?" I couldn't help the instinctive crouching over as I shielded my face with my hand, throwing worried glances at the ceiling.

Quinn nodded, like it was okay she was in the middle of a mountain with large carnivorous beasts trying to be the first in line at the all-you-can-eat human buffet.

"And this is a . . . normal occurrence?" I asked, hoping the aliens just beat their ugly mugs against side of the mountain in some futile instinctive animal ritual.

"No, it's worse."

Great, no need to panic.

"Quinn." I lowered my voice, the thunderous pounding had

ceased, and I needed to make sure she received my next question with crystal clarity. "Can they get in?"

She shook her head and shrugged one shoulder. "They haven't yet."

"Oh, very comforting, Quinn. Very comforting. Am I the only one who is beginning to panic here?" I threw my hands up in the air. Was there no such thing as platitudes in this century? I would love to hear an "it's all gonna be fine" about now.

"Listen, you have to help him, no matter what. You have to help him!" She crossed her arms, hugging and rocking herself as if comforting a small child.

"Help who?" My hands grasped her shoulders, stilling her motions. At the same time I wanted to shake her, because once again Quinn and I were having *two freaking different conversations.*

Quinn's head was bowed mere inches from mine. She tilted her face up, her gaze fixed on mine—hiding nothing. The soft blue of her eyes had been hazed over by dark rolling storm clouds obscuring the whites of her eyes with a muted blue.

I sprang back and released her as if her skin had scorched my palms. "What the—"

A loud noise crashed through the room. I whipped my head around as a soldier burst into the infirmary with enough force to bang the metal door against the adjoining wall. He stood with one arm braced against the backlash of the door, the other holding his gun. His brown crew cut matched his café mocha eyes that could've been appealing if they hadn't harbored such trepidation. He scanned the room and quickly locked stares with Quinn. "Where have you been? I . . . we need you at the center. We're going up."

The conversation was a mere formality. Quinn was already racing toward the door. With a turn of her head she glanced back at me. "Kris, don't forget what I said, please."

"And what exactly was that, Quinn?" I yelled to the swinging door. Religion was wrong—hell wasn't pitchforks and fire; it was never getting a straight answer to your questions.

Jeezus, going up, really? Where exactly was UP? The only *up* I knew was where the aliens were. A synapse in my brain fired caught and then . . . *God, please no.*

I raced after Quinn.

I ran toward the command center, and before I even turned the corner I could tell something had happened. The volume had been raised to a low roar. Men shouted orders, boots marched on hard ground, and guns were being locked and loaded. I'd never been in the army, never seen a battle or even volunteered for the Red Cross, but the symphony of sounds I heard for the first time in my life was unmistakable. It was the song of war.

My feet slowed as I took in the chaos of men readying for battle. The room, thick with adrenaline, resonated with a low buzz sending goose bumps across my flesh. A blur of green and black camouflaged uniforms merged with faces smeared black with paint. Weapons crisscrossed backs and strapped onto bulging biceps, pockets were being loaded with ammunition and grenades, then Velcroed shut.

There were two groups of men preparing to go topside. The ones in the front were heavily armed and had communication devices wrapped from ear to mouth. The second group consisted of five men, equally armed, but forming a protective circle around a woman in a long, flowing white gown. Though

I'd never seen her, I'd no doubt what she was. Soldiers hovered, encircling, though careful not to touch her. A goddess.

She was quite a bit younger than the goddess who had done the mind-invasion on me—barely out of childhood in truth. Her black hair was swept back into a messy thick braid that swayed down her back. She looked nervous, though she tried to hide it. Her white teeth worried on her bottom lip as she twirled whips of hair around a finger and shuffled from foot to foot. She all but screamed, "I'm scared." I couldn't blame her. In a room full of men armed to the teeth (one man was actually carrying a knife in his mouth), she was the only one without a weapon or armor. Just long, flowing white robes like a homing beacon in the sea of black and army-green camouflage. An unease blossomed in my stomach; it was like watching a virgin being taken to the sacrificial altar.

Everyone seemed to be running to their destination and duty. And yet there was calm among the chaos, as in the eye of the tempest was one man—ConRad.

He stood apart, distancing himself. The quiet air surrounding him vibrated with authority. The crazier things got, the more heightened—it didn't seem to matter to him. All the madness seemed to get sucked into his personal black void, leaving him with no emotion, except calm control.

I glanced back over to the goddess. She was licking her lips, which seemed overly red against the paleness of her face. Regardless of the cause, children shouldn't go to war. My decision made, I rushed into the fray and almost ended up on my butt after crashing into a soldier. I maneuvered through a line of men and ran over to where I'd last seen ConRad. He was barking orders at a few soldiers.

I softly placed my hand on his arm. I knew I had no pull with ConRad, so it couldn't hurt to drizzle my words with a little honey. I put on the charm, kicking my voice up a notch, hoping I came across sounding sexy and a bit helpless. "ConRad, I mean Commander, where are these men going?"

As soon as I said the words, I knew it had been a mistake. His arm tightened as if I'd struck him. He stopped talking midsentence, and with the precision of a surgeon, cut his hardened ice-gaze to mine.

I removed my hand, letting it flutter self-consciously at the base of my neck. In self-defense? I felt my throat move hard as I swallowed the lump that had formed. "I mean, I know why they are going up, but I'm not sure there could be a strong enough reason to the allow men—and one child," I said, emphasizing the word *child*, "to go topside and . . . fight?"

I couldn't break the gravitational pull of ConRad's glare. But out of my peripheral vision I saw one soldier's mouth slack open. Quinn's face loomed behind ConRad's, eyes huge in her panic-strickened face. It was as if someone had hit the mute button; the volume quieted.

"Are you inferring that I don't place the life of my men in high enough regard?" His voice was all taut control. His jaw muscle flexed, probably at the thought of snapping small, delicate finger bones—like my own. Honestly, I hadn't meant to question the Commander in Chief of the compound, but that's exactly what I'd done. In front of all his men no less.

I shook my head. The thunder clouds were brewing, and I knew what every experienced sailor knows—sometimes you need to cut the sails and ride out the storm.

"It sounded to me like you were questioning my authority.

Because I assure you," his eyes narrowed, and the creases at the corners deepened into grooves, "I've weighed every life and take no man or woman's sacrifice to be worthless. But as to the 'why now, why this time'—well, that's an excellent question."

He lifted his head and surveyed our transfixed audience, seeing if any wanted to join our two-man play. "Would anyone be willing to let Ms. Davenport in on why after ten years of meticulous and covert operations we are now going up to engage the aliens?"

There was a silence that no one wanted to fill, except for me, yes . . . stupid, *stupid* me. He had addressed me as Ms. once before and I hadn't corrected him. But now . . . "Doctor."

I sucked in my breath. I hadn't meant to say that out loud, really. It's just that the pathway from my brain to my mouth is way too short—it is a disease, a condition. I should come with a warning label.

"Excuse me, Ms. Davenport, I didn't quite catch that."

Probably because I had spoken under my breath. "Um . . . doctor. I passed my medical exams three months ago, so that would be . . . um . . . Dr. Davenport."

He paused for a number of heartbeats, his eyes widened, and his hand came to rest on his chest. "My apologies, please forgive the misrepresentation."

He waited for a response, so I mumbled something, but my voice broke on the word "fine." My face felt uncomfortably hot and my ears, I knew, were turning a bright crimson color.

"Well then, please let me be the one to inform you why all my work has disintegrated, and why the aliens are trying to find their way into the mountain." He crossed his arms and lowered his voice to a menacing whisper. "The aliens have gone berserk over their first smell of a woman in over ten years. So I need to lay bait, a decoy, to lead them away from the drugging, all-consuming, addictive scent . . . of *you*."

The word "you" was launched like a fiery missile and dropped right at my feet.

I was the cause, the reason a mere girl and a dozen men were about to risk their lives to prevent the aliens from breaking in. I opened my mouth to protest, but what could I say? Apparently I'd already said enough. I stepped back. My leaden feet were heavy as I dragged them across the floor. I turned slowly, keeping my sight on the ground. I couldn't bear to see the soldiers' faces. I didn't want the memory of them burned into my brain.

With each step I took the volume rose, and soon the march of men was loud enough for me to glance over my shoulder. The men were on the move, one by one crawling through the tunnel. I knew ConRad was there crawling somewhere among them. He'd never send his men and stay behind, but I couldn't quite pinpoint him in the sea of black. My eyes caught sight of Quinn. To my relief I realized she'd be left behind, since she was busy talking into a com-phone headset and pounding on a keyboard in front of her.

Soon the teams were gone, and a charged hush fell over the compound. The soldiers left behind were pumped with anticipation, and I held my breath, waiting without even knowing why.

"Got it," Quinn shouted excitedly, followed by a loud crackle over some sort of PA system. "Commander, you are all on Broadcast now. Do you copy?"

There was silence and loud crackling, then "Copy" came

across the speakers. "All units are out of entry tunnel. Team One is in defense mode guarding the entrance. Team Two will proceed to the targeted area," ConRad said.

A sigh of relief swept through the command center. It seemed the most dangerous part of the mission had been leaving and entering the tunnel—logical since the tunnel was only wide enough for one man at a time. If caught, the odds were those of shooting fish in a barrel.

Stillness settled thick among those of us left behind. We all began to breathe as one, straining to listen for any words between the crackles. Then there was a burst of noise—gunshots? Men screamed, some yelled profanities and others just in pain. Then I heard it—I remembered from before and would never forget—the inhuman roar of an alien. The call reverberated throughout my body and seeped into my very bones. Somewhere in the blueprint of my genetic code, a code older than I'll ever live to be, my response to the primitive message was clear . . . I was the hunted.

The sounds of battle were deafening, but through the noise were phrases. "There're coming from behind! He's gone . . . leave him . . . leave him!" And the worst two words in the English language heard over and over . . . and over. "Oh God! Oh God!" And something more terrifying than even the screams.

Silence.

CHAPTER ELEVEN

"We've lost contact," Quinn whispered.

A hush settled in the room, thick with fear. What had happened? Could the men not hold the line? Did we break? The sound of rocks clashing and falling echoed behind the steel door of the tunnel. Someone or something was coming. Soldiers prepared for the worst. The noise of magazines being slammed into the chambers of machine guns sliced through the air. Whatever was heading down the tunnel wouldn't be getting in without a fight.

There was a pounding, a curse, and then a shout from behind the entrance. "Open the damn door. Now!" It was ConRad.

The men recognized their commander and immediately opened the steel door. A small sigh of relief slipped past my lips as I watched ConRad step out. He was hunched over carrying the goddess, whose head was listless, robes no longer white, but dingy like she'd taken a crash course in falling from grace. Two other soldiers stumbled out, blood soaked and haggard as they half-carried, half-dragged a fourth man who bled from the stomach. Two others crawled out on their hands and knees. One wheezed and fell to the ground, holding a wound on his side that oozed black-like tar through his fingers. A smell of singed flesh and hair caught me as another solider turned his head, and I glimpsed an ear and scalp melted as if made of wax and held too near a flame.

All too soon the men stopped coming. The steel door was closed with a resounding thud that echoed through the mountain. A large locking wheel was spun by a soldier and a thick steel bolt slid home with a screeching finality. So few, only six including the young girl, compared to over a dozen that had left.

I watched in horror as ConRad's gaze searched the room until his locked with mine. The rest of the men followed suit. All eyes on me, pinning me with their stare.

I froze. A kaleidoscope of thoughts swirled through my brain. Why had I made such an issue about being called Dr. Davenport earlier? I wasn't really a doctor. In the real world I wouldn't even be able to apply a butterfly Band-Aid without a resident breathing down my neck.

But there they stood. Their eyes huge, faces smeared with blood and dirt. They looked as if they expected miracles, and I was their latest savior.

Savior? Miracles? Didn't these people know I couldn't figure out the bill at a restaurant without using the tip calculator on my cell phone? It didn't seem to matter. I was the only option these people had. A rush of adrenaline pushed the bile back down and sent goose bumps coursing across my skin. I turned and raced toward the infirmary.

"Quinn, I need your help." But she was already ahead of me, waiting with the door open.

I was nervous, okay scared to complete constipation. I knew trauma medicine—at least on paper I did—but this was a primitive environment, and I was working alone. I scoured my hands through my hair, trying to figure out my first step.

Get it together Kris. You're the only chance these people have got.

I did a super quick look over the soldiers and decided most of them could be helped later. The solider with the abdominal wound was in the most critical condition.

"Lay him down gently . . . careful. Don't move his head . . . good." I went over to clear his C-spine, not that it would've made a difference since he was literally thrown about before he got to me, but I relied on my saving mantra—*follow protocol.*

His face was stained with red, a hematoma swelled, sealing shut one eye. I did a quick exam, which was super quick, considering I didn't have an X-ray machine, blood pressure cuff, or oxygen monitor. Regardless, the injury was obvious; blood pooled around his midsection and flowed out onto the table. I needed to stop the bleeding, but I couldn't do it on my own. I quickly surveyed the sea of anxiously waiting soldiers. I pointed to the first man I saw, the one I'd named Tank. "You . . . get a clean cloth and put pressure on this."

I gestured to the gaping wound and ripped open my patient's shirt to get the field clear. ConRad stepped from behind and placed a restraining hand on my shoulder. "The girl first," he said, his voice low, but firm.

"What?" I tried to shake off his grip. I couldn't spare him a glance. I knew I would have a hard time figuring out the source of bleeding. Were the intestines involved, the liver, the spleen?

He didn't release his hold, instead squeezed harder. "The goddess first. You need to treat the goddess first."

Thinking the girl might have gone into cardiac arrest. I ran over to the girl who'd been laid out on the next table. I'd started on the solider first because of the excessive bleeding, but maybe I'd missed something. There was nothing obvious, but a quick check revealed a steady pulse, good respirations, and pupils even and reactive to light. There were no wounds, no bleeding or distorted limbs. She was unconscious, but seemed stable enough. My gut reaction was possible trauma to the head, but it was impossible to tell without doing further tests, of which I had none. With a snap judgment born to all good emergency personnel, I determined the girl was less critical than my first patient. The decision made, I jumped back to the soldier who had already soaked the first cloth and was starting on his second.

The Commander didn't appreciate my decision. He stepped in front of me blocking my access to my patient. "You need to completely finish with her treatment, before starting on this soldier."

"Negative," I said, holding my hands in the air placating my illusion of a sterile field. "He is the most critical patient. If I treat her first, then he'll die before I can get back to him."

"It may not matter."

My heartbeat skipped a beat. "What do you mean . . . may not matter? Of course, it matters."

"He failed his duty," he said, pointing to the girl.

Really? I widened my eyes in disbelief. "The way I see it, he protected her with his life. How is that failing his duty?" I pushed my way past ConRad and continued to work. The man bleeding out on the table was my patient, regardless of what the Commander said.

"It's out of my hands. The Elders will decide, but the *status level* needs to be followed." His voice was monotone, as if he'd repeated this line of crap at least a dozen times before.

I was stunned. Who were these Elders? And exactly why did they get to decide? "If you weren't going to allow me to treat him, why did your men bring him back? Why not just let him die in the field?"

Out of the corner of my eye I saw ConRad glance down at the solider whose blood had spilled onto the floor and started to pool toward our shoes. His gaze drifted back toward me and for a brief moment I saw regret flash in his eyes. But then the emotion was gone, replaced with blue ice. "He's a good man. And there may still be hope for the goddess."

I looked around the room. Despair dripped like water from a sodden blanket. Quinn's face had grown pale with worry, eyes huge with fright. The other soldiers stood motionless, not sure whose orders to obey. Each face was etched with pain, eyes dead and hollow.

"But your men thought there was hope for *him*. That's why they risked their lives to save his. And I think there is hope, so until I have none . . . I expect full cooperation from you and your men. Cut off his clothes, I need to see what I am working with." As far as I was concerned, the discussion was over. My ER doctor persona had raised its ugly head. I shouted orders and expected to be obeyed. But ConRad's presence was doing its standard assault on my brainwaves. I needed him gone.

"Commander, unless you're going to help, you need to get

out of my way." My voice was sharper than I intended, but I could detect his scent underneath the blood and gore, and to realize how aware I was of this man sent panic coursing up my spine. Expecting resistance, I was relieved when he took a huge step back, allowing me breathing room.

"You need to know, you are disobeying a direct order from the Elders."

His words had the same effect as if he ran ice down my naked spine. I glanced down at my battered and torn patient, and then the pale goddess. I wasn't sure I could help either of them. But were they worth the risk? I shook my head; it wouldn't come to that. I'd be gone before the Elders, or whoever they were, could find me.

I nodded. I understood what he was saying; the responsibility was all mine. ConRad stepped closer to me and whispered in my ear. "I will protect you as much as I can, but they could ask for retribution instead."

My only reaction was the slight stutter in my heartbeat. "It doesn't matter."

I lied; it sure the hell did matter—a lot. He stepped closer. His shoulder brushed my back, his breath tickled the fine hairs along my neck. "I didn't think it would."

I sighed. What did he know? Apparently nothing, because I had a plan. Try to save both of my patients and then get the hell out of Dodge.

A spasm found a home deep in my shoulders and neck as I struggled to knit flesh and bone together. Hours had flown by and now only Quinn and I were left with our patients. In the harsh glare of the infirmary the blood glowed orange and soaked the gauze as it seeped through my clumsy attempt at stitches. The work was tedious, his wounds extensive, and to top it off, I wasn't sure my stitches would even pass for surgery. I strained my Hippocratic oath with the "first do no harm" part, not knowing if, after I was done, he'd even be able to take a leak without squirting himself in the eye instead.

My God, please let him be able to take a leak. Panic caused my hands to shake. I wiped wetness from my forehead with a shrug of a shoulder. If I had been in a "real surgery," I would've been thrown out of the OR for such a non-aseptic move, but then I would at least be wearing gloves instead of bearing cuticles stained orange with gore.

"You're doing fine," Quinn said as she wiped my working field clean.

I nodded, unable to speak. I was so tired. I'd crossed the line of hopelessness into the prolific state of despair hours ago. But there was one saving grace; whatever had cut him had been sharp, so the severing was clean. Except, grace wouldn't be enough. I needed a butt load of antibiotics and a couple hundred liters of blood.

I glanced up at my patient, his eyes were closed and he seemed to be resting comfortably. Quinn earlier had stocked the infirmary with supplies that she received from the morning shipment from Earth. Sterile drape cloths and an anesthetic were among the stockpile, of which I was grateful for, possibly the only thing. After she'd cleaned him up a bit, I recognized him as the soldier who had searched out Quinn earlier. I remembered his coffee eyes, but with them closed I could tell the rest of him wasn't too bad either. He still had too much softness in his chin and cheeks to make him age appropriate for me, but he was definitely in the "handsomer as he gets older" category.

"Do you know him?" I was drawing on my reserves. I needed to make him more than flesh and blood. I needed to make him human.

Quinn's ocean-blue eyes popped up and regarded me over a particular stubborn rib bone. I broke eye contact first as I maneuvered the bone back in place, praying I didn't puncture vital organs in the process.

"We're not allowed to have contact outside of work. Relationships between men and goddesses are strictly forbidden."

I wasn't born yesterday. It was obvious there was more going on with these two than Quinn was telling me.

"So you're a goddess then?" I had my suspicions, especially after the creepy, swirling eye thing.

Her shoulder lifted. "A goddess-in-training. I wasn't a very good pupil. The Elders wanted to send me to the work camps, but the Sisters at the school convinced them to port me to the front lines instead. It was their hope that the experience would jar latent powers."

"So it's worked."

"To a degree, but . . . ah . . . you're the only one who knows." Her fingers tried to smooth down a pucker in my stitch. Damn, that one's gonna scar.

I nodded. I knew acknowledging herself as a goddess would sentence her to sensory isolation and no teenager, no matter what century, would look forward to that. I tried again. "What's his name?"

"I think his ID number is 215-67 . . ."

"I didn't ask about your relationship or his ID number. I want his bloody name!" The stress had gotten to me. I took a deep breath and lowered my voice. "What do his friends call him?"

Silence. She wasn't going to answer.

"Look, I know you know it . . . just tell me." Maybe it wasn't fair to push her, she had a lot to lose, but I was desperate. I realized there was a chance I might not find my way home before the Elders came. I needed a purpose and this man's life was it. So he better as hell be worth my efforts and have more than just a number to speak for him.

"Zimmion."

I nodded with relief. He had a name; somewhere, somebody loved him.

I threaded the now blunted needle through the connective tissue and pulled too hard, tearing the flesh. I dropped the needle in frustration and massaged my cramping hand. I checked over my stitches—some held and some didn't, springing leaks along the jagged suture lines.

A choking sensation bubbled in my throat. The quiet of the room was deafening. With it I could hear the voice in my head repeating—*just give up, you weren't good enough to save her, and you're not good enough to save him.* I shook my head, trying to clear my mind. "Quinn, I need you to talk to me."

"About what?"

"God, I don't know . . . anything. Tell me about the older men, the Elders that ConRad was concerned about."

Quinn heaved a heavy sigh. "It's a long story."

"I've got time."

"I guess you'll find out sometime. See, we are all followers of The Way. It has become our life—what saved us. After the Global War, humans were scattered throughout the planet. Most found their way to the same place due to the limited amount of dry land. But there was no civilization, no laws or order, just chaos. Women especially became threatened because of being so few, the aliens were particularly fond of females. Fights broke out; wives and daughters were kidnapped. That was when the older men came together and created a new doctrine. Order was established and the weak given protection. The Elders' punishments were harsh and their justice swift, but the religion worked. More and more people came to follow The Way."

I reached up and checked Zimmion's pulse; weak, but steady. My recent sutures were holding. My technique wasn't pretty, but it was working. "Go on. But if you tell me that one of these older men are descendants of David Koresh from Waco, Texas, I'm out of here."

"Who?" her brow furrowed.

"Nothing." My sense of humor was lost on these people. Pity.

"There are rules that affect almost all areas of our lives. Laws about procreation, marriage, birth order, and workstations, but the main beliefs govern the anti-tech laws. The Elders believe the alien invasion was a direct result from God's displeasure about the advancement in science and technology. So though we have the knowledge for greater technologies, we choose to live a more simple life outlined for us by The Way."

I nodded. That explained the advanced microbiotics and also such primitive surroundings. "Are they bad men?"

Quinn's expression darkened. "No, at least not in the beginning. But power corrupts men, and the Elders are powerful."

A sense of foreboding swept through me. These were the men who could determine Zimmion's fate and mine? I tied the last knot and almost wept with relief. "Thanks Quinn . . . for everything."

She smiled. The lines of fatigue accented her eyes. "Do you think he'll make it?"

I hated that question. "He needs a huge dose of antibiotics just to give him a prayer of a chance."

We both looked at each other; volumes spoken between us, but I still asked. "You don't happen to have the key to the microbiotics?"

Quinn shook her head. "Remember, you promised."

Ha, I'd done no such thing, but the line had been drawn when I made my stand with ConRad. The question now was how far across was I willing to go? Dread washed over me in waves. I couldn't think of a single thing I wanted to do less than fight over the stupid key to the metal box. Without a doubt there'd be a fight, but did I really have a choice? If Zimmion didn't get the microbiotics, there was no way he'd survive.

I'd kick my own behind if I could've reached it. I knew the rules, knew microbiotics were strictly for the goddess, and decided to go through with the surgery anyways. All that work, all that meticulous care, and I had no way to treat the infection. I was getting sick of all the rules here, rules I seemed to be breaking at an alarming rate.

ConRad was probably up in his command center laughing his head off, knowing that there was no way I could save his life. Okay, so maybe that wasn't fair. I knew he wouldn't think this was any joking matter, but still he'd never give the microbiotics to me.

"You should check on the goddess," Quinn said. I looked up, surprised to see she was slowly stroking the hair off of Zimmion's forehead.

"Yes . . . yes . . . I should do that." Watching Quinn I realized this was the first tender affection I'd seen anywhere in this compound. The gesture seemed strange, out of place in such a harsh society. After washing my hands, I walked over to the goddess and checked her vitals. Everything seemed stable and she was resting peacefully. I still believed my first instinct was correct, possible head trauma. If she sustained a blow to the head, hopefully it would be nothing more than a concussion. But if there was hemorrhaging in the brain, then there was nothing I could do. I was definitely no brain surgeon and absolutely not under these primitive conditions.

"I think she needs the microbiotics," Quinn said, not bothering to remove her tender gaze from Zimmion's face.

I shook my head. "I don't think antibiotics would help. There doesn't seem to be any sign of infection. There could be a possible concussion, but only time will tell."

"I still think we should get them for her though." This time Quinn did look up and gazed intently at me.

"What are you trying to say?" My chest tightened. I knew she wasn't contradicting my medical advice, but something else all together.

"All I am saying is that you need to go and get them."

"For the . . . goddess?"

"Yes." Her eyes lowered to Zimmion, then back at me. "For the goddess."

"No, no." I shook my head, throwing up my arms in defeat. "I'm done. I did what I could to save him. I've already pushed ConRad as far as I can. I'm not willing to put myself any more on the line. I'm sorry, Quinn. I know how you feel, but I just can't. I need to concentrate on finding my way home, *before* the Elders are notified. I'm already in too deep."

"You can do this," Quinn stated. "ConRad's just a man like anyone else."

I was aghast. "Have you seen him? The man's a killer! I think he rips heads off of small children for pleasure."

"There *is* a reason we don't have small children running around the compound."

I threw a deadpan gaze at Quinn. "Was that a joke?"

"I don't know. Was it funny?" A spark of light flashed in her eyes.

"No, not really." If she wouldn't laugh at my jokes, then I wouldn't laugh at hers. "Besides, if you haven't noticed, I'm not exactly his favorite person."

"I'll help you," she said, her face blank, all signs of teasing gone.

"How?" I didn't have to ask to what she was referring to. I knew. I focused in on the possibility of a way home like a surgeon's precise incision. If I was going to commit to this, I wanted more than just a point toward the door and a pat for good luck.

"I can get you out of the compound and limited protection through the dark, if that's what you really want." Her voice was barely a whisper, as if we were plotting sin in secret. I didn't know, maybe we were.

I nodded. This was what I wanted. The thought of racing

the open, dark land with aliens on the attack sent my heart pumping. But I could feel this world sucking me in, drawing me down. There was a sense of losing myself, relinquishing my control if I stayed. I needed to get away soon; if I didn't, I may never leave. Or else leave zipped up tight in a black body bag.

Great, I knew what I'd have to do, and I knew I wasn't good at it. Like every kid, as a teenager I did a bit of lying to my dad . . . teacher, boss, therapist. (By the way, lying to your therapist is beyond stupid. I mean what's the point?) Okay, I lied quite a bit, but it doesn't mean I had an easy time with it. I'd always get a little sick to my stomach, my heart would race, and my mouth would go dry. This didn't mean I'd never pulled it off, but then again the people in my world are not nearly as intimidating as ConRad.

I wouldn't consider myself a master liar, but I had picked up a few tricks along the way. What seemed to work was to catch people when they were busy, off guard. If they were too distracted to stop and look me straight in my eyes, then I was golden. That was my plan with ConRad, to avoid his assessing look. Otherwise, I would squirm like bait on a hook or . . . pant like a dog in heat. I swallowed and shook the thought from my head. *Professional, I am calm and professional.*

Having made my decision, I wanted to get the conversation over with, but tracking ConRad down became an irritating lesson in persistence. Asking the men in the compound got me one of two responses, blushing and stammering, or outright rudeness and blatant dismissal. Finally, after many inquiries and dead ends, I found a soldier who was courageous enough to talk with me. Though his stutter was thick, I was able to discern that the Commander's shift was at night and he slept days. So, more than likely, I'd find him in his quarters. When asked where that was, the solider turned the shade of smashed beets and explained that my room and his were one and the same.

How's that? The man tricked me into sharing his bed without me even knowing it.

CHAPTER TWELVE

Conniving, manipulating, controlling . . . jerk!

"What?" I screamed at the red-faced solider, whose name I didn't bother to remember. My voice echoed off the steel beams and bounced down the tunnels.

He scampered away, not bothering to answer my question. Fine with me. His head wasn't the one I wanted to see roll. I was angry and embarrassed. No wonder I felt like people were talking about me behind my back, because *they* were. I bristled at all the ceased conversations as I walked by and the awkwardness previously in the cafeteria. It wasn't hard to imagine why. It was my second night here, and I was already sleeping with the boss.

I had a hard and fast rule about coworker affairs. I may have had a reputation as a party girl, but I kept sex out of the workplace. When I was a young and just beginning my internship, I broke that rule . . . once. I fell hard for the head cardiac surgeon. It wasn't really my fault. He was tall, handsome and he could talk the pants off of any woman, me included. Of course, not every woman found herself being screwed up against the supply closet wall with a smelly mop bumping against her head. If that wasn't enough, I fancied myself in love. A love that was split wide open when his wife and two kids showed up at the hospital. I was brokenhearted and humiliated. My reputation was ruined. As a female intern working in a male-dominated field, I couldn't be as good as the men; I needed to be better. Instead, I was labeled "easy," the girl who wanted to make her way to the top . . . on her back.

In my eyes, ConRad had done the very same thing. Double standards for men and woman, no matter what century, were unfair but real. In this world of men I had to have a stellar reputation, and being perceived as someone who sleeps around was a weakness I couldn't afford to have.

I stood seething at the door to my . . . *his* room. Should I knock or just burst in? Crashing in on him in a dead sleep would be rude and childish. My lips turned up at one corner. Right up my alley. I pushed the door wide, slamming it into the opposite wall, hoping to catch him off guard.

Instead, it was me who sucked in my breath at the sight of his broad back as he stood half naked, muscular shoulders gleaming with only a barely-there towel wrapped around his waist for decency. He stood in front of the sink, and in the reflection of the mirror I could see the bottom half of his face was covered with shaving cream. The top half contained a chilly stare that pierced me through the mirror.

By the expression on his face, I could tell not too many people burst through his door uninvited and lived to tell about it. I would've made an excuse, but I got sidetracked. I was mesmerized by a drop of water, fallen from his damp hair and slowly caressing the ripples of his spine. I held my breath as the drop eased lower, over the dip in his lower back, and melted away beneath the towel. Damn, to be jealous of water.

"Do you need something?" He didn't turn around when he spoke, and I realized that I had been standing there staring for only God knows how long.

"Yes," I said. It was a simple word; I just answered his question really, but it came out all breathless and needy, like I had infused a mountain of meaning in that one tiny syllable.

He heard it too. He lowered his razor and slowly turned to face me. His eyes widened and grew all liquid blue on me. His face softened, and I could see his mouth part slightly . . . invitingly.

I pinched my leg hard, stopping myself before I drifted over there, wiped off the shaving cream and feasted on his lips like a woman starving. "Yes . . . I . . . I need to *talk* to you. What did you think I meant?"

There might have been a flash of disappointment in his eyes, but I didn't dwell on the thought. Instead, I muscled up my indignation.

"I can't believe you put me in here, in *your* room, in *your* . . . bed. Whatever gave you the idea that this . . . this room was okay?" I said gesturing to the walk-in closet of a space.

To ConRad's credit he didn't seem taken aback, since it probably wasn't every day he had a woman screaming at him while he stood half naked in his own quarters. "What's the problem? I provided you with a room and a bed. What else do you want?"

What else? Only like a hundred other things popped into my mind. Like a shower for starters, but I wasn't going to be sidetracked.

"The problem is . . . that it looks like . . . to everyone else . . . that we are, that we're in here sleeping . . . *together*." I couldn't help but whisper the last word as if the secret wasn't already out.

"So . . . you are worried about what everyone else is thinking?" He shook his head as if the mere idea was foreign to him. "Well, don't worry. I . . . am . . . the . . . Commander . . . here." He said this real slow like I was simple or something. "This means no one should bother you. You will always be treated with respect. If not, report the soldiers to me immediately, and they'll be taken care of."

As if signaling the discussion was over, he turned and went back to scraping the blade along his cheek.

Wow, I took a step back, just so I could admire the most perfect incarnation of male arrogance.

"Uhhh no . . ." I said, drawing my words out like he was the one who was simple. "That's the problem. I don't want special treatment just because everyone thinks we're sleeping together."

"Sleeping together? Oh no, trust me, everyone thinks we are doing way more than just sleeping." Catching his expression in the mirror, I watched as his eyebrows went up in a you-know-what gesture. ConRad had scraped his face clean and began splashing water from the sink to rinse. He seemed so calm, while I could feel the burn creep across my cheeks.

"That's just it," I cried in frustration. "I don't want them to think we are sleeping together, because we aren't."

"Ahh, but we could be." He pivoted back toward me and flashed a predatory smile. Privy to the full frontal assault with his wicked smile was akin to being dropped from a twelve-story building . . . with no parachute. My breath caught. And I had thought his back was arresting.

He was all wide chest and broad shoulders. A light dusting of blonde hair narrowed down over a washboard stomach and disappeared, causing a riot within my imagination. Though his body wasn't perfect, far from it. Thick scars puckered the otherwise smooth skin. A circular mark of an old bullet wound hollowed the flesh beneath his ribs. A branding in the form of an S had been burned into his right peck. But the body beneath was rock hard and solid. A refuge one could cower behind in a storm.

He glanced around the room with a renewed interest toward the bed. "I wouldn't mind. I just thought since you were from another time and all that, I would give you a little space to adjust to our ways before we, you know, . . . co-inhabit. But if you'd prefer not to wait, then now works for me also."

Oh please, the time "now" would work for any guy I knew.

"No." I gritted my teeth together and tried to focus on the task at hand. "I don't want to, not now, not at anytime in the near future." Okay, so that was a small white lie, but for some reason it didn't seem to bother my conscience.

"Why not? It's not because you would like to co-inhabit with another soldier, is it?" His eyes narrowed slightly. Arms crossed over his chest, his biceps flexed.

"No, it's not! Listen . . ." I said, trying to take a deep breath and pull patience out from the bottom of my toes, "I don't want to co-inhabit with anyone. But regardless, if that ever changed, then *I* will be the one to decide, not you."

"But you already are." He raised his hand in a gesture of resignation. "You're co-inhabiting with me."

"Not any longer!" My God, could anyone be that obtuse? I know he is a male and all—thus the weaker sex—but it was almost if he was trying to. . . . I stopped and drilled him with a look. "You're pulling my leg, aren't you?"

"Pulling legs? What?"

"You're kidding me, you know, having fun at my expense."

He laughed. "Got you real mad for a minute. Sorry, I just couldn't seem to help myself. You walked in all self-righteous. It was just too easy."

I was surprised. He didn't seem to be the joking around type. There was a glint to his eyes that I'd never seen before, a relaxed stance where before he'd been spine-crushing straight. But my surprise turned to shock when he stepped over to the bed, picked up his clothes and . . . dropped the towel.

A loud gasp sounded in the quiet of the room—it was me. I quickly turned around and felt my cheeks flame with embarrassment. I knew I was acting like a school girl, instead of the sophisticated woman I wanted to personify. My fears were confirmed after hearing him chuckle.

That's it. I was done with this locker room mentality. I was a doctor on a serious mission and it was time he was reminded of that. Of course, having an entire conversation to the back of a door does something to one's professionalism.

"Oh, so you thought it would be funny to get me all riled up when I've been up all night trying to save a soldier's life." Immediately a cold front blew into the room, dropping the temperature to downright chilly. Did those words actually come out of my mouth? I hesitated, then turned and saw a completely dressed soldier with the usual deadpan expression back on his face.

"Of course, I apologize. How is he?" Iceman was back. All eye contact was gone, all the warmth in the room frozen.

Kris, you are such a jerk. He was actually smiling, and I had to go and shoot him down.

"Look, I'm sorry. I didn't mean it that way. I can take a joke, really." But all I got from him was a slight nod in response. He was in commander mode now.

"How's the goddess? Has she awakened?"

"No, not yet." I took a deep breath. I'd been prepared to lie to him, but I wanted to give him the benefit of the doubt—that he'd do the right thing, before I'd just assumed.

"I'm not sure if there's really anything I can do. It may be some type of brain injury, but again, I'm not sure. All we can really do is wait and see. But Zimmion might have a chance. I need the key to unlock the microbiotics. It's his only hope."

ConRad sighed. "That's too bad."

"If you're saying that you're not authorizing the use of the microbiotics just because he is a soldier and not a goddess, then you are going to have a real fight on your hands." I needed to hear his motive. It was just too awful of a concept for me as a doctor, as a human, to realize someone would sit back and watch another person die.

ConRad shook his head. "If you're sure there's no chance for the goddess, then I don't think Zimmion has a chance either."

"But that's just it. I do think he has a chance, if only you could just trust me." *Please, please don't be this man.* Please have a heart somewhere hidden far beneath the ice you've capsulated it in.

ConRad walked over to the door and prepared to leave, which signaled to me this conversation was quickly coming to an end. "There are very strict rules regarding the use of micro-biotics, and all of them refuse the application of them on any soldier, regardless of the reason."

I opened my mouth to argue, but he put his hand up to stop me. "I know you are not aware of all of our rules and some of them might even seem callous to you, but they are in place for our survival and for the overall good."

Before I came in here I already knew how this conversation would play out, but I had to give him the benefit of the doubt. Knowing this was a losing battle, I switched tactics. "Fine, you win. I'm not backing down because I think you are right. It's just I don't want to waste the precious medicine unless I know it will work. More than likely, Zimmion will not make it through the night."

He nodded assuredly, happy that I wasn't going to put up more of a fight. "You did the best that you could. He had more of a chance with you than he would've had without you."

I nodded my head with sorrowful acceptance and waited for the appropriate moment. "But you know . . . there is some-thing . . . I may have overlooked a possibility."

"With Zimmion?" he asked, beginning to look like he was impatient with the conversation.

"No, the goddess."

Immediately his eyes lit up. "The goddess, really? If there is any chance at all, then you need to try it."

"Well," I said, trying to sound as if the thought had just occurred to me, "it could be an infection that's keeping her un-conscious."

"Could a blow to the head cause an infection?" He sounded doubtful.

He had every right to be doubtful, but he didn't need to know the truth. "It's possible. See, sometimes when a person is hit hard enough, especially in the head, the blow could dislodge a bacteria or virus and possibly contaminate the bloodstream, causing an infection. If bad enough, it could lead to loss of consciousness."

My God, that was the stupidest thing I have ever said, but would he buy it? I could see him watching me with narrowed eyes, trying to figure out if what I said made sense. I fought the urge to give him more information, knowing from experience that liars always got caught up in the details.

"All right, if you think there's a chance."

I nodded as he walked over to his locker, unlocked it, and grabbed the key. Relief swept through me, but it was quickly taken over by panic. What if I got caught? What if someone found out? I didn't know what the consequences were, but knew it wouldn't be good. Regardless, I got the heck out of there, not wanting to wait around and find out.

When I finally made my way back to the infirmary, I found Quinn sitting on Zimmion's bed, his head in her lap. The gesture was a little too intimate for simple workmates, but I said nothing. ConRad had told me that administering the drug sublingually was the best method, and since I had no knowledge about the medicine, I couldn't disagree. So, before I could change my mind, I administered the medication. There was nothing more I could do except wait. I wanted to tell Quinn to go on ahead to bed, but one look at her haggard, worried face and I didn't bother.

The exhaustion I had kept at bay fell on me like a lead blanket. My head felt fuzzy with fatigue. I needed to lie down, but

I was still unsure of whose bed I would be sleeping in. Was it really such a bad thing to share his bed, curl up against his chest and sleep soundly for once? I scrubbed my hands over my face and shook my head. That was fatigue talking. Sleep, my sorry white butt. More like sexual assault. Of course, heavy on the sex, light on the assault.

Ahh, stop it, Kris.

I always got punchy when I was tired. I decided I could work out my living arrangements better with a clear head. Was sleep worth the risk?

When I stumbled into ConRad's quarters, I thankfully found them empty. Thankful or slightly disappointed? No . . . no definitely thankful.

I rallied myself with a Scarlet O'Hara moment by deciding that tomorrow was another day. Tomorrow I would find other living quarters; tomorrow I would find a way back to my time. Tomorrow I would fight the fight, but tonight . . . I would curl up in sheets that smelled of ConRad with a smile on my face.

Chapter Thirteen

My vow was broken in less than twelve hours.

I didn't find new living quarters, I didn't find my way home, and I sure as hell didn't fight the good fight. Instead, the days passed in a parade of sameness, me avoiding ConRad, and everyone else for that matter, as I hid in the infirmary. I'd wake up every morning, stifle a scream at my reflection, and shuffle over to the infirmary. Then I'd send Quinn to get my breakfast (I was not going to step a foot into that cafeteria) of bitter coffee and bland goop that tasted like oatmeal minus any of the good stuff like salt, butter, or sugar. The rest of my day would alternate between monitoring my patients and daydreaming about fried cream-cheese puffs from my local Chinese restaurant that I used to frequent more than my own refrigerator.

Today I was in a particularly bad mood as I sat hunched on a metal stool and watched Quinn flit around our two patients, Zimm and the goddess, as if she'd been doing this her whole life. Quinn had a *Mona Lisa* smile hovering at the corners of her mouth as if all her secret dreams had been answered. And why not? Zimm was healing rapidly, his color was excellent, and though he slept most of the day, he woke to take solid food and shoot goofy grins in Quinn's direction. Even the goddess seemed stable, though no real change in her status—still unconscious.

I lifted my mug and finished off the last dregs of what I nicknamed stomach cancer in a cup. Coffee grounds slipped between my teeth, I crushed them, enjoying the bitterness—it suited my mood. Where did Quinn get off being all happy and helpful? It wasn't as if anything had changed, she was still a goddess-in-training and Zimm was still a soldier. Relationship aka heartbreak.

I wanted to snap my fingers in her face and yell at her to wake up and smell the disgusting stuff that was brewed in the cafeteria every morning. Whatever. I didn't really care if she got hurt. It wasn't as if I had anything invested here. Sure, I was leaving (God, please let me be leaving), and she'd realize soon enough what a mistake it was to wear her heart on her sleeve. A twinge of guilt settled between my shoulders, telling me that years of lying to myself still pricked my conscience. Grrr. Okay, I did care, but why?

Maybe I had a thing for pathetic, love-sick creatures, though at this moment Quinn and Zimm were pushing my limits. Watching them act like school children with their first crush would annoy even fans of the Hallmark channel. If I had to watch her lift his head so he could sip some vegetable broth and then pat his mouth dry with her napkin one more time, I might grab the bowl and throw it against the wall.

That wasn't the only thing that had me feeling as if someone pissed in my Wheaties. For the last several days I had been trying to get Quinn to divulge her plan for my escape, but all she would say was the time would come when I could make my choice. What kinda crap was that? I'd made my choice. About three seconds after I came here. But pushing her harder didn't work; she just shut me down like a frigid wife with a headache.

"Are you going to sit there and sulk all day?" Quinn asked as she tucked the sheet snug up around Zimm's chin.

"I'm not sulking, I'm observing. It's what doctors do." I pushed my goop over to the side, no longer interested. Maybe I'd go on a diet.

"Is that what you call scowling and snapping at everyone you talk to?"

"Since you're the only one I am talking to at this moment, I guess that means yes." I crossed my arms over my chest and threw a darkened glare.

"Why don't you go talk to the Commander?" Her tone was the same my mother used when I told her I wanted to learn how to pee like my brothers—standing up.

"I'm not talking to him right now." Wow, was I really picking a fight with Mother-Teresa-in-training? A new low, even for me.

"Maybe you should."

"Maybe I don't want to." Brilliant comeback, Kris.

"You're acting like a child," Quinn countered.

She was right. Quinn wasn't nearly as fun to fight with as ConRad. When I shot a sarcastic response, she would merely shrug or smile at me in some knowing way as if she knew my inner child was really a grumpy old man. How do you fight with someone like that? The answer—you didn't, it just makes you feel like a loser.

There wasn't much I could do here anyway. Zimm was in

more than capable hands. When I'd originally given him the single dose of microbiotics, I planned to cut the dose in half and give a little to each patient, but the amount was so small it seemed pointless to jeopardize both of their chances. And there was no way I could convince ConRad to give me more medicine. Even though I knew I'd made the right decision medically, I couldn't help the feeling of dread, like I was missing an important piece.

But the benefits . . . a medical wonder. His vitals were normal, perfect in fact, and his coloring, not what one would expect after losing so much blood. His complexion was pink, rosy as if in the prime of health. I'd checked his incisions, once, twice, a thousand times, and was still in complete disbelief. They looked weeks old, not days. The flesh had started to mend together, and the scabbing was sloughing off.

I'd peppered Quinn with every question of how this was possible, but she knew even less than me. In her world the "how" wasn't the concern, just the "if." She told me the microbiotics killed infection and helped speed up healing. How could I argue, Zimm had been close to death mere days ago and now . . . the evidence was too convincing.

Of course, the goddess wasn't fairing as well. I let my gaze roam over my other patient, assessing, for the thousandth time, how I could help her. She was so young, a pretty thing really. Her black hair had once been shiny and thick. Now it lay limp against the dingy cot. From checking earlier I knew her eyes were a soft brown that reminded me of warm tequila. A sense of hopelessness washed over me. She was sleeping so peacefully it almost seemed like nothing was wrong. I went over and did the same exam I'd done throughout the week, in case I missed something. But with such limited diagnostic tools I was guessing more than diagnosing. All I could do was wait and see.

"What's her name?" For some reason it always felt wrong not to know even the most basic information about your patient.

"She's known just as goddess."

I shot Quinn one of my specialty looks.

Quinn shrugged. "Some people call her Sari."

I broke my rule about not getting too involved with patients and started to stroke her hair. She seemed so young, and this place was so cold and sterile.

"I can't believe no one has come to visit her." No one had been in to hold her hand or talk to her besides Quinn and me. There was something fundamentally wrong with a child dying alone.

"Her mother's been here."

"What?" My head snapped up to look at Quinn. "Her mother? Who? Where? Here at this compound?"

Panic flashed across Quinn's face, and then she quickly busied herself straightening the supply closet. "What? Ah . . . no."

"Quinn, look at me! Is Sari's mother here?"

Quinn turned and put her palm up to ward me off. "Kris, stop. You need to let this go. I slipped up. I can't tell you anything else."

"Then who can?" I was undeterred. I wanted to let Sari's family know that they could be with her. That she didn't have to go through this alone.

"No one. This information could get people killed. Is that what you want, another death on your conscience?"

My breath sucked in cold and quick. A stab of pain shot to my heart. Whose death was she talking about? No patient of mine had died, yet. Was she talking about the two soldiers who died during my rescue attempt? But something told me that wasn't it, either. The images of my reoccurring nightmare popped into my head. My small incompetent fingers, shaking as I tried to put the bits of skull back together. My sheets soaked with sweat so often that my closet could be mistaken for a linen warehouse.

"What do you know about my conscience?" Then another thought hard on the first. "Have you been using mind-invasion on me?" I stalked her around the flimsy wood table. If she had, I was going to tear her from limb to limb, no half measures for being a nice, sweet girl.

She backed up, her eyes wide as she shook her head with denial. "No I haven't. It was a lucky guess."

"I don't believe you," I growled. Trust didn't come easy for me. I had a hard time opening up to anyone, and to think that someone could peer inside my brain and poke around was unforgivable.

"You have to. I don't have those types of powers. Besides, I could never do that without you knowing."

"She's right, Kris," Zimm said from behind me. "Only the most powerful goddesses have access to mind invasion."

I whipped my head around at glare at Zimm. His concern for his puppy love interest had him propped up on one elbow, looking as if he was ready to fling himself between Quinn and me.

Maybe they were right. I could be becoming paranoid. I was more on edge than I wanted to believe. More than likely her comment was just a coincidence, but something didn't feel right. Quinn was too perceptive. I narrowed my eyes in suspicion at her. "Stay out of my head, Quinn. I mean it. You have no right."

Her head bobbed a fraction in acceptance. I turned on my heel and fled the infirmary. I'd had enough. This damn mountain was closing in on me, ratcheting up my fear of being buried alive to the top ten least appealing ways I wanted to die.

I needed to assume control of my life, start making decisions again. Not only were my thoughts being probed, but I had no peace in my living quarters. ConRad's presence was everywhere. Yes, he was neat, probably to the point of OCD, but now that I was aware he lived there, I couldn't un-aware myself.

Hiding out in the infirmary wasn't cutting it. My living arrangement wasn't cutting it. Sleeping in the same bed as ConRad and smelling him on the pillow *wasn't cutting it.* Just this morning I'd woken in a flush of heat, not from a nightmare, but from something else that had a dampness forming between my legs, which had nothing to do with the stifling humidity.

It was best to have it out with ConRad. Clear up my living arrangements, start talking about a way for me to get back home. Of course, wanting to find ConRad and actually doing so were two different things. But dogged persistence was one of my virtues. Granted a more useful virtue would be patience, but that trait didn't seem to swim in my Polish-Hungarian gene pool. After numerous attempts at locating Mr. PITA himself—the code word we used at the hospital for a "pain-in-the-ass" patient—I was directed to a back pathway, a place I'd never gone before.

I wound my way through tunnels and crevices. The temperature spiked and the telltale sulfur/rotten egg smell under-scored the musky air. The heat hit me in the face, and within seconds I wanted to rip off my clothes and run screaming back to the coolness of the upper levels. In no time my army-green tank top was darkened with sweat, and when I ran my hands through my hair, I could feel the frizz at least a foot in all directions. Grrr.

Just when I was about to give up, I caught a flash of glistening skin through a split in the cave wall and skidded to a stop.

My heart jumped as the reptilian part of my brain woke up and raised its ugly head. I bit my lip in anticipation and rounded the corner.

I had every intention of announcing myself—really. I wasn't into sneaking up on people; most people's secrets were best left undiscovered. But nosiness—or curiosity as I like to call it—was also another enduring link in my DNA chain.

I mean, I just wanted to know what the hell he was doing down here all by himself. Did he skin small children and eat them for lunch? No, that was unfair. He probably tortured un-willing victims for mere practice.

Whatever he did, darkness surrounded him, a coldness that kept him shuttered from the world. And why, I had to ask myself, did I find that quality appealing? It was plain and simple: I had a sickness that only years of therapy could cure.

I caught sight of him. With profound regret, I realized no amount of therapy could save me; I needed a complete lo-botomy. The primitive beast in my head purred and my mouth watered like a damn Pavlov's dog.

ConRad wore nothing but low-riding cotton pants, even his feet were bare. I mean, didn't the man own an f-ing shirt?

How hard was it to stay dressed? He stood in the middle of a black exercise mat performing some type of martial arts. His movements were quick and deliberate; his body performed like a machine made up of rippled muscle and taut skin.

Sweat ran off him like water, shimmering and reflecting with each movement. His hair, slicked back from his face, showed off his chiseled profile. Jaw muscles clenched with each blow and kick as his breath came in with hisses, tightening his stomach.

I watched in a trance. He was dangerous and fascinating, and on some basic level I found myself wanting to respond to his authority. *Whoa!* Where the hell did that thought come from? A throwback from a Stone Age ancestor? If I didn't watch it, next thing I'd know I'd be asking him to drag me by the hair and take me back to his cave, which reluctantly, when I looked around the carved out mountain, wasn't very far from the truth.

He came to a stop and closed his hands into a prayer pose and did a thankful bow. He turned his back toward me and walked over to get a drink from a metal canteen alongside the mat. "You do know it is against the rules to walk in on your Commander without permission. I'm quite sure even in your time it is considered rude."

Heat flushed my face; it was like I was twelve all over again and my mother had just caught me kissing the neighbor boy. "I'm sorry," I stammered, "I didn't mean to catch you unaware."

"I wasn't unaware," he said, then added softly, "quite the opposite."

I wasn't sure exactly what he meant by that, but a little flame lit up in the center of my belly. "I wanted to talk to you," I said, not bothering to hide the pull of my lips into a stupid grin.

"So talk," he said.

He still wasn't facing me, and I demanded eye contact with any conversation. I walked closer and peered over his shoulder. "I wanted to finish our conversation we started the other day."

He turned and fixed me with the bluest of eyes, like an Arizona pool during a hundred and twenty degree summer. "You're still upset about the sleeping arrangements. You didn't seem to have a problem this past week."

"I've been . . . exhausted and you haven't been in the room." I wasn't about to tell him each night I buried my face in his pillow and savored his scent.

"We haven't been in my room together since you got here. So what's the difference?" He unscrewed the cap from his canteen and poured the water over his head and neck.

My tongue went dry. I was suddenly so thirsty. "Yes, but I didn't know it was your room until the other day."

Focus Kris, focus.

"So now that you know, or more importantly, now that you know what other people know, it's a problem," he said with his famous half smile.

Was the smirk on his face a little annoying, or was it just me? But the small flame that was glowing warmly only a moment ago was now out. "I don't care if you agree with my reasoning or not. I just want my own quarters. And . . ."—in for an ounce in for a pound—"I want a unit to escort me back to the portal."

"No." And with not even a glance he got down on the floor and started to do push-ups.

My teeth slid edge to edge. The impressive display of rippling muscles was getting . . . less impressive.

"No? No to the escort or to the new quarters?" Stay calm, do not get baited.

"No to them both." He sighed, obviously unaccustomed to explaining himself. "An escort is too dangerous at this time, and there are no other quarters available."

"Fine." I said, knowing it wouldn't be easy. Unfazed I pushed ahead. "Then I'll move in with Quinn." I hadn't actually asked her yet, but I knew I could plead and beg my way in. I'm sure she wouldn't hold a grudge over my threat of physical dismemberment.

"Request denied." Another round of push-ups, but this time one handed . . . show off.

"Why? I'd prefer it and would feel more comfortable." I stood above him, hands on hips, my scowl wasted on his back.

"Simple," he said. His voice muffled as he continued talking to the floor mat. "She's a goddess-in-training and needs sensory restraint in order to hone her skills. With a goddess down, we need her active as quickly as possible."

"So Quinn's a goddess huh? What kind of powers does she have?" Maybe I could pump ConRad for information to see exactly what she could do—mind-invasion perhaps? The hairs on my neck stood at the thought.

"Good question," Conrad growled. He had flipped onto his back to do sit-ups, and I could see the flexing of his jaw muscle. "Since she spends most of her time in the damn infirmary, and not in sensory restraint, it's hard to know for sure."

Guilt flared up at the thought of what really was drawing Quinn to the infirmary. I decided to move on.

"The infirmary then. I could stay there at night and crash

on one of the cots." It wasn't my first choice, since there was no privacy, but I could manage for a time until I left.

He stilled and threw me a raised-one-eyebrow look. "You really want to sleep in an open room, with no locks, in a compound full of men? Some who haven't been with a woman their whole lives?"

Small point. Damn, but my options were diminishing fast. Of course, *his* way would have me in his room, door locked, and with only one horny man.

"Look," I said, my voice edgy as I tried to steer the conversation back to my objective. "There has to be another way, some sort of compromise."

"Look." His tone sarcastic, was that supposed to be an imitation of my own? "There is something you need to understand."

He propped himself up to rest on his elbows, which showed his abdominals off to their best advantage. He looked . . . um . . . inviting. My eyes must have glazed over because both of his eyebrows raised and that devastating half smile softened his eyes.

"See something you like?"

"What?" I snorted. "No." My voice sounded lame even to my own ears. But I was not about to tell him that he had just replaced Brad Pitt in all my late night fantasies.

"The invitation is always open."

I narrowed my eyes. I'm sure it is, buddy. Then I did a circling gesture with my hand to have him continue our original conversation. Between the two of us, someone had to keep us on track.

ConRad flashed me a full smile this time as he continued

on with his denial of my request. "See, the thing you're worried about, not wanting everyone to think that you belong to me, it's already happened."

He put his hands behind his head and started to crunch to the side, working his obliques. The sight of his washboard stomach flexing and relaxing must've rendered me stupid because I found I needed clarification. "What exactly are you saying?"

"I am saying I've already claimed you. It was over the first night you slept in my quarters."

"And claiming is . . . ?"

"A provision made for available women. I've claimed you, and so it's my responsibility to protect you with my life."

"How can you have claimed me without my permission? Without my knowledge?" I blinked rapidly as each word sputtered out of my mouth.

He shrugged. "You came to my quarters willingly enough. That's all that is needed."

"Because you ordered that I be taken to your quarters!" I shouted, stepping closer and glaring down at him. I was surprised at how much I enjoyed the rush of power from standing over him. He must've realized this and quickly jumped up to come nose to nose with me, or more like his shoulder to my nose.

"Look around you, *woman*. How many unattached females do you see walking about here?"

"There are at least a dozen or so goddesses here," I countered.

"They're not unattached . . . they're *unavailable*. No relationships with goddess are permitted, not of any sort."

"But there are no other females," I protested.

"Exactly, females are at a premium here, and we all want one. If I hadn't claimed you, then someone else would've. And trust me when I tell you they wouldn't have been nearly as nice. In fact," the tilt of his head was decidedly arrogant, "you should be thanking me instead of berating."

"Really and why is that?" I asked unbelievingly.

"Because I am the highest ranking officer here and no one, I mean no one, should be giving you any trouble."

"Does that include you?"

"Well . . . almost no one." His eyes licked my body like hungry flames. I began to question my place on the food chain.

Irritation didn't begin to touch what I was feeling. I'd been manipulated into a position I neither wanted nor was able to control. My defenses slammed up, and like my grandfather used to say "there she goes gettin' all prickly."

"Everything about this," I used my hands to encircle the whole crazy place, "goes against everything I believe in. Everything that makes up . . . me. What right does any one person have, male or female, to *claim* another? Especially without their consent? This goes against basic human rights. It's archaic."

ConRad stepped back and shook his head in pure disbelief. "Are you actually arguing, what's the word . . . *ethics* with me?"

"Yes," I said, excited to finally be getting somewhere. "Ethics, principles, morals—the structure of what all thriving societies are based on. What happens here is a total regression of human rights, not to mention women's rights. . . ." I would've gone on, but his expression of utter bewilderment made me hesitate.

"Woman, you don't get it do you?" His voice rose and echoed off the high cavern as he began to prowl aggressively. "Who the hell do you think you are anyway? You've been here a total of what . . . one week, and you feel the need to lecture me on, what did you say, oh yes, basic human rights? What kind of bloody crap is that? Wake up. Look around. What society do you see here? Whose rights are you trying to defend? People die here *every day!* This isn't living; this is survival. Be glad, or better yet *thankful*, that I've *claimed* you or who the hell knows what would've happened to you. You should be kissing my feet that you're still alive. So when you have a real problem, then you can come and ask my permission to interrupt my workout and see if I'd be willing to help you. And until then . . ." He paused dramatically, his nostrils flaring with a deep inhale. He let his hardened gaze slide over me. "You need to work out."

I was stunned. My brain froze in blankness. Of all the things he said, of all the reactions I could have, the one thing my mind stopped on was "you need to work out." Did I mention I was vain?

"Work out? Work out! I will have you know that I am a runner. I've completed my third marathon. Yes, that's the number after two, muscle head. I work out every day, well . . . almost every day. I am in damn good shape, and I take offense that you're implying otherwise." Alright, so it's been a while since I'd actually done any running, but my blood still boiled on principle. Screw human rights. This man basically just told me that I was fat. Did I mention that I was defensive about my weight?

"So you can run," he shrugged. Then plopped himself back down and started leg raises, this time I could've cared less.

"Run . . . run! It's a lot more than . . . it's twenty-six point two miles of running. It's endurance. It's . . . it's . . . it's a hell of a long time to run. And why am I arguing about this with you? I'm fit, damn it, not fat, but F-I-T and how dare you tell me otherwise."

"What?" He ceased his excessive exercising and stared at me as if I was the star of one of those daytime talk shows and just told him he was my baby's daddy. "Are you . . . I don't know what they call it in your time, but in mine it's called lacking intelligence or slow?"

He was serious. My mouth fell wide open and my brain had a hard time wrapping around the fact that he had just called me fat and stupid.

"I never said that you were fat. I said YOU-NEED-TO-WORK-OUT." He spoke as if I was hard of hearing and . . . stupid.

"That's the same thing, you moron." I yelled back.

"No, it's not. You may be able to run from danger, but what if you need to fight? Claiming works both ways, and so because I don't want to die anytime soon, you need to work out. Do you have any defense moves or combat training?"

I shook my head no. I wondered if we were both speaking English.

"You're under my protection, and I will protect you, but I can't be there all the time. You need to be able to defend yourself. And maybe then you can do the same for me." Then for the second time in my life I heard his horse bark of laughter.

He jumped up and put his shirt back on. "Tomorrow, be here at oh five hundred hours. We'll begin your training."

He started down the exit tunnel, while I stood there still dumbfounded.

Before he turned the corner, he glanced over his shoulder. "Oh and Kris, in case there is any confusion, this claim is forever. Don't be getting any ideas."

Chapter Fourteen

Alright, so maybe my idea wasn't the best thought-out plan ever. I am a doctor, people, not a secret agent. My arms ached as I clasped all my stuff—soap, towel, change of clothes, and a metal chair. This wasn't helping my goal of being inconspicuous as I hovered around an adjacent corner to the community showers.

A shower. A true, honest to goodness shower instead of the small sink I was making due with in my room. I raised my shoulder and did a cursory sniff of my underarm. *Wow.* My eyes watered. Nope, a spit bath was no longer an option. I was ripe and heading at Mach speed toward foul.

I peeked around the corner at the large metal door down the hall that sported the words "COMMINITY SHOWER" in spray-painted block letters. I'd discovered it while poking around when I first arrived. The word *shower* was used very broadly since it was basically a series of holes, bleeding rust and water in a stall-less metal room.

Boots pounded on the hard packed dirt as soldiers rounded the far corner. I quickly ducked behind the wall again, narrowly missing detection. If found out, no doubt I'd be immediately marched in front of ConRad, since I seemed to be his problem to solve.

And rightly so. It was all ConRad's fault, really. I could've gone one more day, possibly two if it wasn't for the butt-kicking, body-slamming, Ninja-warrior workout that had me contemplating faking a stroke before I called "uncle" and he released me.

This morning we'd worked out in the bowels of the mountain where the heat and humidity bordered on inhuman levels. I'm surprised I'd survived, considering the conditions were perfect for inducing a heart attack. Then ConRad sauntered off, back to commanding the world or torturing unwilling victims, I couldn't say for sure. This left me panting, flat on my back and scraping my hair—sweat soaked and dirt filled—off my face.

So here I was, in desperate need of soap, playing P.I. as I staked out the showers in the heart of the men's quarters. Of course, the word "COMMUNITY" wasn't lost on me. I wasn't a complete idiot, though one might not realize that from my current situation. I had no intention of giving a whole group of testosterone-laden men a peep show for free. Hence, my semibrilliant plan.

Nervousness flip-flopped in my belly as I hefted the metal chair high on my shoulder. I'd originally thought I could take my time to check the room and make sure it was empty and then slip in without being seen. I'd brought the chair—a stroke of genius if I do say so myself—with the idea I could prop it against the door from the inside in case there was no lock. Growing up in a household of brothers I knew I could take a true three-minute shower. I'd be in and out before anyone, especially ConRad, found out.

My plan would've worked, except I didn't take into account how busy the hallway would be. There hadn't been a second in all of the fifteen minutes I'd been standing there where there wasn't some bone-brained man lounging around or running through. Didn't these people have a planet to save? I wasn't into making a spectacle of myself, and in a world of men, one thing I learned was never offer an open invitation if you weren't willing.

I was having second thoughts, okay more like third and fourths. It wasn't as if I hadn't tried other options. I'd asked Quinn where the showers where, thinking there may've been other women only showers, but she'd given me that "look" and pointed me in this direction. I don't know, maybe goddesses here don't stink, but I was a mere mortal and had sweated like a whore in church.

The sound of booted feet had faded, and I did a cautionary glance. The coast was clear; but once I started, I'd have to commit. Swallowing hard, I made a run for it. I shuffled as fast as I could with arms full and a chair banging against my leg with every stride. Damn, but the hallway was long—didn't seem such a distance from the safety of my corner. The sound of men's laughter bounced off the walls a distance away. I didn't have much time. I'd have to count on Lady Luck that the shower was empty. I opened the door and ran through. *Come on baby, just this once.*

Lady Luck hated me.

In another life I must've been her bastard stepchild because standing under a spray of water and a lather of suds was a broad back, a magnificent pair of buns, and thick, muscular legs that would've shamed a Tour de France cyclist.

Time slowed to a crawl. The door slammed closed behind me as I saw his head start to twist my way. In my mind's eye, I'd turned, opened the door, and ran down the hallway before I was even noticed. But reality was different. My feet stuck to the floor like all the swamp mud in Florida had contrived to attack my boots at this precise moment.

My eyes widened and my mouth slacked open. My cheeks burned as an undignified squeak slipped out of my gaping mouth. Having such exquisite control over my vocal cords, I tried my feet. I turned so quickly I nearly knocked myself out with the door. Desperation had me seeing spots. I tried to find the knob to facilitate my escape, but the universe conspired against me . . . or maybe the damn chair, my towel, the soap, and everything else I was carrying.

"Hey, what's your hurry?"

I knew him. We hadn't been formally introduced, but I had seen him before working closely with ConRad.

"Um, listen I'm sorry," I said, holding up my hand as a gesture and feeling stupid because I was talking to a door instead. "I didn't mean to barge in on you. I didn't know anyone was here."

"Well, I'm not quite done, but I'd be more than willing to share."

Oh, I'm sure you would, buddy. I heard his cheesy smile even though I was missing the actual visual.

"Ha," I said, forcing a fake laugh. "Really, I'm okay." I was still working on the door knob and becoming increasingly aware of how bad this whole situation could go for me. Being stuck in a small room with a naked man twice my size that I didn't know was becoming progressively uncomfortable.

"Don't worry, sweetheart. ConRad would never have to find out."

Like hell he wouldn't, because I'd be the first one to tell him. The bloody door knob was stuck, how the hell could a door knob get stuck? "Do I need to remind you I am under ConRad's protection?"

And how's that for my life. Less than twelve hours ago I was bristling under his high-handedness and now I was grabbing for it like a lifeline.

"No, I got that, but sweetheart . . . ConRad's not here."

How achingly aware I was of that fact. Then, as if I could summon him by mere thought, the door was lifted out of my hand and off its hinge. And there stood ConRad. He completely filled the doorway. He took the door and flung it down the hall. I heard it clatter what seemed like yards away. His feet were shoulder width apart, hands on his hips, his face a mask of pure rage.

"What the HELL is going on here?" He didn't yell, his voice was actually quiet as he spoke through clenched teeth, his lips barely moving.

"She walked in on me, Commander, while I was here, just taking my shower."

Ahh . . . what a snake, he threw me under the bus, before I could even form a word.

ConRad took two seconds to switch his gaze from me to the solider and roared "OUT!"

I glanced in the soldier's direction. I'd never seen a man move so fast. He grabbed his clothes, covered himself fig-leaf style, and scrambled out the door, but not without ConRad giving him a shove for good measure.

I looked on with longing. I too wanted to make an escape and peered around ConRad's shoulder to check the possibility. Horror flooded my brain as I realized the entire command center was behind ConRad ogling the scene before them. A few soldiers in the back were actually jumping on other men's shoulders trying to get a better view.

Thick, hot embarrassment settled on me, causing a low roar in my ears. God, let this be it. Let my life end, let the floor open and swallow me whole.

"I asked you a question," he growled.

"I . . . I . . . I" Was that me stuttering? For Pete's sake, Kris, just spit it out. You have nothing to feel guilty about. But my tongue disagreed, sticking to the roof of my mouth. I swallowed hard and tried to dislodge the afflicted organ. "I was trying to take a shower."

"In the men's shower?" he shouted. His body was rigid, a block wall of authority. ConRad had learned the art of intimidation well; he used it to control dozens of men with a mere withering glare. But I wasn't under his command. Besides, his tendency to control brought out my tendency to rebel.

"It's a community shower!" I shouted back.

"It's a community of MEN!"

He had a point, but a small one in the face of such need. The silence stretched a bit past uncomfortable, until I realized he was waiting for some type of rebuttal. The truth was I couldn't think of a single answer that made any sense. That is well, except the truth.

"Well, what did you expect me to do? I haven't taken a real

shower in over a week and . . . and it's starting to become obvious." I clutched my shower accessories as one would a security blanket.

"What?" He seemed baffled, my explanation beyond him.

"I am starting to stink. I can barely stand myself and if you weren't so self-absorbed, you would've helped me with my dilemma before it got to this."

With that there was a bark of laughter from the peanut gallery. ConRad, just seeming to notice we had an audience, turned around and glared at the men behind him. Bodies went flying in every direction, and within seconds we were alone. I didn't know if that was better.

"You can't take a shower here," he said. I could hear the sound of teeth grinding together. I am sure he'd be eating flecks of enamel for weeks to come. He took a deep breath, as if drawing from patience he didn't know he had. I could sympathize.

"You don't seem to grasp how precarious your situation is. I'm trying to fight a war that could determine the existence of the entire human race, but instead I hear shouts 'there's a woman in the men's shower.' My entire command disappears. Instead of trying to catch the enemy, my men are trying to catch a peek of a naked woman. I had to wade through soldiers ten deep just to get to this door."

Well, the mystery of the jammed door knob was solved.

"These men are holding on by a very thin, very frayed thread. They all know their lives are short lived. Many of them have never been with a woman, much less seen one naked. So when one seemingly extends an open invitation, there's only going to be trouble."

"It wasn't an invitation," I shouted. "It was an accident."

"Do you think they care?" He shouted back. "Hell, they're willing to take anything they can get."

"So what? Women are not supposed to take showers here?"

"Well, you don't see the goddesses taking showers here, and they're not stinking up the place."

I sucked in my breath. His comment aimed true. Did my embarrassment know no bounds? "Fine then. So what does a goddess do?"

"Hell if I know. Do I look like a goddess?"

"Well neither am I, you ass!" I was so pissed I threw the only thing I had as a weapon. The soap bounced off his chest, not even causing a flinch. We stood staring at each other, neither of us willing to back down.

I couldn't remember the last time I'd been so angry. All I wanted to do was rip his head off, and by the look on his face, he felt the same way.

"Quinn!" He roared so loud dirt rattled loose from the ceiling. Before the dust settled I heard footsteps running toward us. We both looked out the doorway into the hall and saw a shocked Quinn skidding to a stop in front of us lose traction on the wet floor and slide right on past, crashing into the wall beyond. Quinn muttered an inappropriate curse, and I stifled a chuckle as she ungracefully stumbled back toward us.

"Yes, Commander?" Quinn said as she tried to smooth her flyaway hair. Quinn's antics broke the tension. ConRad ran a hand through his hair and sighed. Believe it or not, I held a little sympathy for him. He had no experience handling women, and I'm sure there was no rule book he could refer to.

"I can't believe this is my life," he mumbled more to himself than anyone else.

"Welcome to my world," I said, my attempt at humor.

He glanced at me. A small smile cracked his face. "Quinn, get her cleaned up."

ConRad took a step and reached out for the back of my neck, pulling me to him. He buried his face into the crease above my shoulder and inhaled deeply through his nose. With his lips brushing my traitorous skin, his husky voice sent a current through my body. "Don't worry. You smell damn good to me."

Then he turned and left.

CHAPTER FIFTEEN

Quinn took me by the hand and led me down a flight of stone stairs. The passage way was lit with smoking torches, apparently the copper wires didn't run this far below ground. At the bottom a cavern was hollowed out, and three small pools filled the room. Steam swirled invitingly above the bubbling water. Smooth black stones lined the pools. Farther back in the darkness was a small crawl space, but I couldn't see where it led to. There was only a slight hint of sulfuric acid so I was hard pressed to know what smelled worse, me or the rotten egg odor. "What is this place?"

Quinn took my towel and placed it on a rock ledge. "We call it the Three Pools. The first one is for washing," she said, pointing to the nearest pool. "The second two are for soaking."

I stared in disbelief. Here was Heaven, smack in the middle of Hell. "Why didn't you tell me this before?"

Quinn shrugged that careless one shoulder shrug. "You didn't ask."

I shook my head. "Ahh . . . yes, I did. Remember I asked where the showers were?"

"Men shower; women bathe."

And our communication barrier strikes again. "What about those?" I asked pointing toward the small tunnels. "Can anything—and by anything I mean aliens—get through?"

Quinn shrugged. "They never have."

"Ah, the comfort you bring, Quinn." But I decided to take a page from her book and not worry about it.

Quinn smiled and headed up the stairs. It took three washes for my hair to feel clean. After a long bath I soaked until my skin was wrinkled and waterlogged. Finally, I forced myself to reenter the real world. I dried, put on fresh clothes, and made my way back to the infirmary to check on my patients.

Once in the infirmary I couldn't help but stare at Zimm. He was up and around and taking solid foods, which was a miracle. Sari, on the other hand, was not experiencing divine intervention. Her vitals were weak—respirations were shallow, pulse thready, and her eyes had sunk, creating deep black circles in her pale face. Her bones were more pronounced, as if their sharp angles could tear her paper-thin skin. I knew if I had a way to check, her blood pressure would be at a critical level. She had all the signs of intracerebral hemorrhage, but there was nothing I could do about a bleed in her brain.

The day crept to late afternoon with minor cuts and bruises coming through the door. Either the word was out that I was a competent healer or there was leftover curiosity from the morning shower incident. I chose to believe the former, hoping I'd gained the trust of some of the men, at least enough to stitch up their cuts.

I groaned and dropped my head onto my folded arms on the table. The day's events had finally caught up with me. Couple that with my latest bout of insomnia had my eyes burning like coals inside my throbbing head.

"Why don't you go and get some rest? I can handle things here," Quinn said. She'd left earlier and had gotten some sleep. "Things should be pretty slow the rest of the night, and if anything happens, I'll come and get you. I promise."

Quinn was right. There wasn't much I could do. So I left knowing my patients were in her capable hands and made my way to my quarters.

I still wasn't sure what ConRad's schedule was, but I'd learned my lesson about walking in before checking. I knocked softly, waited, and then carefully cracked the door. The room was empty. I sighed with relief. The last thing I needed was another confrontation with ConRad. I wasn't quite sure what my feelings were concerning the Commander. It was like a weekend in Vegas—fun while there, but afterwards, hung over and broke, the self-loathing begins.

I pulled the rough blanket over my legs and threw my arm over my eyes. I needed just twenty minutes and closed my eyes in relief.

The room was dark, but very familiar. The smell of roses and fabric softener told me this was my mother's room, though I couldn't see the slightly worn bedspread and antique cherry wood dresser. Even without the familiar scent I would've known where I was at. I'd walked this path a hundred times, maybe a thousand. At the far side of the room, the bathroom door was outlined with yellow light, a beacon in the darkness. My princess pink slippers didn't make a sound as they stepped on the thick carpet. I told myself, like I did every time—*stop, don't take another step.* Maybe this time I'd listen. But even as I screamed at myself to turn around, my child-sized hand reached for the tarnished gold doorknob.

In a flash, I was on a cool beach. The sun shone bright and hot as it poured down from a brilliant blue sky. A clear turquoise ocean sung its lullaby as a cooling mist sprayed light kisses on my neck, arms, face. The mist lingered on my lips and coaxed them to part. A petal-like spray cooled my sun-warmed body. Chills spread down one side of my neck and arm like the effects of a good wine. I purred in the back of my throat, contentment—treasured and rare—spilled over me.

The mist changed into fingers and restless hands—nips from sharp teeth, then soothing administrations from soft lips. A glow grew in the base of my belly and spread warm like brandy. A sigh slipped past my lips and was caught by an opened mouth, hot and wet. In one kiss I was drunk—intoxicated by a single stroke of tongue. The flavor of male sparked a connection to the heated pool between my thighs.

Moans purred in my chest. This was like no beach I'd ever been on. My eyes fluttered open. No beach, no white sand, *no swirling freaking mist*. Just a solid mass of muscled chest.

My brain hurried to assimilate the reality with my dream fantasy. An incredible glorious man lay on top of me doing things to my neck that was deliriously distracting. My body recognized him before my mind did. It was ConRad. His hard body pushed me into the rough military mattress bringing different parts of my anatomy alive with slow purposeful friction. Ahh . . . that friction—it fed an insatiable heat. The more friction, the more burn. My body was always such a slut, but my brain had saved me on more than one occasion.

"What the hell do you think you are doing?"

The question sounded more like a reverent plea than a shocked outcry. His mouth came down, effectively stopping any more prudent questions. Our mouths were open and hot. Tongues danced, licked, and tasted. I smelled him—raw, musky, primitive. He growled, and I responded to the command. My body arched to meet his, and my legs wrapped around his hips and back. His teeth gently sunk into the softness of my lip, while I ran nails down his naked back.

Naked? When did he get his shirt off? And better question, when did I? All that was separating us was the thin cotton of his army fatigues. The barrier was not enough to placate my logical mind, but my body, on the other hand, wanted to rip it off with my teeth. My constant battle—sensible brain meet gluttonous body.

"Wait . . . wait," I said, breathlessly. This was too fast. I needed a moment to think, though he didn't seem to hear me. He trailed a sequence of hot kisses toward my already sensitive breasts, and I knew if he made it to his destination, I'd be more than willing to go down with the ship.

"Stop, damn it." This time for emphasis I boxed the side of his head. It had the same effect of hitting a brick wall with a rubber mallet. Christ, he gave thick skulled a whole new meaning, but he did get jostled and raised up on one elbow to look at me. That was all I needed. With his momentum working against him I pushed hard, throwing him off balance. He landed hard, on the floor, with a resounding thud, flat on his back. The bed vibrated from the impact.

"What the—?" He lay still, shaking his head, trying to clear the effects of my ninja move he'd shown me earlier.

"I would ask you the same question." I jumped up and

threw an extra-long shirt on, not wanting to lose a minute of his stunned reaction. "I mean, what exactly did you think you were doing?"

"Damn . . ." He rubbed his head. "I know it's been awhile, but I didn't think I was that out of practice." He threw himself back on the bed and scrubbed his hands over his eyes.

So the ruthless man did have a sense of humor after all. Unfortunately, I was in no mood to entertain it.

"You know what I meant," I said crossly, putting on my pants and fumbling with the drawstring.

"Hey," he said, rolling onto his side and popping his head on one hand. "You were the one who issued the invitation, not me." With arched brows his face was a sham of innocence.

My mouth flew open. "Issued a . . . I was asleep!"

"Yes, but in my bed." His half grin was in full force and showed a whisper of a dimple.

I stared at him. Was that really his argument? "Since when did sleeping in *that* bed become an open invitation for molestation?"

"Molestation!" he sputtered. "Damn, I really am out of practice." He flipped onto his back with a heavy sigh. "How about helping a poor solider out, honey, and giving me a one-on-one coaching session?" His head tilted to one side, his fervid gaze cloaked behind deceptively long eyelashes.

My rolling eyes must've said it all as far as his coaching session went. In his dreams.

ConRad sat up in bed and with a guileless expression on his face. "Woman, if you're in my bed during my hours of use, then that's an open invitation as far as I am concerned."

Annoyance didn't begin to touch what I was feeling. Considering I was maneuvered into bed by *him* and had a sleepless night due to *his* previous ministrations.

"Let me tell you something, Commander. If I ever issue an invitation for sex with *you*, you'll know it. There'll be no need to assume, because it will be so obvious that even someone of your intelligence could grasp the concept. And by the way, if there's ever going to be a chance of that invitation being issued, then I suggest you never call me woman again."

I grabbed my boots and slammed out the door. I sulked down the hall and was sure I could be heard doors away, forsaking men and naps for a long time to come.

I turned the corner and headed in the direction of the infirmary. Gnarled fingers reached out from a darkened doorway and clasped my wrist. For such a fragile hand, the strength it exerted was enough to stop me mid-stride. Startled, I glanced up and started to pull away, but instead was dragged into the shadows. A hand quickly covered my mouth.

"Shh . . . don't scream." I recognized Aura's voice. My eyes quickly adjusted, taking in her long gray hair and dingy old robes that hung from her shoulders as if from a wire hanger. I nodded my consent, and she lowered her palm. "I've heard you want to make your way back to your time. If you still do, then meet me at the command center at midnight tonight."

"But . . ."

Aura shook her head. "No time. Just know the journey will be dangerous. I cannot guarantee your safety, but I can get you through the tunnel and will escort you to where you came through to Dark Planet. After that you are on your own." She glanced in the dark behind her. "My guards will be frantic; I must go." She turned to leave down a poorly lit side tunnel, one I'd missed previously.

I couldn't leave well enough alone. "But . . . why?"

She paused, her hand resting on the ragged rock. Her head bowed to the floor, then rose slightly. "You gave my daughter a fighting chance at life. For that I am grateful."

"Who? What . . . you mean Sari? But you're a goddess. I thought relationships were forbidden?"

Her profile caught the light as she glanced toward me. A glimmer of a smile hovered around her mouth. "You're not the only one who breaks rules." With a swish of robe she disappeared into the mountain.

By the time I made it to the infirmary my palms were sweaty, and the pile of snakes that was my stomach was awake and snapping. This was what I wanted, right? My chance to leave. Then why did I suddenly feel ill at the thought of going back to my quaint patio-home and Sleep Number bed?

My conscience couldn't have picked a worse time to rear its ugly head. I pushed through the doors of the infirmary, and with one look at Quinn's face, I knew the snowball of my life had just picked up speed, going downhill.

From habit my eyes scanned Zimm, his face expressionless and void, but otherwise healthy. I took a breath for courage and turned to Sari. I could tell from where I stood she was already dead.

I dragged my feet to her bedside and gazed down at her peaceful features. Death had a way of easing away years, erasing pain and stress, even from one so young. I stroked her forehead—cold and smooth. Just a body, a vessel, her life force already gone. She was so young, but I'd realized long ago that death had no prejudice, being an equal opportunity employer.

"ConRad needs to be told," Quinn whispered from across the room. I nodded. The knowledge of the conversation I needed to have with ConRad came with a pitted feeling in my belly. Losing a patient was always piggybacked with a sense of failure, but I felt more than personal guilt. I wasn't sure what the consequences of losing a goddess were, but I didn't want to find out.

Quinn sat next to Zimm, she cupped his hands in hers and slowly raised them both to cover her face and wept. Zimm's eyes shuttered and looked away as if the display of grief was too much. Even mourning in this place seemed subdued. No loud screaming, no wailing, just stoic acceptance.

I sighed, heavy and long. I'd never had to tell a family about a loved one's death. An intern wouldn't be trusted with such a task, but this time there was no one else. Fear constricted in my heart and then dropped lower. I'm sure the duty was one doctors never relished, but then again, they had never been told their life could be sacrificed in return.

Sure, the threat to my life was nerve wracking, but deep in my heart I knew ConRad wouldn't let anything happen to me. Who was stronger than the Commander in Chief of the compound? No crusty old Elders could get past him. There was something else though, something I was missing. I let my mind drift over the previous events when Zimm was brought to me. What had ConRad said? "Zimmion's life doesn't matter anyways." If his life didn't matter, then why bring him in to get medical attention in the first place? Why not let him die on the front lines? Or did his life only matter if the goddess survived?

I pulled the sheet over Sari's face, but stopped mid-motion. No, that was ridiculous, simply barbaric.

I had to think. What was Zimm's role before he was injured? What was his position in connection with the goddess?

Oh my God. My stomach cramped. I doubled over and shot a glance at Zimm. His face was a complete mask of acceptance. He knew. Of course, he knew. Everyone did except me, the only idiot who didn't put it together. Zimm was the defender of the goddess Sari. He'd sworn to protect her with his life.

My vision blurred. The only sound was the quiet whimpering of Quinn. Her tears weren't for Sari; this place was too cold for weeping over a mere acquaintance. It was for Zimm that her heart broke.

I won't believe it. I won't believe it. My mantra broke my frozen stance. I pushed the swinging doors open and ran down the hall. Tears streamed from my face. *I won't believe it.* Even if you pushed aside all human decency, putting to death a healthy and trained solider was a complete waste of resources. There had to be a place for logic in this society, if not for compassion.

I halted in front of ConRad's quarters. My breath came in short gasps—palms slick with sweat. I stood motionless, unable to bring myself to open the door. The simple act of turning the knob would start a domino effect of events spiraling out of my control.

I planted my hands on either side of the door jam and leaned my forehead on the metal door. What had I done? Did I just produce a healthy human sacrifice to satisfy the bloodlust of this society? A wave of nausea swept over me. I turned and threw up.

My retching did what I lacked the courage to do. The door was thrown open.

ConRad stood in full commander mode—stoic and dead-panned. We froze and stared at each other—me doubled over and gasping, him with hardened resolve. I saw his emotions flash in his eyes before I could even speak. It was all there; the decision was made.

I whipped my head back and forth, eyes pleading. He said nothing, just pushed me aside and headed toward the infirmary.

I stumbled after him, wiping away the tears and snot with the back of my arm.

"ConRad please." I begged. *I begged.*

His strides were long, his legs eating up the distance. ConRad slammed open the infirmary door and stood stock-still, assessing. ConRad had seen the face of death a million times, so I couldn't understand his sudden hesitation. I peered around his massive frame. Then I saw it myself. Hope along with blood drained from my body. I grasped the door frame as my knees weakened, and I slowly folded to the floor.

Zimm and Quinn were locked in a passionate, sorrowful embrace. Their mouths open and consuming, hands clutching and grasping as if trying to burn a brand that stayed even after death. Completely in their own world, they were oblivious to us, oblivious to the fact that they were committing the ultimate sin. A relationship of any kind with a goddess was against the rules. But kissing one went beyond comprehension.

Doing my ER rotation in some of the most debased places leaves you privy to the whole range of human emotions. A mother's deep sorrow for the loss of her child. A father's rage at a drunk driver. A gangbanger's thirst for vengeance after a "duty kill." But as I glanced toward ConRad, I'd never seen a rage so powerful, yet calm and terrifying in its ability. Shards of ice coursed through my veins, chilling my blood. I saw death in ConRad's eyes.

I would witness a murder.

ConRad roared. The sound vibrated in my bones. He charged toward Zimm and Quinn. Cots and chairs flew out of his way. Zimm pushed Quinn behind him, barely having enough time to raise his arm in defense. ConRad descended on him like the Archangel armed with God's vengeance. He grabbed Zimm by his shirt and threw him. Zimm crashed into the cabinet across the room, and fell to the floor with a thud. The cabinet door hung precariously. Then ConRad was on him like he'd never left. He picked him up and threw him against the corner wall.

Crazy burned in ConRad's eyes. The violence and lack of control terrified me. When ConRad's hands went around Zimm's throat, I knew Zimm had drawn his last breath.

Thoughts of self-preservation flooded my mind. I saw myself turning and walking right out the door. I'd hide until midnight and crawl my way back home through the hole in the mountain. I would take my chances with Aura and the aliens.

God had forsaken this place and so could I. Instead, I pushed myself to my feet and walked straight into the turbulent storm.

CHAPTER SIXTEEN

M_y fingers trembled as I placed a restraining hand on Con-Rad's forearm. "Please ConRad, stop." My voice broke. I didn't know if it was enough. If I was enough.

Time was measured in heartbeats. Then ConRad came back. The crazed anger retreated like a low tide leaving clean sand in its wake. ConRad was himself again—strong, emotionless, detached ConRad, and I'd never been so grateful.

His fingers pried loose from Zimm's throat. Zimm buckled to the floor gasping and choking, his face beet red.

I stayed glued to ConRad's side, infusing sanity through my touch. He blinked and took in his surroundings. If he was surprised that the infirmary was filled with soldiers who'd come in to investigate the commotion, he didn't show it.

His gaze found Zimm's. "Was it not enough that your own life is forfeit? Did you have to take Quinn along with you?" ConRad said.

The blood trickling from the corner of Zimm's eyes showed an eerie orange in the copper lighting. He shook his head and tried to massage away the marks left behind by ConRad's fingers. "Her goddess status will protect her."

"Are you sure about that? Hard to keep an eye on her from the grave. Take him away," ConRad said. "Throw him in the cell to await the penalty."

Zimm was pulled up by his arms, hands tied behind his back. His head hung low as if resigned to his fate as two burly men dragged him out the door.

"Same with her." He looked directly at Quinn. "She broke the goddess code. She will suffer the same."

Panic sliced though me. "ConRad no, please, she's just a child." Though in that moment she seemed to have catapulted into adulthood.

His gaze whipped around and pinned me as effectively as his hand that found itself clamped around my arm.

"Enough," he growled, and pulled me aside as they took Quinn away. Within minutes we were alone, and within a second of that he pushed me against the wall. He placed his mouth hard against my ear, his voice dangerously low. "Don't think I don't know what you've done. It didn't escape my notice that Zimmion was quite active and vital, when just a few days ago he was on death's door. I know you gave him the microbiotics, and I hold you partially responsible for this relationship. You saw what was going on and did nothing to stop the crime."

A tremble went through me at his words. How many transgressions were to be piled upon my head?

ConRad slid his forehead to mine, his breathing harsh. "You have no idea what you've done. The Elders will be notified. There'll be an investigation and people will be put to death. I just don't know if you'll be one of them."

Fear chilled my blood. I knew he'd be angry, but I didn't expect this.

"But . . . but you promised you would protect me." I'd held on to his promise the whole time during the committing of my crime. Somehow I believed ConRad would make it all right.

"This . . . this is beyond me now. Even if I wanted to, Kris, I couldn't. You knew the consequences and deliberately disobeyed me." His hands wrapped around both of my arms and shook. Fury rolled off of him and crashed around me like waves. "You lied to me. What were you thinking? Even I can't go against the Elders."

I blinked hard, pushing back the tears I knew shined in my eyes.

A small crack broke through the ice-hardness of his face. "What do you expect me to do? To look the other way as Quinn and Zimm flaunt their relationship? If I break, if I become weak, then I lose the respect of my whole command. My duty is toward Earth. The human race couldn't survive without us."

He released me and I stumbled, less from force and more from weakened knees. He headed for the door, but then turned and settled his deadeye stare on me. "I can't afford to be weak. From now on Kris, for both our sakes, call me Commander."

The infirmary doors swung in his absence. A mocking wave goodbye to my broken life.

Like burning arrows, his words found their mark and pierced my heart. I'd been hurled through time and deposited on a foreign planet. I'd been chased by aliens, imprisoned, and held at gunpoint. I'd been treated like a spy and forced into mind-retrieval, but through it all I'd never been so scared and alone as I was now. In the back of my mind I'd known ConRad was always there, despite everything. ConRad had made me believe he'd be willing to die to protect me.

Self-delusion was a luxury I'd given up since my arrival. I knew his protection wasn't because of some undying love he harbored for me. It was just his makeup. He took his claim on me seriously. He couldn't live with himself if he did anything less. He was my protection in this hostile world, and I'd severed the tenuous ties. Now he was gone.

I was alone in a world I didn't understand. The threat to my life had crystallized into hard reality. Sinking to the floor, I drew my knees into my chest. What had I done? My self-confidence had shattered. I didn't trust myself to make the right decisions. In fact, I'd made things worse. Zimm and Quinn would be sentenced to death, and I'd be right behind them.

Why was I here? Why be sent to a place that was ruled by absolutism and then die by capital punishment? The rhythmic thudding of my head against the wall didn't provide an answer. Was there something blatantly obvious I was missing? My head fell in defeat against my folded arms.

Images flashed like a bad movie trailer. Her presence right after my interrogation, a coveted key to the microbiotics for my wound, her plea for Zimm before his battered and war-torn body showed up in my infirmary. Then I knew. Clarity crashed in like a drunk ex-lover—unwanted, but hard to ignore. My head popped up and my gaze took in nothing of the vacant, gray room. *She* had the answers. Curse her lying mouth, but she had the answers all along.

A bitter taste of irony bit my tongue. I laughed. God's grace worked even in this forsaken place. Those bars of steel that imprisoned Quinn were the same thing that kept her protected from me.

Because I was going to rip the answers from her bare throat.

My determination prevailed in my quest to access Quinn. The word was out that ConRad had withheld his protection from me. My status in the compound dropped like a supermodel who'd fallen off her diet. If previously I had too many takers to count, now I was a leper with a death sentence on my head. In the end I played Quinn's goddess card and lied. I convinced the soldiers guarding her cell she needed medical attention, and if she died, it wouldn't take much to load another round of bullets and use them both as target practice.

Of course, there was absolutely no hope in seeing Zimm.

My anger dissipated at my first sight of Quinn. She sat cross-legged on the floor, staring blankly into space. Her long blonde hair lacked shine, forming a dull curtain that obscured her eyes. Her skin had lost the rosiness of youth and lay flat, hollowing her cheeks. Quinn had never donned the traditional white robes, since she never declared herself a full goddess. But even her standard-issue military uniform was too large, swallowing up her petite frame. Uncertainty had me biting my lip. Maybe I'd mistaken her age after all. I'd originally thought she was around seventeen, but middle-age seemed to have crept up with a vengeance.

"Quinn?" I rushed the cell. "Are you all right?" I glanced around her prison. She wasn't as bad off as compared to the rest of us. Her cell had the same homey quality as ConRad's room, but with rusty iron bars across the front.

"Quinn, really, are you okay?" A nervous tingling started in my belly at her silence. Maybe she was suffering from shock. She continued to sit and stare off into nothing. I bent lower, trying to catch her line of sight. Clamping my hand over my mouth, I stifled a scream. Her eyes were filled with black, churning like a restless sea. As long as I lived, I'd never get used to eyes that had the look of death.

Quinn blinked and her eyes snapped back to baby blue. "You're The One."

I knelt before her, desperate to understand. "The One what? I'm not special, Quinn."

"But you are." She spoke with such conviction, it was hard to disbelieve.

I'd come here for answers. I had to be willing to listen. "One what? I don't even know what that means. Wouldn't I have some sense of purpose?"

Quinn shrugged. My feelings to her were inconsequential. "I'm not sure what you'd feel, but it doesn't change what you are."

My forehead was flush against the bars, my hands wrapped around the rusting metal. "Which is what, Quinn? Give me some damn answers so I can figure this out and preferably not get all of us killed in the process."

Quinn sighed and shrugged again in that irritating and unassuming manner everyone here used. Was nothing here worth getting excited about? I gritted my teeth as she turned her body to face the wall, dismissing me with the dignity of royalty.

This was getting me nowhere. If anything, I'd learn patience while I was here. "Quinn, I'm sorry. Just please explain. Can you please start from the beginning? Pretend I'm an idiot and you have to lay out the whole thing to a simpleton."

Quinn tilted her head and flashed me a half smile. "Fine, that won't be hard at all."

Sarcasm seemed to be taking root.

"Good," I said. If my tone was a bit drier than before, she didn't comment.

"You have to promise to just listen. There's not enough time for pessimism and distrustful arguments. You're going to have to take a lot of this on faith."

Faith? I'd rather flaunt my cellulite in a string bikini. But hadn't my BBD said I needed to be more trusting?

Quinn scooted closer to the bars. With a quick glance toward the long stone steps, she lowered her voice. "I'm a goddess, a powerful one. I've been hiding my abilities for some time now. I never wanted the goddess lifestyle, to be all alone, no relationships, no human contact. It was more of a prison sentence than a gift."

I nodded. The life of a goddess seemed cruel.

"But if you have powers, you don't have a choice. The value placed on goddesses is too high. Of course, each goddess's gift is different. Some see in the dark. Some can sense the aliens. Others read minds."

I nodded again, shuddering at the memory.

"But me . . . my gift is powerful and multifaceted. I can read minds, foretell events, and read or see energy. My gift was inconsistent in the beginning, but that changed when I met Zimmion. My gift became more controllable, more powerful."

If what she was saying was true, then she was the most

powerful goddess to be sure. Way too essential to be put to death. I saw hope for Quinn. I just had to inform ConRad.

"I could never tell anyone this. The rules we have are too ingrained. No one ever questions them. That is, until you. My people here wouldn't have believed me, and Zimmion would have been put to death. So we've kept this a secret."

Quinn pushed her hair behind her ears and massaged her neck. Exhaustion pulled heavily on her. "It wasn't Zimmion's fault, not really. It was just I could read his thoughts so clearly, and soon he could read mine also. We were too connected not to be together. I believe our lives are vitally intertwined. If one of us dies, the other will also. That's why I could never risk going out into the field. If I died, it would be like holding a gun to Zimmion's head and pulling the trigger. I couldn't do it, regardless of the Elders' rules."

"Quinn, I had no idea." I relaxed my grip on the bars and sat cross-legged in front of her. Certain pieces came together. The way Zimm and Quinn could communicate without words. Her desperate plea for me to save his life. Her willingness to court death by kissing him in public.

"But now what? What's the point, Quinn?" Nausea rose up. There was a small hope the Elders could be persuaded to pardon Quinn, but there wasn't a chance in hell Zimm would survive.

"Kris, we are caught in a time warp. These events keep happening again and again. You send yourself here from the past to either change something or finish something. And before you ask, no, I don't know the answer to what needs to change. I don't have memories of any previous cycles, but I have dreams . . . or impressions, maybe?" Quinn shrugged. "All I know is that it feels like we have been here before. As you can see, I'm aging at a rapid rate, deteriorating before my very eyes. I can only guess my body is the one gauge that time isn't standing still. I'm scared, Kris, scared that we have been caught here for years. And all I can do is pray that this time you'll learn what you need to do in order to break the cycle. I can't even fathom a guess of what will happen once my life span gets to the end."

My heart pounded in my chest. Things that my future-self had told me, things that I'd dismissed as ramblings of a crazy person, rushed back. What did my BBD know that I didn't? She had talked about a prophesy, saving ConRad, and evil men. Then I shook my head. No. I was her. All the knowledge that I needed was inside me. A wisp of anticipation swirled in my gut, because now I knew. Everything she had said was true. No more self-denial. I swallowed hard. "What's The Prophesy, Quinn?"

A smile broke over her features, as if she had waited for this moment. "The Prophesy was first spoken during the rebel movement over thirty years ago. The Prophesy says that she will come from the past and be protected from the wild beasts. With the wisdom of old she will save the lives of men and drag the doings of the evil ones into the light. And they will hate her and seek to kill her. But a mighty warrior will be called upon to save her, and he will become an outlaw to her rescue. And she will incite a small nation to rebellion. A final sign will be given to all of you, so that you may know she is The One. A miraculous birth will be bestowed upon her. This sign will be hers and hers alone, so all may know she is The Chosen One. By means of her body, she will save the world."

Shock zipped along my spine. For some reason, I never

thought The Prophesy was about *me*. "And you think I'm that woman?

"You have fulfilled the requirements. Who else has come through time? Who else has been saved by the wild beasts or aliens, and used the older knowledge of medicine to save soldiers here? It could only be you."

Even I couldn't deny that I had traveled through time. And by any standards, that was pretty unusual. But my resolution of putting away self-denial was fast losing its appeal, since the last part didn't sound too promising. "Um, my mind got tripped up on 'means of my body,' smacks of sacrificial death, don't you think?"

Quinn broke eye contact to finger her bootlaces. "Ah . . . I don't know. Over the years I've had visions concerning The Prophesy and some details have become clearer . . . some not. All I really know for sure is that you are The One."

"So you don't really know if I die on this alien-infested planet or not?" I got to my knees and resisted the urge to reach through the bars and shake her.

"Kris, I don't have all the answers. My gift doesn't work that way."

"Why the hell not? It's not like you've been shy about manipulating events to fit your agenda."

"Manipulating is a strong word. I prefer leading." Quinn raised her hands in a take-it-easy gesture. "Calm down, I don't think you are going to die anytime soon. I haven't seen that. Since you've been here, my visions have been more frequent and detailed. So I'm sure we're on the right path. I can't explain it, but you're going to have to take some things on faith."

"God, I don't believe any of this, not really." I rubbed my

hands over my face. I had a sudden headache. But I did believe, kinda—the sense of déjà vu I had since coming here. The way I had known ConRad when I'd gazed into his eyes, the feeling that I had come home.

"You are so stubborn." Quinn's "princess of the castle" tone was back. "But what you believe is irrelevant. There are things at work here that are greater than you. You need to accept that."

I studied Quinn. The crinkles around her eyes and grooves at the corners of her mouth hadn't been there when I first met her. The truth was staring at me in the face. But she was wrong. I was no leader.

"One more thing." Quinn stood and began to pace her eight-by-eight cave cell. "When I see visions of the future, they're only in black and white, foggy, without much definition. But since I've been down here, I keep glimpsing the same images over and over again. I can smell the gunpowder, the burn of flesh, but I just don't know what it means."

Another vision of death and destruction, how original. I stood and stretched my lower back. God, I was tired. The emotional upheaval of the day had drained me, leaving me numb. "Tell me about it. Maybe I can help. Or at least by putting the images into words can help make things more concrete."

"I see terror and death. Man and alien. And . . . *you* in the middle—you're the key." In a flash, Quinn threaded her hands through the bars and grabbed my tank top, pulling my face a mere inch from hers. "It's now . . . it is happening now! You have to go up and help ConRad."

ConRad was the last man on earth I wanted to help. "Why would I help that bas—"

"Stop! No questions. His life is in danger."

The wild look in her eye broke my mind's fog. Could this be true? Did ConRad need me? Was this why I'd come here? I backed away, turned, and started up to the main base.

"Kris!" Quinn shouted. I glanced over my shoulder to see Quinn staring into nothing, eyes clouded over with inky black. "You'll need a grenade. Don't forget the grenade," she whispered.

I started to run.

CHAPTER SEVENTEEN

The echo of gunfire ricocheted off the metal doors that lined the passageway. The ceiling rumbled, pouring dirt and pebbles down on me. I threw my arms up in cover and ran toward the command center. Screams of men in pain broke through the low roar of battle. Then an ear-splitting shriek—high in pitch, deafening in volume. Not human. Not machine. Terror struck my body like lightning. I turned and threw myself to the ground, clamped my hands over ears, and squeezed my eyes shut. My head shook in disbelief. Only one thing could make that sound. I've heard it before. Would never forget. Alien.

There were aliens in the compound. A sob broke as I turned back and crawled over rocks and fallen debris. *Run. Hide. Live.*

But ConRad needed me.

I swung my head back and forth. *No.*

"NOOOOO!" My scream echoed down the deserted tunnel.

I glanced behind me. The monsters were close. With just a turn of one corner, I'd be at the command center. A spasm shot through my bowels.

On hands and knees I hung my head in shame. *I can't. I can't.*

I heard Quinn's voice. *I pray you'll learn what you need to do this time.*

I closed my eyes and looked within myself. Past the thick tar-like fear, deep beyond my churning intestines and my blood drunk on adrenaline was a small pocket of light. I dug deep and tentatively grasped the glowing ball. *Heat. Strength.* The ice of fear thawed from my muscles.

Turning, I belly-crawled forward.

Hard gray scaled bodies towering ten feet tall were attached to elongated oval heads. Wide front-facing eyes shined like tiny black mirrors. A double-hinged jaw, racked with razor-sharp teeth opened to half a grown man's length. Viscous white slimed their bodies and dripped from stubby arms and claw-like fingers. Mucus mixing with blood whipped about as they moved at inhumanly fast speeds, coating the dead and walls alike.

The outside tunnel had been breached. The men who'd been guarding the entrance lay below in pieces. One by one, the aliens slithered out through the narrow entrance, crawled over bodies, and attacked.

I cowered, hovering on the side lines. The scene was like nothing I'd ever known. Machine guns fired and sprayed the room, hitting some targets, bouncing off the majority. Aliens swooped, dismembered, and beheaded soldiers in seconds. Bodies slid apart on their razor claws like tissue paper.

A man, a few feet away from me, was unloading his machine gun at the enemy. Quicker than an inhaled breath, a claw reached out. His gun dropped with a clatter by my feet, blood sprayed across my face.

The warmth along my cheek set me to motion. I dropped to the floor and using a headless body as cover—*don't think about it*—I scanned the carnage for ConRad. The majority of soldiers left were defending the two double doors opposite the tunnel. I remembered ConRad telling me what lay beyond the heavily guarded doors. The Earth Portal.

I knew what this battle meant. If the aliens got to the portal, all human life would be lost. This was survival. It was them or us. My choice: Die here or die later. There was no in between.

Sweat rolled into my eyes. I swiped at my face, grabbed the gun, and crawled to a nearby overturned metal table. A small band of soldiers were somewhat successfully protecting the red double doors to the portal. Peering over the barrier, I saw ConRad in the forefront barking orders and firing guns. He was so far away. My heart sank. We were separated by a dozen feet, but it might as well have been oceans. Piled between us were the dead, both human and monster, and, of course, live killing-efficient aliens.

A grenade was thrown, exploded, and killed off two of the closest aliens. Cockroach bits flew. I swallowed burning bile back down my throat. *Grenade!* Quinn had said I needed one. I wasn't sure what to do with it, but having an explosive was as good of a place to start as any.

"ConRad!" My voice was hoarse, I tried again and succeeded. His head snapped around and his eyes caught mine. A stricken look flashed across his face, and then it was gone. He whipped his head forward, refocusing on trying to stay alive.

"I need a grenade," I screamed to be heard over the noise. An emphatic shake of his head was my answer.

I ducked back behind my metal barrier, lying as close to the ground as possible. The air was thick with smoke, dust, and the hot smell of gunfire. I tried, right? I asked and did not receive. The Prophesy must be wrong, or at least Quinn's most recent vision. I'd done my best, tried to do what I was supposed to do, but the continuation of the human race was not up to me. My eyes were already plotting my escape route as a grenade flew over and hit the opposite wall, bounced, and rolled slowly, as if hand-delivered, to my feet.

A second of paralysis, then a bloodcurdling scream as I covered my head. This was it. *Death by being blown to bits.* A few stilted breaths later and I found the courage to peek through my fingers. The little doodad with a small ring-sized circle was still wedged in the top. I'd never handled a grenade, much less seen one in real life, but I'd watched plenty of movies, and they were educational, right? Linda Hamilton threw dozens of grenades and never blew herself up. Besides the mechanics seemed simple enough. Clamp down the lever, remove circle-thingy with teeth, then throw and release toward target. Under no circumstances were the steps to be reversed or, God forbid, done out of order. Of that, I was quite certain.

My sweaty fingers shook and wrapped themselves around the cold grenade. *Don't think.* If I gave myself a second of hesitation, I'd chicken out. I jumped over the table and ran in the opposite direction of the battle—toward the entrance tunnel itself.

Time slowed. The compromised entrance seemed a mile away, when in reality it was only a few feet. Aliens poured out of the tunnel like rats leaving a sinking ship. Crouching low, I used the body carnage as cover. I grasped the gritty metal pin with my teeth and spat it on the ground.

For a split second my courage faltered. I needed to throw the grenade as far into the tunnel as possible, ideally pitching it over their heads so it wouldn't bounce back and blow me up instead. My plan was to execute a triple front flip, stay suspended in mid-air, while simultaneously hitting my mark. This was possible, I knew, since I'd seen every *Matrix* movie at least twice. But maybe only high-paying Hollywood actresses could pull that one off. So I decided to do what I did best—run like hell.

I ran and leapt with all my strength toward the hole in the mountain. There was a loll in the incoming alien bodies. I threw the grenade into thick blackness. I crashed to the ground and slid to a stop when my head thudded against the wall. A loud explosion, flames burst out of the side of the mountain. Then my vision narrowed to black.

I woke to find three ConRad's staring down from above. My head hurt too badly to try and merge them together, besides something was wrong with his face. He was all pasty white and grim looking. If I didn't know better, I'd say he was scared. "What happened?"

"You're awake?"

"Yeah, but I don't want to be." I groaned. "My head. Did I hit it?"

"That and every other body part. How do you feel?"

"Like I hit my head and every other body part." I raised myself up on one elbow and glanced around. I'd somehow been carried from the command center and was laying in one of the many adjoining pathways. ConRad was kneeling besides me, his hands clenched on his thighs.

"What happened? I remember throwing the grenade, an explosion, and then not much else."

He turned his attention to the ground, and took a deep breath as if he needed a moment to focus himself. "When I first caught sight of you, you were flying through the air within inches of an alien's razor-sharp teeth. I thought I'd see your head leave your body for sure. But you made it, by the goddesses, I don't know how, but you did. Then the grenade went off inside the tunnel."

I nodded. That must've been the explosion I remembered.

ConRad shook his head in disbelief. "How did you know to do that?"

"Do what?" My body hurt and for some reason I wanted to burst into tears.

His mouth twitched at the corners. My treasonous heart responded, skipping beats at ConRad's version of a smile. "You triggered an earthquake of sorts and collapsed the whole tunnel, sweetheart. All the aliens in the tunnel were crushed under a thousand tons of dirt and rock."

"And the rest?"

"With no new recruits we were able to take out the remaining aliens, and still maintain the integrity of the portal."

"In other words we kicked butt?"

"If that saying means like it sounds, then yes." He smiled fully—this one reached his eyes.

I cut my glance away and swallowed hard. "The wounded . . . they need my help," I said, trying to push myself to a sitting position.

ConRad shook his head. "There are no wounded. They're dead or alive, not much of an in-between with this battle."

I closed my eyes in regret, but decided to get up anyways. "I feel better. Let me try to stand."

"Good." He helped me to my feet. "We're evacuating the compound in fourteen hours. This place was barely habitable to begin with and now it's toxic."

I searched the area around me, trying to find anything familiar in the destruction. Debris was everywhere. Overturned tables and chairs, and computer monitors were thrown about and broken. Live copper wiring crackled and swayed from the ceiling. And of course the bodies. Blood flowed from alien and human alike. Unidentifiable parts were strewn about like a scene from the gruesome underworld.

I could never have imagined anything so horrific. Instinctively, I looked toward ConRad, trying to reach out for comfort. He stared at the same scene, but with his concrete mask in place. I reached for his hand, knowing he'd lost good men and very likely friends today. My fingers brushed his. He clamped his hand around mind. A surge of desperation waved through me. Then, as if it never happened, I was released and pushed away.

"I am glad that you are all right," he mumbled, turned, and walked down the corridor.

How could he be so cold? He'd just walked away like he could barely tolerate my presence. Stunned at his callousness, I leaned against the wall. Hot tears found their way down my cheeks. Angrily, I wiped them away, pissed at my sign of weakness.

My head pounded. I squeezed my skull with my hands, hoping to keep it from bursting apart and spraying against the wall. My legs shook. The adrenaline that surged through my body crashed, leaving me below rock bottom. I bit down on my bloodied finger, hard, and tried to get a hold on myself.

I needed to get out of here. Away from the blood and smell of death. My hope of escape with the goddess Aura had crumbled along with the destruction of the command center. I would never go home, never leave this hell.

I needed to be safe. If only for two minutes, I needed protection. Hadn't he promised he'd protect me? He said the "claiming" was forever. He couldn't just pull his protection whenever he felt like it. It didn't work like that. In seconds, I was going to lose my blasted mind. And if I was, then it best be on the one man who could handle it, iceman himself. ConRad.

Chapter Eighteen

A tingling started at the base of my spine, crept over between my shoulder blades and took root in my brain. A red haze diffused the perimeter of my vision as I stumbled down the hallway on shaky legs. I burst into his quarters and kicked the door shut behind me. My body was braced, hands on hips ready to attack.

ConRad sat behind his wooden desk, elbows on the top, head in his hands; grief and defeat were heavy in the slump of his shoulders. The venom I wanted to heap upon him shriveled and died in my throat. At my entrance, his gaze slowly rose. The piercing blue of his irises had turned dark gray. Purple hues ringed his eyes. The responsibility he bore was shown in the creases of his face, aging him ten years in the last ten minutes.

My breath hitched and the tears I'd ruthlessly pushed back broke through. I cried for all the soldiers lost, the violence of their sacrifice, the hopelessness of their cause. I wept for me, misplaced and scared in this unforgiving world. I wept for him grieving and alone, knowing he couldn't weep for himself. There were no words, so I said nothing.

His gaze finally silenced my sobs, but the hot tears continued down my face. The moment stretched out into another and another, until time slowed with nothing but our breathing to number the seconds.

His defenses had crumbled, leaving a brutal rawness pulsing from him. For the first time he allowed me to see past his wall, down to the core of him, into his soul.

And his soul was black, the blackest I'd ever seen. The pit of loneliness and despair would've been too much for a lesser man. And then something else altogether. Need. A want so primitive that fear rose inside me like a self-preserving shield. I pushed myself back against the wall, my hand fumbling for the handle.

Mind changed. Want out. I'd seen this man's tightly reined control, and I'd seen him snap. I was no match for the power that rolled off him. I couldn't play this game and win. To engage was to submit. The strength of his will would consume me with one lick of its flame.

ConRad rose. Cords in his neck stood out as he braced himself with his hands on the desk. With a savageness borne of a man of action and few words, he flung the desk aside, a mere obstacle to the object of his desire . . . me.

With no barrier between us he stepped forward. I courageously held my ground. Being that the wall pushed against my backside and prevented retreat was of little consequence. He stepped forward again.

A fish on a hook, a rat in a trap, I had sympathy for them

all. I stretched my hand out to preserve the distance between us. Shook my head in feeble denial.

Instantly upon me, he pushed my futile objections aside. His hands pinned mine to my sides; his mouth captured my own. An arc of lightning shot from my lips to between my legs.

His hand savagely wound in my hair and pulled. My head yielded for his easier access. I let my lips part for one cautious taste. He took what I gave and then more. His tongue invaded, swept across my teeth and palate, sending my senses reeling. At the first hint of his familiar flavor, a whimper escaped from the back of my throat. *I knew him. I knew this.* This was home.

By the rapid rate of his breathing, he fared no better. I ran my hand through his hair and grabbed on. I wanted to crawl up him. Crawl inside him. Reading my thoughts, his hand ran down my side, across my butt, and grabbed my leg. He lifted me to meet him, mouth to mouth, breast to chest, hip to hip. A growl sounded deep in his throat. My body responded to his primitive call. We were like two animals in prime heat, licking, biting, clawing. It was a natural progression from what we just witnessed. We were slaughtered like animals and now we needed to rut like ones.

The thought had me rearing my head up and gasping for sanity. *Breathe. Dammit, just breathe. Reason will return.* Was this what I wanted? I was too close. I couldn't go down this road and still leave that vital part of me protected. He was like a lion seeking to devour. He'd always demanded more than I could give. ConRad may think we were two animals heady on bloodlust and survival's guilt, but I had to stop being so naïve. This would change everything.

Scared. Too scared. My well-constructed defenses that protected me were no match for his assault. I'd been strong enough to close myself off from everyone, my family, my own flesh and blood, but with one hushed word he could destroy me.

I struggled, gently at first, then with earnest. He didn't notice. He rained kisses on my neck, the soft spot behind my ear, and the hairline by my temple. Fresh tears blurred my vision. His lips brushed the wetness at the corner of my eyes. The tender gesture had me biting the inside of my cheek to keep my focus. I slipped my hand between his tempting mouth and my traitorous skin. I need space.

He looked up; my breath caught. His face etched with pain, tortured and starved. My heart rose in my throat, and I swallowed hard to lodge it back into place. With my legs still wrapped around his waist, I gently placed my hands on either side of his face and gazed directly into his eyes.

"What are you doing?" I whispered.

ConRad closed his eyes with a heavy sigh. "God, I was really hoping it was obvious."

I smiled. I couldn't help it. Underneath his callous demeanor he was still such a guy. "I mean, why are you doing this?"

"You don't know the answer to that either?" ConRad's mouth twitched in a smile that didn't reach his eyes. "I'll weep with gratitude later, but please, sweetheart, let me show you now." His hips rubbed against mine in a way that had me biting my lip for another reason all together.

"Damn it, ConRad." He was nowhere close to weeping. I on the other hand was shaking. "If you want to get me into bed, being obtuse is not the best way of going about it." This wasn't my best argument being that his hands were on my butt, and I was resting on something extremely hard and apparently very large.

ConRad sighed again and lowered his forehead against the wall behind me. "Sweetheart, I'm a patient man; I know this. Really, I do. I'd not be where I am today, Commander in Chief of this compound, if that wasn't so. But damn it to hell if I'm not scraping for the last dregs of tolerance I have left. So let me explain the blaring obvious to you. The last thing I want to do with you is argue. Hell, I don't even want to talk, and I'm really hoping you have other uses for that tongue of yours, except flaying me alive. I just want to lose myself in your soft body. A body that smells so damn good that I haven't let my sheets be washed since you've come here. I work out three times a day, just so I have a hope of falling asleep. And even when I do, it doesn't matter because I spend the whole time chasing you in my dreams and wake more enslaved to you than ever. And I just . . . just want to forget that this day ever happened."

Enslaved? ConRad enslaved to me?

He'd been whispering in my ear, and he now raised his head and stared straight into my eyes. I saw something in his gaze. Something small and fragile, could it be hope? I wasn't sure about anything anymore, except no one had ever looked at me the way he did in that moment.

Conrad's glance traveled down to my nose and lips. His mouth followed, bestowing feather soft kisses to each. "I've seen and done things like I have today so much and so often that I've become dead inside." His voice grew husky as if he had a catch in his throat. "I walk around all day and live my life feeling nothing; no hate, no anger just . . . nothing.

"I thought that was how life was . . . and then you came. And I started to feel. Mostly pissed off, mind you, but a feeling nonetheless, and it meant that I was alive." He broke eye contact as if he couldn't face me and rested his forehead in the nook between my head and shoulder. He shuddered. "Kris, I've never asked another human being for anything in my life, but I am asking you. Please let me feel alive with you for just this one moment, this one time."

Breathe. For the love of everything that's holy. Breathe. This was the longest he had ever spoken to me at one time. But was it enough? Trust for me was a territory uncharted, unlit, and uncomfortable. It was like jumping off a cliff . . . in pitch dark. I'd been on the precipice and now the rocks were crumbling beneath my feet. Was I ready to give this man my everything? To hold nothing back?

No, I could hold the line. I could give into him and not lose myself in the process. I was strong enough. In my mind I walled myself up tight. Then dove in.

I groaned into his mouth and opened wide. His tongue stroked mine, thrusting in and out, sending a warm liquid to pool down where I wanted him the most. I traced his lips with my tongue, wetting them, and then reveled in the spontaneous shiver that went through his body.

He strained his hips into mine and rocked in the most maddening rhythm. If he was the most patient man, then I was his polar opposite. I'd always been open for the quickie, but this couldn't get moving fast enough. He locked my ankles around his waist and slid his hands under my shirt. With a few quick moves he bared me completely to his mouth, open, sucking, sending me to a place where thought didn't exist. My breasts were so sensitive they hurt. He lifted me up like I weighed nothing to place each nipple at mouth level. I dug my hands in his hair to better direct his delicious, hot mouth.

Someone pleaded; I think it was me. His heat burned me, flushed my skin. A want rose deep inside me. I moved my hips so there was no question, the invitation was clear.

He got the message.

ConRad swung us over to the bed and laid me on my back. In record time he stripped off his shirt, boots, and pants, leaving him standing there, impersonating an ancient warrior, ready to ravage. I bit my finger to keep myself from losing all self-respect by begging, but then did it anyways. "Hurry. Please."

ConRad seemed to agree, and I was way overdressed for this party. He attacked my military boots first, grabbed hold and tugged hard. I nearly flew off the bed.

"Um, you'll have to untie them first," I giggled. Crap. I clamped my hand over my mouth. I don't giggle. With exaggerated patience he bent down to the task of undoing the seemingly hundreds of holes and laces. He got to about halfway, tugged again, and nearly pulled my hip from its socket.

I laughed. "You have to undo them *all* the way."

"Damn these boots," he growled.

"You're the one who made me wear them," I said, laughing again.

"Stupid mistake. From now on you'll be going barefoot."

"And naked?" I couldn't resist.

"Not if you plan on ever leaving this room," he shot back.

I couldn't help but smile. To think I had this effect on such a powerful and controlled man had me feeling heady in my own right.

Both naked and both out of patience, he slid on top of me, grabbed my thighs, and pulled me closer to fit him better. Tasting, licking, biting. I struggled free and sunk my teeth into his shoulder. He might have gotten first blood, but I'd get my due.

The taste of smoke, sweat, and man lingered as I bathed my tongue over the small bite marks. I buried my face in his neck and imprinted his scent on my brain. His wet mouth . . . warm tongue circled my ear flicking in and out, igniting chills throughout my body. A crazy whimpering sounded deep in my throat. *Enough. No more.* I ran my hand down the length of him. Clasping his rock hardness, he was all warm steel, soft silk, and I was crazy for him.

ConRad was breathing hard, and holding me so tight a weaker woman would've crumbled. He whispered in my ear sweet, gentle things like how soft my skin was, how the smell of my hair made his mouth water. Then his words turned naughty. Raw sex talk threw me over the edge, making me moan with need. I drew him toward me, and wrapped my legs around my waist and pulled.

"God," ConRad rasped as he pushed into me. And I allowed him in, all the way in. He chose the pace, held me down, and made me take him. The tempo we followed was all our own. Then our rhythm quickened, and I threw my head back. Colors exploded behind my eyes. He stiffened and groaned.

We lay there, chests heaving, sticky with sweat. The air was thick with the scent of sex, mixed with our heavy breathing. ConRad's weight bore down on me, and I shifted to a more comfortable position. My movement must've brought him back to the moment, and he quickly rolled off to his side, drawing me into a classic spoon position. He threw his leg over my hip effectively staking his claim. Purring my contentment, I closed my eyes. I'd done it. My vulnerability, bloodied and tarnished, was still my own.

I would've been fine, even as his lips brushed against my throat. But he whispered one word, reverent and prayerful, in the silence. "Kris."

And I was lost, tumbling over the cliff.

Chapter Nineteen

I woke with a smile and breathed into a deep contented stretch, letting the rough blanket slip down around my waist. My range of motion was limited due to the big hulking man passed out on top of me. ConRad's leg was thrown over mine and his arm wrapped protectively around my middle. It felt glorious. I smiled even bigger and wiggled my naked little bottom against his groin, secretly delighting at his low moan. I could feel him grow hard and loved the thought that it was me he was reacting to.

But that wasn't the only thing bouncing around in my head. Shocking as it was, I couldn't help but think of what beautiful children we'd make together. I groaned inwardly. *Don't do this. Don't start planning your wedding to a man that you barely know.*

My father's voice chimed in. *"Kris,"* he said disapprovingly. *"Now why would any man buy the cow if they're getting the milk for free?"*

Ahh, mental head slap. I always hated that expression. Who'd thought it was okay to start comparing daughters to farm animals? Then all nagging voices were silenced because

ConRad opened his beautiful intense eyes, framed with the longest lashes I'd ever seen, and bestowed upon me the most devastating smile. After that, . . . what father?

"Hi," he said.

"Hi."

He had a silly grin on his face, and I was pretty sure my face mirrored his.

"You're beautiful," he said. "Did you know that?"

Ironically, I was thinking the same thing about him as a flood of warmth pulsed through my body. "If I said no, would you tell me again?"

It was shameless to fish for a compliment, but it wasn't as if I had far to fall, considering I was lying naked with a man I barely knew.

His smile faded and a look of seriousness sobered his eyes. "I'd tell you for the rest of your life if you'd let me. In fact, plan on it."

I sucked in my breath at his words. A thrill shot through me. See dad, I wanted to shout, you are not always right. ConRad seemed to be waiting for an answer. I searched my muddled brain for some smart, witty response, but couldn't find one. Instead, I settled for a stupid grin and a dumbfounded nod.

Embarrassed, I broke eye contact. I wasn't ready for this conversation, too many implications. Feeling the need for coverage, I pulled the blanket up under my arms. I rested my head on his chest and concentrated on taming the unruly butterflies in my stomach. I ran my fingers over his chest and traced the S-shaped scar on his right peck. The mark was ugly, the skin still puckered and red from the burn. Needing to change the subject, I asked, "What happened?"

He stiffened beneath me. Long moments passed and I thought he wouldn't answer. If I was more trusting and confident, I'd tell him to never mind, but I wasn't. Our previous conversation exposed too much of my vulnerability, and I grasped at the opportunity to have a little balancing of the scales. I knew nothing about his past, nothing about who he was. We had to start somewhere.

"It happened a long time ago." His voice muted as the caressing stroking of my hair stopped. "When I was a kid, I was given up by my family. Since I was male, they really had no use for me. I couldn't create an alliance through marriage or be sold for money, so I was taken to the military for training. As with most of the young men at the age of twelve, I was slotted for the corps nicknamed the Killing Fields. We were merely speed bumps to slow the aliens' progression down. There was no chance at survival."

His fingers massaged my temple as he paused, trying to find the right words. "There was a custom. Not a good one. The last night before our big battle we were given a no-holds-barred chance at freedom and a small bottle of whiskey. I guess the leaders' thought they could turn us into men overnight so they wouldn't have a guilty conscience of sending children to their deaths.

"Regardless, among us boys the custom was called Hell Night. Older boys hunted in packs for the smaller, younger ones. It wasn't until much later I figured out why. I guess I was considered pretty, and was definitely young enough. I spent most of that night hiding and running."

At his words I stilled. I could only imagine in a world full of men behaving badly, what teenagers, desperate and knowing they were going to die, would do to a younger, more helpless boy.

"I found my way into the sleeping quarters of a high-ranking Elder. At that time I thought he was my savior. He protected me through Hell Night and took me in as his page, preventing me from going to the Killing Fields. Everything started innocently enough: cooking, keeping his quarters clean, and in turn he taught me about political intrigue and espionage. Then things turned personal." His voice was controlled and neutral as if he was relaying what he ate for lunch the day before. "I'll spare you the details of the seduction."

My breath shallowed, and my insides tightened. I was afraid any sudden move would close him down, cut any tentative bond between us.

In a monotone, he continued. "I tried to escape numerous times and ended up being shackled to a metal post in his room. Those months are dark, huge gaps in my memory. But I do recall him believing himself in love with me, and it infuriated him that I wasn't willing. He called the sessions 'Breaking the Boy.' After one such session I got sick, delusional with a high fever. He must've realized he'd gone too far because I was anonymously dropped off at the infirmary. After I got well, I made my escape, but in that last session he had already branded me with his mark. And that's why I carry the first letter of his name, Syon, on my chest.

"It wasn't inconsequential that when choosing my last name—Smith—I chose one that began with S. I refused to let his mark shame me forever."

Silence hung heavy between us. He'd just bared his soul to me and it scared me to death. I was used to living my life on a superficial level. This went way beyond. "I don't . . . I mean . . . I'm . . ."

"Shh. I told you because you asked and because you need to know I have a dark side. You need to know how dark I can get."

I scooted off him and busied myself with a frayed hem of the sheet. This was going in a direction I had no hope of being able to control.

"This is supposed to be where you say that you're not afraid of the dark." There was humor in his voice, but underneath was something else altogether.

"You make me nervous," I said. *Coward!* I shouted at myself, as I wished fervently to backpedal the conversation to safer ground.

"I make a lot of people nervous, sweetheart." There was a sly smile in his voice, but I refused to glance up to confirm.

His utter stillness had me fidgeting even more. But he deserved more from me. He deserved the truth. "ConRad, I don't think . . . what I mean is, this is going too—"

A sudden loud pounding on the door had us both jumping four feet, straight into the air.

"Commander sir. Urgent, sir," a solider said from behind the door.

ConRad was up and dressed before I was even out of bed. Apparently seeing no need to wait for me to get my clothes on, ConRad cracked the door and peered out.

"The Elders are here and looking for you. The word is that they aren't happy."

ConRad gave a nod and began to close the door.

"Sir?"

ConRad looked back to the solider.

"They're looking for the woman."

ConRad went dead still for a mere heartbeat, but it was

enough to send my mind racing. He closed the door and shifted his gaze toward me.

"Get dressed," he stated coolly, then sat down and pulled on his boots.

"What's going on?"

"The Elders are here," he said simply.

"The Elders?" I squeaked. I hadn't really believed they'd come.

"They're here to investigate the death of the goddess. I thought I would have more time, but their spy network must run deeper than I thought."

"Do they know about me?" Sweat prickled underneath my clasped arms.

"If they don't, they will soon. An unattached female, who appeared out of nowhere, is hard to keep secret."

I hadn't moved, still naked and wrapped in a blanket. My heart rate was picking up fast and the familiar taste of metal coated my tongue.

"Listen—" he took my face in his hands and drilled his gaze into mine, "the Elders control all of civilization . . . and everything in between."

"Does that include you?" I whispered, my throat suddenly dry.

"Oh yeah . . . especially me. Do us both a favor, stay low, out of sight." He let me go and walked to the door. "Get dressed and go and find Aura. She'll hide you if she can. I'll meet you at what's left of the command center after I get rid of them."

It wasn't his words that sent ice mainlining into my body, but the desperate look he gave me before he left.

ConRad was scared.

Chapter Twenty

---

*T*he Elders were here.

My hands shook as I pulled on my clothes. The boots took the longest, since I had to stop twice to dry my palms as I laced the millionth hole. I paused before opening the door, remembering the look in ConRad's eyes. *He'll protect me. He promised.*

I threw the door open and fast-walked down the hall. I was torn between not drawing attention to myself and doing a full run to get the hell out of here. Find Aura, my white butt; I was in full-out hide mode. The small crawl space down past the three pools seemed a perfect place.

I turned the corner toward the tunnel leading to the infirmary, and stumbled to a stop. ConRad stood underneath one of the numerous metal support beams, his back toward me, blocked by the four men surrounding him. Three of the four were young, maybe in their mid-twenties. They were dressed in identical crude black robes, with V-necks that were low enough to reveal their hairy chests. Their muscled arms bulged from gripping the heavy machine guns, and just in case that wasn't intimidating enough, long glittering swords were strapped to their backs.

The fourth man was different. He stood in the center, the position of authority. He had neither bulging muscles nor a sword. Instead, his thin graying hair snaked past shoulders rounded with age. His pale face was a maze of lines and broken blood vessels. Like holes cut in a wrinkled sheet, his shifty eyes peered out black against the pasty skin, and missed nothing. His onyx gaze caught mine, and his reddened lips thinned into a straight line. His face didn't move, didn't betray one emotion, but his eyes flashed. It a blink it was gone, but not before I read what was in them—jealousy, pure and hot.

All motion slowed, yet everything happened in a span of seconds. ConRad's body stiffened. His spine went ramrod straight as if the iron in his blood solidified. A roar in my head drowned out all sound, but I swear I could hear the inhalation of ConRad's breath.

"Is that her?" I saw the old man's lips move, but the voice sounded a long way off. ConRad turned, his movements rigid and stiff. He looked straight at me with eyes as barren as the landscape outside the mountain. "Yes . . . that's her."

Pain shot through my chest and bloomed. I looked down expecting to see a gaping wound, but betrayal only leaves its cuts on the inside. Black shadows pulsed along the borders of my vision. Then everything inside quieted. My vision focused crystal clear and one loud red message shot off inside my brain. *Run!*

My legs weighed a hundred pounds each. My feet slipped as I backpedaled and dug in for traction. A swoosh sounded as the swords were pulled from their sheaths, drawing an invisible arc in the air. Reflecting red in the light, the slick metal gleamed high above the heads of their masters. Then their sharp tips lowered and aimed directly at me.

I turned. Fell on my knees, slipped and fell again. I dug my fingernails in, losing a few to the dusty ground below. I crawled back up, gritted my teeth, and forced my legs to move. One step, two steps, three . . . a fist caught my hair from behind. My head snapped back as my body rushed forward. I bit my tongue; my mouth filled with the sweet metallic taste of blood. Hauled back up, I was slammed against the wall.

The men tied my wrists behind my back and rough hands patted me down. Words slipped through my foggy brain. "Direct disobedience and violation of the use of microbiotics." "Improper use of health care protocol." And one phrase that really stood out: "punishable by death."

I craned my neck trying to catch a glimpse of ConRad. I knew if I could just see him, if I could look him in the eye, he would help me. He'd sworn to protect me. He'd told me he wanted to spend the rest of his life with me. He loved me. He hadn't spoken the exact words, but after baring his soul like that, I knew he did.

"ConRad," I screamed. I caught sight of him. He was stiff. Even from this distance I could see the flex of his jaw. His face was pale as beads of sweat glistened against the smoothness of his brow. Gone were the eyes of burning blue that an hour ago had both heated me and had me whimpering in the same breath. In their place were eyes made up of nothing more than ice and snow.

"ConRad, please help me," I pleaded, my voice barely a whisper. One robed man attached himself to each arm. As they dragged me down the hall, my legs buckled and my boots dug deep trails in the dusty ground.

I struggled in my captors' grip to look behind me, and at that moment something inside me died, as ConRad slowly turned and walked away.

I woke in a dark room strapped to a metal chair. My hands were tied behind my back, my fingers numb. The few memories I had were colored with a daze of shock and pain. After being given up by ConRad, the men in black robes had dragged me through the prominent double red doors in the command center. The doors swung open to a huge swirling vortex of lights. Bigger than the side of a house, its circular shape sucked at me, pulling at my clothes and hair like a greedy lover.

The portal to Earth increased its pull the closer we came to the energy field. My hair whipped at my face as I fought against the force. The men on either side of me tightened their grip and strained their bodies. They ducked their heads and sucked in a huge breath of air. We stepped through the vortex. My chest burned, as I tried to claw at the metal band that seemed to be clamped around my lungs.

I must've passed out, coming to only when the scream in my head rose to the audible level of a shrilling siren, and broke through my unconsciousness. My tongue stuck to my palate like a dried piece of leather, two times bigger than normal. Molten heat shot down my shoulder to my wrist, making me groan out loud.

"She's coming around," a voice said from somewhere in the thick blackness. Instinctively, I knew it would be better for me to slip back into the quiet sea of nothing. I let myself go, half hoping never to surface again.

Cold shocked my system as ice water slapped my face. I sputtered. Adrenaline flooded my blood; fight or flight sharpened my senses. Above me a mess of copper wires washed my vision in crimson, shining down on me, keeping the rest of the room's occupants in shadows. The small circle of light didn't allow me to see much—a dirty concrete floor, my boots bound with thick rope, red splotches showing bright against the camouflage of my pants. I found myself in the classical interrogation scene from every spy movie I'd ever watched. Hero beaten and tied to the chair, 100-watt bulb swinging overhead, dark mysterious voices in the background. The muffled rustle of cloth on cloth and heavy breathing sounded loud in the darkened room. Knowing I wasn't alone didn't comfort me.

I was scared out of my f-ing mind.

"That was a surprising show of defiance you put on earlier. I hope you aren't thinking of pulling anything like that again," said the Voice. Its owner was male, his voice husky and sickly sweet at the same time.

If this were Hollywood (which is based in reality I'm sure), this would be the part where the hero/heroine pulls out a hidden nail file, cuts the ropes, and does an impossible Kung-Fu move that simultaneously frees herself and kicks butt. Me, on the other hand, I couldn't swallow my own spit. No worries here, Voice, no show of defiance, at least not from me.

He seemed content to take my silence as a response. "I guess we'll have to convince you to talk. But don't worry, we're good at that."

I shook my head, but blazing white pain shot to the base of my skull, ceasing all movement.

"Ahh . . . defiant to the end. Excellent." Without hesitation he raised his fist and swung. Bam! Right across the face. Pain exploded in my orbital bone, my head snapped back and to the right. Warm fluid filled my mouth and I waged a war with my stomach to keep from vomiting. The battle was quickly lost with another solid hit to my abdomen. Vomit spewed projectile style over the robed figure, onto the floor, and my boots. Objectively, I realized my nose had been broken since blood trickled down my face, soaked my shirt front, and began pooling between my legs on the chair.

No! I wanted to shout. Not defiant. But the piece of leather that was masquerading as my tongue wasn't cooperating. Then it was too late. I heard a door close and he was gone.

I hoped, at a later time, I'd be able to tell him I was a cooperative prisoner. I'd be willing to say anything he wanted. Hell, I'd gladly sell the soul of my own mother, because no matter what my strong suits were, courage was not one of them.

But what I didn't know is that when later came, all my confessions wouldn't matter anyway.

CHAPTER TWENTY-ONE

Braided hemp cut into the flesh of my already chafed skin. Blood oozed out between the rope and my skin. I watched a small red stream trickle down my upraised arm, find its way past my ribs and finally fall off my big toe, contributing to the growing pool beneath me. Stripped naked, hung from an iron hook by bound wrists, I'd been left to "cool my heels." They were cool alright, my heels and every other part of my body. I had long since ceased the protective response of gooseflesh, and now was blessedly numb.

Can't breathe. I couldn't fully inhale hanging like I was. *Can't think.* I had no more fight left. I'd lost. The dark shadows were mocking and dancing on the sidelines whispering cruel whispers. *You're gonna die die die. They're gonna kill kill kill you.*

For the hundredth time I glanced around the room. Concrete walls, a window barred with wooded shutters, the zigzag of copper wires overhead, a small bowl of heating coals, and me. Numerous iron hooks were bolted into a wooden beam across the ceiling. Brown-stained concrete beneath each hook stood as a witness to the men's sweat and blood that came before me. I'd have shuddered at the thought if I had any energy left. After weeks of beatings, starvation, and sleep deprivation I couldn't imagine what more could be done to me.

Kill kill kill you. I was ready.

The door opened timidly as if the intruder had been taught a recent lesson in manners. A robed figure slithered in, silent in slippered feet. If I hadn't recognized him by his thinning hair and pasty face, then his lecherous stare would have sealed the deal. He was the Elder who had ordered my arrest back at the compound. The same older man ConRad had given me up to.

My heartbeat skipped. I'd thought I used up my quota of fear, but its prickling wormed into my belly anyway.

"I've heard some very interesting things about you in the past few weeks." His voice wasn't what I expected from an old man; instead, it was sweet, calm . . . seductive. "Time travel, prophecy nonsense, location of another portal. Seems like you haven't stopped talking since you came to visit."

He walked over to the window and methodically opened the shades, securing each to the wall. Dusk was approaching and a fading pink light fell across the concrete floor.

"I've wanted to see you like this." He turned to face me, sunken black eyes sweeping over my naked body.

"Ever since I heard about you, I wanted to see what ConRad had been so protective of. After years of steadfastness, what had him dividing his loyalties?" He lifted one shoulder in a half shrug. "Can't say I'm impressed though, but I have heard some of the other men talking." He circled my suspended body and with a well-manicured hand brushing the curve of my back ending with a squeeze to my bottom. He paused in front of me. "Did he tell you who I was? No? Typical. ConRad likes to keep our relationship secret."

I could see his eyes had softened at the mention of ConRad's name. A small forlorn smile touched his lips.

I'd heard numerous times that when an animal is caught in a trap, he gnaws on his limb for days to escape. My eyes shot to my bound hands. I kicked my legs, trying to reach my mouth to my wrists.

"Ahh, like bait on a hook. Cliché, I know, but I still love the classic saying. Don't you? But maybe not quite fitting for this situation. You're not bait really, more like retribution. ConRad knew the consequences. I'm just shocked he took the risk." He stepped away and began to unbuckle a thick black belt he had cinched around his waist. The wide leather strap cracked as he snapped the folded the halves together and placed the belt along the floor. He reached into his robe pocket and withdrew a foot-long metal rod. On one end was a leather handle, on the other was metal formed in the letter "S."

There was something I should be piecing together. Alarms of warning were going off inside my brain, but I couldn't think past the red horror that was brewing in my mind.

"Did you notice the view?" He turned to the window and rested one elbow on the small sill. "I had this chamber made specifically for this reason—spectacular sunsets. I always get a little thrill as the last of the sun dips below the Earth."

He shook his head and came back toward me. "Have you heard of the Winter Solstice? It's the longest night of the year. They say it happens only once every three hundred and sixty-five days. But they're wrong. The longest night is every night we spend here." He chuckled quietly and placed the metal rod, letter side down, in the center of the heating coals.

"I thought about placing the window so we could watch the sunrise instead, but I found that my guests were more concerned with when we would begin than when we'd stop. Of course, I've had more grown men weep at the last ray of sunset here than any other place. But I must confess I've been moved to tears more than once by such creations."

He stretched his neck from side to side cracking the joints back into place. "Kind of embarrassing to be babbling so, but I haven't been this giddy in a long time."

Waves, alternating hot and cold, rushed over me. My gaze shot to the perfectly framed sun as it sped to its setting. My insides turned to liquid. If I had anything left in my stomach, I would've lost the remains on the floor.

He turned his back toward me. I watched as his black robe fell in a puddle around his feet. Shirtless in black cotton pants, he reached behind and secured his stringy hair with a tie.

He faced me.

On his upper right peck was a pink puckered scar—forming a large letter "C."

The brands. Suddenly, it clicked.

Oh God, Syon.

I screamed.

Chapter Twenty-Two

My eyelids scraped open as if made of sand paper. I was lying on my side, cheek smashed against the concrete floor. A deep breath . . . white fire burned across my ribs. It hurt to breathe. It hurt everywhere. My fried nerves woke and sent messages of pain to my boggy brain. The world, fuzzy and out of focus, seemed strange, but oddly familiar. Familiar because this was my life now and had been for weeks.

I moaned and closed my eyes, hoping to lose consciousness again before full awareness set in. No such luck. I'd caught a glimpse of blood congealing around my face and pushed away, disgusted despite it being my own bodily fluids.

My gaze swept the surroundings for the thousandth time: four gray concrete walls, one concrete floor, and a pail to piss in. The stench of warm metal, strong urine, and fear had me glad I'd asked for the upgrade to a luxury cell. Here was my new home. Or I'd found the answer to one of religions' most pressing questions. Hell wasn't a place; it was a time, decades in the future.

The air was thick with heat and stench, but that didn't stop the cold from seeping into my body, racking my bones with a deep ache. But that pain was mild compared to the throbbing mass that was my face. I forced my brain into "doctor mode" and tried to objectively access the damage. At least one of my ribs was broken and more than a few fingers smashed. Cautiously, I reached up to palpate my nose. A large bump had formed on one side. Again? My nose kept getting in the way of someone's fist.

I didn't think. I just pushed . . . hard.

A sickening crack. Blood, warm and thick, covered my top lip and chin. A potent wave of nausea rushed my insides. I closed my eyes until the light-headedness passed, and tried to breathe. With shaking courage I checked again, my nose seemed straight enough. There was a lot to be said about my vanity, which raised its ugly head even under the worst circumstances. Though I liked Owen Wilson as an actor, I didn't want to look like him.

A blanket of hopelessness settled over me. What was the point?

Tears rolled silently from the corners of my eyes, finding a home in the hollows of my ears. Why was I here? Why be sent forward in time, why be tormented about a prophecy, why be sentenced to death? And why, most of all, did I meet ConRad?

I hadn't forgotten what my future-self had said that night in my bedroom. *You have to save him.*

Save him? I'd rather watch him burn.

ConRad. It all came back to him. Before, our situation was complicated. Him believing I was the enemy, and me not willing to trust him.

But things were much clearer now. No misguided emotions clouded my judgment. No naïve romantic longings. He'd claimed me, sworn to protect me, with his own life nonetheless, and hadn't. Not even a cursory fight or half-hearted objection. No, I was freely given up without a second glance. Shame filled me at the memory of being so scared, so terrified that I'd called to him for help.

I'd begged him.

I controlled my relationships. I kept aloof, kept myself protected. But with ConRad, it had been different. Despite his warnings, I'd believed he would protect me as he had with the aliens, as he had with the other men in the compound. His ability to keep me safe struck me in a fundamental way. It spoke to something deep within my bone marrow. Something feminine that I refused to acknowledge. And to my lasting disgrace, I had believed him.

Why bother with the "for the rest of my life" speech? ConRad couldn't marry, that privilege was left to the Elders and the ones in power. His words were a lie, and I'd sold myself like a hooker for a testosterone grin and a crappy line.

What had I expected? Weakness was a family trait. My father left my mother and us three children for a younger, more beautiful trophy wife. My mother—first place winner for cowardliness—couldn't handle the embarrassment and gave up by putting a bullet in her brain. Considering my family, I could go nowhere but up.

Should I fight the darkness? Or do I give up like everyone else in my life had. Like ConRad had—on me.

Fear, I'd learned over the past weeks, was a funny thing. The key element to a good torture plan is the anticipation. The *knowing* is what makes the pain ten times worse. The knowledge of what is going to happen . . . knowing how much it's going to hurt.

At first, I had been so scared. Every time the guards came for me I'd pleaded and begged. They had to drag me kicking and fighting because I soon learned that my cell was the safest place I could be.

Syon had been right. Here, every night was the longest night of the year. I hadn't been conscious to see if the sun had come up that night. I was pretty sure it hadn't. The night never ended, not here in hell. The sun had ceased its shining and the whole world existed only within these four walls.

Even though there was no light in hell, it sure had its sounds. And in the darkness my hearing heightened. Not a good thing. No, probably one of the worst things the darkness brought.

The screaming. It never stopped, but went on and on, sending lurid waves roaring through my head. I'd covered my ears, but it didn't work. I could still hear them, the cries from grown men—trained for battle since infancy—who were stronger than I.

But the prayers were the worst. "I'm telling the truth . . . Oh please, God . . . Help me, Jesus!"

Prayers weren't answered here either. In the beginning I had prayed. Asked to curl up and die. Just stop breathing, stop existing. At first I thought my prayers were answered. I felt nothing, was nothing. But then God had played me for a fool because there was something left inside my nothingness. A burning hot coal flickered inside me. The flame had a name, and its name was Hatred.

After that, all my tears turned bitter as something changed

deep inside of me. Some gear clicked over and the light I carried in my soul fired red. Red with unholy anger at ConRad.

If I didn't have courage, could I use something else?

People say strength comes from the heart, but that's for heroes. Not for people like me. No, I needed to go beyond that faulty organ. So I dug deeper. I dug past the liver, pushed the kidneys aside, and went right on through to the small intestine. No, not there either, but deeper, in the bowels. I found my strength in the gut. Yep, there it was—down deep—my fury at ConRad paving the way.

My rage became a living, breathing thing—so powerful I'd almost choked on it. It kept me warm during the long cold night. Pushed me to keep myself strong physically and mentally. It gave me the courage to fight back and not to just lie on my cell floor and wait for the next round of beatings.

So I decided to live. I decided to eat.

The food here was brown mush and given on a tray that was slid through an opening at the bottom of the door. At first I could only manage to slither across the floor on my elbows and shovel the goop in with dirty fingers. I didn't chew, didn't taste, but swallowed before I lost the desire. Most times my stomach would rebel, pissed off at the force feeding after being idle for so long. The foul substance would crawl back up my throat. But desperation was a funny thing, so I covered my mouth and swallowed my own vomit.

Time crept and I healed. The beatings were regular, but not made of quite the same stuff as Syon's. I did sit-ups, or the best I could with ribs in different stages of healing. One-handed push-ups at first, since during one beating I'd raised my arm in protection and got two bones crushed in my hand, which destroyed my hope of ever becoming a surgeon.

Only my changing body marked the passage of time. During a self-inflicted grueling series of yoga poses, I glanced down and didn't recognize my own arms. Blood and sweat mingled together and flowed down forearms all sinewy with muscle. Veins and tendons stood prominently among bruises and cuts. I looked past clotted blood and whip marks and saw a physique that wasn't my own.

This was me. I'd become the crazed, buffed out woman I remembered. My past finally caught up with my future. And now I was her, more animal than human.

Sure, I could hate Syon, and I did. Sure, I could hate all the other men who beat and tortured me, and I did. But ConRad was different than all of them. Not one of them had cherished me with their bodies or whispered words of endearment under the cover of intimacy. Not one of them had made me fall in love with them. And for that ConRad needed to pay.

So I nourished my rage, fed it a lush diet of hate-filled thoughts. And in return, the emotion filled me, warmed me, and gave me a purpose. The holy grail of purposes—revenge on ConRad. I was obsessed with what I'd say and do the next time I saw him.

And yet, when that day came, I did nothing.

CHAPTER TWENTY-THREE

In my defense I was barely conscious. I'd just been through a particularly savage beating and hadn't had time to heal. I was lying on the floor, drifting in and out of awareness.

The sound of muffled gunshots reached me behind my four walls, then a loud crashing outside my cell door. My dreams had begun blurring with reality, and I had a hard time distinguishing between what was real and what was fantasy. So I didn't immediately believe my own senses.

My cell door broke open and there stood a terrifying warrior, appearing like he'd just crawled his way back up from the Underworld.

I dared not move, not even breathe. I couldn't tell if he was some new form of torture I was meant to endure or Lucifer himself coming to drag me to another layer of Hell.

"Oh God . . . Kris?"

I inhaled sharply, recognizing the voice. Only one person on Earth ever whispered my name with such deliberate reverence—ConRad.

He was ConRad, but not quite him. He appeared different, more wild . . . more volatile.

The same piercing blue eyes stared at me, but from a more chiseled face. His hair was longer and plastered back with sweat and grime. His face was smeared with black and weeks' worth of growth. His body, though never soft, was carved down to its most basic elements—muscle and bone.

A large bowie knife strapped menacingly to his outer thigh and a machine gun slung over his back. Ammo belts haphazardly crisscrossed his war-painted chest. A red blossom spread on his camouflage pants from a gaping wound in his right leg.

ConRad, who always wore the mask of the calm and the controlled, was teetering on the razor-sharp edge of crazy.

I didn't know if he was here to save me or finish me off.

He stepped forward. With my remaining strength, I pushed my beaten body farther away.

"Kris, it's me . . . ConRad."

That didn't change a damn thing for me. In the however long I'd been in Hell, I'd lost any fragile hope I had for the human race. I trusted no one.

ConRad stepped closer. I pushed backwards.

"Can you walk?"

I didn't answer. I couldn't figure out why he was here. Why give me up and then come in for a rescue? It didn't make sense.

Without another word he picked me up, cradle style, in his arms. Pain exploded in my ribs, coloring my vision red. A scream died behind my clenched teeth. The shadows danced again, laughing. *Heehee Heehee. He's gonna kill kill kill you.*

We quickly exited the cell. ConRad crouched low, keeping his back to the walls. There was a shout and then a blanket of gunfire. He slung me over his shoulder into a fireman's hold to free his hands and reach his weapon.

The pain broke me. I screamed loud and primal. I just alerted anyone who didn't know to our whereabouts. But it didn't matter, they'd already found us. My screams couldn't be heard over the machine-gun fire anyway.

Bullets flew. Semiautomatic gunfire bounced off walls and metal doors. ConRad got hit, stumbled, and threw us into an adjoining hallway. I went flying from his hold and finally skidded to a stop when I hit the opposite wall.

ConRad flipped on his stomach and returned gunfire around the corner, while I laid in a stupor and fought for breath. A bullet whizzed by and nicked his shoulder. He slammed himself back behind the wall as he slapped another magazine in the lower compartment.

"Damn, they're close," he said, and then seemed surprised to find me still on the floor next to him. "Go, run down the hall! Quinn's there."

But I wasn't quick enough because he grabbed my shirt like the scruff on the back of a dog's neck and propelled me in the direction he wanted me to go.

The idea of escape finally snapped into place and I moved.

I pushed to my feet, took a step, and fell flat on my face. Apparently, I'd lost all control in my left leg. I looked down and was shocked to see I'd been shot just above my knee. Using my hand to stem the flow of blood, I once again struggled to my feet.

The hall was infinite, doors and doors of endless gray. I leaned against the wall for balance, my leg smearing blood along like a trail of bread crumbs in some twisted fairy tale. My vision faltered, at times showing me two hallways, and two paths leading out. I didn't trust either, I just followed the wall.

I saw Quinn huddled by a black metal staircase and almost didn't recognize her. She, like ConRad, had changed. Gone was the long flowing hair that crowned her innocence and youth. Gone was the seventeen-year-old I had known, in her place was a hardened soldier ready for battle. She was dressed in dirty army fatigues, hair chopped short under a black cap, and a machine gun, with the safety off, pointed at me.

Her fingers white-gripped the gun, and her eyes shimmered as she held back tears. I saw in her face when Quinn recognized me, and with a sigh of relief, she lowered her weapon. Which left me wondering how willing she was to shoot it. Playing female warrior didn't seem to sit too well with her.

I couldn't blame her, it was hardly a childhood aspiration of mine, but I felt left out being the only one without a gun.

"Where's ConRad?"

I nodded back toward the hall. "He's trapped."

She nodded and turned to the two men who were kneeling behind her. I hadn't realized there was anyone else with her, but when the two men stood, I recognized them from the compound. They were the soldiers I'd nicknamed Red and Tank.

"The Commander needs help. Leave him here for now," Quinn said.

I didn't know what *him* she was referring to. There was no one else here except us. Us and a pile of bloody rags the two men had left at her feet in their pursuit of ConRad.

Quinn dropped to her knees and murmured quiet calming

things to the pile. It wasn't until she stroked at something that looked like hair that I realized it wasn't rags at all, but a human body at her feet.

In the emergency room I'd seen horrors. Knife and bullet wounds, bodies wasted away from drugs, and even the sickness of child abuse, but I'd never seen a human body mutilated to the point of what was lying on the floor.

My stomach churned at the thought. There was only one person Quinn would risk her life and come here to save.

Zimm.

Whatever torture they'd put me through, whatever beatings I'd endured, they were like slaps in the face compared to what they'd done to him.

"Is he alive?"

She nodded yes.

I didn't feel comforted. The poor man would never recover from this. The human body could take only so much. Sickened and unable to watch further, I turned away.

I glanced up and saw the two soldiers and ConRad running toward us at the end of the corridor. Tank risked a look behind him and shot off some half-hearted rounds one-handed. Red supported ConRad as he limped down the hall.

"Run. It's gonna blow!" screamed Red.

That was all I needed to hear. I hauled myself to my feet and hustled my butt toward the stairwell.

"Wait," Quinn pleaded. "Help me." She had one of Zimm's bloodied arms around her shoulder, but couldn't even budge him. Dead weight was heavy.

I looked up at the stairway with longing. There was no way the two of us could carry him up the stairs; I could barely make it myself. The chances of Zimm living after such abuse were nil. To ask me to drag a dying man up a flight of stairs, in my condition, was impossible.

I checked behind me. ConRad and the soldiers were barreling down still a few dozen feet away. But I heard ConRad as if he were shouting right next to me. "Leave him! There's no time."

Quinn had heard too. She sobbed, pleaded with Zimm to wake up. He didn't move. Probably dead already.

I looked back toward the stairwell. I could make it. It would be close, but there was enough time.

My gaze caught sight of Quinn, sobbing on Zimm's battered chest. I knew there was no way we could get him out.

And I also knew she'd die here before leaving without him.

Panic rushed my muscles; a split second of acute clarity. I was already dead. I'd died in that cell. My body just didn't know it yet. Might as well make the death worth the sacrifice.

I kneeled before Zimm. "Get up!" I screamed right in his face, using my most commander-like voice. I grabbed what remained of his tattered shirt and shook him, snapping his head back and forth. If his C-spine wasn't clear, then he was dead to us already. "Get on your feet *now*, soldier! MOVE!"

He moaned and began to come around; to help the process I slapped him . . . hard. "Get up off your ass and climb up those stairs. Now, soldier!"

Against all odds he moved. Quinn and I both pulled on each shoulder as he crawled up each step.

We'd barely made it to the top when ConRad swept down on me like a deadly bird of prey. He picked me up and hurled us through the door. He didn't check to make sure anyone else made it out, just threw me against the opposite wall and covered me with his body.

The world shook.

For a moment I thought we'd made it out just to be buried alive. The entire dirt house we were in quaked and trembled, raining debris on top of us. A huge fire ball burst through the stairwell, incinerating anything on the stairs. No one would've survived.

I crawled out from under ConRad and tried to see if anyone else had made it. To my relief all four were huddled in the adjacent corner, singed, covered in dirt, but alive.

Shaken and disoriented, I couldn't believe I was out of prison and alive. I'd accepted the only way I'd leave was with a blanket thrown over my body. Now, I couldn't seem to process what to do next.

ConRad didn't have any such problem.

Seconds after the fire cleared he began shouting orders. We exited the mud house, leaving the place in much worse condition than when we entered.

ConRad leaned on Red, and Tank had Zimm thrown over his shoulder like he was a mere inconvenience. They led Quinn and me to the three horses that were tied off in a struggling-to-survive forest. Tank tied Zimm to the front of one saddle, while Quinn slipped up behind Red. Zimm had mercifully gone unconscious, and I for one, was jealous.

It quickly became apparent that I'd be left sitting in front of ConRad. My mind positively balked at the idea of being jostled on horseback. And being jostled so intimately next to *him*.

I hesitated.

ConRad gestured with his hand for me to come on. I contemplated asking Quinn to switch places with me. My intention must have showed, because ConRad's face distorted to a whole new level of pissed. His teeth smashed together, his lips barely moved as he growled. "If I have to get down off this horse to get you . . ."

The threat was implied, yes, but effective nonetheless. With the old ConRad, I might have pushed things a bit. Doing so with new Crazy ConRad? Well, that was just stupid.

I couldn't get up on the horse fast enough.

Chapter Twenty-Four

How does the saying go? It's never as bad as you think it's going to be. No . . . it's far worse. We started riding at dusk and didn't stop until well past dawn. By this time I was beyond exhausted and nauseated from the pain. I'd thrown up twice. (Mind you, throwing up from trotting a horse is not a skill I should ever have had to acquire.) I thought of killing myself just to get off, but honestly I don't think it would've made a difference. ConRad would've dragged my poor dead body to the end just out of sheer spite.

As the hours crawled along we traveled deep into a dense forest. There was no civilization, only thick foliage and sparse signs of wildlife. We veered to the left, and on a small rise there appeared a vine-covered hut. The dwelling so effectively blended into the surrounding area that I took notice only because ConRad announced, by finally stopping the damn horse, that we were there.

As ConRad slipped down, his breath hissed through clenched teeth—and this coming from a man who didn't even groan when he got shot. I didn't think I'd be quite as brave.

ConRad reached for me, and I flinched from his touch. He jerked like I'd slapped him and then closed his expression down all together. I didn't get a second chance to brace myself. He just hauled me down like a sack of horse feed. My feet touched solid ground, the bullet wound burned, my legs buckled, and I crumpled in a heap on the dirt. I was in no hurry to get up. My stomach still churned, but I was more than grateful to be off the moving beast.

ConRad left me groaning on the ground and limped away to take care of the horse. No one talked. There was an eerie silence, except for my harsh breathing and Zimm's moans. I wasn't sure if the silence was a security measure or the permanent air of indifference in this future time.

Red and Tank carried Zimm into the green-leafed house, while Quinn began to rub down and water the remaining horses. I decided I was of better use inside and pulled myself up to see about helping with Zimm.

I pushed past the creaking wood door and limped into what appeared to be the tenth century. Dirt floor, an open cooking pit in the corner, equipped with only a cast iron pot and a wooden ladle. Moss and mud insulated the walls and roof. The only furniture was a long pine bench and a table by the hearth. And in the far corner were three straw pallets, one of which Zimm was lying on.

Hovering over Zimm were two other women I hadn't met. One was very old and gnarled. Her shoulders hunched over a weathered walking stick, her gray hair hung in clumps, thin enough to allow generous amounts of pink scalp to peek through. The other was much younger. She stood straight as if her spine was incapable of slouching. Her hair, thick black,

was plaited and swayed rope-like down to her incredibly tiny
waist. Both of the women's backs were to me. At my entrance
the younger one whipped around to pierce me with a fiery black
stare. Her presence seemed too large to be contained in such a
small room. I broke eye contact, uncomfortable, not sure if I
should smile or bow.

The older woman slowly creaked and kneeled over Zimm,
then began placing her hands over his body. She mumbled and
hummed in some unknown, and possibly ancient, language.
The air around us stilled. My skin felt tight. There was a drawing on my lungs as if all the energy in the room was being fun-
neled through a narrow opening.

The rest of us watched, transfixed, as she placed her hands
on his head, heart, and stomach. At one point I thought her
eyes clouded over in a milky white, but she bowed her head and
obscured my view.

As softly as I could, I moved over to the younger woman,
hesitant to disturb the quietness in the hut. I lowered my voice
and spoke in her ear. "I'm a healer of some sorts. I may be able
to help him."

Her head came up, revealing eyes shrouded with hopelessness and fatigue that I immediately placed her years older than
I originally guessed.

"My grandmother," she nodded to the ancient woman, "is a
great healer, and he is even beyond her help."

I had known, of course. Surprised he'd made it this far.

"You can't give up!"

The cry startled the quiet room, and I turned toward the
source. It was Quinn. She'd walked in behind us and had overheard our conversation. She had a wild look about her. Her eyes

were deep set and highlighted with black circles. Her hair stuck out oddly at all angles with the terrible cut she'd given herself. She seemed barely able to hold herself up in the overly large warrior clothes and too-big boots. She looked scared as hell.

I didn't want to be a witness to the blatant desperation so evident on her face. To the pain I'd seen so many times before, when a family member lost a loved one, but this time was different. This time was personal.

Quinn ran over to the healer and fell to her knees before her. She wrapped her arms around the old woman's legs and buried her face into her thighs.

"Please." Quinn looked up with tears streaming down her face, making tracks on her soot-covered cheeks. "Please, I beg you with my life, please try. He has . . . he has to live." She lowered her head and paused, seemingly unable to find the words. "I can't, simply *can't*, live without him."

The scene was too intimate, the emotion too raw. In a place where cold-heartedness ruled and any tender flames of compassion were extinguished, her desperate plea was downright sinful. My eyes stung as I watched her beg for her lover's life, and I couldn't help but wonder if there was anyone who would beg for mine? My throat constricted and I covered my mouth with my hand to prevent a sob. I turned away, unable to stand the sight a moment longer . . . and stared right into ConRad's eyes.

He'd come up from behind, having entered the hut without my knowing—his face a familiar crag of rocks. He'd also watched the scene unfold, but there was no compassion softening his features. His gaze raked over Quinn, with eyes like liquid ice. "You're a goddess. Where's your pride?"

Shock rippled through me. I inhaled sharply and turned away to hide my reaction, my stomach ablaze, like I'd swallowed a thousand burning flames. How could he be so callous, so ruthless? Didn't he have a heart? Was he even human?

Fortunately, ConRad wasn't in charge; the old healer was. She gently ran her arthritic hand over Quinn's sobbing head and looked to her granddaughter and nodded. The young woman, needing no words, understood her grandmother and emphatically shook her head in denial. But the old woman would have none of it and raised her hand to stop any objections before they started.

The old woman gently helped Quinn to kneel beside her and bent once again over Zimm. Without a word or sound she placed her hands on his body. With feather-light touches, she moved her fingers from head to toe and finally rested one hand on his head, the other on his heart. The healer closed her eyes and filled the room with a deep, raspy breath. The sound bounced off the mud walls and hung heavy in the open spaces. Finally, her lids fluttered open, and where her eyes should have been there was nothing but a blanket of white.

For a time nothing happened. Then I watched in amazement as Zimm's skin pinked up with her touch. His breath before had been rapid and shallow, now deepened. Zimm's eyes moved rapidly under closed lids. Broken fingers straightened, bones snapped into place as if made of Lego's instead of cartilage and marrow. Blood stopped oozing from his ears and nose, and open wounds knitted together right before my eyes.

I lowered slowly to my knees and shut a mouth that had long ago dropped open. I could scarcely believe a body that had previously been a bloodied pile of broken bone and tissue now resembled a healthy man.

The old woman was steadfast in her position for what seemed like an eternity with her hands on Zimm and eyes closed. Finally, her face lifted, her eyes, a normal brown color, fluttered back into her head. Before anyone could react, the old woman's head rolled and she collapsed onto the floor. Her granddaughter ran to her side, gingerly picked her up as if she was no more than a husk of skin and cloth, and placed her on a nearby straw pallet.

"Will she be alright?" I asked. I still hadn't moved. Exhaustion swept over me like a torrid storm.

"Healing him took everything she had. She may never recover from this." The younger woman stroked her grandmother's forehead and pushed the gray hair back from her face. "She knew the risks, of course, but decided that those two were worth it. Whatever her reason."   I stole a glance to where Quinn cradled Zimm's head in her lap and lovingly wiped the blood from his face.

"She won't be able to heal anyone else. You'll have to mend the old-fashioned way." Her black eyes studied me as if seeing me for the first time. "Forgive me, it seems like you've been through an ordeal yourself. I know what a toll healing takes from my grandmother, and I tend to resent the intrusion. But regardless, you're a guest here. There's a place to wash up and some clean clothes in the shower house out back. You're welcome to whatever you wish."

"Thank you," I said, and extended my hand as an offering of peace.

"MaEve," she said in way of an introduction, her lips in a thin smile that didn't reach her eyes.

"I'm Kristina Davenport, but please call me Kris." After a while I withdrew my outstretched hand that had laid there like day-old fish.

"I know," she said, and dismissed me with the turning of her attention back toward her grandmother.

The small hut behind the house was empty and for that I was grateful. I had no desire to see anyone, especially ConRad. I shuffled in the door, bracing my ribs with my arms and gingerly stepping with my left leg. The shower house was surprisingly well hidden and more modern than the vine house. Though it too had a mud exterior, the structure was sturdier and the floor was laid with smooth, pale flagstone. On one of the walls were panels of long thin sheets of shiny metal and on the other was a hole plugged with straw and cloth, from where I presumed water flowed.

I knew the metal sheet acted like a mirror, and with a mixture of hesitation and curiosity, I walked over to glimpse at my reflection. The sharp intake of breath sent a slicing pain through my left side. I didn't recognize myself. My blond, curly hair was matted with dirt and blood. One side of my face, eye included, was swollen and my lower lip was blown up to twice its size. My stomach clenched at the thought of examining further, since I had taken the worst of the beatings to my back and midsection. I slipped my tank top off of my shoulders, knowing I didn't have the strength to raise my arms above my head.

I tried to prepare myself for what would stare back at me from the dull reflection. I forced my brain into "doctor mode," but I struggled to remain clinically detached.

I couldn't help but gasp. Twenty pounds of fat, muscle, and tissue had been beaten away. I'd finally achieved the gaunt model look I'd always envied, except, of course, every inch of skin was marred with a collage of bruises, abrasions, and dried blood. My breasts had shrunk at least two cup sizes and my navel dipped hollow. And, of course, the bullet wound. I gently probed the rip in my pant leg, cautiously joyful to find it was a graze with no residual bullet lodged inside.

As my heart beat, my pain pulsed in rhythm. Nausea rolled through my empty stomach and an overwhelming sadness swept through me. I couldn't believe this was my body, my life. Just a little over a few months ago I was bemoaning my grueling internship and a few pounds of weight gain. What I wouldn't give to go back to my Sleep Number bed, small townhouse in an upper-middle-class neighborhood, and two-sizes-too-small skinny jeans.

Wetness tickled my chest and neck. I glanced up, surprised to see tears trailing down my cheeks. At least torture hadn't beaten all the emotion out of me, leaving me a shell of a person. I could feel; therefore, I was human.

The door opened and ConRad walked in carrying a glass bottle and some cloth bandages. The bruises, cuts, and make-shift tourniquets tied around his shoulder and thigh didn't do his gruesome appearance justice. He looked like hell.

Startled, I crossed my arms in front to cover myself, knowing I didn't possess the strength to bend and pick up my tank top.

He stopped and stared, barely moved. He seemed to have forgotten how to breathe. I did too.

His hand was white knuckled around the bottle, while his gaze assessed every blue and purple mark, every jagged cut, and every piece of ravished flesh. He drank my body in like penance, missing nothing.

I remembered when he'd looked upon me with reverence and awe. Now half of me didn't want to see the flash of pity in his eyes. The other half wanted the knowledge of his betrayal to burn forever in his psyche.

I wanted . . . *needed* him to say something. To recognize my torture—my pain. I studied his eyes like they held the secrets for my redemption. I scrutinized the face I was intimate with, the one so rarely betrayed by emotion.

His lips trembled. The muscle in his jaw contracted and released as he ground his teeth. He inhaled as if to speak, but swallowed hard instead.

I was surprised. I'd never known ConRad to hesitate. His actions were executed by cold logic, every sequence planned.

"I tried to come sooner." His voice, always strong, came out raw, as if torn from his throat.

"I shouldn't have been there at all," I countered, my defenses coming up like a clumsy brick wall. The anger I used to keep alive in prison was the same I used to dam the torrential flow of emotions. I only had a few precious seconds before I'd break and lose whatever self-respect I had left. All I wanted was to run to him, bury myself in the curve of his neck, and plead with him to help me.

"I know," he whispered.

His words were too intuitive, and for one brief moment I thought he could reach the little girl inside of me who still believed. But then I remembered that the Elders had broken me, cut my humanity out with their knives. I'd never be whole again. I couldn't ask or beg ConRad to fix me when the screams from the prison were still inside my head . . . and most of them were mine. The confession would splay me open and gutted like a trout for dinner.

"You gave me up. You left me." I broke on the last words, my fear of abandonment too ingrained not to hurt.

"I'll never forgive myself."

I hardened my gaze as I stared him down. "Neither will I."

He made a move as if to step forward. I panicked at the thought of his touch, decent and gentle, the first of its kind in weeks. *Save me. I'm afraid.*

He took one look at my face, and then stilled his movements. "I failed to protect you. You have the right to ask for my life in return."

A few weeks ago I would've been sickened by the thought, but now I realized how worthless life was here. Rage flowed through me like a powerful river. I drew from the burning ebb and drank the fury like a cactus would water in a desert terrain. *No pity. No remorse.*

"In prison I wanted nothing more than to curl up and die. Let the pain go away, sleep forever, but I couldn't. That would've been too easy." I said, my voice betraying no emotion. But despite my best efforts, my vision blurred as my eyes filled with tears. I had to get him to leave, and it needed to be now. I drew on my last strength reserves, which cost me in flesh. My fingernails gouged my palms, cutting the skin. My chest wheezed as if I had a pack-a-day habit, but my voice barely shook as I faced ConRad straight on. "I would like nothing better than to have your head on a platter. But that's the easy way, and you don't deserve the easy way. Instead, I want that every time you look at me, every time you see my face, you remember, you *live* with what you've done."

I heard his sharp inhale of breath, then he stiffened. "And so I will."

And then I got my wish and was left alone.

CHAPTER TWENTY-FIVE

I folded inward and melted down the wall into a fetal position. The strength I drew from my need for revenge was gone, depleted from my last stand with ConRad.

I didn't hear Quinn approach over the sound of my cries. But she was there, pushing my hair back and murmuring nonsense in my ear. She helped to remove the rest of my clothes and led me over to the spray of water that poured from the wall. Silent, she washed my wounds and then my hair. I watched as the water mixed with dried blood and turned into a light pink stream that trickled off the stones and seeped into the ground. I waited patiently for the water to run clear, but instead watched as my shadows danced, this time mercifully quiet.

There was something scratchy on my back. Wool? Straw? It took a moment for me to realize I was on a straw cot in someone else's cotton shirt and my hair dry to the touch. An incredible thirst assaulted me. My tongue, coated and rough, stuck to the roof of my mouth. I tried twice before I could dislodge and crack out the word *water*.

Someone gently lifted my head and placed a cool cup to my lips. Bitter water flowed down my throat, barely satisfying, and I wondered absently what herb was mixed in. Then it didn't matter because my shadows were back. *Don't care. Go back to Dark Space. Nothing matters in Dark Space.*

Something cool was on my face. My eyes and forehead were washed. A cloth, soft and pleasantly heavy, was placed on my eyes. The scent of lavender rose around me.

Blindfolded. Don't like to be blindfolded.

I struggled to remove the cloth, but I couldn't find my arms. I couldn't feel my body. Fear tingled through my veins. I moaned. Then bitter water slipped past my lips and a shushing sound was whispered into my ear.

"Mom?" I couldn't place the voice, but something seemed . . . comfortable. I must be back in my four-poster canopy bed. I could smell her perfume—White Lily.

"You're all right. You're safe now. Go back to sleep."

"Mom? Mommy? You came back? You didn't leave?" A rush of tears slipped from the corners of my eyes. Why couldn't I see? I wanted to see her face. Just one glance. I couldn't remember what she looked like. *How could I forget my own mother?*

"I'm here. You're okay. Go to sleep. I've got you now." The voice didn't seem right, a little too gruff, but the words did. And why didn't she touch me? I wanted her to touch me. Her skin was always so soft—like flower petals.

"Where were you? I was so scared. I called for you. You

didn't come. Mom, why didn't you come?" A heavy weight bore down on my chest. Something black and deep sucked out my insides. I felt like I'd been screaming her name forever. I missed her so much. Why had she left me alone for so long?

There was silence. A hesitation.

"*Mom!*" I cried hysterically. I tried to move. My arms flung widely at my sides. "Don't leave. Don't leave me. Don'tleaveme don'tleavemedon'tleaveme."

"Shh. I won't leave. I promise you'll never be alone again."

I believed. I believed her. My mother would never lie. Not *my* mom. My coiled insides relaxed. My arms, so heavy, fell like stones. More water. I drank as much as I could. The darkness thickened, but this time it brought peace.

My stomach's loud growl and the overwhelming urge to pee pulled me reluctantly from my coveted Dark Space. I wanted to go back. I loved my Dark Space; inside were my shadows. They didn't mock me anymore; instead they whispered sweet things. Things that calmed me and made me feel loved. I was cherished and never alone in my Dark Space. But a bladder is an insistent organ and will tolerate being ignored for only so long.

I opened both eyes and was surprised at the lack of pain. My hand gingerly traveled up and examined my face. The swelling seemed to have gone, and breathing deep caused only a minor twinge. I patted down my leg and felt the graze of the bullet. A rough crisscross stitch marked the wound, but no signs of infection.

How long had I been lying here?

I glanced around the small room and tried to get my bear-ings. A trickle of memory came back. A hut covered in thick vines. Zimm lying on a straw mat dying. Quinn begging. An old woman healing Zimm. ConRad's callous eyes.

I sighed. So tired.

I turned at the feel of a light breeze. A thatch window was thrown open, allowing sunlight to spill across the floor and bathe my straw cot. The fire in the corner was banked and the other pallets were empty. I was alone, but had a sensation I'd been watched over for a long time.

I struggled to a sitting position and was slapped in the face by a wave of dizziness for my efforts. I would've given up, if not for my damn bladder. I rose and stumbled to the door. Bare-foot and covered only in a man's long T-shirt, I pushed the door open and was nearly flattened by the strength of the sun. The white light burned my eyes, but my skin hummed, reveling in the feel of its heat. I hadn't seen daylight in weeks.

My eyes narrowed protectively, and I braced my hand on the frame to steady myself. Focusing, I saw Tank and Red and several other soldiers sitting in a circle murmuring among themselves. Quinn and MaEve were busy cooking over a large open fire.

And then there was ConRad, off by himself cleaning a deadly looking machine gun. He looked as dangerous as I re-membered. Army fatigues, hair wild and long, face shadowed with whiskers as if he shaved only when the mood took.

I meant to turn around and go back to my cot. At least that was what I told my legs to do. Instead, they buckled and dropped me like a newborn foal. Twelve pairs of eyes turned toward me. All motion stopped. They stared like I was Lazarus brought back from the dead. Maybe I was.

ConRad moved first. He stood and took a step toward me. "Kris."

Something was wrong with his face. If I didn't know better, I would've said he was worried. I flinched. It wasn't conscious, just a knee-jerk reaction. ConRad looked too menacing with a weapon in hand, muscles bulging in his chest and arms. My wounds, physical and emotional, were fresh. I couldn't risk being hurt. Besides, I still hated him. *Hated* the way he said my name. The way it rolled off his tongue all whispery and rough.

Never say my name.

Something in his eyes flashed, and then blinked back to familiar cold blue.

Thank you God. My protective shield was up, but wobbly. I didn't need missiles of pity fired at me. Quinn glanced between ConRad and me and came to my rescue.

"Kris, you shouldn't be up. You're still too weak," she said and put her arm around my waist to support my weight.

"I need . . ." My voice trailed off as I took in that I was barely clothed in front of a group of men I barely knew. Gratefully, Quinn helped me back inside. Crawling into bed, I realized my Sleep Number bed back home had nothing on the straw pallet on the floor.

Quinn made quick order with all my needs. She sat next to me, fed me broth, and told me I'd been unconscious for close to two weeks. The old healer had done what she could for me, but healing Zimm had weakened her considerably. All she'd been able to do was speed up the mending of broken bones and stop the infection of the bullet wound.

I nodded like I understood, but I didn't really. I missed my Dark Space and quickly closed my eyes to find it.

The days passed and my stamina improved rapidly. The conditioning I did in prison had strengthened me. After being in solitary confinement for weeks, the busyness of camp was oppressive. There was too much noise, the clicking of metal, the incessant chatter, and even the subdued laughter. Couldn't they just shut up? Didn't they know I was on the edge, barely holding on to my sanity?

Dusk approached and Quinn and Zimm had left to forage for firewood. I needed to get away. We weren't allowed to leave without an armed escort, but I was bristling for a fight and almost begged someone to stop me. No one did.

With no real destination, I limped through the forest. The bullet wound continued to fester causing a shooting pain with every step. The end of the summer was approaching, but the meadow grasses still grew long and most of the trees held on to their foliage. A slight breeze rustled through the branches, shaking the leaves like a hundred green hands. Soft murmurings caught on the gentle wind, and I stilled, instantly afraid. I hid behind a large oak tree and peered toward the sound. There was Quinn dressed in a simple cotton dress, hips swaying, hair short and pixie-like as she cast a scorching glance behind her at Zimm.

He had suffered few aftereffects of prison. His hair had grown out into soft brown curls. Muscles moved with grace under his taut army-green T-shirt. It was damn annoying how quickly he bounced back to full health. And not only health, but happiness. Darkness didn't dog his step like it did mine.

Zimm's movements ceased, then he dropped the armful of twigs and branches. His footsteps crunched along the forest floor, thick with fallen leaves, as he chased after Quinn. Picking her up, he swung her around like some cheesy commercial for douche advertising a "fresh, clean feeling." Quinn threw her head back, her laughter melodious and soft.

The sound cauterized me like a heated blade pressed against open wounds.

I was that girl once, carefree and sexy-comfortable in my own skin. I couldn't remember when; but I knew at one time, I'd laughed like that. But no more; my youth and beauty had been spilled along with my blood onto a dirty prison floor. I guess it could've been worse. Syon could've given me to the men in prison, but with his obsession with ConRad, he wanted to keep me for himself.

Quinn's laughter turned to a soft moan. Her back arched like an elegant bow as Zimm's open mouth kissed her breast through the thin dress.

"You shouldn't be here."

I whipped around at the sound of ConRad's voice, my face blazing at being caught spying on a lovers' tryst. He was decked out in the standard-issue uniform, so tight it seemed to have been painted on. The brilliance of his eyes stood in contrast to his darkened whiskered face and mussed hair that swept across his forehead. There was no evidence of the bullet wound. Everyone seemed to have healed except me.

"I didn't mean . . . I wasn't . . ."

"I don't mean those two bloody fools." He nodded toward Zimm and Quinn, who were oblivious to anyone else. "Him, I can understand; he's just a man. But her? She's a goddess and has no right to jeopardize her gifts for mere bedsport."

"They're in love," I said, jumping to their defense, even though only a moment ago I had been bitter about their display.

ConRad shook his head. "They'd still take her back, the Elders. They'd consider her too much of an asset not to."

"You'd want her to go back to *them*?" I could barely believe him. His callousness knew no bounds.

"What you always fail to remember is that we are in the middle of a war. If we don't win, we're all dead." He adjusted the strap of his machine gun that slung across his back and patted it securely—his constant companion.

I turned around and started shuffling back to camp. ConRad and I would never agree. He was genetically programmed to "Serve and Protect." I was programmed to survive and grab some chocolate along the way. Besides, talking to ConRad made me crazy. How could I have insane notions of my fingers running through his hair when I hated him? I steeled my voice. "What do you want, ConRad?"

"You can't leave camp without protection."

His words were like a scalpel to my wounds, splitting the tender flesh and letting the venom rise to the surface. My body may have begun to heal, but my heart was still a ravaged organ, pumped full of rage. I whipped my head around. "Protection! Your protection? I had your protection and barely survived it. No thanks. I'll take my chances on my own."

His face softened. "Kris, please."

He reached for me. I flinched. My weakened leg gave out and I landed on my butt. ConRad rushed toward me and tried to help me up.

"Don't!" My hand outstretched to prevent his touch. The word, much harsher than I intended, lingered between us. Syon's sickness may sway toward boys, but it didn't mean I'd been spared. He had his own brand of hate reserved for women who his men betrayed him with.

A muscle in his jaw twitched. "Kris, can't you just listen—"

"No. I can't. Won't. Will never be able to." I was panting now. My rational mind warred with the instinctual need of my body to turn and crawl to safety.

We froze, ConRad hunched over, arms extended, and me, cowering in fear.

"You think I'd hurt you? You really think I'm that person?" Raw hurt flickered in his eyes.

He waited for my response, and I gave him one. "I've changed my mind. I want your head on a platter."

I couldn't breathe for the silence. I waited for him to shut me out, shut the pain down. He did, but it took a few heartbeats longer. ConRad backed away, hands up in surrender. "You win, Kris. You win."

I nodded and watched him walk away.

About time I won something. But there was a shaky feeling that had me folding my arms across my stomach—like I'd lost the only hope of ever being whole again.

Chapter Twenty-Six

ConRad was gone. Again. I tried not to notice, but my spine had an internal GPS where he was concerned, tingling whenever he was near.

It was late. An oak stump had been placed on the fire for the night. Almost everyone was curled in their bedrolls asleep, except the guard who was stationed by the tree line. I postponed turning in for the night. Night terrors stole my strength and had me quivering in the dark. But knowing that ConRad guarded my door gave me the courage to face them. Ironic really, since he was the cause of them in the first place, but it wasn't something I wanted to examine too closely.

I looked up and noticed Quinn watching me, concern plain on her face. She was always checking on me, and insisting I get rest. She stood, brushed the dried leaves from her skirt and walked toward me. She lowered herself on the felled log beside me and straightened her legs toward the fire.

"They would've taken you anyway. After killing him for interfering."

Her voice had been quiet, but my heart leapt just the same. I didn't want to hear this. The calming aroma of burning wood and fresh pine had me bristling at the intrusion. I stared straight ahead, hoping if I ignored her she would take the hint and leave.

"He knew he was the only hope of getting you out of there alive. He resigned his post and went AWOL. No one's ever dared to go AWOL before. If they catch him, they'll hang him and his men. No trial, no leniency, just the death penalty. He's lost everything, his career, his position in society. He'll be an outlaw forever. Only the few men that you see here remain loyal to him. They left in order to help with the rescue mission." She moved her feet back from the fire, giving her toes a reprieve from the heat.

I shot her a quick glance, stunned. "I thought the rescue mission was your idea."

"It didn't have to be. I knew he'd be coming after you." Her one eyebrow arched slightly. "I just made it so he couldn't leave me behind."

"And how did *you* know he'd come?" My voice was caustic. How had she known when I didn't? I was left in hell with no hope. If I had a small sliver of faith, then maybe I would have made it out with a tiny piece of myself intact.

"He's leaving. For good." Her hands rested lightly on her knees as she stared into the flames.

A black sickness rolled in my stomach at her words. He was leaving me? "When?"

"Soon."

I nodded at her answer, but my palms were slick with cold sweat. I swallowed hard. The air was suddenly thin. I never thought he'd actually leave. Hate me—yes, never talk or touch me again—fine. But to abandon me?

I leaned over and picked up some roasted rabbit meat lying on a stone slab. Since my recovery, I'd been ravenous. One night I absently made the comment I preferred rabbit meat to squirrel. Afterwards there was an unlimited supply by the campfire.

I gestured toward the food. "ConRad?"

She smiled. "We think he almost eliminated the entire rabbit population in about two weeks."

I nodded, not liking what the implications were. I tried to logically sort out my feelings. I tried to calm myself with the platitude that I'd be alright.

He's leaving.

I shook my head. I'd never been afraid of being alone before, but a sticky, black sensation had me hunching over my stomach, arms wrapped around my middle.

I couldn't deny the truth; it was too bold, too ugly. I never gave him a chance, never even let him speak. He told me in no uncertain terms if I used the microbiotics on Zimm, he'd no longer be able to protect me. But I'd made my choice regardless, thinking I could handle the consequences. And now I was alone. "If I asked, do you think he'd stay?"

Quinn didn't answer. She didn't have to. I could feel her censure. She thought I'd pushed him too far. Maybe I had.

I bit on a ragged thumbnail. Over the last week ConRad had avoided me even more than I had him. I needed a way to make sure he couldn't ignore me when he got back.

I saw his bedroll across the fire. Apprehension rose in my stomach as an idea formed. *How weak did this make me?*

I should just let him go. It was simpler.

Something deep inside tore at the thought. A silent scream vibrated against the walls of my gut. I rushed over and slipped between the blankets. I needed him just a bit longer. When I was stronger, I'd let him leave.

"What are you doing?" Quinn whispered furiously.

"I have no bloody idea." Maybe this small gesture would be enough. Maybe I wouldn't have to ask.

Quinn shook her head. "You're playing with fire."

I couldn't help but agree. I just hoped I could survive another burn.

I rubbed my face into the cool cloth of the pillow and drew the covers up to my chin. I hadn't expected to fall asleep, but the scent of him—musky, woodsy, male—calmed me, made me feel safe, taking me to a place where my dreams couldn't follow.

A rough hand shook me awake. ConRad loomed above. Concern etched in his brow, the fire throwing gruesome shadows across his face. "Are you alright?"

A bit groggy, I had a hard time following his question. "Umm . . . yeah, I'm fine."

"Good."

He bent, took hold of the edge of his bedroll, and pulled . . . hard. I flew through the air and tumbled to the ground.

"Hey . . . ," but before I could stand and brush myself off, he had his bed secured and pack on. "What are you doing?"

No answer. Typical. He turned and walked out of camp.

"Wait a minute. Dammit. Just stop for a second. We need to talk." I tried to keep my voice down, but panic bordered the edges.

He ignored me, his form quickly being swallowed up by the night.

Did I have to chase him? Seriously? Crap. I didn't chase well. And I was nervous. It was so damn *dark* out there.

I threw on my boots in record time and ran after him. "ConRad, please, I just want to talk." Couldn't he make this easy?

"I'm done talking."

Breathless, I jogged after him. Damn, he moved fast, but I had to keep him in sight. "Okay, then I'll talk."

"You've said enough, thank you."

Not good. "I think you took the whole 'head on a platter' comment wrong. I didn't mean it literally, but more in a meta-physical, slash, artistic, slash, humorous way."

He whipped around, glared, and took a few menacing steps in my direction. Dried leaves crunched underneath his booted feet. Then I took a few menacing steps . . . back.

"That—is exactly what I'm talking about. Everything's a joke, a . . . what do you call it . . . sarcastic response. Nothing's serious. This," he gestured, pointing to me, then himself, "is not a joke. This is serious."

I didn't want to get into whatever was between us. I just wanted us to go back to camp, so I could fall asleep with the knowledge that he was there, watching me. But I was fast running out of options as he turned and stalked into the night.

"Alright, so I did mean it literally. But I take it back. Your head looks great, right where it is." I was getting tired of running after him. Chasing sucks.

ConRad stopped; with a resigned sigh he dropped his pack and turned to face me. "Fine Kris, let's talk." His voice infused with steel. "Say what you need to say and be done with it, because, God only knows, there'll be no peace until you do."

He waited for my response, his eyes the most uninviting ice. My throat went dry—the sides stuck together. My hand splayed against my collarbone. I was supposed to ask him something. Maybe this wasn't the best time. "I just wanted to say . . . um" *Don't leave.* "Umm . . . thanks for getting me out of there." *Don't leave.* "Out of prison, I mean." *Don't leave.* "And, well . . . I owe you one." *Please. Don't. Leave.*

"Fine." He turned, picked up his pack, and walked away.

I poured my heart out—kinda, sorta, in a roundabout way—and he was just going to walk away. "Fine? Fine! Is that all you have to say?"

"I'm not the one who wanted to talk," his said, voice low, back toward me. "I don't have anything else to say."

Anger had me clenching my teeth. My fist knotted at my side. "Fine. Go ahead and go." I turned to head back to camp, but true to form I had to have the last word. "Coward."

As soon as the words rolled off my tongue, I regretted them. I sucked in a breath and readied myself to turn and apologize, but didn't get the chance. ConRad was on me like fire to fuel. He grabbed my arm and swung me around so fast that my feet left the ground.

"What did you say? Did you call me a coward?" he roared, his face mere inches from mine, nostrils flared, eyes fiery blue.

I swallowed hard. Staring down the beast inside the man was never easy, but I'd grown some claws myself.

He grabbed both of my shoulders. "I went to Hell and back for you. I lost friends. Good men trying to get you. I sacrificed everything, my career, my freedom, my life, my . . . honor." The words were spoken as if metal burrs shredded his tongue.

"Now I'm sentenced to live like this . . . like a criminal." He shook me so hard that I thought my neck would snap.

I shook my head, pleading. "I didn't mean it. Please, I was stupid . . . angry."

He talked over me as if I had said nothing. "Since the moment I saw you mere seconds from the alien's claws, I've given everything I had to protect you. And at every turn . . . every sardonic turn," he shook me again, "you've resisted me. I told you what to do with Zimmion. I *told* you there were consequences, but you didn't listen. Instead you lied to me. You knowingly *lied* to me."

The man of few words had hoarded them to hurl at me all at once.

"And you call *me* a coward." He sneered, and a wicked laugh had the hairs on the back of my neck stiffen. "You're the biggest coward I've ever met. You think I don't know? You talk in your sleep. A lot. Why are you out here, Kris? What's got you so scared that you're willing to run to me?"

I couldn't go there. Wouldn't go there. "ConRad, I don't know what you're talking about? I just—"

"Oh no, you wanted to talk? Let's talk, princess. What happened to you? And don't tell me prison. You were screwed up before then. Having nightmares back at the compound. Screaming about blood on your hands. What happened?"

I wedged my hands against his chest. "Shh, don't talk to me like that. I don't—"

"I don't. I won't. I can't. I am SO bloody sick of your whining. Talk to *me* about being a coward. You're so damn scared; you're a mess. What do you want, Kris?"

I shook my head and tried to break free.

"Where's my mommy?" His voice rose in imitation of mine. "Do you know you screamed for your mommy over and over like some pathetic child? The men were nervous, thinking you'd lost your mind. The only way I could shut you up was to rock you on my lap and whisper calming nonsense in your ear."

His words were like a slap, stunning and brutal.

"Liar! Liar!" I pounded his chest with my fists. He wouldn't do that. I'd never let him, never need him like that.

He ignored my blows, invaded my space, and shoved his face in front of mine. "Oh, I'm a liar now, huh? I've been nothing but honest with you, but you've lied to me from our very first meeting. About who sent you here, about Zimmion, about how you feel. About knowing more about The Prophesy than you've let on."

I was scared now. Real fear had invaded the fluid around my spine—owning me with its power. "I don't know how I feel."

He laughed, white incisors flashed. "You're such a liar, Kris. You've lied to yourself for so long you don't even know what's true. Guess what? It's truth time." His voice was rough, boarding on ugly. "*What happened to you?*"

I whipped my head back and forth. "ConRad, please! Shh."

Tears burned, I blinked them back. I needed a different tactic. Reaching up to his face I pulled his mouth to mine. The kiss was bruising. I couldn't tell who was doing the punishing, me or him.

He jerked his head back. Eyes threw shards of ice. "Oh no. I'm not going to let you push this away with sex—let you cower from your fears. You want to screw so hard so fast that you can forget. Well, I'm sick of this game, sick of you pushing me away. We're having it out here and now. What happened to your mother?"

"Shut up!"

"You think I don't know? Say it." His fingers bit into my flesh. "Goddamn it, SAY IT."

I broke. Red exploded in my brain. A sharp-knifed pain drove to the base of my skull. "She blew her head off. She killed herself in her bathroom, and I heard it." I screamed the words in his face. "Heard the gun. It was so damn loud. And I found her. *Found her.* Is that what you want me to say? Pieces of her on the white tile. I tried to put the bits of skull and brain back inside her head. Scooped them up like a puzzle and tried to fit them in place. And I couldn't save her. After all that I couldn't save her!"

Tears streamed; my nose ran. My hands were fisted in his shirt. Fabric ripped beneath my fingers. "Screw you! Is that what you want me to say? That she never said goodbye. That she freaking left me! LEFT ME! My mother left me when she promised. Promised that she loved me!"

I fell sobbing to the ground, sharp rocks imbedding in my knees. He followed, holding me tight to his chest. "And then YOU were leaving me. You *wanted* to leave me. How could you ConRad?"

"I love you."

"Shut up. SHUTUPSHUTUPSHUTUP. Don't. Lie. To. Me. You were leaving. I saw you turn your back and walk away."

"I wasn't leaving. Not really. I would've been back. Even if you didn't chase, I would've been back."

"LIAR!" I screamed. My hands fisted in his ripped shirt and pulled it tight around his neck.

"Marry me."

If he took a gun and shot me, I would've been less surprised. I crumpled and buried my face in his lap. "You are so cruel. Why are you so cruel? Don't say that to me. You can't mean that. Nobody can. I know what I am. *I know.* I'm damaged at best, broken at worst. You can't want me."

Silence. The truth was out. I said it. I didn't lie. For once I didn't lie.

"You're right."

A kick in the face. A knife in my heart. I looked up. He was giving up on me? That was it?

He laughed. And it wasn't that hoarse laugh I'd heard before. But one that came from the heart, one that came from a place of joy. "You're such an insane mess, but you're a beautiful mess. You're my beautiful mess. I'd never let you go."

I wiped my face with the back of my hand. I didn't know how I felt about being called a mess or crazy. "Well, you're no bed of roses yourself."

"Atta girl." He smiled at me.

A few words of praise and my skin hummed. We were inches apart. His hands moved over my neck, his thumbs stroked the underside of my jaw. And then I knew. He filled the emptiness. Made it smaller, easier. And I was okay.

"I love you." I rushed the words not wanting to lose courage. My declaration hung heavy in the air, but my relief was greater. Finally, my heart was laid bare, there were no more secrets. "It's the first time, you know. I never said it before."

The liquid blue in his gaze burned hot as it trailed slowly down to my lips. "Me either," he whispered.

My lips opened in invitation. Hunger flared in his eyes; my only warning.

He crushed his mouth to mine—open and wet. He drank from me like I was his personal savior, and I let him. I opened myself to him, dropping all my barriers, exposing as I'd never done before. No more games. This was real.

I ran my fingers through his hair—*finally, yes*—and grabbed on for leverage, pulling closer, grinding my hips to his. He sucked on my tongue, drawing me into his mouth, then pulled back, gently biting my lip. The taste of him—so unique it branded and claimed me as his forever.

ConRad groaned deep, the sound resonating on a primal level within me. His hands cupped my bottom and traveled lower to stroke my heat. I moaned, resenting the clothes that separated us. He grabbed me and pulled me onto his lap. I wrapped my legs around his back.

Our hips meshed and ground together, an inciting tempo that only we could hear. He pushed up my shirt, exposing my breasts to the chilled air. They puckered instantly. His mouth, hot and wet, pulled on one nipple, creating a heat that seared a path from his lips to down deep between my legs.

His mouth was brutal, sucking, pulling, nipping. Emotions rippled off him, and I felt them like they were my own—punishment, redemption, need. Ah God, the need—it hovered on the edge of pain. Tears flowed unhindered. I loved this man. I wanted to take all he had to give.

ConRad's mouth came back to mine, crushing, forcing his way in. The saltiness mixed with the musk of him and created an aphrodisiac for my palate. ConRad must've tasted my tears. He pulled away and gazed at my face.

His breathing was ragged. He touched his forehead to mine and rested. I could feel him fight for control. A deep sigh. An illusion of calm. Then he caressed his cheek against mine, brushing my tears away. His lips—quiet, gentle—kissed me. His eyes leveled with mine, and I saw ConRad. Gone was the wall of solid steel he had forged around himself for protection. And inside was a man, a man who had never loved, one who had never been loved before.

ConRad trembled.

I understood completely. Vulnerability is terrifying. The complete exposure of one's soul is gut-wrenching.

ConRad broke eye contact and nestled his face against my neck. It was too much. He wasn't ready to go there with me yet. I stroked his hair as one would a small child. "It's okay. It's okay."

"No, it's not," he shook his head. "Give me a moment."

I nodded, trying not to let the pain of his withdrawal show in my face.

Instead of walking away, ConRad reached for his pack and undid his bedroll. He spread the blanket on top of dried pine needles and fallen leaves, and knelt down. He raised his hand and clasped mine, tugging me toward him. We knelt there facing each other, my hands wrapped in his, resting both on his heart.

The lines on his face deepened, furrows creased his brow, his eyes simmered. "I pledged my protection to you once before and failed. So I pledge the only thing I have left: my life. As an exiled man I cannot legally ask to be your husband. But with

God as our only witness, I devote myself, my heart, my soul, my life to you until the day I die."

His chest heaved. Hands shook as they clasped mine. "Do you accept?"

My breath hitched. In the span of a quick inhale I was humbled. I didn't deserve this fierce, strong, proud man. "You asked for honesty and I gave you lies. Lies that almost killed us both. I make a vow to you that from now on only truth will be between us. I give you my heart, my soul, my life until the day I die. Please, ConRad. Let me be your wife."

He sighed, just a whisper, but I heard it down in my soul.

This powerful man wanted me. Amazing.

My hands trembled as I lifted my shirt. Most of my cuts and bruising had healed. Only along my ribs was there a slight yellowing.

He traced my colored flesh with the pad of his rough thumb. "I'm so sorry."

"Shhh—no more. All that's behind us now."

No more hesitation. His shirt fell beside mine, and he gathered me into his arms.

The skin-on-skin contact rushed through me. My breath came in shuddered gasps. My nipples hardened, pulse quickened. His arms were strong and corded, his strength barely contained below the surface. I felt his stomach quiver against mine.

I skimmed my hands over his biceps and shoulders, up his neck, and rested one hand on each cheek. The feel of his week's growth of beard was rough and slightly painful to my sensitized skin. With my thumbs I outlined his lips, full and slightly parted. His mouth opened more and gently teased the pad of my thumb and then soothed the skin with his tongue. I was mesmerized by his mouth—white teeth, pink tongue. A groan formed deep in my throat. I wanted that mouth on me—my lips, my breasts, my everywhere.

A rush of heat sent my attention, my want, my need there. I needed him *there*.

I pulled his mouth closer. His tongue mated with mine mingling our tastes—metal, musk, heat.

He broke the kiss, locked his hands in my hair and arched my back, offering my breasts up like the sacrifice on an altar. His mouth sucked one peaked nipple and then the other, sending currents straight to my center. I rubbed myself against him, needing friction, needing relief.

I tugged on his head, needing him lower. He moaned and with startling speed picked me up and lowered me onto the blanket. He made quick work of my boots and yanked on my pants, not even bothering to undo the snap.

I was naked. Then his body flowed over mine like rich cream into hot coffee. His mouth was hot and wet against my concave belly—then headed lower. His fingers stroked the inside of my thighs, the pad of his thumb tracing the palm-sized "S" branded into my skin. All motion stilled.

"I'll kill him."

My trembling fingers settled over his. "He's not worth it. I'm yours now. My body's branded with your name. Not his."

He lowered his mouth and kissed the mark that joined us in more ways than one. "You humble me." His tongue bathed the scarred flesh, and then blew cool air to torment my senses.

And from one second to the other I was embarrassed. He wanted everything. I wanted to give him my all, but I was afraid. Letting him make love to me this way exposed me, shattered my last defense.

His gaze snapped up and pinned me with the clearest of blue. He shook his head. "No, don't. Do this for me. I want all of you." He pushed himself up and kneeled before me. "Kris, look at me. It's time to trust me, time to let go."

"Open for me," he said in a whisper. He brushed the back of his fingers along my thigh, caressed my hip. Seconds ticked by, then minutes. I trembled, but not with fear. The power in letting go and trusting completely had my breath coming in gasps. My back arched. Small whimpers escaped and in minutes I was bursting apart from the sheer intensity. But it wasn't enough. I wanted him—all of him.

I reached for him. Both of our hands met at the button of his pants. Mine frantic, his shaking.

ConRad pushed his clothing down toward his knees, to impatient to remove his boots and be free of his clothing all together. Then he was there, above me, over me—thank you God—inside me. My legs wrapped around him. I bit his shoulder. Drew my nails down his back.

He buried his hands deep into my hair, holding me hostage to his pounding heat. I threw my head back to the sound of my name on his lips. And the world exploded.

CHAPTER TWENTY-SEVEN

Hours later I lay warm and cozy on ConRad's chest, wrapped tight against him inside his bedroll. We'd both fallen asleep, but upon waking I wished to prolong the afterglow. Tucked in a cocoon of peace and serenity, joy bubbled inside me. This was my wedding morning, none like I'd ever imagined, but I didn't want the outside world to intrude. But the presumptuous rays of early morning sun and the insistent twitter of birds were the world's evil reminders that life didn't stand still, even for a time traveler.

One moment ConRad was sleeping and the next he was up on his feet, ready for battle.

"What?" I asked, still huddling down for warmth.

"Shh," he said, cutting me off with a hard hand gesture. He stood feet apart, gloriously naked and dangerous, with a machine gun in his hands, his finger easy on the trigger.

"Commander, stand down. It's Red . . . um, I mean 00273." Red and Tank had gotten used to their new names during my recovery. There was a rustle in the trees and then the curly red-haired man with a full copper beard appeared.

"You alone?" ConRad asked, not lowering his weapon.

"No, Tank's with me, but he doesn't want to come out on account of the . . ." his voice trailed off but his head nodded in my direction.

ConRad's eyes scanned the area, then grunted his consent. He set his gun down, within easy reach and turned to dress. I pulled the covers securely under my chin.

"We need to move," Red said. "They've found the hut."

"Where's Quinn?" My concern for her safety overrode my embarrassment.

"They're a mile or so south. We'll meet up with them in about an hour." Red's eyes flicked over me nervously, then back to ConRad. Having a naked woman in his midst seemed to make him skittish.

"The Sanctuary then. We'll catch up." ConRad had finished dressing and was chewing a piece of jerky. He glanced at me and flashed a boyish smile. My heart forgot its normal cardiac rhythm and hitched. He threw me a strip of chewing leather. It plunked soundly on my stomach. With resolve, I placed the dried hunk of meat in my mouth to begin the softening process. A pang of longing for a five-star breakfast in bed and a real cup of coffee—the way my honeymoon was *supposed* to have started off—had my eyes blurring.

"You okay?" ConRad squatted closer to my eye level and stroked my cheek.

But in all my wildest wedding fantasies, I never got a guy like this. I smiled my tears away and nodded.

"Let's go then." He stood and started packing his gear.

"I'm not dressing in front of an audience."

"Red's gone," ConRad said, without taking his eyes off his pack.

I glanced around at the empty meadow.

Within five minutes, ConRad had broken camp, and I'd barely gotten my clothes on. ConRad grabbed my hand, loosely lacing our fingers. The gesture was small, but possessive. I belonged to ConRad. I took a deep breath and swallowed. The thought still had the power to release a fresh batch of butterflies in my stomach.

We walked over to where Red had tethered the horse for us. ConRad helped me on and then mounted behind me. We started forward at a fast walk with ConRad letting the horse pick its way through small trails that wound deeper into the forest. Birds sang cheerfully and sunlight flickered through leaves, playing across my face. I rested my head against the hard plane of ConRad's chest and closed my eyes. I sighed. I vaguely remembered a girl who avoided the sun for fear of wrinkles. Never again. I'd lived through a night that never ended. Daylight wasn't something I'd take for granted again.

I could block out the world only for so long. I had to know. Gone was the girl who spent her lifetime ditching reality. Ignorance was death; it was time to start living smart. Resignedly, I opened my eyes. We were still a ways behind the group so I felt free to talk. "Who are they?"

ConRad didn't need to ask for clarification. He knew what I was asking. "The Elders."

"They found us?" I couldn't keep the tremor out of my voice. Cold fear flooded into my veins. I sat forward, prepared to run, even if in my mind I knew it was illogical.

"No, they haven't. We're still one step ahead of them. Relax, sweetheart." His arm came around my waist and then gently pushed my head back to his chest. "I won't let them take you. I promise."

His words were meant to comfort, but they didn't. This was no fairy tale. This was real life. My body still showed the scars of how very real it was. "You can't promise that."

"No, you're right. I'm sorry." There was a long pause, then he inhaled deeply. "I wonder if you'll ever feel safe again." His voice was low, as if the comment was made for his ears only.

I wondered the same. The question haunted me ever since ConRad carried me, half dead, from my concrete cell. There was an answer—not easy, but my life had taken a complete detour from easy. I thanked the fates that I wasn't facing him. I'd never have enough courage to ask otherwise. "There is something."

My tone must've spoken volumes. His body stiffened. The horse sped up in response to what it felt was a command. ConRad realized what he'd done, took a deep breath, and relaxed the pressure on our mount.

"I'm not having this conversation."

I shouldn't have been surprised he'd guessed what I meant. He knew me better than anyone else.

"I'm sorry." I really was. I never thought I'd put this burden on anyone. "You're the only one I know who can do it."

At first I didn't think he would respond, then . . .

"Don't ask this of me," he growled. I could feel the muscles in his arms tense.

"ConRad, I can't sleep . . . couldn't bear to take my next breath if I thought for one second that the Elders getting me was a possibility. You're the only one I can trust, the only one who *knows*."

His hands squeezed my arms and shook. "How do you know I can do it?" he said in my ear. "Do you think I have no soul? No heart? Didn't I lay myself bare to you last night? Sweet goddesses, what do you think I am?"

"Man enough." Thick emotion clogged my throat. "Man enough, so I won't have nightmares. Man enough, so I can feel safe."

"Man enough to kill you?" His voice rose, his arms lifting me and turning me so I could see the glaring pain written across his face.

There were no tears. I couldn't cry. The fear of capture had frozen them inside me. I had to get him to agree—to understand. "Please, ConRad, they can't take me alive. I can't go back there. I need to know you'll end it before it gets to that. I need your vow."

His hands slid up my arms and cradled my face, his thumbs smoothing my bottom lip. "The only way they'd get to you is if I were dead. You have to know that."

I shook my head. "It's not good enough . . ." I swallowed hard, knowing what I asked went beyond the bounds of humanity; it went straight to the heart of pure sin. "You need to stay alive to make sure I don't."

The horror on his face shattered my heart and almost my courage.

"Kris, have mercy." His voice was beyond a whisper, more of a shearing rasp. He had the look of a man burning alive. He released his hold, not wanting to touch me, and then scrubbed his face with his hands. "Ahh, God, woman, you ask for the last bit of my soul. I'll make you your damn vow, but only because I know it won't come to that. I'll make sure it won't. But I decide when, not you. Understand?"

I nodded, relief flooding through me. My body unfroze as blood began to thaw my veins. Moments of silence lengthened as I nestled back into the wall of his chest. He seemed as happy as I to drop the subject.

"What's the Sanctuary?" I asked, more to break the quiet than for any real concern.

"A safe place," he stated. Bitterness underlined his words. I couldn't blame him.

I doubted there was such a place, but didn't want to question. I found that for the first time since ConRad had broken me out of prison, I didn't have the need to plan. I'd gotten my reassurance. I trusted him.

Within half an hour we'd met up with the group. ConRad and I were the only ones sharing a horse. Quinn and Zimm stayed close to us, and Red was in front while Tank pulled up the rear. We moved quickly, our pace slightly below punishing. We stopped only when it was too dark to travel, and by then ConRad had to peel me off the horse.

It wasn't better the next night, or any night thereafter. Exhausted from the riding, I would crawl from our horse to our bedroll face first. ConRad would massage my limbs and sore behind. It was the only way I could contemplate getting up and doing the whole thing again the next day. Unfortunately, it always stopped there. My honeymoon: ruined by a bunch of snoring soldiers and open sleeping arrangements.

On the third day we left off following a river, and within an hour broke through the forest to open land. Stationed on top a small hill was a brown stone fortress. Thick walls flushed the front and extended quite a way behind, encapsulating a good portion of land. The fortress loomed two or three stories, with a rectangular tower extending, like a phallus, from the center. Double wooden doors, edged with thick metal brackets decorated the face. Brown-colored glass lined the upper levels, barred with rusted iron and thick metal pegs.

The tree line ended close to a quarter of a mile from the stone fortress, allowing any approaching guest to be seen. Our ragtag group rode through the meadow and pulled the horses to a stop a few hundred feet from the entrance. ConRad continued to the wooden doors, and then halted our mount. We sat on the horse and waited. Trying to practice patience, I was impressed I waited a full three minutes before turning to eye ConRad. "Is this it?"

Without answering, ConRad slipped from his horse and turned to haul me down. Reaching for my hand, we walked to the side of the huge fortress and turned the corner out of sight of the group.

I cut a glance to ConRad's face, which held the familiar resigned look. I knew "that look." "That look" never boded well for me. "ConRad, what aren't you telling me?"

I rested my back against the coarse stone wall, while ConRad stood in front of me, his gaze assessing the open grassy area. He was always on alert, always on guard. Finally, he turned and made eye contact. "This is the Women's Sanctuary. No men allowed."

"No men? Then why are we here?"

"Kris, please, this is a safe place." His eyes were hard, mouth in a grim line. "This is where men can bring their women. Where they can be protected. No one can hurt you here."

"I'll be safe with you." Wings of fear began to bat against my rib cage.

He shook his head. "The arrangements have been made."

Realization was slow, but when it came, it was like a physical blow. *He meant to leave me.* I whipped my head back and forth.

He grabbed my face between his hands and pinned me with his gaze. "Kris, stop. This isn't about you. I'm not leaving you. You have to trust me."

"I won't go. I'm your wife. You can't just leave me here. You made a promise! Or do you break them as easily as you make them?"

I heard his quick inhalation of breath, but I was hurt. To be abandoned so quickly after his declaration stung.

His fingers bit into the sides of my skull. "Damn woman! You wield your words like a weapon. No, I don't make promises easily, nor do I break them. Apparently, not nearly as easy as distrust comes to you. I made you a promise to protect you with my life, not to never disagree with you. But I will give you a choice. You can either walk in the Women's Sanctuary on your own two feet, or I can carry you kicking and screaming like a child."

I'd seen the expression he wore before chiseled on his face. His mind was set, the decision made without my consent. "But I'm your wife." To my shame, my voice trembled.

He sighed and his expression softened. His fingers relaxed

into a caress. So he wasn't as indifferent to me as he wanted me to believe. "I'm not used to having to explain myself."

"Time to get used to it."

"Apparently," his tone dry, but there was a small lift to the corner of his mouth. "We're being followed."

I nodded. "The Elders."

He released his hold and braced one hand on the wall behind me. His head bowed as if the patch of grass between his feet held the answers to the secrets of the ages. "It's Syon. He has a group of men. Men loyal to him and his agenda. He wants to hurt me and that means everything that belongs to me."

His eyes pierced mine, holding me captive as much as his physical body. "Syon will never cease hunting me, and that means hunting you to get to me."

Cold sweat broke out across my skin. I splayed my palms against the back wall, fingers finding the grooves in the stone. "But why didn't he kill me when he had the chance?"

"It's complicated."

"Try me."

Then his famous sigh again. "Word got out about you, where you supposedly came from, how we saved you from the alien. And, well . . . people, people started to talk about The Prophesy and how you might be The One.

"The Elders needed to show the people that you're not the one to fulfill The Prophesy. They wanted to break you— control you, so they restrained Syon. But now you're an es- caped prisoner—a walking death sentence. And Syon couldn't be happier."

I hadn't thought about The Prophesy in what felt like a

thousand years. I was by no means convinced of its authenticity, but if other people and the Elders were, then my beliefs didn't matter much. Regardless, my concern right now was for my husband. "What are you going to do?"

"Hunt him back." His voice deep—low. And if I had blinked, I would've missed the flash of pure rapture in his eyes.

For one second my confidence rattled. How precarious was the line that ConRad walked, separating good and evil?

Then my ConRad was back, gathering me into his arms and kissing me gently on the forehead. His breath shuddered slightly as he inhaled deeply. "Kris, please believe me, I don't want to leave you. But I can't protect you."

I shook my head not wanting to hear the rest.

"You're a liability to me. You're exhausted. You've barely eaten in three days, and I don't have a horse for you. I can't do what I need to do and worry about you at the same time."

Everything he said was true. I could barely sit in a saddle anymore, but I wasn't willing to give in yet. "No," my voice broke. "I'm stronger than you think. Stronger with you."

"Kris." He shook me again, his face mere inches from mine. "I can't protect you. And the goddess knows that it rips me apart to admit it, but I can't."

Pain clenched at my throat. I swallowed tears. "But Quinn, she's not staying." It was a childish plea, but I was desperate.

"No one is trying to kill her." His final words secured the last bar in my prison.

I broke his gaze and took in the peaceful looking meadow and sporadic yellow and purple wildflowers scattered about.

"You need to know that if I fail, Syon will not give you up." My eyes cut to him at his words. "He can't breach these walls. If he does, he'll have mutiny on his hands, but he'll try whatever he can to get you to leave. Kris, do you hear what I am telling you?"

I did, but there was something about his urgency that scared me. Something I needed to understand, but my mind was too fumbled to comprehend.

"Whatever happens, you cannot leave. You can't leave. Even for me." His hands cupped my face, pinning my head to maintain eye contact. "Dammit, tell me you understand what I am saying."

I nodded, but he must have seen the heartbreak in my face because he pulled me into his arms and held me tight against his chest. I breathed in his scent—woodsy, sweat—one so achingly familiar. After a moment he pulled back. "I'll come back. Do you trust me? Do you believe that I'll come back for you?"

I nodded again, mute with emotion. I trusted.

His lips met mine in a powerful kiss, forcing my head back as he held me steady with his arms. A low growl escaped from the back of his throat. I opened my mouth wider, crazy for the taste of him. Then he broke away and turned the brick corner. I gave myself a second as I clasped my hand over my mouth to squelch the plea for him to come back. When I turned the corner, ConRad was on his horse and riding away.

He didn't look back.

Chapter Twenty-Eight

The draft was what finally forced me inside. The wind had picked up, beating at my shirt and slashing my hair around my face. Searching for a way inside, I walked to the wood door and pounded to be heard above the rising howl. A small metal plate opened, revealing a pair of brown eyes surrounded by sagging skin and deep lines.

"Thought you'd stay out there all day. Ready to come in now, are you?" said a voice, muddled with a thick accent.

I nodded, not up to having conversation.

Metal protested as it slid against metal, shrilling its displeasure. Then a large double door opened, squeaking from lack of use. An old woman appeared, black hair shot through with white and cut in short style that framed her smallish head. Her heavy gray robes seemed cumbersome as she struggled to encourage the door open.

She waved me in, and with a grunt indicated that I needed to help with securing the door. After the awkward metal bar was jimmied into place, she turned. Her perceptive eyes assessed me from head to toe. "Eh, you look like you've had a hard time of it. Your owner needs to take better care of ye."

I bristled at the "owner" comment, but let it pass. An overwhelming fatigue gripped me, and the mere thought of enlightening limited views was exhausting.

She beckoned with her hand and shuffled forward. "Follow me. We'll get you rested up. Feelin' like new in no time."

Grateful, I followed her down a shadowy corridor that opened into a common room of sorts. High, vaulted ceilings were accented with airy sky windows that let in the soft afternoon light. Lush, bright-colored rugs and body-sized pillows were thrown on the floor, inviting long afternoons of lounging and hushed intimate conversations. Bright intricate paintings lined the walls, depicting nature and various tasteful nudes. In the center was a circular fountain bubbling fragrant water, scented with jasmine and lavender, among floating flowers.

I breathed a sigh of relief. Women were here. Civilization was here. We *had* crawled out of the swamp and evolved. I choked back my embarrassment as tears sprang to my eyes. I hadn't known how the gray utilitarian environment had affected me. I needed this oasis, this sanctuary. The rough ride over the last few days had depleted all my energy reserves. ConRad said this was a safe place. I had to believe him, believe I could let my guard down and stop being hunted.

"Nice, yes?" The old woman stopped and turned once she realized I wasn't following. "The women decided that if they were forced into the Sanctuary by their owners, then they'd sure make 'em foot the bill." She laughed a deep and cackling sound, her eyes almost lost behind excess folds of skin.

"Your room's down here. We're too full up for single ones

so you'll have to share with Mistress Ana, but she's due any day now so you'll get the room to yourself soon enough. When are you due?"

"Do what?" My mind must've slipped. I couldn't seem to follow a regular conversation.

"Your baby. When are you due to give birth?" Her eyes traveled to my flat belly.

"I'm not pregnant," I said, surprised at how defensive my voice sounded. Surprised, and some other emotion mixed in that I didn't want to pinpoint.

She snorted as if not believing me. "Your owner sure paid enough for your entry. Thought for sure you'd be breeding."

Guilt and shame washed over me at the thought of ConRad having to hand over his own money. I had no idea what Con-Rad's financial situation was, but I hated the thought of being a burden.

"My name's Kris. And yours?" This conversation was too personal not to be at least on a first name basis.

"I'm Mother of the House, but everyone just calls me Mother."

I grunted an affirmative, but I would *not* be calling this woman "Mother." I was led down a long corridor and taken to a small airy room with twin beds covered in thick patchwork quilts and a skinned dead animal thrown on the floor as a rug.

Sprawled over one of the two beds that lined the walls was presumably the overdue Mistress Ana. Her hair was pulled up in a messy knot on top of her head. Dark wisps stuck to her flush cheeks, round from pregnancy. One hand rested on an overly extended belly as her other hand whipped a fan furiously in front of her face. Her toes, pointed in my direction, had the look of five pork sausages plumped to near bursting.

"Lord, I hope you brought cooler weather with you. I think I'm gonna pass out from this heat."

I hadn't noticed the heat, and in fact, it had been a little chilly outside, but then again, I wasn't the one who looked like an overfilled water balloon.

"Mistress Ana, let her catch her breath and then get acquainted," said the Mother of the House, then she turned to me. "You can rest now. Dinner is served at the seventh bell chime down in the dining room past the fountain. If you'd like to wash up, there's a bathing chamber at the end of the hall."

I nodded again, my only thoughts—naked, bath, bed, and maybe not necessarily in that order.

During the first few days after ConRad had left, I railed against the separation. Would ConRad be okay? Would he be able to slip past Syon and his men, and finally extract the justice he craved? For days, my worry for ConRad's life kept me pacing the common area and running up the circular staircase to the lookout tower. I alternated between praying for ConRad's return and terrified of Syon's arrival. I couldn't relax enough to grasp the concept that I was safe. That Syon couldn't touch me here.

A week went by with no incident, then two, and finally, the Elders came. But not for me. Ana had gone into labor and according to custom only the holy sect of the Elders could attend the birth. The bell in the tower was rung, and I helped carry

Ana to the birthing room off the grounds. The dank, airless structure was small, bearing only a stiff straw cot and leather straps attached to the wooden walls.

With a tightening sickness in my stomach, I watched as the other woman tied Ana to the bed. Her face was pale and drawn with worry, but she patted my hand anyway. "Don't worry, it's better this way," she said. "The Elders want to make sure I don't fight and hurt my baby."

I nodded past the lump in my throat and swallowed every medical opinion I had. I'd learned from my episode with Zimm. There were times when my knowledge could help a person, and then there were times when it killed.

"It'll be okay," I said, promising, despite my concern.

But it wasn't. Less than forty-eight hours later Ana was back in our room exhausted, drugged, and without a baby. Her daughter had been stillborn, and was already buried in the Sanctuary's graveyard.

In the following week I saw very little of Ana, since she spent all of her time in the Sanctuary's small chapel, and I spent all of mine in bed. The shroud of heartbreak Ana wore was impenetrable, and besides, I was worthless. A perpetual exhaustion dogged my steps like a bad habit, making me realize my recovery from prison would be hard won.

There was a lazy quality to my days and as much as I missed ConRad, I couldn't help but agree that the reprieve had been good for me. In the four weeks I'd been at the Sanctuary the hardened muscles in my neck softened. My jaw stayed unclenched for hours, and my night terrors? Well, they were still there, but less, more like a silent movie than full-colored cinema. I watched now as a spectator, no longer the lead role.

Cloudless skies had warmed the last few days, and this particular afternoon was sticky. Windows throughout the Sanctuary had been flung open. And a light breeze tickled the fine hairs along my brow as I indulged in the sweet smell of summer as it made its last hurrah. I laid wallowing, guilt-free, in a recently discovered luxury—afternoon naps.

"Kristina. Kristina Davenport, come out now."

My name swept through stone corridors and painted vaulted ceilings, hitting me like an attack from a tender lover. More painful because of its unexpectedness, more brutal because of my lack of preparedness.

I'd been lured into security and safety, by soft textures, beautiful surrounding, and sweet feminine laughter.

Stupid. Beyond stupid. I crossed into the land of too dumb to live. I should've known better. Should've . . . damn it.

"KRIS-TIN-A."

Only two people had ever called me by my full name. One was my mother, long in the grave. And the other—Syon.

The adrenaline floodgates opened, the toxicity making me queasy. I froze. Stiff. So tight, my spine cracked. My breathing shallowed into harsh pants.

Then, between one second and the next, I became motion. Bare feet sliding on cool uneven stone. My hands slapping on stone steps as I half ran, half crawled up the circular staircase. My body slamming against the unyielding walls as I rushed up to the second floor tower. Finally there, I pushed my face against the brown, cool, distorted glass.

ConRad. ConRad. ConRad. Please God, not ConRad.

From the second floor, I could see the meadow below where wildflowers dotted the muted green rolling hills with spots of color. Where the horses tied in the distance chewed lazily on the grass. Where the sun shone high and bright in a blue sky and the Elders, anonymous in brown robes and cowering in their shadowed hoods, encircling a form humbled in defeat.

The man inside the circle had been brought to his knees, in more ways than one. His hands were tied behind his back, his head low and heavy with submission. The sun kissed this one more freely. Rivulets of sweat streamed down his shirtless body, his glistening skin exposed and raw.

I knew even before his head, with painful effort, lifted. I knew before I saw the ice blue of his eyes, dulled to an imitation of the ones I loved. I knew because I'd kissed every scar, every jagged cut, that this was my ConRad.

Dried blood caked the one side of his face, crusting a swollen eye shut. Spidery fingers of red wrapped around his neck and mixed with the mud sprayed across his chest.

Information streamed high speed into my brain, but my mind slowed, unable to categorize the images. ConRad—on knees, beaten and tied. ConRad—eyes fixed straight ahead. ConRad—defeated.

The Elders all had weapons. Some of them carried guns, others wooden clubs. All concealed their faces, all except one.

The bareheaded Elder positioned himself in the front of the others, self-assured in his power, unconcerned with repercussions. His face—God, *his face*—was carved on the inside of my scorched eyelids. All I had to do was close them to see the etched lines and folds of skin sagging under his chin. See the gray hair that had thinned, leaving a small pink circle, evidence of the sun, and his lips thin and abnormally red against his pasty face.

This man owned a part of me, and my body responded to his call. Muscles tightened and quivered, ice-sweat wetted my ribs. I sank, following the floor-length window to my knees. I watched the robe snap around his feet as he paced behind the broken man before him.

Memories mingled with reality. I remembered how he moved before me as I hung from the ceiling, naked, withering on a metal hook. The scent of his stale breath. The leer that spoke of the thin demarcation between his hatred and his obsession. The face that held the same pleasure when executing a caress as with the sting of a whip. Eyes that had me screaming before a hand was ever laid upon me.

"Kristina Davenport, you need to come out." His tone held a song-like quality, as if this was all just a childhood game of hide-and-seek. I almost expected him to finish with "come out, come out, wherever you are."

Acid sloughed off layers of my stomach lining. My fear turned to a sick and twisted thing. I'd come from a place of no more guessing, no doubt—all the blank spaces were filled. I knew what torture was, and I'd rather die than go back. I'd meant every word when extracting my promise from ConRad. But would I have enough strength to keep my promise to him—my promise to not leave the Sanctuary? To stay here and watch him die?

I slammed myself back against the wall, away from the window—away from the image I was drowning in. I couldn't breathe, couldn't get on top of it.

"You see, Kristina. We know you're here. Where else would you be?" His clear voice penetrated the stone and dirt of the walls.

My gaze darted all around, trying to block his words yet hanging on every one.

"KRIS-TIN-A."

My ears singed at his audible fondle, as if he knew me, had every right. But my body didn't lie, even if my mind recoiled from the truth. He and I were intimate, as only a torturer could know his tortured. He'd seen me beg. Seen me willing to rip out my soul for a reprieve—seen the core of me, parts of me even I hadn't know existed. And I hated him for it.

"It's all very simple. All you have to do is come out. Your life for his. No strings attached."

The world swam. My vision was reduced to snapshots: the uneven window ledge, a diagonal crack in the brick, Ana's head shaking, and her lips forming words I couldn't hear over the rushing static in my ears.

I closed my eyes. What abominable sin did I commit to deserve this life?

"I realize this is a difficult choice to make, so we'll give you some incentive," Syon said, a smile in his words.

I heard a thick thump and then a muffled grunt. I turned and opened my eyes, straining to see through the barred window, my hand already over my mouth to prevent the scream.

There was ConRad face down for an excruciating minute. Then with a determination painful to watch, he pushed one shoulder into the ground, then the next, and lifted himself upright. Lastly, he raised his head, straightening his spine as if infusing it with liquid metal, and stared straight ahead.

His hair, longer and sun-bleached, fell over his eyes. With a flick of his head, he whipped it away. For one stilled second, his eyes found mine behind the colored glass that prevented the view from outside. Intense blue ones sent unspoken words to mine. I understood. He remembered my promise to never leave the Sanctuary and expected me to keep it.

No matter what. The words hung heavy between us.

The man with the club swung again, catching ConRad's right rib and kicking him in his face as he fell forward. A scream sounded behind me. I turned and vomited in the corner.

ConRad lay there at an odd angle, sprawled face forward on the dirt. Blood soaked the grass around his left ear.

My mind snapped; reality fuzzy around the borders. I ran toward the staircase. I'd pray for a merciful death later.

A solid human wall stood before me. Ana's hands grabbed my shoulders and shoved me against the back stone wall. White noise clamored in my head, loud and roaring. Only one thought cut the static—I needed to save ConRad.

"Kris! Kris, you need to stop." Ana's wide brown eyes hovered before mine. Her forearm pressed against my chest; her whole weight held me against the wall. Two other women held down each arm.

I shook my head, vocalizing anything was beyond me.

"I'm sorry, Kris. I can't let you go. He wouldn't want you to sacrifice yourself for nothing. It's too late."

"Let me go." I struggled. There was no way I could stand by and do nothing. "They're going to kill him."

"He's already dead."

Her cold words hit like a sucker punch. Someone screamed, but it sounded far away, as if happening to someone else.

"He's already dead," she repeated. Her voice rose to be heard above the clamoring. "It just hasn't happened yet."

The truth struck me with a resounding accuracy, but I

didn't want to accept it. Ana's words accomplished what all her strength couldn't do. Defeated, leached of all hope, I lowered to the floor.

"Please . . . I can't live without him," I said, my voice raw. To even express that thought ripped my soul.

Ana took my wet face in her palms and wiped at the tears with her thumbs. Her forehead touched mine. "You can't go with him. No matter how much you want to."

"It's my choice." Damn her, this was my decision. She couldn't take that away from me.

"No, it's not." She shook her head.

"The hell, it's not." I tried to pry her hands away from my face. I didn't need her comfort, or her permission.

But Ana held firm and refused to relinquish eye contact. "Kris . . . stop . . . think of the baby." Her eyes shuttered with pain, the grief of her recent stillborn baby coloring her words.

Baby, what baby? Bright lights exploded behind my eyes as the realization hit. The excessive tiredness, the queasy stomach, the barely acknowledged missed period. I was pregnant—I carried ConRad's child.

The weight of the thought sunk me. My options folded in on themselves like a broken tent in a torrid storm. I lowered my head in my hands. Ana was right. I might be able to forfeit my own life, but never that of my unborn child.

My beautiful ConRad. Panic seized me. I needed to see him and, God help me, say goodbye. Maybe somehow I could absorb his pain, give him strength through sheer force of will. I crawled, no pride—nothing, but endless black before me—but I needed to get to the window. Needed to see him one last time.

ConRad swayed on his knees. He leaned at an odd angle favoring his right side. I could see his stomach expand and flatten, sucking air in with each labored breath. He swallowed, his Adam's apple pronounced in his corded neck, jaw clenched, and shifted trying to find a new spot to grind.

I could see, so close, no more than thirty feet away. Might as well have been the distance of the Milky Way.

A quick kick to his right rib made him exhale with a whoosh, spurting blood from his nose and mouth in a spray of red. His eyes glazed, then refocused.

I knew what he was doing. ConRad had tried to teach me, tried to show me how to leave your body. How to rise above and hover on the outside. He hadn't managed the pain yet, I could tell, as his eyes blinked rapidly and refocused to a spot right above my head.

Then a blow to the left kidney. A hiss. His eyes fluttered back, showing white.

"Now we're getting somewhere. Let's make some noise," Syon said, his voice sickly sweet.

A small pop. A rib broke. ConRad screamed and crumpled to the floor.

Noooooooooo. The thought of him dying was bad enough, but the guilt of him still drawing breath in the midst of all that pain was more than I could bear.

In here, ConRad . . . right here . . . focus on me. I'm here. I'm here. I'm here. I'm here.

He rolled back up, swayed, fell, then finally pushed to his knees. Eyes blurred with torment, he searched the colored windows.

He'd heard me. Somehow our connection crossed barriers and locked. ConRad couldn't physically see me, but our eyes caught regardless.

I'm here, baby. Sweet husband, I'm here. You're okay. You're not alone.

His breath evened. Gaze fixed, then softened to quiet. His jaw relaxed, mouth parted slightly.

He'd left. *Thank you.* I breathed a sigh of relief.

A hit to the side of his head. Head snapped back. His body crumpled, still—dead.

A piercing scream rang out on and on—then my shadows didn't wait. They rushed at me until blissful Dark Space.

CHAPTER TWENTY-NINE

Something tapped my cheek softly, then harder. "Kris, wake up. Wake up."

I opened my eyes. Ana's face wavered above mine. Her brown eyes wide, her full mouth pressed into a tight line. For a split second my mind was blissfully numb, blank, and then in a painful shock, reality screamed in.

ConRad was dead.

The thought was like a millstone being tied around my neck before being pitched into the open sea. I was drowning, the waters closed over me. Couldn't rise above. Couldn't breathe.

"Kris, they've taken the body." Ana's big hazel eyes were soft with concern.

The body? ConRad's body?

I pushed myself up and fought my way past the tempting darkness that promised oblivion.

"Where?" My voice scraped my throat raw.

Ana shook her head. "I don't know, but they didn't have any supplies with them so maybe their camp isn't far. They headed south to the rear of the Sanctuary."

I struggled to my feet. My whole body seemed foreign, over-taken by some alien life-form. "How long ago did they leave?"

"A quarter of an hour . . . maybe longer. They waited awhile hoping you'd come out. The leader kept calling your name, taunting, but we thought it best to let you sleep." Her hand touched my knee and gave a light squeeze.

"Did ConRad . . . did he wake . . . or move? Anything?"

Ana's eyes lowered and she shook her head.

I didn't expect anything different. Glancing out the tinted window, I saw darkness creeping over the horizon. I dragged myself to my feet, my body barely responded. I started toward the circular stairs, but this time at a much slower pace.

"Where are you going?" Ana asked, ready to body-check me again.

"I need to see his body . . . I need to know."

Ana bit her lip, and then nodded. "Careful, Kris. Don't let ConRad die in vain. Stay alive."

Stay alive . . . stay alive . . . to what end? To never see my family again? Never love again, to live alone, and raise my child alone? But I couldn't think of that now. I had to find ConRad's body and give him a proper burial. When my mother died, she'd been cremated. There was no gravesite, no tombstone to visit, no comforting ritual to go through to help process the grief. I found myself desperate for a marker to place on his grave, a place I could visit with my child and show him or her where a great man was buried.

I struggled with the heavy metal bar across the front door. Using my foot, I braced myself against the door jam and pulled. The heavy door finally gave and I was out. I walked toward the dense forest line, but soon broke into a light run.

My heart was pounding, not only from the excursion, but from something that wouldn't die. Syon loved ConRad; twisted and sick as that love was, would he have killed him? A hardy seed of hope planted in my gut, one I couldn't uproot unless I was sure, until I saw with my own eyes and felt with my own hand.

Quiet. A voice hushed me in the back of my mind. I was too panicked for stealth, but self-preservation made me avoid the pile of dry leaves and stay close to the brush cover. I soon picked up a trail of some sorts. Not that I was a tracker, could be a deer, could be the Elders. My only saving grace was that I knew what direction they had headed.

Night fell fast within the depths of the forest. Clingy shadows blanketed any semblance of a path. My mind played upon my fears of slivered orange eyes and muted growls. I was glad when the tree line finally broke, and I saw a camp that kept the night at bay with its muted fire. Simple white tents were pitched in a circle within the small clearing. The campsite seemed subdued. Could the guilt of killing a man weigh on the Elders, or was it just exhaustion from beating a man to death?

I glanced around. There didn't seem to be any guards. And why would there be? Their only enemy was dead, and within their midst. They had no fear of repercussion.

I had no idea what I was going to do, so I settled for observation. The night deepened into silence and lanterns inside the tents created perfect silhouettes against the backdrop of fabric. I circled the camp, looking for anything, something that would give me a clue to ConRad's whereabouts. It didn't take long for me to find a man huddled inside a tent, over a large darkened form. I watched as the man lifted someone's head and carefully administered a cup to the still form.

My heart slammed with a painful beat against my chest. ConRad. It could be no one else but him, and if ConRad could drink, then he was alive!

I watched as the shadowed form tenderly stroked his hair, and placed silhouetted lips against his forehead. I knew those movements, had memorized his mannerisms as a key to my survival—Syon. He was the only person sick enough to administer care to the same soul he'd just tortured. My nails dug into my palms, and I bit my tongue to keep my screams behind my teeth.

My reptilian brain reared its ugly head. *Mine!* Syon couldn't have him.

But I had no idea how to get to ConRad. Syon would never let his guard down, wouldn't even leave his side. And I had no weapon. What could one lone woman do against a band of armed men? So I waited. I'd learned patience in prison, a requirement of survival. Opportunities revealed themselves to the ready.

The hours passed. I sat cross-legged, still as death, and bided my time. I watched as the moon traveled across the sky and finally set. My fingers stroked the pointed side of a rock I'd found as I primed my mind. A body had dozens of vulnerable spots; I knew them all. A stab into the smoothed tender skin of the temple was easy enough. David had brought down Goliath with such a well-placed shot, and Syon was no giant.

The lantern flicked to life after hours of sleep. The light was faint, but shined as a beacon in the thick night. The silhouette I'd pegged as Syon moved. His body hunched over ConRad's, stilled and then rose and pulled his shirt over his head. The pants went next. His darkened form hesitated, looming over ConRad's unconscious form.

My fist clenched, the rock's sharp edge cutting into my palm. I watched transfixed, like the unfolding of a tragic train wreck, unable to look away. *No . . . no . . . no.*

Syon's silhouette covered ConRad's. I rose to my feet.

No plan formed in my mind, just a cool blank space.

Then ConRad's silhouette moved. His head connected with Syon's, making a terrible thumping sound like two watermelons thrown together at high speed. Syon crumpled, so did ConRad. I raced to the tent, using my rock to tear an opening in the heavy-duty cloth.

Syon lay naked on ConRad, face torqued to one side, blood oozing from a cut on his forehead. ConRad was still, eyes rolled back into his head, fresh blood flowing over his already red-caked face.

The image shattered my mind. Simple, blank, nothing. My thoughts hiccupped and I lost a few precious seconds. One moment I was standing there, the next I was straddling Syon's limp body, and had pinned his head to the side with my hand. My forefinger and thumb splayed, framing the fleshy part of his temple. I raised my stone high above my head. Fire and ice flowed through my veins. My heart pounded so loud, I was sure it could be heard outside my body. My arm shook with pent up energy. So easy. Just one downward motion. Just. One. Blow.

My hissed breath blew wet through clenched teeth.

He'd tortured me. Beat me and cut me with his knife. Watched me sweat and bleed. Laughed, as I trembled with fear at his touch. Almost killed my husband, and then . . . almost did more. No. He deserved to die. I could do this. I was stronger now, no longer the weak, pampered girl. I would extract justice for both of us.

Vengeance is mine.

I am a killer.

And damn it felt good.

I raised my hand higher, fought to still the shaking. My eyes targeted on the pulsing blue of a vein covered by the thin membrane of skin.

I smiled.

And swung.

CHAPTER THIRTY

A swift upper cut connected to the soft underside of my solar plexus. Air whooshed from my lungs. I doubled over in pain as Syon took hold of my shoulders and threw me over, head first. I rolled, but didn't come up in time to prevent him from launching himself at me. Our roles were reversed, him on top now, knees pinning my arms, his flaccid junk splayed between my breasts.

For an old man, his strength was deceptive. His arms were sinewy with muscle, legs corded and hard. His long hair straggled past his shoulders and the ends brushed at my neck.

"I knew you'd come. He said you wouldn't. But you did," Syon said. It was hard to make out his features in the dim light, but I knew he was smiling.

I strained against his powerful thighs and tried to kick my legs high enough to reach his head with my booted feet. He was quick with the back of his hand, a powerful blow across my cheek. Not enough to break bone, but enough to remind me of who was in charge.

Pain painted my vision red. My head snapped to one side.

I bit my lip and tasted blood. I stilled myself, lay limp. His ragged breathing was loud in the quiet of the camp. I felt his pulse as it rushed through the arteries in his inner thighs.

I knew how this would play out. Been here before. There were no more blank spaces. But fear is a funny thing. Because inside fear were kernels of something else—power.

Pain didn't scare me, not anymore. I'd been schooled in agony.

I harvested the terror and pushed it through my veins, intoxicating me with its power.

My breathing slowed and I relaxed my fisted hands. My senses heightened to an almost supernatural acuity as my eyes adjusted to the dimness. I could see the woven fabric of the tent's material, distinguish three different breathing patterns in the silence, feel the slow warm drop of Syon's blood as it rolled off his face and landed in the hollow of my throat.

I straightened my head and smiled at him from behind hooded eyes. I licked my lips, as if preparing for a delicious meal. And with a deep growl that vibrated in my belly, I raised my head and sunk my teeth into the fleshy part of his thigh.

An animal screech sounded. Blows rained down on the back of my skull. Iron warmth filled my mouth, but I held on.

A well-placed punch to my jaw had me rolling to protect my face, but I wasted no time. I sprung to my feet, spit on the ground, and faced him. I was a wild thing, animalistic in my ferocity. I'd fight him to the death.

Today . . . today was a good day to die.

We circled each other like wild dogs. All that was missing was the yapping.

He bared his teeth. I laughed in his face. "Oh yeah, old

man. It's you and me. You've got no whips and chains to make you powerful. It's all about who can take the most pain, and I've had the best teacher."

Something darkened his eyes and it wasn't triumph. I smelled fear. Yeah, I was that crazy.

He went for a quick jab to my face. I blocked, but he got a punch to my ribs. I hissed and came back with a smile.

He came after me and then we were locked in a battle of strength. My hands wrapped around his wrists as they loomed over me. My arms shook, every muscle straining to keep him at a distance. We were close, caught in a deadly dance, his bare feet inches from mine. My back slowly began to bend to his superior strength, pushing me to where he wanted me, on my knees. In a desperate move, my steel-toed boot crashed hard on his instep. A small pop. A low cry. His body bent forward, my fingers threaded through his hair, my knee swift to connect with his face.

Syon crumpled to the ground like a lifeless doll.

I stood gasping, shoulders hunched, arms limp in victory. My body was drunk on blood and hate. I shook. I was power. *End him NOW.*

In the distance, someone shouted. A light flared through the thin fabric at the entrance of the tent. My vision cleared. ConRad. My God, what was I doing?

I dropped to my knees beside ConRad and pushed the hair off his face. With a clinical eye I surveyed the damage. Hands tied behind his back, one arm bent at an odd angle. Chest smeared with blood and raised welts. His face was smashed in, the facial bones crushed beyond repair.

But his legs weren't broken and that meant that he could walk.

And God knew we needed to run like hell.

I raised one of his eyelids. The white of his eye was shot with red, his pupil was heavy and rolled back into his head. "Move solider! Up on your feet."

Nothing. I slapped the good side of his face.

More lanterns were lit. The camp was now engulfed with light. Through the ripped back of the tent, the dark shadows beckoned. Panic pumped through my body as Syon groaned, coming back to consciousness.

"Elder Syon, do you need assistance? Is everything alright?" A man called from the front of the tent.

We were out of time. I placed the heel of my palm on the indented part of ConRad's rib cage and pushed.

"Get UP!" I hissed in his ear.

He moaned and rolled his head. I stood and kicked his booted feet. "On your feet. Move!"

"Elder Syon, I request an answer immediately." I could hear him scratching at the door, as he fumbled for the inside tie.

I took hold of ConRad's broken arm . . . and pulled.

ConRad screamed, but he was on his feet. I pushed back the ripped tent fabric and pulled him into a run, hell bent for the thick darkness of the forest. He stumbled once. I twisted his arm. He moaned, but pushed up into a run.

I looked to the sky and prayed for the delay of dawn. We'd have a better chance in the dark. Fickle divine intervention seemed to sway in our favor because ominous black clouds descended with a vengeance, blocking the stars and slowing the onset of daybreak.

It had to be enough.

CHAPTER THIRTY-ONE

"Come on," I panted, as ConRad fell for the umpteenth time. I had no idea where we were going, just knew we needed distance. We'd never make it back to the Sanctuary, and even if we did, they'd never take him in. Offering ConRad protection would bring the wrath of thousands upon their head. The Elders would declare an all-out war.

I stumbled to the ground, taking ConRad with me—and stayed. Despair weighed heavy on me like my veins pumped lead instead of blood. The adrenaline rush had ended. I knew the physical responses. Shaky limbs, chills, a queasy stomach, and foggy thinking. My body was simply replacing the epinephrine hormone with norepinephrine, helping my system establish a balance from the survival response of fight or flight to normal functions. Except, I'd never be normal again.

We couldn't go any further. This had to be far enough—safe enough. I hoped.

I scooted my back against a tree trunk and gently laid ConRad's head on my lap. He hadn't said a word during our clumsy journey, just hissed and groaned at each fall and rise up. Absently, I stroked his head and listened to his labored breathing slow, and then turn into the rhythmic sound of sleep. Asleep or unconscious—regardless, it was a blessing.

Every urge screamed to flee, but I'd pushed ConRad as far as I could and besides, I had nowhere to go. I was lost. If there was a plan for me, then God had better show me because I'd run completely out of ideas.

My fingers played with the crusted hair along ConRad's gashed scalp. With a skilled ear I listened for any change in his breathing. It'd slowed, but not in a good way. And if I blocked out all other sounds, I could hear a wet sucking sound with each inhale. He had fluid in his lungs, an almost sure sign of internal injuries.

My tears wetted ConRad's hair, my harsh sobs loud in the muted sounds of the forest. I wiped my nose on my shirt and took in the scent of sweat, rotting leaves, and blood. Why was I here? What was the reason for my coming? To watch my loved ones die? To be helpless and lost? I didn't know what was worse, watching him die or knowing that if I was in a hospital I could've attempted to save his life. I bent my head over ConRad's and rested my cheek on his chest, finding comfort in the continued beat of his heart.

The sound of rustling leaves woke me. My eyes opened to the lightening gray of predawn. My neck screamed in protest as I shifted from the odd angle I'd slept in. The crashing sound was getting louder. Someone was coming and not caring if they were heard.

I froze like a rabbit caught in the crosshairs of a rifle.

Should I risk moving us or play possum and pray the quickly disappearing night was enough to cover us?

I glanced at the sky. The clouds had rolled on leaving open stars peeking through the leaves of the trees. I cursed the lack of forethought on my part not to find better cover. I hadn't meant to fall asleep, but now . . . it was too late.

The crunching of footsteps drew closer. The metallic taste of fear sprung up in my mouth—a little too familiar.

"Kris? Kris is that you?"

Quinn. My breath flowed; I could swallow once again. Thank God. "Here, I need help. ConRad's out cold, and I don't think we should move him."

"Let me see," Quinn said. Then a soft click and a small flame appeared. The light grew as it touched a wick attached to a crude lantern. A soft glow encircled us and I glanced up and made out Quinn's slight figure and a taller, sturdier one. From the protective stance as he hovered around Quinn, I could tell it was Zimm.

"How did you find us?" I'd never been so happy to see two people in all my life. Despite myself, hope bloomed in my chest. Quinn kneeled beside us, and then grinned at me. "I have my ways."

Her smile was familiar. I'd seen it before when I'd gone on my "European tour," courtesy of my father. He wanted me to soak up Old World culture. I did a lot of soaking up, but most of it German beer. In a more sober moment I did go visit the *Mona Lisa*, and though smaller than I'd imagined, her smile was mysterious and serene just like Quinn's was.

"What? How?" I asked, but then I remembered Quinn's clouded eyes and shut my mouth. Zimm stepped forward and placed his finger over his closed mouth indicating a need for silence. His brown eyes didn't rest long on my face as they scanned the landscape, wary and alert for danger.

"He looks bad," Quinn whispered. Her gaze accessed Con-Rad's body, taking in the damage. I wasn't sure how well she could see, the lighting was poor, but it didn't stop me from noticing the graying around Quinn's temple. Both Quinn and Zimm had a feral look about them, like they'd made the forest their home for a little too long. I turned my attention back toward ConRad.

"I don't know if he'll make it." My voice hitched as my mind steeled itself for the possibility.

"But he's alive?" she asked, seemingly hesitant for the answer.

I nodded. "For now."

"Let me try." Quinn kneeled at ConRad's side and placed one hand on his forehead and the other over his heart and breathed deep. Her eyes fluttered close and a quiet humming sounded from between pressed lips. I watched as wrinkles receded from her face and her skin glowed with a white light.

I threw a questioning look at Zimm, but he just raised his eyebrows in acknowledgment and placed his finger to his lips, again assuring silence on my part.

I nodded, having no intention of breaking Quinn's concentration. The dim yellow light from the lantern and the more powerful one from Quinn's face revealed the miracle I'd never grow tired of seeing. Bruises faded, a broken arm snapped into place. Ribs cracked into alignment. Open cuts mended, then scabbed and flaked off, revealing pink new skin underneath.

And ConRad's face—my beautiful ConRad's face—popped back out and un-disfigured before my eyes.

Twenty minutes passed as Quinn worked. Sometimes quietly, sometimes with a low hum. At one point her brow furrowed and sweat formed along her upper lip. Zimm came from behind and placed his hands on her shoulders as if giving her strength. The gesture seemed to help, calming her almost immediately.

Soon Quinn released ConRad's head and scooted back. Her healing had worked, and now ConRad seemed to be sleeping peacefully instead of unconscious.

I stared at Quinn in amazement. "You're a healer?"

"My powers have grown." The *Mona Lisa* look was back, albeit more tired.

"How?"

"With lots of great sex," Zimm answered. I could hear the smugness in his voice even in the dim lighting.

My mouth dropped. He couldn't be serious. I shot Quinn a questioning glance.

"I prefer to call it making love, but I'm not discounting the benefits." She smiled and raised her eyebrows.

I laughed, feeling lighter than I had in days. "Are you saying that great sex has made you more powerful? Actually evoked your healing ability?"

"That's what I attribute it to. I'm stronger after physical contact from Zimmion. I can feel his strength and tap into it when healing."

Well, if that isn't a case against "sensory deprivation," I didn't know what is. "Regardless, you need to rest." I said, remembering the old lady's weakened state after she had treated Zimm.

Quinn shook her head. "I'm good. He did have some internal injuries." Her gaze flowed over ConRad's still form. "You were right. He wouldn't have made it."

Tears welled in my eyes. "Thank you."

This time a real smile broke across her face, and for a blinding second I could see exactly why Zimm risked his life to be with her. "Just helping The Prophesy out."

I sighed. It all came back to The Prophesy. What had Quinn said back at the compound? Something about dragging the evil ones into the light and they would seek to kill her. Her or me? I thought of the murderous look on Syon's face. Yeah, that part was true. But there was more. *A mighty warrior will be called upon to save her, and he will become an outlaw to her rescue.* I stroked a stray hair off of ConRad's forehead. He could definitely be classified as a warrior, and now my heart hurt at the realization, an outlaw. *And a final sign will be given to all of you, so that you may know she is The One. A miraculous birth will be bestowed upon her. This sign will be hers and hers alone so that all may know she is The Chosen One.* I placed my hand protectively on my stomach. I took solace in the fact that The Prophesy spoke of an actual birth, because the last part sent chilled apprehension through my blood. *By means of her own body, she will save the world.*

There was more at work here than just me. And regardless if I felt up to fulfilling The Prophesy or not, it was time to finish the damn thing once and for all.

Zimm sat down with his back to the tree and grabbed

Quinn, snuggling her in his lap. "We should rest. We'll stay here till full morning, then leave."

I nodded, not really caring where we were going. I was just glad for the possibility of another day with ConRad, because, as much as I closed my eyes to it, something told me my days with him were numbered.

Small kisses to my neck woke me from a fitful sleep. I'd lain down next to ConRad before drifting off, determined to steal some of his body heat. He must've rolled over since his arm and leg were protectively thrown over my shoulder and hip. Something hard and solid nudged me from behind and began a slow sensual grind against my rear.

Oh, he had to be delusional.

My eyes were gritty from lack of sleep; dirt grew as an additional layer next to my skin and my latest bath seemed so long ago I think I'd become immune to my own body odor. And he really was poking my behind with intentions of doing it here, no more than two feet away from Quinn and Zimm. Typical male.

I turned to give him a small piece of my mind, but lost my momentum when I took in his dazzling blue eyes. A silly grin split my face. He was alive. In the deep of the night I'd thought I'd lost him and then to see him in the morning, looking at me like I was the best thing that ever happened to him, made my heart skip.

"Hi," he said, as he bent and kissed the tip of my nose.

"Hi back," I said, blinking my eyes, trying to clear my sudden watery vision.

"What happened?" he asked, stretching his arm overhead, testing the feel of his ribs.

I told ConRad the events that happened after he'd passed out and how we were found by our new traveling companions.

ConRad took the knowledge of Quinn's new healing abilities in stride. He did mumble something along the lines of "about time," but his welcome to Zimm was decidedly cooler. He actually growled in his direction. "Why's he here?"

I stood as ConRad did and brushed the dried leaves from my backside. Quinn overheard—it was hard not to—and shot me a pleading glance to pacify ConRad. I rolled my eyes and held up my hand for patience. I knew the practice of sensory deprivation, so ingrained in this culture, would be hard to overcome, but we needed to get to safety before debating the issue.

"ConRad, please, they saved your life. Let's go and we can discuss this later," I said, tugging on his arm.

"*Quinn* saved my life. All he is—is a distraction." ConRad stood and took a menacing step toward Zimm, and at the same time scowled at Quinn. "He put your life in danger by showing no regard for the laws that kept you safe. Now, because of him, you are hunted just like the rest of us."

"He loves me, and we're getting married." Quinn shot back in the same defensive stance.

"Over my dead body! No goddess and soldier of mine are going to marry. With healing powers you have an obligation to society to focus, and you can't do that by playing house on the run."

Zimm stepped forward, teeth clenched, ready to charge.

Quinn threw an arm across Zimm's chest, telling him to back off. This was her fight—she'd handle ConRad.

"Well, I wished you'd have mentioned the death wish before, I could've arranged that last night." Quinn's voice rose with each passing word.

"Don't push me, Quinn, because I'm still your guardian. I'll drop you off at the Sanctuary so fast you'll think time stood still," he growled. ConRad and Quinn stood nose to nose, neither one ready to back down. Both of them mirroring each other, arms crossed, teeth bared.

"Enough," I broke between the two. "We can discuss this at a later time when we're safe, and when I'm sure the Elders aren't chasing us. Zimm, lead the way. And ConRad, since you seem to be fit enough—carry the bags." I lifted Quinn's and Zimm's bag and threw it at him. "March."

Quinn had stormed off, and Zimm followed. When there was enough distance between us, I turned to ConRad. "What was that all about? They've both risked their lives to save you."

Zimm had given him an extra shirt, a size too small and he pulled on the collar, irritated. "They'll never be accepted. They'll be ostracized and hunted by the Elders. Any offspring of theirs will be tainted. Nothing good can come from their spitting in the face of convention."

My heart broke for Quinn. "But things are changing. And you've broken with convention also. You would've never been allowed to marry, and yet we did."

"Not legally," he said, shooting me a glance. "You're the wife of my heart, but no laws bind us. I might've broken the

Elders' laws, but not religious taboos. Plus, neither one of us is a healer. We are not depriving anyone of our abilities."

"Yes, but neither is she. They're stronger together, and she even attributes her new powers to Zimm."

"You'll be hard pressed to make society believe that."

I sighed. This was not the conversation I wanted to have. Quinn would have to fight her own battles. God knows, she let me fight mine. There was other more pressing information I wanted to know. "How did the Elders catch up with you?"

ConRad sighed and rubbed the base of his neck with his hand. "That's another reason I'm upset with Zimm. Originally there'd only been five horses, one for each person. But a few days after we left you, Zimm—reckless idiot—wasn't paying attention and his horse stumbled and went lame. We had to put her down, which meant Quinn and Zimm were riding double. Syon had us on the run. Damn bloodhound didn't let up for a minute, having fresher horses and better supplies. I should've followed my instincts and gone off on my own. I would've found him and killed the bastard already. Instead, I'm running. Again."

I hadn't told ConRad about my own failed attempt at murder. If he knew, it would be one more reason for him to lock me safely up in the Sanctuary. And Lord knows he didn't need another. My hand fluttered over my belly. This child would be my one-way ticket to nine months of confinement. I couldn't bear being separated from ConRad. And child or not, The Prophesy would never be fulfilled with me tucked away somewhere safe.

"What happened?" I needed to hear the rest.

ConRad adjusted the pack to his opposite shoulder. He

shrugged his shoulders as if easing stiff muscles. His movements were subtle, but I knew him. ConRad was tense.

"It was early in the morning and we were exhausted. The night before we believed we'd covered our tracks enough so we could rest till dawn, but they found us. In the end there was no choice . . . I knew who they were after. I gave my horse to Zimm and led the Elders away from the group on foot. I was able to avoid capture for three days, but the lack of food and sleep took its toll. I was finally caught."

I'd thought he'd end the story there with his face an impassive mask, and his body closed off from all emotion. But he took a breath and pushed through as if the words were poison and he had to expel the venom.

"When they caught me, Syon had his men tie my hands behind my back. Then . . . Syon forced me at gunpoint to walk with him alone into the forest." ConRad stopped talking and, for a long moment, we walked in silence. He wouldn't look at me, but stared straight ahead putting an emotional distance between us with each step.

I wanted to reach out and touch him, tell him it was okay, but the barrier between us was too thick. "It doesn't matter. Whatever you had to do to survive, I understand. I'd never think less of you because of it."

He pierced me with the blue of his eyes. "You think I'd *let* him? You think this was about me? Some things *are* worse than death, Kris. He knows that and it sickens me. And yet you think I wouldn't take a little pain to prevent *that*? Do you even know me at all?" He looked at me with disgust and my gut tightened with shame.

"He didn't just want to rape me. If he did, he could've done so at any time. He wants me willing. That's his game. And he knows that the only way he'd get that from me is through you. But the link between us works both ways, and I knew what he'd do. So that's why I had you promise to never leave the Sanctuary."

My heart broke at his words. I'd almost betrayed him. Almost betrayed him by giving Syon the means to break him, bend him to his will.

ConRad stopped walking and stared out into the horizon. He swallowed hard and dragged a ragged breath deep into his lungs as if to steel himself with courage. "I had to make you promise, because, Kris, everyone has their limits. And—God please forgive me—but mine . . . is you."

Chapter Thirty-Two

By mid-afternoon we'd made it to a ragtag camp, thrown together with battered tents and scanty lean-tos. Clothes were hung on branches and the smell of cooked squirrel and unwashed bodies ripened the air. I was surprised. When I'd last left the group, Red and Tank were the only soldiers, now over forty men milled about. Some of the men I knew from the compound; others had the look of being farmers. As ConRad and I walked into the camp, men still loyal to their Commander in Chief stood in respect. ConRad was greeted with salutes and pats on the back, and even I received a hug from Red, which had ConRad arching his brow.

ConRad and Zimm left quickly after they showed us to our new camp to meet with some of the higher-ranked men. Quinn led me toward a fallen log that was used as a seat around a low campfire. We watched as our lunch sizzled in a flat iron pan and passed a canteen of water back and forth, content to observe the other soldiers work. The camp hummed with repressed energy. Guns were cleaned, knives sharpened, and weary guards patrolled the perimeter, their fingers never far from the triggers.

"Where did all these men come from?" I plucked at the collar of my damp shirt and blew down the opening to cool my skin. The afternoon was hot and the clearing provided little shade.

"All over," Quinn said, in her typical non-forthcoming manner. She sat beside me, legs out stretched and crossed at the ankles, hair tucked behind her ears. For wearing such a male getup, military uniform and black combat boots, she looked decidedly feminine.

I threw her my famous deadpan look, which spoke multitudes about my lack of patience.

"Sorry," she said, with a sheepish grin. "I communicate with Zimm simply by thinking the conversation in my mind. I forget with others I need to talk. Some have left their farms, others their posts—the word's spreading."

"And exactly what word is that?" Pulling information from Quinn was an exercise in persistence.

"Kris." She shook her head in disbelief. "Look around you. This . . . is the Rebellion."

The words made me edgy. Her tone was light and awe inspiring, as if she were witnessing a thing of beauty.

And she will incite a nation to rebel. The word *Rebellion* made me uneasy. The term was a synonym for death. "Why?" I asked, not sure if I wanted the answer.

"Look," she said, pointing to an older man, his shirt taut against the swell of his belly, his face already reddened from the sun. He seemed awkward with his weapon as he adjusted the strap numerous times, trying to find a good fit. A less likely warrior would be harder to fine. I wondered why he'd leave his life of comfort to live as an outlaw.

"That's Ana's husband," Quinn said, reading my thoughts again. "Word spread of the Elders' corruption and the torture that is going on in the prison. People are sick of being under the Elders' heavy yoke, tired of their daughters being sold to the highest bidder. And . . . ," her words trailed off as she cleared her throat, "there's suspicion around the number of stillborn female babies."

Stillborn female babies. I remembered the deadened look in Ana's sunken eyes after she came back from the so-called birthing room. As per the custom, she'd been alone with the special sect of Elders. And now with Quinn's implication . . . the thought was too monstrous to comprehend. "You don't think?"

Quinn shrugged. "I don't *know*. Not for sure anyways. The Prophesy is fulfilled by a woman. What better way to keep it from happening than to prevent the child from ever living?"

I gasped and wrapped my arms around my middle. I barely had time to acknowledge the life growing inside me, but a deep primal instinct to protect had already roared awake.

Quinn's sad eyes found mine, and she patted my knee with her sun-spotted hand. "That's only my theory. Most people, if they have any suspicions at all, think it's a way for the Elders to keep control over society. What better way to keep men under control than by doling out females to only the obedient?"

I looked around at the camp. "It must be more than just a suspicion for all these men to become outlaws."

Quinn nodded. "There is no more noble cause than safe-guarding our children, fighting for the chance at a better life.

The men heard of you and your band of rebels. Many came to pledge their loyalty."

My heart quickened at the thought. *My band of rebels?*

"They thought the sacrifice was worth it," Quinn said, her voice solemn, the rounding of her shoulders no longer casual. Her blue eyes found mine. "Kris, we all have sacrifices to make."

I came to my feet. "What exactly are you saying, Quinn? I've made sacrifices. I've given plenty for a cause I wasn't even sure existed." How *dare* she? Quinn had no right to ask any more from me, and I was about to tell her where she could stick her damn Prophesy.

Then her irises darkened, and blackness invaded the white sclera like a poison. Her eyes clouded over and, I couldn't help it, my body tensed in response.

Her breathing slowed, barely discernable to the untrained eye. Her gaze fixed in the distance, the black of her eyes disturbingly gruesome against the white of her skin.

"You need to go back," Quinn said, her voice monotone, almost trance like.

"Back?" I didn't need to ask to where. The walls of my defenses locked into place, fortified with the steel of my spine. "I'm not going anywhere."

Prophesy be damned. I made my own decisions.

Quinn's eyes bled quickly back to simple blue. She shook her head while pink returned to her pale face. She turned away and stared out over the milling crowd a small distance away. "You won't come unless you go back."

I knew what she meant. The night before I came forward in time I was visited by me, but an edgier, harder, older me. I knew that my transformation had taken place. I was her now, gone forever was the young, pampered intern I'd once been.

"No," I shook my head, "this is the cycle where I get it right. And by the look of your face, it seems like it couldn't be quick enough."

Quinn when I'd first met her was a young girl. Now, her age had fast-forwarded to old. Her hair was gray and the lines around her eyes had deepened.

My heart ached as I watched Quinn self-consciously smooth the wrinkles in her forehead. "I hoped. I really did, but if this was the end, then I wouldn't still be getting older. I'm not sure if I'd go back to being a young woman or not, but the rapid aging should stop. This isn't it. You need to go back and try again. Your daughter needs to live."

Her words had me restraining myself from wrapping my hands around her throat and squeezing. How did she know I would have a girl? But I didn't waste my question on what was now such a mundane issue. "Tell me everything you know about my daughter," I asked, not willing to allow Quinn to play her cryptic card.

Quinn's eyes saddened. "I had a vision. I'm so sorry, Kris."

Emphatically, I shook my head. "I don't believe you. You've lied before."

She sighed. "Please, let me show you."

I wanted to say no. Whatever she saw, she could bloody hell keep to herself, but I'd put naïveté away for good. I swallowed hard and nodded. Quinn reached out her hand and grasped my wrist in a vise-like grip. Her eyes fluttered closed as she began to hum.

Something slow and hot leached into my skin from our point of contact. Seconds passed and the heat grew until my muscles tightened in resistance. In my mind's eye I saw black fill my veins like boiling tar creeping steadily toward my heart.

I gasped and used my other hand to clamp down on my upper arm, trying to prevent the spread. But the blackness wound itself forward, and inflamed my shoulder. I cried out as my knees buckled.

"Quinn?" I whimpered through clenched teeth. Lines of fire traveled across my clavicle, encircling the bone like a serpent, making my neck twitch in pain. I tried pulling from her grasp, but she held tight with a deathlike grip. My breath came hard and fast; lungs blazed. Quinn hummed louder and seemed to push. In one heartbeat the black flames engulfed my heart and burst through my whole body.

My vision erupted in crimson colors against the darkest sky. My eyes, open and wide, saw nothing of the camp full of men, but only what Quinn forced upon me.

It was night, but almost as light as full day. Fire ignited all around. The world burned. Trees exploded like bombs in the distance, carcasses of both man and beast littered the red-soaked ground.

ConRad's body lay beside me. His head torqued at an odd angle and limbs twisted in a horrifying way. I wanted to go to him, but couldn't. Two robed men pinned me down, one at each arm, while a third cut my shirt, exposing the huge swell of my pregnant belly.

I screamed, but I couldn't be heard above the roar of the fire. A knife rose high and gleamed in the red light. The blade, poised in eternity, hovered with the tip aimed at my heart—then moved lower. With the precision of a surgeon, the blade pierced my womb and sliced in a downward motion.

I screamed as my flesh parted with sickly ease. Then loud sucking sounds as the fetus was ripped from me. With detached clarity, I witnessed the murder of my baby—saw the umbilical cord savagely cut, saw the wrinkled, wet body as my daughter was held high above my face.

She made no sound, no cries, didn't even open her eyes. My daughter's blue body was dead, before she even took her first breath. A grief, greater than any I had known, raged through my body. My heart crushed under the weight and with divine mercy, gave out.

The pain grew smaller and my vision clouded, folding in on itself. But there was one thing, one thought I needed to take with me, to stow down in my heart and never let go. I struggled to take my last inhale and strained my eyes to focus on the man who held my daughter and murdered my family.

Pale face, blood-red lips, Devil-black eyes—Syon.

I came to, screaming and sobbing on the ground, rocking myself in a fetal position. ConRad loomed above me, lips moving frantically, trying to get my attention. Then, as if a switch flipped, my hearing came back and his words filled my head.

"Kris! What's wrong? Wake up! Damn it, answer me!" His hands were clamped around my shoulders shaking me. "What's wrong with her? Quinn, what the hell did you do to her?"

There was no more breath left to scream. I launched myself into ConRad's arms and sobbed into the crease of his neck.

He stroked the back of my head and murmured in my ear. "Shh baby, it's okay. Tell me what I can do. How do I make it better?"

Shaken didn't begin to touch what I felt. The vision was so real I still felt the burn across my belly, the pain of losing my husband, the devastating emptiness of a world without my daughter in it. "I need to go back. I'll never be safe here."

I felt his body stiffen. His breath shuddered, and he shook his head, but my mind was set. The vow I had made to ConRad as we knelt before each other on our wedding night tasted bitter in my mouth. *Only truth between us, Kris. Forever.*

My mother's words came back to haunt me—tell the truth, baby girl, and shame the Devil.

"You can come with me. We'll go together, be a family in my time." My hand fluttered up to cover my face that burned with regret.

Or not.

Of all the sins I committed, I knew this one was unforgivable. May God save me because ConRad never would again.

Chapter Thirty-Three

The ground was red and cracked from the heat and the thin air, but still heavy with humidity. Sweat ran like a river stinging my eyes and tasting of salt as it ran into my mouth. It was so much harder to breathe on Dark Planet than it was back on Earth. I dropped to my knees, unable to go any further, even if my life depended on it. And it did—mine and everyone I loved.

ConRad collapsed to his knees beside me, panting in the paltry atmosphere. He let his heavy pack and gun fall to the ground beside him. We had timed our return to Dark Planet in accordance with the planet's rotations. Every forty-eight hours there was a graying hour, when the planet's moons came together and glowed enough to give off a dim glare similar to dusk on Earth.

I tried to breathe through the stitch in my side, then gave up. I shot a glance at ConRad to see how he fared. The vision stilled my heart. His eyes brilliant blue spheres of color in his tanned, rugged face. Green army fatigues wet and dirty, bare chest peeking through an opened flack vest. Sweat poured down his face and neck, covered in a week's worth of stubble, making him look like a Greek god just emerging from the sea.

Determined, I etched the picture of him in my mind—my beautiful warrior.

Sweet lord, he was gorgeous. And MINE. But not for long.

"We don't have a lot of time," he said, voice calm and sure under pressure.

God, how could he even talk? I was beyond even swallowing.

His hand reached out and stroked my cheek. His eyes searched mine. The tenderness warmed the blue, softening him.

This was the first time we dared to stop since our mad dash across space and air. I told ConRad that Quinn had a vision of us traveling through time, back to the past to prevent the invasion of the aliens. I told him we'd be safe. I told him we'd both go through.

I lied.

But my lies worked like magic. Within a week we were ready, armed with a plan to pay off the guards at the portal and enough fire power to blow ten aliens to kingdom come. But something I hadn't counted on went wrong—the Elders had been tipped off and an army of men loyal to the Way were after us.

When I had destroyed the passage from the compound to outside by throwing the grenade to stop the alien invasion, I thought I'd collapsed the only tunnel to the outside. But ConRad had taken me the back way. Apparently the small crawl space behind the three pools was a little-known tunnel, barely big enough to walk through, which led to the outside.

But the Elders had dogs. And we hadn't had the time to cover our scent.

ConRad's fingers trailed across my lips and outlined the fullness of the bottom one. Tears welled up in my eyes despite the promise to myself not to cry until later—later I'd have plenty of time alone to weep my heart out. My stomach churned with a familiar sickness. I couldn't believe I was going to go through with this.

"We're going to make it," he said, misreading my face.

Nodding quickly, breaking eye contact. I couldn't afford for him to see too much. I pushed myself to my feet. "We'd better keep moving. They're not far behind."

We started off at a much slower pace, neither one of us able to maintain a run anymore. We traversed the rough landscape of shadowed holes and hidden obstacles much easier with the faint light of the twin moons. I was so caught up in trying to determine the landmarks of our previous desperate flight that we almost fell into the hole I had originally time traveled through. ConRad's booted toes hovered over the edge as he lit his florescent light stick and peered in.

The hole was no bigger than a small swimming pool—and I was surprised to notice—only a few feet taller than ConRad, but in my mind I'd imagined such vastness. Terror had a way of playing with one's perceptions.

"Are you ready?" He looked worried, his unease stemming from the unknown.

God, how I wished for the bliss of ignorance.

"Whatever we are going to face, we will face together," he said, reaching over and squeezing my hand.

I nodded. I couldn't speak, couldn't help the tears that leaked from my eyes. I clamped my jaw shut to keep the sobs, piling up within me, from spilling out.

And then we jumped hand-in-hand . . . fell . . . and landed at the bottom of the hole.

"What happened? I didn't feel anything," ConRad said, as he looked around at the now familiar lava and rocky landscape. "This is the right place, the same place that you originally came through from?"

I nodded and wiped at my face with my free hand.

"Why didn't it work?" ConRad asked. Confused, he glanced at me for answers. The tears turned into streams and dripped off my face. Shame ate at me like an acid as I cowardly turned away.

"What aren't you telling me?" His voice cut with razor sharpness.

I shook my head, how could I speak when my whole life was ending? He dropped his weapon and grabbed my shoulders with both hands.

"What the hell aren't you telling me?" He began to shake me, his frustration tightening his grasp on my arms. "Answer me, dammit! Answer me!"

I'd seen ConRad in life-or-death situations before, but I never heard his voice seared with such panic.

"*We* can't go." My voice broke.

His face was a mask of confusion trying to absorb what I told him, but not wanting to hear it. "What are you saying?" he whispered.

"*We* can't go . . . just me."

"No," he yelled. "I won't do it. That's not what we planned. I won't allow it."

"ConRad, please. You have to listen to me. This is the only way." I swallowed hard. "This is the only way The Prophesy can be fulfilled."

"Hell no, if you think I am going to let you travel through

space and time, to hopefully the right place, but who the hell really knows, by yourself. Think again. It's not happening."

"ConRad, please, please listen. We don't have much time." I begged, I'd given up pride long ago. I couldn't leave him like this, not this way. "You can't come with me. *It* won't allow you to."

"Then we'll fight. I have enough ammo. I'll hold them off and you can run . . ."

My finger came gently to his lips cutting off his words. "No, my love, that's not how this will end."

"End? My God, you knew this all along. You knew what you were going to do the whole time, didn't you?" He flung my arm off and pushed away. "You lied to me . . . again! After all that we've been through, our vow, you lied to me anyway."

His words pierced my soul. I was amazed I could still stand—still give the appearance of being whole. "You have to understand there was no other way."

"No."

"Do you think for a second you'd let me get this far if you didn't think you could come with me? Come and protect me?"

"Then let me protect you now." His fists clenched at his sides. "You don't have to go."   His back was to the wall literally and figuratively. He would plead with the Devil himself to keep me with him.

I knew this would be hard. I knew I needed to believe in The Prophesy enough for both of us. But was it enough? Was I willing to give up ConRad's and my happiness based on a mere vision? Was I really a bloody martyr?

I wrapped my arms around my middle and squeezed. If I held on tight enough, maybe I could keep myself from exploding. "If I thought in the heart of selfish hearts that I could have it all, I would. But you and I both know you'd never let them take me if there was breath left in your body. And I know I can't watch you die. You can still make it back to the compound if you're by yourself."

"That's my decision, not yours."

"No." Calm settled in my voice. My palm cradled my stomach. I had to do this. The decision was the right one. "This is my choice. You have no control over this. I am so sorry."

ConRad turned and slammed his hand into the packed earth. Dust and rocks fell. A moment passed, then he placed his forehead against the impassive rock.

Silence settled around us. The barking of dogs whispered in the distance, the euphoric braying of hounds on the hunt.

ConRad didn't seem to notice. "This can't be happening."

A sliver of panic sliced through my despair. My sacrifice would be too great if I knew that ConRad wasn't safe.

"ConRad, you need to leave. You can still make it. You'll be faster without me. I have to go back to my time and send myself forward. I'll get it right this time." But even as I said the words I doubted the truth of them. How many more times did I have? I knew my time was running out.

He didn't move. Neither one of us did.

"You're The One, aren't you?" He looked up to the sky and shook his head, as if saying that the gods were cruel and unjust. "You've been The One. This whole time I fell in love, this impossible love. A love that went against all laws of God and nature, because I fell in love with The One."

He turned around and finally let me see him. Tears rolled down his cheeks, his face a portrait of anguish and despair . . .

hopelessness dulled his eyes. "No matter what I say or what I do, you have to go back. Neither of us is in control. It was destined that I would love you before I even found you."

My shoulders shook with the effort of holding myself erect. My sniffles were quiet against the increasing backdrop of howling dogs.

He pulled me into his arms, then shifted and cradled my face between his palms. His lips caught the rain of tears streaming down my cheeks and soothed them away. He whispered reverent, prayerful things against my cheek. I strained to hear his words, wanting his voice to be the last thing I heard before I left. "You're The One. You can change all this, make all of this go away. You have the power to change the past, to save mankind."

I shook my head. That wasn't true. I wanted to tell him that was part of the lie, but I couldn't find my voice.

Then he smiled. That devastating smile that would make some other woman go weak in the knees. Another woman, because I wouldn't be here with him.

I sucked in a ragged breath. "I don't want to be The One. I just want to stay here, love you, and have your babies. Be your wife."

He groaned, then kissed me like we'd never kissed before. His mouth was hungry, devouring the very essence of me. I poured myself into his embrace, wanting to physically imprint myself on his body, become a fundamental part of his DNA so he'd never forget me. ConRad slammed my body against the dirt wall and hooked my legs over his hips.

I went wild.

My hands reached under his shirt and clawed his back. He

groaned and retaliated by ripping my shirt down the front, pushing the sports bra up, and sucking on my nipples so hard that I screamed.

I wanted more.

His hand shot down my pants and his finger entered me with no warning, no foreplay. The invasion made me wet with two thrusts, my inner muscles clenched, drawing him deeper. Pleasure shot through my quivering thighs and out my toes. My feet briefly touched the ground as his hands came around my waist and ripped my pants off, throwing them to the side. He forced me back against the rough stone and lifted. My skin scraped against the rock, but I didn't care. The pain didn't touch the burning centered between my thighs.

I fumbled with his pants button. He helped by pushing the offending clothing away. My hand closed around him—rock hard and throbbing. I led him to my core and in one thrust he buried himself to the hilt. Fast and quick we rocked. I couldn't hold back and exploded in his arms. I screamed as he whispered, "I love you."

Aftershocks still rocked my body as he left me on shaky legs and then shoved my pants to me.

Dogs howled, men shouted.

He held my face once more, his gaze boring into mine. "I am so blessed to have loved you. I'm a better man because of you. You are my redemption. You are The One."

Then he lifted himself out of the hole and was gone.

And then the ground opened and I fell into the black hole of space.

Chapter Thirty-Four

Cold. Bone aching cold. Weird since the oven-baked earth was pressed hard against my face. Then the pain came, hard and fast like a bullet to the brain. Every ligament hurt, stretched, like I'd been sawn asunder, then hurriedly slapped back together. Sucking wind, I tried to rise above the pain. Tried to leave the body that lay on the ground, with clothes wadded tightly against its chest, ripped shirt, underwear lost in some vast darkness of time and space.

There was no oblivion. I knew exactly where I was. Back on the mountain preserve in Scottsdale, back in the past, back before I knew about The Prophesy. Before I loved ConRad.

ConRad was dead—there was no way he could've survived. He would've taken his own life before letting Syon take him and be tortured.

And I couldn't blame him, even as in the same breath I screamed for him to survive.

I saved my child, but killed my husband.

God, what've I done?

I screamed. Desperate loss weighed on my heart. I couldn't

live without ConRad . . . but I didn't have to. I could fix this. I had to go back. Had to try again. I could reinitiate the cycle. I had the chance to change the past, to do it better this time.

I pushed myself up as the world spun. Wetness tickled my nose. I wiped, surprised at the amount of blood smeared across the back of my hand. I'd no idea at what cost time traveling extracted from my body, but didn't care—last ride, for me anyway. My younger self was fresher, less damaged.

The burden of what I had to do enveloped me in its thick velvet coat of guilt. It was hard to alter a life in such a harsh way, even if that life was my own. A bitter laugh escaped. I never had a clue, never really had a choice. Time for a reality check; life is hard and about to get harder. I'd no idea how many times I could restart the loop, but I needed one more chance to get it right.

I fell twice putting on my pants. My heart raced with the need to hurry. Time, my ever elusive enemy, had me frantically glancing up at the sky. The first time I'd time traveled it was at sun break and I wanted to follow the exact pattern to increase the chances of sending myself back. The current sky showed no signs of the breaking dawn, but I'd no doubt I was in a race.

I increased my speed and stumbled down the mountain path. My house was about two miles from the preserve. Previously, I was driven here by my crazed future-self and had traveled through time, but this time I didn't have the luxury.

On the deserted paved city streets I broke into a jog. I'd never have tempted a run, alone, in the middle of the night before, but I'd been through hell, and this world was not it. Nothing scared me anymore.

I reached my single-story patio home and braced my hands on my knees, catching my breath. The world seemed so much clearer now, newer. It was simple to take in all the small details I'd never bothered with before. The way my potted plant drooped on the step from lack of water, the dirt caked on the ledge of my deco security screen door, and how a person could peer into my kitchen through a gap in the blinds from a certain angle.

Maybe I should water my plant first?

Stupid Kris, do what you've come to do.

I knew what I had to become—scary, tough, no mercy. I was ready to start myself on a new, painful future. I bent over and reached behind the terra-cotta pot, searching by feel, for the spare key.

With a deep breath, I steadied the key with both hands and slipped it into the slot. I hesitated. Instead of turning the key, I plucked the bright orange flyer that was wedged between the jam of the door. I unfolded it as my brain reared at my delay. My heart screamed at my need to go and save ConRad as another, detached part of me, read the advertisement like I'd just come from a morning walk.

On the top of the ad was a logo of a cute cartoon puppy going around and around in circles trying to catch his stubby tail.

Does housework have you chasing your tail?
Let us help. We'll clean up your mess
so you can get on with your life.
Call us for free quotes.

A gear so long out of place slid into its groove. A new neuron synapse found its way, cutting a painful pathway into my soft gray matter.

Oh God. Oh God. Oh God.

No. No, this wasn't the way it was going to go. This was NOT the answer. But the cold reality of the years spanned before me. Me walking the halls alone with a crying newborn, me going to teacher conferences as a single parent, me handing the car keys over for the first time to my daughter, to worry through the long night by myself.

In order to stop the cycle, I'd have to stop igniting the cycle. I couldn't send myself forward. I couldn't change a damn thing. Couldn't save ConRad.

I folded in on myself, knees buckling under the weight of what I'd just realized. Gut-wrenching sobs shook my body. I quelled the sound by stuffing my fist into my mouth.

There are moments when words ceased to describe life. Where time flatlines into nothing. Where only the functions of the nervous system keep your heart beating and your lungs pumping, because, if it was up to you, you'd breathe your last breath just to stop the pain.

I'd no idea how long I sat curled into myself, but a person can cry for only so long—the tears finally run dry. My insides cauterized, scraped raw with only bite-marked knuckles as my permanent souvenirs.

Certain senses slipped under the dark abyss that was my life. The way the desert night spoke of peace with its sound of crickets and muffled roar of traffic. The way the stars dimmed as dawn approached and the comforting setting of only a single moon.

Closing my eyes I inhaled the smell of sage, mesquite, and heat. The scent of Earth. No rotting alien smell, no smell of blood and death. I sighed, as a stubborn tear leaked from behind my closed lids.

The sun rose. Darkening the horizon with shadows first, then painting the surrounding mountains with purples and reds. Warm colors spilled forth like liquid gold from a bucket God had labeled "SUNSHINE" in big block letters.

Then a ripple, like the whole world was superimposed on a still pond and someone tauntingly threw a pebble in just to watch the effect. The atmosphere shimmered, then solidified into reality. If I'd blinked, I'd have missed it. But I hadn't, so I didn't, and therefore I knew. Time had caught up. The continuous skipping of the record had stopped. I'd broken the loop.

It was over.

My mission was never to save ConRad, but to have his baby. And keeping with my choice, my future self caught up with my past self. I knew this like a person knew where their legs and arms were at all times. I knew before I stood. Before I turned the key, pressed the alarm code, and walked to my bedroom. I knew I was alone. There was no one here to send forward.

I flipped on my bedroom light, then the bathroom one and even the one in my closet. I was so sick of the dark. I didn't think I'd ever be comfortable with shadows again. I stood in front of my full-length mirror and peeled my clothes from my body.

The image that reflected back was disturbing on so many levels. Two inches of dark roots from the regrowth of hair, face crusted with blood, and a still board-flat stomach. But it was my eyes that had me worried—cold, hard, calculating. I'd seen eyes like them before, in ConRad's face, and remembered wondering what suffering did a soul have to endure to get such haunting eyes? Now I knew.

Just lose everything that you'd ever cared about.

This time the tears didn't stop for a long time.

Seven and half months later.

I lay in bed and watched my ceiling fan lazily cut through the cool night air. At least I'm not pregnant in the middle of July—yep, there's always a silver lining. Some lining. Being a single mom was so not what I'd planned. I was going to have a daughter who'd never met her father. I shied away from the memory of the ultrasound tech telling me my baby was a little girl. I knew it, of course, but knowing the sex confirmed the vision Quinn had forced into my mind. I thanked the tech and then proceeded to lie on the table and sob until the doctor asked if I needed a sedative.

I stopped the memory from looping again and again in my brain.

No more. No more self-pity.

I relocked the thought tight in the steel box in my mind, then threw another lock on the latch for good measure.

But that was why, once again, I was revisited by my good friend insomnia. There was something else that needed to go into that box, but it kept slipping out.

The Prophesy.

The words ran around and around in my head. When Quinn first spoke them to me, they seemed vaguely famil-iar. At the time life-and-death situations were exploding all around us, but now, after seven months of relative peace, my mind couldn't help but replay every moment.

Had I really heard the words before Quinn mentioned them to me? Or had they become so much a part of me that they always seemed familiar?

Who wrote the words? Who could possibly know the future to such an extent to be able to pen the details? Why was I chosen to have ConRad's child? And for what purpose?

I still didn't have any answers. When I'd first come back, I tried to derail any type of new advancement toward satellites. Stop the contact between us and any alien race. Stop Armageddon.

But I was no scientist and had zero connection with NASA. I didn't even know if it was the United States that had made first contact with their super satellite. Most likely it was China and China sharing its top-secret information with me was hopeless.

Not that I didn't try. The great World Wide Web was a beautiful thing. After a few weeks I was able to pinpoint some scientists at NASA who were working on satellites. Of course, I didn't get anywhere. After numerous emails I realized I was coming across like a crazy fundamentalist with words like "technology was evil" and "stop all work on satellites because it could trigger the end of the world."

Yeah, it was time I got smarter.

So I set up the premise that I was a student doing my thesis on space technology and the possibility of being able to expand a satellite's reach. I hadn't received a response yet, but my emails weren't being blocked anymore. I took that as a good sign.

I wasn't even sure what I was looking for. I remembered

ConRad talking about atomic power being used to power the satellite and the use of UFCs, whatever the hell that was.

Way out of my league, but at least it gave me key words to look for.

Deciding that sleep was again my elusive partner tonight, I jumped—no, more like rolled—out of bed. On swollen, fat feet, I padded down the hall to my office and switched on the computer. It'd been weeks since I sent the email, but I couldn't help checking daily. Regardless, my new issue of *Science Times* would be sent via electronic delivery. Gone were the days of *In Style* magazine and recorded episodes of the latest reality shows.

The Internet connected and began downloading email messages into my in-box. My heart raced as a message from Dr. Robert Edwich at NASA.gov popped up on my screen. My finger tapped restlessly on the mouse as the damn hourglass symbol mocked my impatience. Finally, the blessed white arrow, I clicked and scanned the note.

Dr. Edwich seemed interested in helping me and wanted me to call him. He gave me his office number and the best hours to contact him. I shot a glance at the clock and did the mental math. NASA headquarters were located in Washington, D.C., and East Coast time worked in my favor. It was early, but maybe I could get ahold of him before his day began.

I dialed the phone and waited an eternity for the interoffice connection to go through. I wasn't sure what I was going to say. It wasn't like I could stop the research, but I had to know how far off the technology was and then maybe. . . .

"Hello, this is Dr. Edwich," he said, picking up on the fourth ring.

"Yes, hi. This is Kristina Davenport. I just received your email and thought I would take a chance and call you right away." My voice sounded steady, but my palm was wet underneath the black receiver.

"Ahh, Dr. Davenport. Yes, hi. I really enjoyed your email, flattered actually, that someone would want to quote me in their thesis. There are so many more experts in the field of space satellite development. Really, I'm just starting my research, haven't done anything yet to put myself on the map."

His nasally voice was annoying, but I decided I could deal.

"Please call me Kristina, and no, not at all, you're exactly what I'm looking for. Someone who has new and fresh ideas." I couldn't tell him that everyone else had written me off as crazy.

"Ah well," he chuckled. "What can I do for you?"

I told him about my interest in satellites and telescopes and asked about the possibilities of expanding their radio range.

"Well, we're always interested in furthering our reach. As of now, the Hubble telescope will be out of commission in few years, possibly sooner. The second-generation telescope will be more powerful, but at this time, with budget cuts, I'm not sure the project will ever get off the ground. Of course, the length of transmission is always a limiting factor, and we don't have the funds to pour money into researching alternative power sources."

I knew all this, of course, but I needed to ask as a segue to my next question. "What about the possibility of using another power source, like nuclear fusion?"

"You're very well informed. We've just started to look into that possibility, but things are in the very early trial stages. I, personally, don't see how it would work. Atomic power is too unstable. For the last fifty years we've tried to use the hydrogen reaction for something other than bombs, but we can't harness the result. Of course, if we ever could control the reaction, theoretically it would deliver ten times more power than what we are using. Mind-boggling, but too risky, especially during the takeoff. Can you imagine the consequence if . . . well, it doesn't matter at this point."

My heart sunk. They were already in the early trial stages. Yet, he made it sound like they were decades away from finding the technology. There was time. I could come up with a plan. Maybe sway public opinion away from spending money on "unrealistic technologies."

"Yes," I said, needing to see where the research was heading. "Of course, takeoff would be dangerous, but tapping into the nuclear fusion of the stars once the satellite was up in space is a possibility."

He laughed. "That is stuff of science fiction, Kristina. You'd be better off peddling your idea to Hollywood, rather than NASA." His tone was decidedly dismissive, and I knew our conversation was limited.

I needed to ask one more question. I needed to see how many years I'd have before the war to end all wars began. "So no plans at this time to use the UFCs?"

It was a shot in the dark. I had no idea what UFCs were, but to ConRad they seemed a viable part of satellite research. If he wasn't familiar with the term, then I could breathe easy, but if he was, then . . . they were closer than they even realized.

There was a long pause. I checked the minute count on my phone to make sure we were still connected. "Dr. Edwich, did I lose you?"

"Where did you say you were calling from, Dr. Davenport?" His suspicion crackled across the phone line.

It didn't slip my notice that he was back to using formalities. "I didn't say."

"This is no joking manner, Doctor. The Ultra Fusion Capacitor is top secret information."

My stomach tightened. He had a name for it. God help us. He had a name for it!

"If your research has come up with a way to tap into nuclear fusion in space . . ." His voice trailed off as I keenly listened to the silence from the receiver. "Oh God . . . but, of course, that's it. There's no reason to have atomic power during launch. The Ultra Fusion Capacitor could extract the power *after* takeoff."

The excitement in his voice traveled thousands of miles to the dark comfort of my office. My hands protectively cradled my baby in my womb.

"What? No! No . . . that won't work." I sat up in the office chair and saw the horror of mankind's future begin to descend down the slippery slope to self-destruction.

"Well, we won't know until we try, but don't worry, I'll cite you if it works. I'm not like some of those scientists who never credit where they get their ideas from."

A loud rushing sounded in my ears. I barely remembered placing the phone back in its cradle.

Oh my God, what have I done?

*O*ne week later. . .

The night was quiet. I'd put this off until the last moment. I left tomorrow. I sat at my kitchen table, one of the few possessions that would stay with the house when it sold and looked down at the words penned on simple white-lined paper. A jagged black line ran across the top where the pen had slipped.

I'd wrestled with this decision for hours, days. Finally I couldn't deny what I had to do.

I knew that I'd failed . . . failed before I had even begun.

But the future generations didn't know. They still thought The One would come and from that hope they made decisions that altered their lives. They believed.

So I had written The Prophesy and with it as much detail as I could. I was too afraid to change anything. One small word could alter so many lives. Prevent someone from believing, from taking action.

And she will come from the past and be protected from the wild beasts. With wisdom of old she will save the lives of men and drag the doings of the evil ones into the light. And they will hate and seek to kill her. But a mighty warrior will be called upon to save her and he will become an outlaw to her rescue. And she will incite a small nation to rebel. And a final sign will be given to all of you, so that you may know she is The One. A miraculous birth will be bestowed upon her. This sign will be hers and hers alone so that all may know she is The Chosen One.

I laid the pen aside and folded the tragic fate of mankind into thirds. My hands shook as I slid the paper into a plain, inconspicuous envelope addressed to Dr. Robert Edwich.

There should have been more. Should have been some ominous symphony playing in the background. Dim lighting and numerous close-ups on my letter, something to signify that in this moment I'd just fated the death for more humans than any one person in the history of mankind. I'd just given Dr. Edwich the final piece to start the Global War.

And with such a simple act, black ink sprawled over white paper, The One and The Pale Horseman become the same.

I had written on the back not to open until after the first satellite was launched using atomic power. I had no idea if he would wait that long or not, but I knew my path was already set.

I'd taken a week to prepare. From the time of my early morning phone call to now had been a whirlwind, but the actual decision was quick. Going back to ConRad's time would complete The Prophesy. I'd go back pregnant, which would be the final sign—the birth. How it would be miraculous, I had no idea, but that didn't stop any of the other signs from coming true. I was taking a lot on faith. Faith that had been hard won.

This would be my last "jump." The previous time travel had messed with my equilibrium; I had vertigo and a bloody nose for weeks, causing an unplanned trip to the emergency room.

Could my body survive another jump? Each trip proved harder to pull myself back together, and this time I had another life to think about.

I'd waited long enough to know that if labor was induced, the baby would be fine. Lord knows, that thirty-six and a half weeks was plenty long. But going back to ConRad's time was risk enough. I was no fool. Life there was hard and would be harder still without ConRad.

This time I was prepared. I was going into battle; I had to fight for my life and my child's now. I'd given the sales clerk at the Ammo&Guns store a shock. His rounded bloodshot eyes,

set in a pimply face, said it all when a very pregnant woman
came into the store and asked for a semiautomatic rifle, sighted
with night vision for deer hunting. He'd almost lost his nerve
when I threw in the request for a weapon belt, size large. I'd
wanted to add grenades to my list, but was afraid he'd call the
cops.

My backpack was full—Twinkies, instant coffee, peanut
butter, and a butt-load of chocolate. I'd been steadily eating for
two and didn't feel like I should rein myself in at this point,
hence, the size large belt.

By Sunday night or early Monday morning, I was ready. The
army fatigues didn't fit anymore, no loss there. So I dressed in
an extra-large pair of sweats, an oversized T-shirt, and tucked
my hair through a baseball cap. I did a final check in the mirror.
Damn, there was a distinct resemblance to a beached whale on
downers.

I jimmied myself behind the steering wheel and drove to the
hiking trail parking lot. My car would have to be abandoned,
no help for it. Fortunately, I'd given myself plenty of time to get
up the trail so dawn was still a ways off. The darkness was good
since there was no plausible reason under the heavens as to why
a very pregnant woman, with a night-sighted rifle, backpack,
and an industrial flashlight was shuffling up a mountain.

I waddled toward the trail head and then huffed and puffed
up the beginning mild incline. Within five minutes I knew I
had underestimated the time I needed to climb the mountain.
Even though the baby had dropped over three days ago, I still
couldn't draw a big enough breath.

It took me forty-five minutes, and the abandonment of
my pack and rifle, to make it to the particular mesquite tree.

Gasping for air and coated with a thin sheen of sweat, I leaned against a large boulder to sit and wait for the first rays of dawn. I circled the beam of my flashlight over the "portal," which showed nothing more than dirt and rock. How many people crossed this place without any thought, without anything unusual happening? Why me? So many others would've been a better choice. And yet here I was.

I didn't have to wait long as the light pink of the sun outlined the mountain horizon. My heart raced in direct opposition to such a peaceful scene. My daughter's elbow jammed me in the ribs, and I pushed back trying to get more air. This was it and yet I hesitated. Both times I'd gone through before was either unknowingly or in a life-or-death situation. Today— today was purely by choice.

Black crackling holes appeared in the atmosphere. First, slow disappearing pops in my peripheral vision, then gathering in duration and mass.

Icy sweat coated the back of my neck as the blackness grew and coalesced into a hole big enough to step through. The cold vacuum of space chilled my skin as my terrified blood heated my veins.

Before me loomed the vast blackened emptiness. My heart pumped so hard it hurt and my daughter's body tightened in response.

For courage, I rubbed my extended belly and said a final prayer. *Please help.*

I stepped forward. Then stepped again.

And fell.

CHAPTER THIRTY-FIVE

Pain splintered my body apart. There was no direction, no up or down, just a pulling outward. A tearing from my center like an elastic band stretched to the maximum and then pulled some more. Muscles slid from bone, ligaments popped from joints. Then I was lost.

Too far gone. Need to fight. Can't remember why? Something . . . someone . . . focus. Piercing blue eyes, hard whiskered jaw, blond hair darkened and slicked with sweat.

ConRad.

Snap . . . I was back. I woke up sprawled out on the cold dirt ground. My head swam, and the darkness spun. Loud sharp bursts of noise rang around me. A scream, high-pitched and deafening, echoed inside my skull.

The scream was bad. Something about it told me I needed to move. I tried, but my legs and arms were disconnected as if broken and laid useless on the ground. I gritted my teeth, fighting through the white fire behind my eyes.

Go small, simple, but move! I tried the tiniest of movements—a head turn—instead a moan escaped from behind my clamped lips.

"Kris? What are you still doing here? Get the hell out of here, now!"

The words didn't make sense, but the voice? Like a tuning fork struck to the note of C, my ears aligned to the familiar sound. I fought with grainy eyelids, too thick to roll back and open. Then slowly the darkness abated. ConRad?

His back was toward me, shirt off. Dirty sweat ran like rivulets down his back. Muscles trembled as he aimed and fired his machine gun.

Oh God, he's alive.

My insides, once a cauterized gaping hole of flesh, unable to heal, beyond all mortal help, slammed shut. I breathed the first full breath in months. I'd come home.

A sharp pain knifed through my abdomen. I rolled onto my hands and knees trying my best to keep my screams behind closed teeth. They sneaked out regardless.

"What's wrong? Can't you go? I only jumped back in because I thought you'd left. Do you need me to leave again?"

I shook my head, but realized he couldn't see me with his back still turned.

"No," I panted.

Wetness trickled down my lip, pooling brown on the ground—a nose bleed. The abdominal pain layered upon itself and I froze. My body was stiff with tension, and then the sharpness of the pain ebbed enough so I could swallow and think again.

I needed to apply pressure to my nose before I lost any more blood. When I jumped previously, it took packing the sinus cavity to stop the bleeding. I pulled my shirt off, thankful I had a sports bra on underneath, and wadded the shirt into a ball. Applying pressure, I bent my head forward to prevent having a tasty little meal of my own fluids.

The dogs' howling turned into whimpering yelps as the piercing shrill of the aliens filled the small hole.

Aliens? Shi—

"Ahh, I can't watch." ConRad slammed his back against the wall and ducked for cover.

I shifted back to my knees and stole a peek at ConRad. His eyes were trained on my bulging stomach, his face a mask of utter shock, and with more than just a little of disgust. "Holy crap, what happened to you?"

"Imph pragnaph."

"What?"

I took my shirt away from my face and tried again. "I'm pregnant."

A gunshot sprayed the dirt by his head. ConRad crouched lower, then turned and fired off a round. He ripped open his side pant pocket, pulled out a clip, and slammed another round into the chamber.

I shoved the already soaked T-shirt back against my nose. The bleeding slowed, but I was feeling light-headed. From lack of blood or time travel, I'd no idea.

ConRad's body vibrated as he laid down fire, spraying the bullets in a sweeping pattern. He paused long enough to yell. "Why didn't you leave?"

"I did. I've been gone for almost eight months."

He turned his head to face me. "Eight months? But you just left!"

But I hadn't. I'd been gone for almost the whole pregnancy. I had no idea what happened, but I couldn't explain the intricacies of time travel any more than he could. "I don't know," I said shaking my head.

"Kris, why the hell are you back now?"

This question wasn't any easier. Because I believed in The Prophesy, because I'm Death and The One, because I needed to be close to his grave, to the life he'd lived. I wanted to tell him about my tortured existence, about the pain of knowing he and I weren't breathing the same air. That even though we lived decades apart, him not being alive destroyed me on some elemental level. If not for his child, I would've never gone on. But that was too complicated and yet not nearly enough, so instead I said, "I thought you were dead."

A scream rang out, more bullets zinged by his head—too close.

"Damn!" He ducked, turned, and fired. "It won't be long now. I took off my shirt and used it to bait the aliens. The scent drew them here. They'll cut the Elders off at the pass."

But he was alive now. My joy was radiant. Yes, bullets flew, monsters beckoned, but I couldn't wait to touch him one more time. I stood to throw myself in his arms when his body slammed me down to the ground.

"Christ! Stay down. Do you want to keep your head attached?"

I crouched down beside him, hard to breathe when your lungs and a baby were competing for the same space. His chin gestured toward my ever-increasing belly. "Is this normal? You're huge . . . I mean it's huge . . . no, your belly I mean, is really big."

The months apart hadn't softened the edge of irritation that this man could raise in me. "I missed you too. And yes, my doctor says my weight is fine. Twenty pounds is normal."

He whistled softly. "Wow, twenty pounds."

I elbowed him hard in the stomach. "Shut up and get me out of here—ahhh." A stab to my stomach had me feeling like my womb was ripping in half.

ConRad jerked back. "What's wrong?"

"I think I'm going to have this baby," I said through clenched teeth, as I doubled over.

"Here? Now?" I heard the panic in his voice.

"No," I hissed, shaking my head. "First labors take a while . . . usually." Another contraction would have me falling to my knees if I hadn't been there already. My stomach tightened and the baby moved, rolling elbows and knees underneath my taut skin like some possessed thing from a freaky sci-fi movie.

"Ah hell," ConRad said.

My thoughts exactly. *Damn, I hated sci-fi.*

He ran a hand through his hair making it stick up in odd angles. "Kris, why are you back? I sent you home to be safe. Why are you here?" His eyes screamed in his tortured face.

It was so complicated, but I found I could sum it up in one sentence. "I believe in The Prophesy."

He closed his eyes and shook his head. "God, Kris, you could've been safe. I had to make a choice. And I'd never go with them, never willingly go with Syon. Kris, do you understand—I had to make a choice?"

His choice, between Syon or the aliens. He had chosen the aliens.

"It's come to that, then?" I asked. An odd feeling of peace

stole over me. I'd been fighting for so long, so hard. I was tired.

I would've never thought I'd think this. I'd blamed my mom for her cowardliness. Hated her for years, but now . . . I could no longer stand in judgment of her actions. Living without ConRad all those months made me realize I couldn't live with just half my soul. There was no other scenario where tempting aliens would have any other outcome, except this one. "It's better this way."

"You can still go back. There's still time," he pleaded.

I shook my head. "I can't. I almost didn't make it here. Last ride, I was prepared for whatever it brought."

The bullets had stopped flying and dogs were silenced long ago. A few men broke the silence with screams in the distance.

He crawled over to the edge of the pit, stood, and peered out. "They're hunting them down. It won't be long now."

He turned and slid down the dirt wall until he was sitting, knees raised, head heavy in his hands. But ConRad was a man of action and it didn't take him long before he raised his head. The lines around his mouth had deepened as his lips set in a grim line. My husband had come to a decision. "I won't let you go like that. I promise."

I read so much in the depths of those blue eyes. How could I ever think they were cold? They smoked and heated with such passion. I saw my entire life reflected back to me—and it was good. I knew what he saying, and I loved him all the more for his courage and strength.

I nodded. *Ah God.* "Do it then."

ConRad crawled over to me and cupped my face with his hands. He kissed me. Hard lips imprinted his brand on me. "I'm so sorry."

"No need, it's better this way." My voice shook, but it had strength, as I stroked his cheek reassuringly.

He dropped his machine gun to the ground and reached behind his back pulling a pistol out. He lowered himself to the ground and pulled me into his lap.

"Do you believe in God?" I whispered.

"I believe . . ." he paused and pressed his lips to my temple. "I believe that no matter what happens, we will be together. No matter how cruel the universe can be, no one can keep us apart." He cradled my face, and I placed a kiss in his palm. He turned so we could gaze into one another's eyes. "No matter how many worlds there are after this. I *will* find you. Wait for me, because I'll come for you."

Tears streamed down my face, but I was content. That was enough for me. I believed him; he'd find me. I spared one last thought for our unborn child. A sob shook my shoulders before I could suppress the shudder, but I would NOT give her as a sacrifice to the locusts that feasted on man and Earth. She'd never leave her safe home. Never know anything other than me. My hand protectively ran across my belly as if holding her one last time.

"I'm ready." I closed my eyes and inhaled wanting my last scent to be of him. My last sense, if I held on strong enough, maybe I could take a small piece with me. I waited for the click of the gun, as the cold metal shivered at my temple.

"Kris . . . I need to ask you one last thing. It's not important, and no matter what you say. I'm still your husband. Nothing changes that. I can't leave you."

My hand came up and stroked his cheek. "ConRad, it's okay. What is it?"

"Did you love him? The baby's father? Did you love him like you did me?"

The bottom of my world dropped out. Did he actually think I would've been with another man?

"I understand," he said, his voice deep, strained. "You thought I was dead. I don't blame you. I just . . . selfishly, I needed to know if I'd be asked to share you in the next life."

He laughed, but it fell short, more along the lines of a gasp. "Because, God knows, I don't play well with others."

I hit him hard, my hand slammed into his chest. "Jerk, she's your baby . . . your daughter. Do you really think I would break our vows so easily? Do you think so little of me?"

His eyes widened in surprise, then a look of awe lit across his face making the impending dark less gloomy. His hands rested on my belly and caressed his daughter. "Mine? A daughter? Then before you left? Before you crossed back?"

I nodded. "I knew at the Sanctuary."

"I never thought I'd be a father. In my life there was no chance. I was in the military. I could never get enough money to buy a wife and have children."

I swallowed hard. And now he never would be.

A scuffling of rocks, loose dirt fell from the opposite ledge.

ConRad jumped up and slammed me back against the wall, him in front. "Foolish, I waited too long."

He turned, grabbed hold of me, and pushed me face first into his chest. His one hand held me prisoner in the crook of his neck, and the other held cool metal to the base of my skull. "Don't look baby; don't look."

My shoulders shook, but I had to get out one last thing. He had to hear my last words. "I love you."

I felt more than heard his quick inhale of breath. I squeezed my eyes shut. A soft click, more like a squeeze, whispered loud in the quiet . . .

"Commander?"

My eyes sprung open. He jerked his hand. A loud band rang deep in my ear. A warm burn to the back of my skull.

I turned my head, one last look . . .

"Kris. No! NOOOO . . ."

ConRad's face swarmed above me. I watched him scream, but couldn't hear the sound. His face, contorted in pain, blurred and distorted into a million fuzzy lines. Blackness crept in around the sides, then with a tiny pop, the circle closed all together.

Chapter Thirty-Six

I woke to the rhythmic jarring of my body, loud pants of air, and quick crunching of gravel below military boots. I opened my eyes. ConRad held me tight against his chest, running across the barren land, sweating like a bear on a treadmill, and sucking air like one.

The moons had almost set. Dusk was thick upon us. I peeked over his shoulder. Men flanked his sides, guns drawn. A few kept glancing behind to protect our six. I could make out Tank bringing up the rear, and Red hovering close to ConRad's side. I couldn't help but smile; they'd come. Our cavalry may be a little rough looking, but they were dependable, and I wouldn't trade them for any other group.

We came to the base of the mountain, where inside the compound was located. ConRad lowered me to the ground, and then stayed braced on his knees gasping for breath. He made a quick circling motion with his finger in the air, indicating that the team should do surveillance. In quiet efficiency, the men scattered and ConRad went back to sucking wind.

"You weren't kidding about the twenty pounds."

Heat rose to my cheeks. "Okay, maybe it was more like thirty. But hey, I eat when I'm stressed."

His head cocked to the right giving me a view of his half smile. "I thought I'd killed you."

I flashed a smile of my own. "I'm not that easy."

He sat, leaning back on his heels and squeezed his thumb and forefinger over his closed eyelids. Moisture glistened on his long eyelashes. He took a deep breath. "I don't know about that. I had you coming up against a wall, screaming my name within the first twenty-four hours I met you."

I rolled my eyes, and for some insane reason I felt giddy. "I didn't scream your name. That was your ego making up a bit of wishful thinking."

He took his hand away from his face. In the middle of this desolate, God-forgotten place called Dark Planet—he gave me an ear splitting grin—and the sun came out. "Ah, my mistake, it was more like 'thank you God.'"

"You are such an ass." But my voice had no heat. I reached behind my head to where it burned. My hand came away red. I knew that head wounds bled a lot, but I'd already lost so much, I doubted I could afford more.

ConRad's gaze followed mine to my bloodied hand. "The bullet grazed your skull. I checked the wound; it's clean and should heal."

I nodded.

"Are you okay?" Despite his previous smile, he looked worried.

"I think so, but I need someplace safe. Safe and soon."

"The baby?" he asked. He spoke like he was afraid of the answer. This was so out of his league.

"Coming."

"How much longer?"

I wasn't sure. The contractions seemed to be getting closer, even though I hadn't been in a position to time them. But my water hadn't broken, so there was still time. "Maybe an hour, I really don't know."

He nodded. "Let's get you back to the compound. We can use the infirmary."

That was the best option, but the thought of hard metal chairs and wooden tables had my teeth grinding. "What about the Elders?"

"Dead, the aliens picked them off. They had no chance."

"And Syon?"

"I don't see how he could have made it. Unless he wasn't there in the first place."

And that was the crux of the matter. We wouldn't know; we could assume, but never know for sure. "And us, how did we get away?"

"The men planted a decoy scent using some of your old clothes, and the aliens went crazy. Seems like I'm not the only one who can't get enough of you."

I laughed as ConRad came around and helped me up. He lifted my one arm around his shoulder and supported as much of my weight as he could.

Going back into the mountain was harder than when ConRad and I first came through the portal. The treacherous tunnels skirted natural springs, their spray coating the already slippery rocks. The path was narrow and I was fat. In the end ConRad had to lower me over the steep parts into Tank's waiting arms.

Treading carefully, we made it to level ground. Curled against Tank's unyielding body, I doubled over in pain as a warm sensation pooled down my legs. Tank's arm and one pant leg caught the brunt.

The look of total disgust on his face made me tighten my arms around his neck. "Don't you dare drop me, Tank. Just get me to the infirmary."

He swallowed, the muscles of his throat working hard on his Adam's apple. If he could hold me without me touching him, he would have. "Yes, ma'am."

Tank carried me through the double doors of the infirmary, and I realized my prayers had been answered. There was Quinn, having taken her place as a real goddess in long white robes, standing next to a bed with clean sheets and a true honest-to-goodness pillow. On a table by the bedside were some sterile instruments, a basin of water, and clean bath towels.

Quinn, beautiful, fresh-faced Quinn, her complexion rosy, radiating one of health and youth. Her smile, one I hadn't seen in months, made her ethereal appearance all the more striking.

"Ahh Quinn, how did you know?" I asked, as Tank laid me down on the stuffed mattress.

"I saw this room in a vision, and when all the men decided to follow you and ConRad, I realized that I'd better prepare the room just like I'd seen it."

"It's perfect, thank you," I said, surprised at the emotion welling up in my chest.

ConRad burst in the room looking like a stark-raving madman. His dust-covered hair stood on end and his face covered in whiskers and grime. He was shirtless, dirty, and caked with my dried blood, but he looked damn fine to me.

"I saw the stain on Tank. Is she bleeding?"

"No, it's okay," I said, stretching my hand out toward him.

He reached me and took my hand bringing it up to his lips for a tender kiss.

Quinn came up behind ConRad. "Sit down ConRad and relax, you did well. No wait, before you sit, go and wash up. You can't expect to hold your new baby as filthy as you are."

The thought stilled him mid-kiss as if the realization of what was about to happen finally sunk in. And with me too, the pain had begun to radiate up my back, in pulsing waves, feeling as if I'd split in two.

I gritted my teeth and tried to breathe through the sharpness. I was no newcomer to pain, but this time around, at least there would be something to look forward to at the end.

The hours passed in a light glow of red haze. Near the end I stopped holding back my screams and just let 'em rip, shaking dust from the ceiling.

ConRad sat beside me and held my hand, whispering encouraging words to my white-knuckled grip. He wiped the sweat from my eyes and laughed as I threw curses at his head. "Oh yeah, sweetheart," he said, "you can do all that and more. Just get through this."

Finally, I wanted to push . . . needed to get her OUT.

Then she was there, with a loud, robust cry that resonated deep into the marrow of my bones. *Mine.*

Quinn placed the wiggling baby on my stomach as ConRad, with shaky hands, cut the umbilical cord. Quinn wiped the trauma of the birth off of her, and wrapped my new daughter in a clean towel.

My gaze rested lovingly on ConRad, my husband. His

warm blue eyes were red rimmed and wet. Pure awe shone from his face. Quinn placed the baby in my arms as ConRad climbed in behind me. There the three of us lay, ConRad holding me, and me holding our daughter. We wrapped ourselves in a protective cocoon of love, with shining sappy grins and whispered kisses.

"So what are you going to name her?" Quinn's voice, though soft, still startled me. The world was sitting up and demanding attention.

I glanced at ConRad. "Do you have a preference?"

He shook his head, his eyes still slightly glazed. "I'm still reeling from the fact that I have a daughter."

I laughed, at least I had nine months to prepare, and he had what? Less than a few hours. I'd thought of names, but they all seemed better suited to the twenty-first century, not really for here, for this new future.

I lifted my shoulder in a shrug, nothing was coming to me. I looked at Quinn.

"It needs to be something special, something that signifies her role in The Prophesy," she said.

My heart sped with trepidation. My new baby was no part of The Prophesy. "Her role? I should know, Quinn, I wrote the damn thing. The Prophesy begins and ends with me. She's no part of it."

Quinn smiled. She wasn't here to convince me, just to state things like she saw them. Either she was right, or I was. Only time would tell.

"You can't deny who she is or the miracle of her birth. The child of our new leader and of The One, she's the dawning of our new era—our hope," Quinn said.

"I like it," ConRad said. "Dawning Hope Smith, it has a certain quality to it."

I nodded. The name rang true to me. Something bright had to come out of all this darkness. "We'll call her Dawn."

I stroked her wrinkled forehead as she peacefully nursed. I refused to acknowledge the foreboding that fluttered in my stomach. I would not place that much responsibility on one small child.

After a few minutes, ConRad stood. "I need to go tell the men that you and the baby are okay. They'll want to know."

I smiled. The responsibility of his leadership was never far from his mind. When ConRad walked out the door with an ear-splitting grin on his face, I could hear a loud cheer rise up.

Once he was gone, Quinn helped me dress in a soft flannel nightgown and stretch leggings. After Dawn and I were comfortable, Quinn came and sat down next to me and took my hand. "Are you up for it?"

"Quinn, damn it. I hate when you do that. Stop asking questions when you know I have no idea what you are talking about."

She laughed and it sounded musical and light. "I know. I'll work on that, I promise, but I was wondering if you're ready to go and greet the men. Some have traveled miles from all over to be here."

She nodded toward the infant sleeping in my arms. "She is their symbol. She is one of the last signs that The Prophesy was fulfilled."

I sighed. This was what I wanted, right? I wanted to show these men the truth of The Prophesy, to give them the strength to take up arms against their oppressors and defend their children. But now that it was here, all I wanted to do was take my baby, and ConRad, and live someplace where I could protect her.

"There's no mistake," Quinn said. "Her birth was miraculous, a full-term baby in less than twenty-four hours. That's the stuff that makes hardened warriors become believers."

I nodded.

"Here, let me help you up." She took my arm and steadied me as I walked on shaky legs, holding my baby girl.

I stepped out of the infirmary and into the now-cleared-out command center. My eyes widened in surprise as I took in the whole area filled with men, and more than a few women. Their desperate faces personalized the rebellion. Dirty, fatigued, some hardened. Some were riddled with pain at the loss of their own daughters sacrificed to the Elders for greed and power. The faces of soldiers who'll never have the chance to have a family, who'll die so others can break free from the ominous yoke, so their children can have a better life. There is no greater cause.

My heart broke for all of them. How could I be so blessed and withhold the one thing that they all needed—hope.

Tears started down my face. *Please God, give me the strength to hold up under this burden.*

My eyes caught sight of ConRad, a strong, virile man. His heart was loyal to his cause and his people, and his devotion to me was humbling. Dawn's father was a hardened warrior; both her parents were. We would protect her. Strength infused my bones. *With him by my side I can do anything.*

"Men and women of the New Rebellion, I give you our

daughter—Dawning Hope Smith." I raised my sleeping infant up so all could see her shiny face.

"The daughter for the People." My voice rang strong. This felt right.

A hush settled over the crowd. ConRad's features settled into a calm acceptance. His hand fisted and then was placed over his heart. He kneeled on one bended knee. "I pledge my life to The One and to the People's daughter. Our new leader."

The air crackled with emotion. Then men fell one by one till the whole assembly knelt, hand over heart, the walls vibrating with their pledged fidelity.

A sense of peace flowed through me. This was right. This was the beginning. With ConRad by my side, I was the woman who'd brought to them . . . a future.

KC Klein is the author of *Dark Future*, a sexy futuristic time-travel. She became serious about writing three years ago and was as surprised as anyone when her stories took a turn toward dark and snarky. Today, she divides her time between taking care of her family and driving in circles around Arizona, too busy creating stories in her head to pay attention to mere road signs.

Be Impulsive!

Look for Other
Avon Impulse Authors

www.AvonImpulse.com